Stormbound
By
A P Bateman

Facebook: @authorapbateman

www.apbateman.com

Rockhopper Publishing Limited

2018

Also by A P Bateman

The Alex King Series
The Contract Man
Lies and Retribution
Shadows of Good Friday
The Five
Reaper
Stormbound

The Rob Stone Series
The Ares Virus
The Town
The Island

Standalone Novel
Hell's Mouth

For my wife, Clair
Without your support and understanding, these
books would take
so much longer to write

For my two children, Summer and Lewis
Without you, these books would be written so
much sooner, but where
would the fun be in that?

Chapter One

Lapland
Five miles from the tripoint of Norway, Finland and Russia

The air was so dry and cold that it had started to freeze his lungs, crystallising and ripping him inside as each ice crystal stuck to one another. It was inevitable. Exertion should have been avoided at all costs. The Sami - the natives of Northern Finland - were not runners for good reason. They paced themselves, breathed through a shroud of folded cotton on the coldest days. And today was cold. As cold as he thought possible on this earth.

With the exertion his breathing rate raised considerably. The frigid air chilled his lungs, and with each exhalation, the lungs emptied of air and stuck together. The freezing air rushed back inside, cooled them further. The effect was like licking a metal pole in the sub-zero temperatures. Only each time his lungs stuck together, there were no pain receptors to warn him, and when they refilled with freezing air, the wet lining peeled away from the frozen layer and bled even more. Not that it would ultimately make a difference to him breathing, it was nothing more than a natural and uncontrollable reflex, but he did not know the damage he was doing to himself inside, and he never would. The damage had already been done. He was slowly drowning in his own blood.

He wiped his sleeve across his mouth, glanced at the blood. His breathing was laboured, becoming wet and thick. The lack of useable air was thinning the oxygen levels in his bloodstream. He didn't know it yet, but he was already dying slowly through hypoxia.

He could hear the incessant motors of the snowmobiles getting closer. He had earlier tried to cover his tracks, take a devious route, but when he had realised how quickly they were catching him, he had made a break for it and broken cover. His efforts had been poor, and although he had once learned about escape and evasion, those scenarios spent on the Brecon Beacons one weekend now seemed trite. Nothing could have prepared a man for this climate. This extreme environment. And he was a deskman now, years after his basic training, he had lost his edge, dulled in reactions. It wouldn't have made a difference though, he had simply run out of time.

The snowmobiles went silent. He ducked down behind a ledge of ice, a series of ridges which had been blown into waves like a frozen sea. The arctic wind, an irresistible force of nature.

He hunkered down, aware that his clothing afforded him no camouflage qualities in the monochrome landscape. His heart pounded, his breathing tearing his lungs apart within him.

A gunshot rang out across the clearing, cracking the heavy, freezing air and sounding like a canon in the stillness. A solid mist of frozen snow dusted into the air just a few inches from his feet. He pulled his feet up, then broke cover and dodged to a wispy pine. He moved laboriously, partly because of the lack of oxygen in his bloodstream, and partly because of the multiple layers that were both bulky and stiff from the cold. He felt a cumbersome, inelegant beast. But worse; he felt like prey. It was a poor tactical move, too. The tree was far narrower than himself, but more solid than the icy ridge and the crusty layer of frozen snow at his feet. The trees were thinner this far North. They only grew for a few months of the year and the forest was both widely spaced and looked like five-year-old plantations of pine, rather than centuries old forest.

He grimaced, the pain working its way up his throat like bringing up gravel. He coughed, but it only made it worse and he started to retch uncontrollably, blood and sputum dotting the snow at his feet.

Another gunshot. The high-velocity crack ringing through the valley. Part of the tree trunk was blown away and the bullet ricocheted into the forest. The tree was frozen as solid as everything else in this landscape and the soft-nosed hunting round merely chipped off the bark, when it could well have travelled through, had they been a thousand miles further to the South.

He slid down the trunk and slumped onto the frozen ground. The snow had frozen, the temperature now -30°C, and was as hard as concrete. He knew he was finished. He had no fight left in him and had reached as far as he could go. He wiped more blood from his lips, marvelled at how it had already frozen on his sleeve. He closed his eyes for a moment, willed images of his wife and son to come into his thoughts. He wanted to be with them as he died, take solace in the warmth of family memories. But then he snapped too. Remembered his training. Hazy days, twenty-years ago.

Another world. Another lifetime.

The tough Scot instructor shouting at him.

Keep moving forward! Or; if you're dying, you can still be useful…

He raised a hand, bit down on the crusty tip of a gloved finger and pulled it free. Another shot rang out. He was aware of a zing in the air as the bullet ricocheted, but he did not falter. Could not care less anymore. His hand felt cold and numb as soon as it met the frigid air. He feebly unzipped a chest pocket, dug his fingers inside and took out a small, orange-coloured lozenge, approximately half the length of his finger. He reached behind him, dug into the frozen snow. He worked away at the crust, his fingers losing all feeling and making the task near-impossible. He broke the crust, found the snow looser a few inches deeper. He tucked the lozenge into the shallow hole, swept the icy granules on top. He raised his hand, saw the blood freezing to his skin. His fingertips were white. He had ripped out two nails in his efforts, but they barely bled. He tried to squeeze his hand into a fist, but his digits had frozen solid. He lolled his head back against the tree. There were tears in his eyes, but they welled and solidified on his cheeks, pointing downwards like stalactites.

There were crunches on the snow behind him. Multiple footsteps. He looked up as two men rounded the tree. He recognised one of the men, shook his head at the indignity of him being there at the end. The man removed the glove from his right hand and held it out in front of him. He looked up at him, tried to stand, but he struggled too much and rested his back onto the ice.

He was beaten and had accepted it.

A smaller man with dark, leathery skin - who the man would have thought looked like an Eskimo, or Inuit before he knew about the native Sami – laid his old and battered hunting rifle on the ground and took off his pair of reindeer skin gloves and bent down, ripped the man's Gortex jacket open, and pushed the man's hands back down as he weakly resisted. The Sami rifled through the man's pockets, then gave up and ripped the man's jacket over his head and went through the pockets one by one. The man shivered, practically bouncing off the ground as he shuddered. The Sami found a fold of paper, dropped the jacket on the ground as he handed the paper to the taller man, who like the man dying at their feet, wore modern ski-wear and thick double-lined boots.

"Is this it?" The taller man read the paper, folded it and placed it in his inside pocket. "Is this all that was taken?"

The man swallowed, but the action looked as painful as swallowing half a brick. He thought of his contact. The asset. The young man whose body lay ten miles South from here, wrought and stiff in the snow. He had veered off course, missed their rendezvous by twenty-hours. He had almost made it but died in the savage night. So close, yet so far. A waste of life. But the asset had got something out. And now he had given his own life for the same cause.

Resigned to his fate, he looked up and beckoned the man to bend down closer. He murmured something incoherent and the tall man straightened back up. He looked down at the man on the ground, saw that he was drowsy – almost out of it completely. He was hypothermic. The cold would kill him, but they needed the wilderness to claim him. He nodded to the Sami and the man reached under the bulk of his reindeer skin coat and pulled out a knife.

The man could see the dull-coloured blade. Not polished, but tarnished and grey. A thin silver line along the blade, which ran from haft to tip, indicated a wickedly sharpened edge. The handle was made from antler. It was a stubby, curved blade. He tensed as the Sami sliced through the fleece under-coat, dug the blade through the muscle wall and opened him up from his navel to his chest. He could hear the blade cutting through the muscle and fat, felt a tugging sensation, but he did not feel the pain of the cut, he was almost too far gone for that. But he did feel the pleasant warmth on his skin as his blood and entrails spilled and steamed in the icy air. The Sami placed the knife on the ground and dug his hands inside. He lifted out the man's entrails and let them trail on the frozen ground. The man looked up at both men, tried to mutter something, but he closed his eyes and took his last breath, the faces of his wife and son finally coming into his thoughts as he breathed for the final time.

The Sami cleaned his hands on the man's jacket, then wiped the blade of the knife on the man's leg, sheathed his weapon once more and put on his gloves. Between them, the two men pulled the body away from the tree and laid it out on the snow. The entrails had stuck to the ice and unwound further as they had dragged the body away. The Sami swung the rifle over his shoulder and adjusted the sling so that it rode over the crude seam in his reindeer skin coat. He nodded to the taller man and they trudged back across the snow. When they were fifty-metres clear of the steaming body, the Sami removed a glove, cupped his hand to his mouth and howled like a wolf. To the other man's bemusement, it was as if a wolf stood next to him. The Sami howled for close to a minute. When a reply came, chilling and distant, the Sami smiled and nodded silently, and the two men trudged back up the slope to the East.

Chapter Two

The car was a ten-year-old Volvo estate. Battered, but well-maintained. An inconspicuous vehicle barely worth a second glance. Its front wheels wore snow chains and had carved a path here on a crust of foot-deep frozen snow. The municipal snowplough had been through the day before, but it had not snowed here in weeks. The wind was cutting through across the Northernmost tip of Norway, bringing the cold, salty air straight down from the Arctic Ocean and through the belt of wispy forest making up the extremities of Lapland.

The heater was on full power, maximum temperature. It had been for six hours. The car was a petrol engine model. Diesel struggled at these temperatures, turned to gel on the coldest days. The idling engine was going through the petrol at an alarming rate, but he needed the heater on full. A quarter tank of fuel had gone in the time spent on tick-over alone.

He checked his watch. He would have to call it. He had a hundred-mile drive ahead of him and the going would be slow. By his calculations, he had enough fuel to make it, but not if he encountered a problem or diversion. He had taken it to the limit and was already cursing having not called it a full hour ago. He would have had a comfortable buffer for his journey.

There were fifty-mile-an-hour winds heading South, a precursor to the arctic storm threatening to swoop down from the North Pole within the next week. The forecasters had pronounced it imminent and unavoidable. They were certain that it would not deviate. He had used a narrow enough window, and he did not want to chance blizzard conditions on the drive back. He was not a young man any longer, hadn't been for some time. No, he was calling it and that was that. He wiped the windows around him for the hundredth time, cleared his vision for the dull monochrome hue outside. It was only daylight between eleven and three, and the Volvo's headlights were both yellow and weak. Still, better than being blinded in the snow by halogen LEDs on modern vehicles. He took the Walther PPK pistol out from between his legs, placed it back in the glovebox and put the car into second gear for a gentle rolling start on the icy crust.

There was no phone signal out here and he would have to call from the car when he escaped the blackspot thirty miles further South. He had struggled making calls for the past two-weeks, before realising his phone would freeze and switch off after three or four minutes exposed to the temperature. There was a landline back at his lodge. Normally he would call the secure line, and his call would be routed through GCHQ and to River House, or what people would more widely know as the MI6 headquarters at Vauxhall Cross, London. Personally, he'd always called it Legoland.

He had worked there for many years. He had done things he'd rather forget, seen things he didn't want to remember. He had seen the best agents come and go. And now, he was out in the field again. The wrong side of sixty, but worn and weary. Older than his years. But still sharp. Because the man he was to meet tonight had called that same number when he realised he was in trouble. And that man had not made his rendezvous. And he would not be making the same mistake.

Chapter Three

Ministry of Defence (MOD)
Whitehall, London

Amherst watched the woman from hospitality services pour the tea, dutifully position the plate of biscuits closer to them, and step back from the table.

"That will be all," Villiers said curtly. "Thank you." He did not look at her as he dismissed her, and he poured in his own milk and stirred the cup thoughtfully.

Amherst picked up the milk jug. "So, we're agreed?" he said.

"Yes."

"No need for our American friends to know?"

"Absolutely not. The less, the better. That goon in the White House won't keep his mouth shut anyway, most likely send a Tweet and tip them off."

Villiers shook his head. "What a world we live in, eh?"

Amherst glanced at his watch. He had known the chief of MI6 for as long as he'd held his own post of that of Director of MI5, or as it was officially known - the Security Service. His opposite number was a cautious man, and one never really knew how the man ticked. Amherst didn't dislike the man on a professional level but wouldn't be inviting him down to the country anytime soon. He never fully felt at ease in the man's company, unsure how much to divulge, or nip at the bait he so often dangled in front of him. It was eleven-AM and the COBRA meeting had finished. Villiers had asked if he could have a word with Amherst on an unrelated matter. Amherst had proceeded with caution.

"What can I help you with, James?"

Villiers sipped some tea, placed it back down on the thick porcelain saucer. In MI5 they used white mugs, similar in quality to most motorway service stations. In Whitehall, they were afforded cups and saucers, but they were utilitarian destined for chain hotels with buffet breakfasts and airport drop-offs every twenty-minutes. In Downing Street, it was fine bone china.

Hierarchy and budget.

"The Russian president."

"Nice fellow."

"Aren't they all?" Villiers said sarcastically and smiled. "Haven't had much of a chance to assess this one yet."

"No doubt."

"The death of his predecessor was, well, sudden."

"Certainly unexpected."

Villiers murmured as he sipped his tea. "If you say so," he said.

Amherst was a liar. He was paid to lie. Half of his personnel were taught how to. Even so, his neck bristled. "Meaning?"

"Your kidnapped agent last year," he said nonchalantly. "Some people of mine did some digging. An agent in our South African station filled in a few gaps. Unwillingly, I might add. But things sort of caught up with him. A wicked little web he weaved for himself. Thought he could handle it personally. A right old pickle it was too. Missing agents, unsanctioned hits, misappropriation of government funds…"

"Things can quickly get out of hand in the field."

"Don't I know it," Villiers agreed. "But your department had a merry little shindig, so it would seem. Where are your agents now?"

"Sabbatical," he replied cautiously. "We thought it for the best."

"Everybody involved?"

"The ones who count."

"For the best, I'd imagine. As you say. Allow them to lay low," he paused. "Like I said, some of my people dug a little, turns out they dug up a whole load of shit."

Amherst leaned forwards conspiratorially. Villiers followed suit. "Say what's on your mind, James. I'm not playing your fucking games."

Villiers straightened, taken aback. "Fine,"

he said indignantly. "I'll cut to the chase, then. There were people connected to your main suspect in a terrorism case, and they all died. Astonishingly, our investigators unearthed some wholly unbelievable anecdotal evidence that the former president of Russia was somehow involved, too. Many years before he straightened himself out and became an upstanding politician."

"Now there's a contradiction in terms…"

"Indeed. But the Russian president had a wicked, insidious past, and it would seem it caught up with him." Villiers sipped some more of his tea. "Biscuit, old boy?"

Amherst shook his head. He sipped some tea for the distraction. He could tell the old spy in front of him was weighing him up. Amherst had come through the civil service. Villiers had worked out of embassies all over the world as an asset. He had run native agents, bribed and cajoled, sanctioned the use of lethal force – even helped the people who got their hands dirty get in place. And out again. He was an old salt, and he made the career civil servant nervous.

"You see, I know there was some off the reservation affair, and believe me, I understand. You had a missing agent, and your team worked tirelessly to get her back, and take out the threat. I get that. But what I don't get, is why you went after the head of state of the second most, or perhaps even the most powerful nation on the planet."

"Who says we did?"

Villiers smiled. "I'm sure it was unofficial."

"We sanctioned no such assassination. Official, or otherwise."

"Coincidence, then?"

"Of course."

Villiers nodded. "I have an issue, I was hoping you could help me resolve?"

"Go on."

"The Russian government's reaction to their president being murdered was to cast their aspersions upon MI6 and the CIA. Our diplomats are persona non grata and the embassies are now empty. We lost our eyes and ears. Our official agents are twiddling their thumbs at home, while we have nobody out there to watch the show."

Amherst shrugged. "It will play down," he said. "We expelled theirs after the Salisbury nerve agent affair. They subsequently were allowed back; the Prime Minister hasn't gone tit-for-tat, yet. With the Russians still here, our expulsion should be short-lived. They'll want your agents out there where they can keep an eye on them again."

"Yes, that's all well and good," Villiers said curtly. "But the Russians are doing some digging of their own. They will find the same link my agents made between these dead Russian mafia bosses and their esteemed former leader. When your missing agent and her heroic fiancé and all ensemble involved come into the fray, well, MI5 had better have the right answers in place. You certainly won't come out of it holding onto the Director General post. And Commons Select Committees are incredibly taxing. The pressure affects your home life, too."

Amherst stiffened. Was there no end to what this old spy could know, or how he could spin it?

"You see," Villiers went on. "Our man in Pretoria met your missing agent, formed a bit of a bond with her. He was there, or rather, we were there when she got in a spot and needed our help. That's fine. Professional courtesy. An agent in need. But he also told my investigators that he knew your agent's fiancé. Knew him from old…"

Amherst knew this wasn't going to be a meeting he left the room in control of. He could feel his career unravelling.

"Some of my more tenacious investigators did a little more digging," Villiers paused. "Actually, a lot of digging. Turns out your agent who was known by a man on a desk in South Africa was a ghost. No employment records, but he certainly worked for MI6 prior to MI5. The digging went deeper. I called ex-employees. A combination of stick and carrot. I got back some surprising anecdotes. Have you heard of the Reaper?"

"Sounds a little fantastical."

"No doubt. But the man that your agent got herself engaged to, was a fully-fledged black ops specialist for MI6 for more than a dozen years. Now, he did some sort of deal with your deputy director's predecessor, Charles Forrester. A good man. But I fear even he went a little rogue towards the end. He took on this chap, signed him up as an unofficial he had brought in from the cold. Got him all pensioned up and PAYE'd and working for the other side. Your side." Amherst leaned back in his chair. He had always had his doubts about King, but he had inherited him. But the man also got the job done and it had not taken Amherst long in the role to see that there would always be jobs that needed doing that few would ever be capable of. He picked up his cup again, but the tea was cold. He chanced it anyway, could feel his throat drying out. "It gets better. A series of unfortunate accidents over a short period not only led to a regime change within the SIS, but sparked suspicion. It also led to the disappearance of the Reaper. The man named Alex King. How about that?"

"You aren't seriously suggesting that Alex King had something to do with that, are you?"

Villiers steepled his fingers and stared at Amherst. He watched until the MI5 man glanced away. He smiled. "I have it on good authority that the top tier of MI6 was as rotten as anytime in history. More so. Forget Kim Philby. Forget Burgess and Maclean. There were men in charge at the River House that made a mockery of what it is we do. The heroes of both World Wars, the Cold War... Everything we've ever done. These men used SIS assets and tried to feather their nests in international business affairs," Villiers paused, watching Amherst for a flicker. He was quite sure that the civil servant knew nothing. Which was good. Because he could always elaborate and build on the situation. "It was a blemish nobody will benefit in making public. Which sort of buys your agent clemency, I suppose."

"Sort of?"

"Yes. You see, I'm quite convinced that this King fellow, killed this top tier of reprobates. I'm also quite convinced that they used him and hung him out to dry. They saw him as a loose end and were foolhardy enough to try and have those loose ends snipped. It did not go well for them."

Amherst shrugged. "No harm, no foul."

"Well, not quite."

Amherst returned his cup to the saucer and placed it back on the table. He glanced at his watch, decided it wasn't too early for a proper drink. He would break out the bottle of Courvoisier when he got back to his office. He had been drinking more lately. It was no wonder why.

Villiers smiled. "I know. It's in the bank. Quid pro quo. I want a favour."

Amherst nodded. He had already decided to put someone on Villiers. Someone's job was now to get something on the director of MI6. No. A team would be on it. He'd get his best analyst and watchers in place. The man's rubbish would go through them before it reached the dump. His wife would be followed. If she wasn't having an affair, then perhaps someone could be coerced to pursue her, a younger man who would sleep with her and put on a good show for the cameras. His teenaged children could be harvested for information somehow. He made a note to check if they were at college yet. University. Maybe drugs would be a way in? Amherst would have Villiers and his family shadowed for as long as the man remained in the role. He checked himself, Christ, what was happening to him? Ashamed, he looked back at his opposite number.

"Go on," he said.

Villiers smiled. All teeth and snide, but no

warmth. "I have a problem. I lost an asset. A Russian who wanted safe passage to Britain in return for what they knew."

"Which was what?" Amherst prompted.

"All in good time," Villiers said. "Only he didn't show. Or, frankly, we don't know if he did or didn't. His handler went to meet him. And that was the last we heard. I sent another man in his place, but he did not make contact with either of them."

"Where?"

"Finland," he said. "Lapland, to be precise."

"Lapland?"

"Yes. Turns out it's not just where Santa has his grotto, but a strategically placed piece of land that meets with Norway and Russia at a single point." Villiers reached into his pocket and retrieved a folded sheaf of four papers. He placed them on the table. "Everything you need is right there."

"What do you want, exactly?"

"Well, the way I see it, your agent went rogue. He has a chequered past, to say the least. He took down Russian mafia, then went on a personal war and killed the Russian president. I'm not interested what the Russian president did; I'm quite sure he deserved it. However, your agent's actions have had all my intelligence agents, assets and support staff expelled from Russia. As well as Britain's diplomats and embassy staff. We have no eyes or ears in the place. But what is worse than all of that, is I have another Russian defector on course with my handler in the frozen Arctic. Now, if my handler's asset was compromised, and it is looking that way, then this defector will undoubtedly be hunted by agents from the FSB or the GRU. The defection is set, so they are effectively on the way and there is no way of getting word to them to halt their migration, and believe me, if they succeed, then what they are carrying with them could well save us all."

Chapter Four

MI5 Headquarters, Thames House

The bottle of Courvoisier had been a gift from Amherst's opposite number in the French counter intelligence bureau, the DGSI, or Direction Générale de la Sécurité Intérieure. The man knew the connotations of the gift when he had given it, and Amherst had known as he had gratefully received it. It wasn't a celebratory drink. It wasn't Champagne. If you were going to have a drink to take the sting out of the awfulness of the job, then you had better have a good one. Amherst was on his third measure of the amber liquid, and it was worrying how well it was going down. To draw a line, he placed the cork stopper back in and put the bottle back in the open drawer beside him. He closed it and moved on.

The man seated opposite him had accepted a glass, but Amherst could tell it had been wasted on him. Should have served him tea. Whether he had accepted out of politeness, gauging his boss's mood, or whether he had wanted to quench a demon or two of his own, Amherst wasn't sure. It certainly hadn't been the man's style to conform, so he already acknowledged that he would probably never know why King had sunk the measure in one go. Perhaps he was toasting something, but as he looked at the man across from him, he could only imagine what that would be. On second thoughts, he knew he was better off not knowing for sure.

At a shade under six-foot, broad-shouldered, trim-waisted and fit, Alex King looked like a light-heavyweight boxer. He certainly had the eyes of someone who could stare down an opponent. They were the coldest, grey-blue that Amherst had ever seen. There were a few scars, thin white lines, that showed when he was tanned. Amherst knew that under the man's shirt was a network of scar tissue, each telling a story. A story about how he was still here, and others were not. He was a world removed from the career civil servant, and those two worlds were never really meant to meet.

King ran a calloused hand through his close-cropped dark hair. It was a new cut. Shaved at the sides and back, a little more left on top. It was the smartest Amherst had seen him. If he wasn't mistaken, he may have shaved this morning, too.

"So, you want me to investigate?"

"Yes."

"And the Finnish police can't, because?"

"In short, there's nobody up there," Amherst said. "They sent one of their officers…" He turned over a piece of paper and read. "Lena Mäkinen. Senior Constable, or Vanhempi

Konstaapeli," he said.

"That doesn't sound very senior," King replied. "Sounds like a patrol officer."

"I gather it was a routine investigation. Our asset was killed by wolves."

"Wolves?"

"Or a bear."

"I think the bears are all hibernating."

"Well, wolves, then," Amherst niggled. "Something tore the poor sod up and left only a few remains."

King shook his head and smiled. "And I thought it was all elves and reindeer up there. Fat guys in red suits sitting in grottos."

"I expect there's some of that up there, too. Or less so now that Christmas has passed, and all the tourists have cleared out."

"Who was the asset?"

"An MI6 agent, or handler."

King frowned. "Not an asset, then."

"He was dispatched to bring in an asset. He didn't show either."

"What kind of asset?"

"A defector."

"Defector?" King paused. "A bit John le Carré, isn't it?"

"An old story for a modern era. We wanted what he had, apparently. It was worth a quiet exfiltration, some sort of financial or lifestyle payoff and a new identity."

"And there's little police presence up there?"

"That's right."

"How far North, exactly?"

"About as far as it gets in Finland. A few miles from where Russia, Finland and Norway intersect."

"Chilly, then." King agreed. "What did the coroner's report come up with?"

"There hasn't been one. The police were called, they turned up a day later. It was a removal and tagging job," he paused. "In their eyes."

"So, what do you want from me?"

Amherst slid the sheaf of papers all the way across the table with a stretch. "It's all there," he said. "Memorise and destroy before leaving the country. Your tickets are waiting for you at the Finnair customer services desk at Gatwick."

King nodded. "Destroy all of these?" he asked.

Amherst nodded. "This is black bag. There are no formal records on this. MI6 have a contact in the area. He will liaise with you and aid with your investigation. You need to find out what happened to their asset and whether the hostiles got what they wanted. MI6 have another defector on route. The first defector's number two. They have the same information and want the same arrangement. MI6 were playing them both, without the other's knowledge. A safety-net. You need to meet them, provide them safe passage to Norway, where an exfiltration will take place. Details to follow."

"Who is the defector?"

"A specialist of some type…"

"Some type?" King interrupted. "That's pretty bloody vague."

Amherst looked at him sharply. He didn't appreciate insubordination, but as he looked into the man's unnervingly steady eyes, he mellowed his expression. King reminded him of a German Shepherd his parents had once owned. Nobody could look into its eyes or it would growl. Linger too long, and it would snap. Amherst's father had taken the dog away one night and returned without it. He wondered whether he would ever be tempted to do the same with King. But then he remembered Villiers' anecdotal suspicions. Amherst dismissed the idea as abruptly as it had come.

"A debt has been called in," Amherst said. "I'm doing this for both you and Caroline, as much as to aid our sister service."

King remained impassive, but his stare was no less unnerving. The mention of his fiancée irked him somewhat. She was on sabbatical with Interpol. Six months so far and no sign of returning to MI5. They had gotten together at Christmas, but it had been different somehow. It had been passionate and a release for them both. But Caroline's experience having been abducted, what she had seen and the people-trafficking links she was now trying to sever throughout Europe, had focused her solely on her crusade. He loved her, knew she loved him, but she had demons to slay. She wouldn't be his Caroline again until she battled them and won.

"Europe? Last summer?" Amherst said. "MI6 did a lot of digging. The Russian's will have too. Links have been made. They are convinced that their president was killed on the back of your operation last summer."

"To get back one of your agents."

"You went too far off the reservation. You had no official remit."

"Do you want my resignation?"

"No, I…"

"Well, brass it out, then," King interrupted. "Tell them it's a load of bollocks and move on."

"Politics isn't always that simple."

"Then it's about time to remember you're not a politician. You are the head of Britain's defence. You hunt the terrorists, the spies and the foreign government organisations who would do our country harm. So, you lie about it. Deny it. Tell them to kiss your arse if you need to. But stand firm."

"We need this done. I need this done."

"I'm doing it," King assured him.

"Well, good luck, then."

King stood up, tucked the sheaf of paper inside his jacket pocket. He knew how unofficial this was, everything else came in various coloured folders, depending on the security clearance and sensitivity. King turned and walked to the door.

"Oh, and King..." Amherst took a pair of glasses out of his pocket and wiped them on a cloth as he looked up at him. "It's probably nothing, but there's a storm on the way up there. It looks to be the worst in years but may even skip right past and sweep back up into the Arctic. The police are a bit nervous in heading that far north unless they can absolutely help it. Just a bit more snow in a cold and desolate place already, I should imagine. It might affect the rendezvous with the defector, though," he paused. "But as I said, it's probably nothing..."

Chapter Five

Kittila, Lapland

King had cleared immigration without a check. Finland was a member of the European Union and the least populated country in Europe. Lapland was technically a country within a country. A region of sensitivity where Finland had to respect its independence for cultural reasons, but that country was also not a self-sufficient one. It needed Finland to maintain its indigenous people. An ironic existence. He had never previously visited, though, and did not possess a word of the language. First impressions were of an independent people, proud of their standing in the world, and happy. King knew the five Nordic countries were self-assured, desirable places to live and among the happiest in the world. He had been to Norway many times. It was where he had completed his mountain and arctic warfare training alongside the SAS and Royal Marines. He liked what he saw in the Norwegians and could tell that there was something similar in the people here as well. Like they shared an inside joke or understanding. We didn't follow the rest of the West and look towards the United States. We didn't fall in with the USSR either. We went our own way, and whose life is better now?

King could see the appeal of countries whose lifestyle and income balanced enough that the people all got to play. The Nordics loved the outdoor life, they made time for cake and coffee, for drinking, for socialising – but without the health and social downfalls. They had better health, less crime and more disposable income. It seemed the sort of place he could happily retire to when he was finished playing cowboys and Indians for MI5. A log cabin, summer swims in the thousands of lakes, cosy winter fires – perhaps neighbours and friends to grow close to? He doubted that, but it was all part of the daydream.

King's first step outside the airport brought all those thoughts crashing down. His breath hung around him in a thick fog and his throat swelled with the sudden rush of icy air. It was three-PM and virtually dark. He stepped back inside, and the blast of warm air thawed him and as the glass doors closed, he thought how soon events could be forgotten. He had spent three-weeks with the SAS and Royal Marines in Norway. He couldn't remember it ever being this cold. He had been younger then, but still. He was in his early forties now, would have been twenty-eight when he took to the frozen fjords and mountains. Could he really have forgotten what it would be like? No. He decided that this was really something else.

Across the ice road, he could see a thermometer on a pole.

-30°C.

Really? He knew his freezer at home was twenty-degrees warmer than that.

He dumped his bag on the floor and opened it, pulled out a pair of black salopettes, kicked off his shoes and pulled the bulky thermal overalls over his trousers. He put on a pair of thick woollen socks over his cotton socks and pulled out a pair of insulated hiking boots. King rummaged through the bag and took out two sweaters. He slipped on the thinner of the two and fastened the bib of the salopettes before putting the thicker sweater over the top. He already felt stiff and cumbersome, but he wasn't finished there. He slipped a hoodie he regularly jogged in over the sweater, then put a navy-blue ski jacket over the top.

King would have been finished there, but for cursing out loud and stripping most of the clothing back off to remove his wallet from his trouser pocket. He caught a glimpse of his expression in the smoked glass. Cursed his rookie mistake. Re-dressed and perspiring at the effort, remembered the car keys and cursed again. Finally, dressed and with everything he would need now placed in his jacket pockets, King put on a pair of Gortex gloves and a black beanie, swung his considerably lighter bag over his shoulder and stepped back out through the automatic doors. The cold still seared his throat and he could feel the beads of sweat from the exertion of changing freeze on his brow.

King found the car as arranged. He had picked up the envelope containing the keys at airport services. There were many car rental companies based at the airport, but none of them operated at this time of year. The whole area had now shut down for tourists. Kittila was the staging post for families taking their children on the ultimate Christmas excursion to see Santa. King had read about it in the in-flight magazine, realised what a magical experience it could be. It was the sort of thing he imagined doing with his own children one day, if indeed he ever had them. King's own childhood had been so poor, so infected and tarnished by poverty, abuse and neglect, that he had never really given in to thoughts of fathering a child. Children and childhood went hand in hand with the worst of his memories and fears. Only in recent years had he warmed to the idea, but now his own relationship was all but on hold, his future uncertain, he had pushed the thought out of his mind.

The car was an old model Nissan Patrol. A sturdy off-roader, or what was commonly called an SUV. It was dented and scuffed but had the meanest set of bull bars King had ever seen.

King popped the boot, but nothing happened. He checked the key fob, but it didn't seem to work either. He used the key but could feel the lock was frozen solid. He abandoned the idea, tried the driver's door but it was stuck also. He could feel a little play and the lock eventually gave. He pulled the door, but the rubber seal was stuck and peeled away slowly. The car was frozen. When the door finally opened, King could see cans of de-icer on the passenger seat, along with a map and a mobile phone. He picked up a can of de-icer and sprayed it on the locks and over the windscreen. He walked tentatively around the car, the ice solid and slippery underfoot, and sprayed some into the lock on the boot. The boot lid loosened, and King opened it up to find a roll of blankets, snow shovel and a can of fuel. He closed the boot lid and went back to the driver's side and got in. He started the engine; the diesel pre-heat light and ignition pause taking a few seconds before the engine rattled into life. King put a little throttle on and cranked up the heaters. The car had been standing for a while and the air rushing into the cabin seemed about as cold as the outside air. The engine would benefit from running for a while, so he used the time to adjust his clothing and look around the vehicle. There was no note. Nothing. He had been told that the keys would be waiting for him and that was as far as it went.

He removed his gloves and opened the glovebox. He could see the pistol inside, along with a spare magazine. He checked his mirrors, making sure nobody was near, and took out the weapon. It was a classic Walther PPK in .32 auto/7.65mm. He could see from the indicator pin above the hammer that it was not chambered. He reflected why more pistols hadn't adopted the feature. He worked the slide, chambering a round, de-cocked the hammer using the safety drop and tucked the weapon into his right pocket. He slipped the spare magazine into his left pocket and picked up the map beside him. There was a clear acetate sheet of A4 tucked into the map. Three points had been marked with a cross using a dry-wipe marker and a route had been drawn over the roads he should take. King saw the pen on the seat next to the can of de-icer. He checked the acetate and could see the road he needed had been highlighted. The destination and two further points lined up underneath perfectly. He had used the practice many times over the years and had been taught the importance of not marking a map from his early days with MI6. If captured by a hostile force or government, the acetate could easily be wiped, and the map held no secrets or tell-tale marks.

King studied the map but could not shift the nagging thought in the back of his mind.

Something about the map and the acetate. Familiar, like Déjà vu. Something in his past he could not unlock. He shook his head and placed the map on the seat. He could see another route that was fifty-kilometres longer and decided he would accept many things from a stranger, but a route for him to travel through the wilderness was not one of them.

Chapter Six

The drive north took a bit of getting used to. King had not driven on snow or ice in many years but was now getting into the swing of it. He just needed to remember to do everything slowly and steadily and anticipate far more than on a tarmac road. He met a few vehicles but allowed up to ten times the distance he normally would and within an hour, he was making swift progress and had managed to close the gap and read the road with more confidence. He had taken a different route, deciding he would call the shots. He always had done.

Another two hours and he entered civilisation at the town of Inakiai. A pretty town with houses constructed of timber or prefab and painted in a variety of primary colours. Bold reds and blues and yellows. Accented with white. King figured white properties got lost for eight months of the year. Most of the houses had a metre of snow on their roofs and all were equipped with a fixed ladder on the gable to clear the snow or maintain it when the snow thawed. Some houses must have been empty for the winter because they were completely covered, but for stainless-steel chimneys poking through.

The roads were clear here. Scraped back to tarmac with the merest sheen of icy sludge mixed with salt and grit. The edges of the road were piled high with dirty snow, now compacted to ice. King drove onwards and stopped when he came to a Spar convenience store. He helped himself to a tea from the machine. It was flavoured with lemon and there was no option for milk. He drank it down as he stood inside the doorway. He held it up in a gesture to the counter staff, showing them that he wasn't going to forget to pay, then finished it and dropped it in the bin beside the machine. He picked up some crisps and chocolate and paid for them, along with the tea. He asked where the police station was but didn't really understand the clerk's broken English/part Swedish answer. He figured it was Swedish because he made out a couple of words but had nothing in the bank for Finnish. He nodded thanks and walked back outside, the cold clawing at his bare face. He pulled the beanie down further until only his eyes, nose and chin remained uncovered.

The car had cooled already, and he started it up and kept the heater on as he polished off a chocolate bar and looked at the map. He picked up the acetate sheet and placed it over the map. The first cross he figured would be a start and he drove out of the parking bay and down the street. The lights within the houses shone warm and welcoming. The street lamps were sporadic, but King could already see that the snow provided enough ambient light to see by. A white background that would never give way to darkness. The headlights from the SUV cut swathes in the night and highlighted the houses further. King had seen similarly painted houses on the shores of Norwegian fjords.

King saw that the first mark on the acetate was a hotel. There was nothing else in the vicinity, so he figured this was where he was meant to stay. He drove on to the second marker and found the police station. There was one patrol car outside. A Subaru liveried as a police cruiser. It was a four-wheel-drive saloon with a handy turn of speed. Next to the car were two snowmobiles. Each looked frozen in the headlights, a thin sheen of ice covering them. There were ice particles in the air as well. The moisture freezing and dropping lazily to the ground. King could see a figure moving around inside the building. He switched off the engine and got out. He walked the twenty-metres or so to the steps and climbed them carefully, the ice forming a lethally slippery layer as the temperature dropped. He had no idea what the temperature was now, but it was considerably colder than it had been at the airport.

King opened the glass door and stepped into the heated foyer. He dusted the ice crystals off his jacket and removed his beanie and gloves, then unzipped his jacket and felt his skin start to breathe through the multiple layers of clothing underneath.

"It takes some getting used to, doesn't it?" A woman's voice behind him. In all his cumbersome efforts to remove the clothing he had not heard her open the door to a row of offices.

He turned around and smiled. "You knew I was English?" he asked, feeling it strange she had addressed him in anything other than Finnish.

"I was expecting you," she said. "Your department called ahead."

"My department?"

"The Home Office," she said, a little irritably. "I waited for you, was just about to give up and go home."

King looked at her. Standard Nordic supermodel. Blonde hair plaited in pigtails and held together with red ribbon, strong features with a sharp nose, blue eyes and teeth as white as the landscape. She could have been on the cover of Vogue, except King had no idea what she looked like under her multiple layers of clothing. Perhaps that was why they were all so good looking and had such wonderful smiles? Maybe you just got to fall for the person before you made decisions about their build. From here, she looked like a fourteen stone power lifter in her snow suit and bib. He glanced at his watch. It was just after seven. He looked back at her and smiled. "I'm sorry," he said. "I thought I'd come and touch base," he paused. He never said things like that, thinking it made him sound like an area sales manager. "My name is King."

Her expression softened. "Lena Mäkinen."

"Senior Constable," he said.

"Yes."

"How senior is senior?" Her eyes flashed, and he knew he'd offended her. "I'm sorry, I don't know how it works out here."

"Senior enough," she assured him. She sighed. "Coffee?"

"Please," King replied. He didn't drink coffee as a rule, but the British Empire was in full retreat and he found he could get tea in less and less places as coffee completed its march towards global domination with a coffee shop on every corner and a paper cup in every busy person's hand. He conceded that anything warm would be welcome and did not want to rebuke her offer. "White and sugar, if that's okay?"

"Sure," she said amiably. "Take a seat through here." She beckoned him into the office and walked over to a weird-looking machine of chrome and red with taps and buttons all over it. She twisted a tap and the machine started to steam and clunk. "Do you watch American dramas?"

King thought for a moment. He realised he didn't watch much television at all. "Sure," he said. He had watched CSI for a while, but realised it was most likely a rhetorical question.

"My rank is like that of a Sheriff," she paused. "I am the law around here…" She had tried an American Wild West accent, but it hadn't really worked. Somewhere between Wyoming and Munich. She flushed red, turned her back on him as she made the coffee. When she walked the cups over she had returned to her pale self. King thought she was as beautiful a woman as he had ever met. The thought made him feel guilty, but, he reflected, not as much as it should have. "I have two constables under me…" she continued. "We are a small department. When we need further assistance, we have police officers and detectives allocated to us. But largely, we do not have murders up here. A bit of drinking and fighting, some thefts of machinery, perhaps love triangles gone wrong. A husband out for some payback…"

"Cold nights?" King smiled knowingly.

"Everybody needs a snuggle in the cold and sometimes there aren't enough single people to go around," she said light heartedly. "But seriously, about your friend… He was killed by wolves. Nothing more sinister than that."

"Personally, I find the thought of wolves eating up tourists quite sinister," said King, sipping some coffee. To his surprise, it wasn't half bad.

She nodded. "I will take you to the medical centre to sign him over to you in the morning."

"Sign him over?"

"Yes, to take him home."

King shook his head. "Sorry, you misunderstand. I am going to look at the body, and then I want you to take me to where he was found."

"But…" she shook her head. "That is not what I was told. And besides, his body was found many kilometres from here. Across Lake Inarijärvi."

"Then we had best do it in the morning. I take it the lake is frozen?"

"Ah, yes. Very much so."

"But crossable on snowmobile?"

"Of course, but…"

"Then I'll get my head down for the night, meet you back here in the morning," he said. "Say, eight-AM?"

She shrugged. "I suppose." She looked perplexed.

"You don't have to check with anyone more… senior?"

It was a cheap shot, but it got the response he was counting on. "No, of course not!" she snapped. "Eight it is."

"Great." King put down his half-finished cup of coffee. He saw some reports on the desk, had them committed to memory before he looked back at her. "Can you recommend a hotel that will have vacancies?" he asked hopefully. He did not want his accommodation planned by someone he hadn't met, either.

She nodded. "The Witch, Serafina," she said. "The only hotel in town."

Chapter Seven

The room was a double with a sofa and a television and deliciously warm. The en-suite bathroom complete with a jacuzzi bath was the highlight of the otherwise plain, but comfortable room. Pictures, paintings and portraits of witches lined the corridors, and some had even made their way into the room. It wasn't the most settling of decors. But King didn't believe in anything other than flesh and blood and wasn't put off by a few pictures. As he had checked in he had read a plaque about an author making Lake Inarijärvi, or sometimes just Inari, the home of his fictional witch, and he guessed the book had done well and had a following, and the hotel had sprung up because of it.

King had delighted in shedding his clothes. He had hung his snow gear in the wardrobe and removed the layers and folded them over the back of a chair. He was down to a T-shirt and boxers and was resting on the bed sipping a bottle of Carlsberg beer from the mini bar as he waited for room service. He had ordered reindeer meatballs in what the receptionist had called gravy and blood sauce. It had sounded intriguing. He always liked to try local food, having spent years on burgers and club sandwiches in hotels all around the world, and one day realising he had been missing a trick. The meatballs were coming with rye bread, pickled beetroot and mashed potatoes. He had added cheese and crackers and a pot of tea, told them to keep the lemon and asked for a pot of milk.

King had casually asked if the hotel was full as he had checked in. He had refused the first room he had been shown to, asked for another immediately. There was only one hotel in town, and his room had been pre-booked by the liaison officer he was still yet to meet. He had taken a different route, although he was aware there could have been a tracker fitted to the vehicle. But he had drawn the line at staying in a prearranged room. It was basic security, what was referred to as fieldcraft. He never trusted anybody and put the fact he was still alive down to his built-in and well-honed lack of trust.

King looked up at the sound of a knock on the door. He slipped his cargoes on and tucked the pistol into his back pocket. He checked the spy-lens in the door, let the waitress in with the tray. He showed her to the table, thanked her and gave her a five-euro note. A little higher than he would like for a simple tray-drop, but he felt uncomfortable tipping in coins.

The meal was excellent, and he polished off the meatballs and strange combination of pickled beetroot and creamy mashed potatoes, drank the rest of his beer and picked at the cheese and biscuits.

The tea was passable, but the milk tasted sour. He wondered if it was reindeer milk, and the thought made him put the tea down and help himself to another beer from the fridge. He couldn't pronounce the name, but it was darker and stronger than the generic Carlsberg. King flicked on the television, selected Sky News and sat back on the bed. It was at times like this that he missed Caroline. He wondered if things would ever be the same after her ordeal at the hands of her kidnappers. Her mission in life was now to sever links in people trafficking and the forced sex trade. He knew she was fighting an unwinnable battle and setting herself up for defeat. But he also knew how badly she needed to do something, to feel she was doing something. If not for her, then for the girls she had been held with that had been moved on before she could help. She had escaped, while they had been lost forever.

King felt lonely for the first time in years. He had been a widower for five years before he had met Caroline. He had become comfortable on his own, never needing a relationship or company. And then he had fallen in love again, fallen into the comforts of companionship. These past two years had given him a new lease of life. He was less cynical, less bitter. He was more patient, far more outwardly looking. And now, he felt all of that changing again. He felt on the cusp of a trough. He'd been there before, but he wasn't relishing the ride. He wished things could be different but couldn't see how he could change the facts. He didn't doubt Caroline's love for him, but he could see a dramatic shift in focus. He never drank much alcohol as a rule, but he had found himself accepting it more and more of late. The Courvoisier in Amherst's office had dulled the ache, and normally he would never have accepted the offer, and tonight he was well towards the end of his second beer and thinking about a third. He had ordered a couple of vodkas on the plane, too. It wasn't much by most people's standards, but it was out of character.

King picked up the map and laid the acetate on top. He could see that his contact had been thorough. The next marking showed the spot where the MI6 handler's body had been found. Nothing else. Simply three points on a map to aid his investigation. He had no contact methods for the person who had provided him with his car and equipment. No way of using them to further his investigation and mission. He would need to find out more about the second defector if he were to chaperone them back to Britain. Technically, once the defector got clear of Russia, then Finland and Norway were safe zones. The Russians ignored the borders regularly, operated throughout Scandinavia, but there were places with a good infrastructure for a Russian specialist with a secret to hide out safely. But they valued Britain for both what they would make of their wares, and the life it could give them. Which meant that what they had would benefit a world power more than a quiet Nordic country with a pleasant way of life.

King wasn't happy with the arrangements. If he needed more from the MI6 liaison officer and he could not contact them, then he would undoubtedly be contacted himself. And that put King at a disadvantage. He liked to call the shots; not look forever over his shoulder and be a step behind. However, he did not need help looking into the MI6 handler's death. He could do that with the Finnish police officer. The female sheriff of a frozen town on a lake famed for a witch.

Chapter Eight

King nodded a greeting to the waitress, who ticked him off a sheet and showed him to an occupied table. She asked whether he would like English breakfast tea or coffee, and he thought about the milk last night and asked for a black coffee. He looked at the woman seated at his table. Having ditched the snow suit and now dressed in a tight-fitting silk blouse and jeans, Lena Mäkinen did not look like a fourteen stone power lifter. He never really suspected she would, but it had been fun guessing. She was slim in a sporty, outdoorsy way. Small-busted, with toned arms and a flat stomach, she looked like she ran a lot. Or perhaps skied. Running wasn't a pursuit to be practised this far into the Arctic Circle.

She smiled up at him, stood up and held out her hand. "I thought I'd join you for breakfast," she said as King clasped her hand and shook it warmly. "I hope you don't mind?"

King shook his head. He could make out a distinctive perfume over the aroma of her steaming cup of coffee. He was surprised at himself, feeling a mild attraction towards her. "Why would I mind?" he asked. "You don't look dressed for a trip across the lake."

She shrugged. "We'll go and see the body first," she said. "Then get changed and head out to where he was found. I have to warn you though; it is an arduous journey."

King nodded. "How far?"

"One hundred kilometres. That's tough on a snowmobile."

"Tougher on skis," he said casually. "I'll be okay."

The waitress came with King's black coffee and took their orders. Lena chose porridge with cloudberries while King chose smoked salmon, scrambled eggs and potato pancakes. He ate some rye bread with unsalted butter while they waited and spooned some sugar into the coffee.

"So, what does the Home Office do?" she asked.

King had decided to be vague and not go into his Security Service status. "My department provides security for the government," he said.

She nodded. "What was Mister Fitzpatrick doing this far north?"

"He was a nature lover," King lied. "I gather he was up here to see the Northern Lights."

She nodded. "Did you see them last night?"

King felt foolish. He'd forgotten to look outside his window. "No."

"They will be better tonight. A clearer sky," she said. "They are quite captivating."

"I can imagine."

Their breakfast orders arrived, and King could already see the salmon was different to anything he'd eaten before. It was flaky and covered with lemon and dill. It looked like cooked fish, as opposed to the bright red, gelatinous texture he was used to. He tried some with a little of the egg.

"Good?"

"Delicious," he said and meant it.

"I find it interesting that you are not a police officer."

"You do?"

"Yes."

King shrugged. "Just protocol."

"We have the internet," she said. "Even this far north."

"Can't escape progress."

"Or common sense."

"Meaning?"

"It is easy to search," she said flatly. "If a British citizen is murdered, in extraneous circumstances, then Scotland Yard may get involved in an advisory or financial capacity. Like that little girl in Portugal, or the missing boy on one of the Greek islands. But Finland has a competent police service. We are more than capable of dealing with our own crime scenes."

"I have no doubt," King agreed noncommittally. He ate some of the potato pancakes. They were a little like a blini and worked well with the scrambled eggs. "I can see a point where we'll just be going around in circles," he said. "You're an intelligent woman…"

"Police officer," she corrected him. "Being a woman has nothing to do with it."

"My apologies," he said.

She shrugged like it was nothing, but King could tell she had not had an easy ride in her career.

"Fitzpatrick was a spook, wasn't he?"

King sipped some of his tea as he eyed her warily. He placed the cup down and studied her face. He decided she could be trusted. Perhaps he would get what needed to be done if he levelled with her, gained her trust? He could already see how suspicious she was. She had pieced enough together, had enough doubts to search the internet and look at Britain's protocols concerning international crime.

"What makes you ask that?" he asked.

"Mister King, there is nothing up there for a nature lover," she said. "The Northern Lights can be seen from anywhere here. A lot further South, even. Up here, at this time of year, it is a fight for survival. The birds have either flown South or are tucked up in their nests. The bears are in torpor, asleep for the winter. What you would probably call hibernation. The wolves are hungry and everything lower in the food chain is prey to something else. The environment is too severe, too cold for nature lovers to be out roaming the woods."

"So?"

"So, he was staying at The Eagle's Nest Hotel. It is built high up on a peak. The highest man-made peak in the world."

"Man-made?"

"Scree and rock moved in from Russia. The Russians built a hydro-electric power station, using rivers that flow to and from the lake for power."

King frowned. "But it's frozen."

She smiled. "The Russians spent millions on the site. Geo-thermal hot rock technology keeps the rivers from freezing. The water powers the turbines, then the water is used for cooling. Apparently, the water comes out of there at almost boiling point. For four-hundred metres from the mouth of the river into the lake, the water is warm all year round. And the river that flows from the lake into the Arctic Ocean leaves the power station just as hot. The dirt and rock dug for the geo-thermal shafts was moved out there across the border at the owner's request and built into a mountain. Like I said, the largest man-made hill in the world."

"So, what's the problem with Fitzpatrick being up there?"

"The hotel is secluded. Like I said, built on top of a man-made mountain."

"It can't be that big."

She smiled. "Trust me, it is. They built the mountain around a funicular. That way, people can enter The Eagle's Nest Hotel in all weathers and besides, any roadway to the hotel would not be safe in winter. Not for paying guests, at least. Snowploughs and all-terrain vehicles can get supplies and maintenance crews and equipment up there, but the funicular adds a sense of drama and theatre for the guests. As if the hotel with its turrets, sat atop the mountain like a medieval castle wasn't theatre enough."

"Well, how big is this mountain?" asked King, marvelling at her English. Just a slight accent that to King sounded more Russian with an American lilt than Finnish, but otherwise flawless.

"I suppose, four-hundred metres. It's shaped like a large mound with a decent ski slope on the northern side. Beginners to intermediates. Chair lifts as well."

"And all built from waste from a power station?"

"Of sorts," she paused. "I suppose nobody really knows how much ground was removed for the geo-thermal aspect."

"Is there Russian money behind the hotel?"

She frowned. "I never really thought about that."

"Better get on that internet of yours again, then."

"You can bet on that."

"So, what's so wrong with Fitzpatrick staying there?"

"It's an ideal location for lovers. The Eagle's Nest builds an ice hotel as well. At the start of winter. It melts away in May. The ice hotel is an extension of pods, really. A place where couples come to watch the Northern Lights. It is built onto the hotel, so guests can walk straight through to the main hotel."

"Does it have to be exclusively couples?" King asked dubiously. "Sounds exactly the sort of place I'd take some R and R."

Lena hesitated. "I suppose not..." she said. "But it would be an unusual place for a man on his own to be staying. Especially a man who was up there simply for nature watching."

"So, what do you think Fitzpatrick was doing?"

She looked at him, her eyebrow cocked slightly. "You have covered a reasonably broad base with Home Office. That department oversees so many things. The police, the Border Force, Revenue and Customs, MI5..."

King could see she had been busy. He could also see that working with her relied on mutual trust. Could he trust her? What ulterior motive could she have?

"Fitzpatrick was working with the Foreign and Commonwealth Office." He shrugged and added, "MI6," King said quietly.

"MI6?"

"Yes. And MI6 believe he was murdered."

"And what department are you with, really?"

"MI5."

"And they investigate murders?"

"I have before."

"But it's not in their general remit."

"There's lots of things that aren't technically in MI5's remit. It doesn't stop them doing it though."

"Them?"

King smiled. Old habits die hard. Too many years working for the opposition. "Why don't you consider murder as an option?" he asked.

She shook her head. "He was killed by wolves," she said emphatically. "You haven't seen the body, yet. Trust me, you will change your mind. When I was twelve, my family dog was killed by wolves. He was shredded to the bone. He was a German Shepherd. A big dog. Aggressive if pushed by other dogs. He wouldn't have been able to put up any sort of fight. Wolves are not dogs..." she trailed off, her eyes glossy.

King could see vulnerability there, a girl at odds with both her age and her status. It made her even more attractive. "Well, let's go and see the body, then."

Chapter Nine

Lena signed them both in at the reception of the health centre and led the way through a door off the waiting room and down a dark corridor. Their snow trousers rustled as they walked. They had left their other garments hung on a series of hooks inside the foyer of the building.

Lena opened the door at the end and they were greeted by an overweight man in his fifties sporting a beard and tousled hair. He wore thick rimmed glasses, and it was difficult to see where the hair ended, and the beard began. Like PT Barnham's Dog Boy. Or maybe Chewbacca from *Star Wars*. King found himself staring, and he was a man not easily shocked.

The man spoke quietly for a moment with the police officer, then looked at King, cocking his head to see up and under his jam jar lenses. "You are wasting your time," he said. "The cause of death was a wolf."

"And you are?"

"What?"

"Your name?"

The man looked surprised. "Doctor Engelmann."

King nodded. "I'm Alex King."

The doctor shrugged like he didn't care, which King suspected he didn't.

"So, Doctor Engelmann, the cause of death would have been from blood loss, organ failure or even asphyxiation." said King. "Death resulting from a wolf attack, maybe. But not the primary cause."

"There is no point in being pedantic, Mister King."

"There are factors that should not be overlooked."

"It was a wolf."

"Just one wolf?"

"Wolves are powerful creatures. Savage."

King looked at Lena, who was nodding in agreement. No doubt remembering the dog from her childhood.

King stared at the man, his hirsute features difficult to ignore. "So, what makes you rule out death due to hypothermia and the body being scavenged by a wolf?"

"Blood loss."

"Maybe he nicked an artery?"

"It was a wolf."

"And not a pack?"

"What difference does that make?"

King shrugged. "I just want to know if you're good enough to identify if Mister Fitzpatrick was killed by one wolf or ten. Because I imagine a single wolf would eat some of him, a few wolves would eat most of him, and a pack of wolves would strip him down to the bone." Engelmann looked at King, was about to say something, but seemed to change his mind. King smiled. "Let me see the body, please."

Engelmann tutted, turned and opened the door behind him. The room was clad in white plastic sheeting with all the joins sealed with trim strips. The floor was vinyl with a mineral element which glinted in the light. It had been laid, fitted and glued a full foot up the wall to allow for deep cleaning and sluicing. In the centre of the room was a stainless-steel table with a gutter running around it and a tap on a metal hose resting in a holder at one end with a shallow sink and ridged draining board built into the table. Engelmann led the way past the table and to a bank of metal doors. There were only four doors. It wasn't a busy part of the world.

The doctor opened one of the hatches and pulled out a trolley. He looked at King with a cynical expression and a wry smile. He had intended to shock him. It might have worked, had King not eaten his breakfast over worse sights in the past.

Lena looked away, took a breath and forced herself to look back at the corpse. Or what was left of it.

"Well, forensics are out of the window," King said. "Transference is already happening from the three of us."

"You're worried about contamination?" Engelmann scoffed. "Look at it!"

"What do you want us to see?" Lena asked, apparently as exasperated in King as the doctor.

King walked over to a counter and pulled a pair of blue rubber surgical gloves from a cardboard dispensing box. He pulled them on as he walked back and eased the tatters of shirt from the sticky flesh. He could see the wolf, or wolves had been busy. The face was gone. As were the ears. Soft tissue was easily pulled and gnawed at, King supposed. The torso was opened-up and the flaps of skin was in tatters.

"Internal organs?" King asked without looking up.

"Gone," Engelmann paused. "As have most of the intestines."

King moved around, bent down and peered into the cavity. He reached inside and gently pulled out some intestines. He let them roll around in the palm of his hand. He looked up at Lena. She had turned pale. She was perspiring, beads of sweat mottling her brow. He looked back at the intestines, then up at the doctor.

"You still think it's a wolf?" he asked.

"Of course!"

"Interesting."

King could see that the man's salopettes had been more difficult for the wolves to get through. There were bite marks and tears, the fibres peeling away more easily in one direction than another. Something to do with the weave.

He pulled at the material, could see that the man's genitals were gone. His legs though, were largely intact. King ran his hands over the body's legs, stopped when he noticed something. He bent down, using the light above him to catch the sight of the material better. He eased his fingers around a patch of blood, a smear.

"You don't believe this was a wolf?" Engelmann asked incredulously.

"I believe he was eaten," King replied.

"But he wasn't killed by a wolf."

"Then what?" Lena asked.

"He was killed by a knife."

"A knife?" Engelmann scoffed, then broke into laughter. "Tell me, why do you think that?" King pulled on the remains of the intestines. The sound was wet, but it was the smell which was most unpleasant. Lena gagged and turned away. She swallowed hard and turned back, her pallor gone, replaced with a blush which radiated heat. King ignored her. He thought most people would have vomited, so she had nothing to prove to him. Engelmann smirked, but his expression became incredulous as King pointed to a link of gut that looked like a length of Cumberland sausage.

"That's why," he said. He fingered a clean slash of four inches or so. "Too clean for an animal to have made. Whether it was one wolf or a pack of wolves. Or even a wolverine," King paused, looking at Lena. "What you might call a gulu-gulu." He smiled. He'd done his research, too.

Lena forgot all about the smell and leaned in. She stared at the slash, looked up at King. "That does look like a clean cut…"

King dropped the length of intestine and walked over to the examination table and pulled on a length of paper towel. He wiped his gloved hands and turned back. He wished he could see some of Engelmann's face under his incredible beard to gain insight to his colour. The doctor's opinion had been called, but King wasn't done yet. He looked closely at the thick nylon salopettes, gently ran his fingertips over the material. "I noticed this," he said. He circled his finger around a patch of bloodstain. "Here, this looks like a smudge. There are bloodstains all over, but this stood out…" He looked at Engelmann and added, "To me, that is."

"What is it?" asked Lena.

"Blood," replied King. "But inside the smear looks like fingertips. There is also a thin, clean cut, as there is on his intestines. Again, four inches or so in length and barely slicing through the material, but you can see a clean slice through the top weave. There is blood either side of the cut." He straightened, removed the gloves and tossed them at Engelmann's feet. The bin was just as near, but he thought the man deserved to be rattled. "I think, or rather, I'm convinced that Fitzpatrick was gutted wide open and left for the wolves. That slash in his guts would denote that." He pointed at the smear and the thin slice in the material of the man's snow trousers. "Whoever did it then wiped their hand and the blade clean. One way, and then the other. Most hunting knives are sharpened and honed on a stone and do not have an equal edge. The blade leans, ever-so-slightly, to one side or the other. The person wiped one way, then the other and the knife edge just kissed the material enough to cut through part of the weave. Not all the way through. The blood smears from thick, through to thin. The marking is unnatural, but the cut in the material confirms that he was killed, murdered." He looked back at Engelmann. "I'm surprised you missed that, doctor."

King turned back to the cadaver. The left hand was missing, the flesh taken clean off the bone all the way up to the elbow. The right hand was intact, although the wolves had chewed most of the way through the thicker parts of the meat and stripped most of the bicep away. Survival was about taking the easiest option, and animals were masters of survival. Fitzpatrick had been disembowelled and that had opened the store cupboard. The animals had taken the pungent and malleable internal organs. Rich in minerals and calories with little effort expelled. The torso was soft and there was plenty to eat without working through bones. King could picture the scene, the carnage. He just hoped the MI6 man had been dead before the animals had started feeding. He studied the intact hand. He could see the frostbite on the fingers, the broken nails. He suspected how that had happened, but he decided not to divulge anything more.

"I… I must have been taken in by the severity of the trauma," Engelmann said quietly. King stared at him for a few seconds before answering. His stare was as cold as the temperature outside, his eyes glacier blue and unnerving. "Yes, that must have been it," he said coldly.

Chapter Ten

"So, have you ridden a snowmobile before?"

Like so much in his life, King had to think. He had compartmentalised much of his existence, put incidents to bed far too often. He shook his head, still unsure. Better to get a briefing anyway.

"Forget anything you've ridden or driven before," she paused, doing her utmost to suppress a smile. "These things are on another level for acceleration."

King studied the machine in front of him. He decided he hadn't ridden a snowmobile. But he had ridden plenty of quadbikes, a couple of fast motorcycles and even driven a Jaguar F-Type. The supercharged one. He was quietly confident.

"Fully automatic," she said. "Neutral select here, press it before you start and when you stop. Accelerator here, or what some people call the throttle. It revs like a chainsaw, so no gears." She indicated a thumb lever. "No front brake as there is on a motorcycle, but the left one is a brake to the belt-drive, and it's severe. Because of the traction of the snow, as soon as you take your thumb off the throttle, the machine will slow dramatically. The brake will be like dropping an anchor."

King had already sussed the controls. Similar in layout and function to the last ATV, or quadbike, he had ridden except for the front brake lever. He had already looked at the starter button and like most utilitarian machines, there was an idiot instructional block of pictures stuck to the frame.

"I'll do my best to keep an eye on you, but take note if you see me do this..." She held up a fist. "That means I'm stopping suddenly. The lake is wide, and we will avoid the islands, but you might still want to ride in my tracks, as the going will be easier."

King nodded. "I think I'll be okay," he said confidently, if with a little arrogance.

Lena shouldered the sling of the Tikka hunting rifle. It was made of polymer composite and the barrel and bolt were stainless-steel. No outer cleaning or maintenance required. He had no idea of the calibre, but the five-round magazine looked wide and thick.

"How long has Doctor Engelmann been here?"

She swung her leg over the snowmobile, looked at him as she straddled the seat. "A year or so," she replied. "Why?"

"And his credentials?"

"All good, I imagine. Nothing to do with the police service."

"Then who decides?"

"The medical centre is a private practice but subsidised through government grants. So those entitled, and that's all Finnish citizens, get free healthcare. The fact it's a private practice is because living this far north has got to be a choice. Private contractors have lucrative benefits. And many of the Sami hold a protected status. They do not earn the levels of income that the Finnish do, so the practices must be equipped with good facilities and amenities, like surgery and x-rays. And then there is tourism. These people are not entitled to free healthcare. There are many visitors up here for the skiing, and although not world class, the snow is guaranteed. And of course, there are the Santa visitors..." she smiled like it was a secret only the people of Lapland really knew.

"And Engelmann's tenure?" King asked. "How did that come about?"

"Doctor Jokela was killed in a traffic accident. He slid off the road and hit a tree. Very sad..."

"So, Engelmann was appointed?"

"I imagine he bought the practice," she replied. "I don't know the details, but that would be his way in.

King nodded. His face was near-frozen, and he pulled his beanie down as far as it would go and pulled the fake fur-lined hood over the top. Lena handed him a pair of goggles and he put them on over his hood once he got onto his machine. Lena started her snowmobile and it throbbed into life, then settled into a surprisingly quiet tick-over.

She adjusted her scarf and hood, shouted above the sound of King starting his engine. "Why? Don't you trust him?"

King shrugged. He said nothing, simply nodded for her to lead the way.

Lena drove steadily out of the parking lot and used the edge of the road for approximately two hundred metres before turning off and heading through a well-used snow path through a belt of forest. King found the throttle responsive, increased it a little to close the gap. Lena slowed and disappeared in front of him. King could see why after a few more seconds, as he caught sight of her heading down a sixty-foot cliff at an angle of forty-five degrees. He slowed, followed in blind faith and found himself gripping on with his knees as if he were on horseback. Lena shot forwards at tremendous speed, and when King levelled out he pressed the throttle and both hands came away from the handlebars and he almost sprawled backwards. He struggled to sit up, then finally got his hands back on the grips when he had slowed enough. He had never experienced acceleration like it, short of freefall parachute jumps. He took a better grip, opened-up the throttle and held on for dear life as the snowmobile shot past sixty miles-per-hour in around two seconds. He hung on all the way up the rev-range but dared not take his eyes off the ground ahead of him to check his speed. The traction was so complete that he felt the machine flexing underneath him. He had ridden a few motorbikes in the past. Several trail bikes and a sports bike with a full race fairing and 1000cc's of tuned engine, but that didn't even begin to feel close to the acceleration of the snowmobile. He knew the snowmobile would top out at around one-hundred miles-per-hour, simple physics would control that, but getting there was the most extreme way he had ever travelled. He caught Lena up, slowed to what he figured was around seventy and settled into her machine's tracks like she had told him.

The ride was flat, and the snow was hard and frozen. King could already feel icy air through some seams of clothing. His goggles had steamed up and he was using all sorts of angles tilting his head to see through the mist. His arms were aching already, and he found the thumb position awkward. It would not be long before his thumb cramped altogether.

Lena held up her fist and King eased off the throttle. He pulled alongside and selected the neutral button on the handlebar. The engines on tick-over were a welcomed break to his ears.

"Okay?" she asked.

"Fine."

"Fast?"

"You could say that."

"I thought I'd give your thumb a rest," she said, flexing her fingers. "I'm used to it, use of these most days, but each winter, it takes a while to get used to."

King squeezed his hand into fists about ten times. "I can see that," he said.

"Clear your goggles," she said.

King removed them and wiped them with his gloves. He could feel the fog had already frozen. He scratched at the ice inside the lens. "I've never been somewhere as cold as this," he conceded.

"I love it," she said. "The air, the clear skies, the feeling of shedding your heavy clothes in a warm room… It's glorious."

King replaced his goggles and tidied up his beanie and hood. The area of skin on his cheeks which was uncovered felt numb. "City girl?"

She nodded. "Helsinki," she said. "Career suicide, I suppose. I'll never be the detective I wanted to be, but I'm happy doing what I do. The community is fun, too."

"A bad break-up, a fresh start?" King asked.

She stared at him, her eyes hostile within her goggles. "Yes," she said. "How did you guess that?"

"It seems the sort of place people run away to," he paused. "I contemplated living in places like this, once."

"After a bad break-up?"

"My wife died," he said.

"And you're still alone?"

"No."

"Married?"

"No."

"Serious?"

"Yes," King shrugged. Despite Caroline's sabbatical, her one-tracked ideal, he wasn't so sure anymore, but wouldn't have answered any other way. "You?"

"No. But I like it that way," she replied. "For the most part," she added. "We all have needs, of course."

King nodded. He wasn't sure if she was dropping hints, or if he had misread it. He chose his usual approach and said nothing. He'd decided long ago that he couldn't get in the shit any deeper if he said nothing. She stared at him, her eyes softening.

"We'd better get going," he said.

Chapter Eleven

He had the edge. Tracking your quarry was one thing but knowing exactly where your quarry would be was quite another. And that was worth everything. Of course, getting there would be difficult. He did not have a huge time advantage, but he did have local knowledge. He would have to travel a little further East for his tracks to remain out of view, but he would do so at full speed. He would not have to slow for an amateur snowmobile rider. His muscles were well-acquainted with the controls and buffeting that would have to be endured at riding at full-speed, and his controls were lighter to use. An older machine, though certainly no slower. Well-oiled and maintained, the parts worn enough to work easily to the touch.

The myriad of islands would work well for him. Keep his tracks from view. He knew his way in the winter, knew his way by boat in the summertime, too. He knew where the rocks were hidden, protruding above the lake ice and just under the snow. Perilous for most, and that was why they travelled in huge tracts of three or four straight lines. But he could weave his way through and gain precious minutes. He had already started out ahead of them, which would give him enough time to set up his hide and watch them through the scope of his hunting rifle.

Chapter Twelve

King's arms ached as if they were on fire and his legs shook with the constant grip his thighs maintained against the edges of the seat. His thumb felt as though it would fall off at any minute. He eased off the throttle and the machine slowed dramatically. As he neared Lena's stationary machine, he applied the brake and pulled up alongside. He cut the engine and the silence was overwhelming.

"Who discovered the body?" he asked loudly, his ears ringing. He removed his goggles and pulled down the hood to adjust his beanie. It was easier without gloves, so he removed them and put them down on the dashboard, which housed the speedometer, rev-counter and fuel gauge.

Lena removed her goggles also. Steam cooled in the air around her face, misty and pulsating as she breathed. "A trapper," she said. "A Sami."

"What else did he say?"

"Nothing," she replied. "He called it in. I suppose we were lucky he did that much."

"Really?"

She nodded. "The Sami are integrating with Finnish society, but some are still traditional. There are families out here, entire tribes even, who live in tents and keep up with their reindeer herds all year. Nomads. Others live wild, off the grid. This trapper phoned it into the central police number and reported it when he reached a large enough settlement."

"You don't find it strange that he did that and disappeared?"

"Not really. He may well have been bear waking, wanted to avoid questions, as it's illegal."

"Bear waking?" King asked, pulling his snow goggles back on. Already, his skin was freezing.

Lena nodded as she did the same and adjusted her hood. She stepped off the snowmobile and crunched through a top layer of softer ice. "See?" she pointed to her boot, an inch into the ice. "It is warming!"

King laughed. The thermometer on his instrument panel showed -22°C.

Lena smiled. "Bear waking is the term used for killing hibernating bears. It's dangerous work."

"Sounds it, what with the bear being asleep and all," King said incredulously. He stepped off the machine and adjusted his clothing. He brushed a hand subconsciously against the pistol in his pocket. "Sounds more dangerous for the bear," he added.

Well, it is more dangerous than it sounds. First, the hunter must find the bear's resting place. Usually a hole dug out of the first fall of snow. The hunter does this by locating a suitable place, then listening for the bear's breathing or heartbeat through a specially prepared stick, that they insert into the ground and hold to their ear. When they find the bear, they must then dig," she paused. "Very carefully. A charging bear will explode through the snow and ice, a three-hundred kilo animal that is scared, and most pissed off." She unhooked the hunting rifle from her shoulder and worked the bolt. King saw the flash of a large brass cartridge leave the magazine and slide seamlessly into the breech. The stainless-steel bolt locked forward as she locked the bolt action down. "But you can't just shoot into the hole or the roof of the cavern. That would mean far too much digging. You need to coax the bear out. Prod at it with your hand, or even a foot if the bear is deep. Wake the bear and get them to come after you. Time it right, and the hunter puts a bullet down through its head as it leaves the tunnel you have dug. Time it wrong…" She cradled the rifle and took a step in the snow. "And the bear gets a mid-hibernation meal. Like a home delivery," she smiled. "A bear is good meat and the fur is invaluable in winter."

King followed but said nothing. He had entered the caves of the Tora Bora with nothing but a knife, a pistol and a pair of night-vision goggles. He had been hunting Taliban commanders at the time. Men holed up, scared and all out of options, and ready to fight to their last breath and drop of blood. The Taliban had not had night-vision goggles. After first contact, when they extinguished all lights, they hadn't even known he was there. It had been butchery. But his experience hunting in those caves gave him a newfound respect for the Sami hunter who would do such things for a pelt of fur and some fresh meat.

They trudged through the snow and ice and into a belt of trees. The forest was sparsely grown. The thickest tree was no more than the average man's waist in circumference. The branches started at around four feet from the ground, around six-inches thick. To King, they looked like wispy Christmas trees, but he could see there were different varieties, although none of the trees were as big as he would have expected. He knew that trees only grew so far north, another fifty miles and there would be no trees at all, merely scrub and tundra.

King stopped walking. He was tuned into his surroundings. Once the engines had been switched off, the only sounds were of their own footsteps in the crisp icy crust of the snow. He could hear no sounds of nature. Now that his ears had stopped ringing at the incessant hum of the snowmobile, it felt was so quiet that he could hear his own heartbeat with the exertion of walking in the cumbersome clothing and thick boots. He could hear Lena's breathing, her efforts, but nothing more. But then he had heard something else. Something out of place. He looked to his right. The same trees. The same monochrome landscape. Snow and trees. Nothing more.

"What is it?" Lena asked, stopping in front of him.

"I don't know," King replied. "I thought I heard something."

"An animal, perhaps?" she asked. "There are arctic foxes, wolves. Partridges roost in the trees as well."

"Maybe."

Snow blew down on them, then as they looked up, the sky filled with diamonds as ice crystals filled the air. The air grew thick, and the trees started to sway. In a matter of seconds, the trees were blowing wildly, ice crystals shut out the light and the already dull sky became darker.

"A storm!" she shouted.

She pulled him by the arm and led the way down an embankment. She continued to pull at him, but he broke free and could already see what she was attempting to do. King powered his legs against the ice and pushed her down into the lee of the wind. She fell onto her knees and checked the rifle's safety catch before she used the butt like a shovel and dug into the bank. The wind was savagely cold, blowing ice over their heads as she dug. Once the ice crust lifted, King got his gloved hands into the snow and dug as hard and as frantically as he could. He could feel the super-chilled wind on the exposed parts of his face, and the clothes were only holding out so much. He glanced at Lena, the look on her face said it all.

"This is the precursor to the storm!" she shouted. "If it hits, it could be like this for days..."

They both dug hard, and soon there was enough indentation in the bank to get themselves flush to the ground. King started spreading the broken ice into mounds beside them, to afford more cover. They tucked up together, Lena abandoning the rifle and wrapping her arms and legs around King as he did the same. The wind howled savagely through the trees and the occasional crack resonated around them as the weaker trees, brittle from the cold, snapped off and fell to the forest floor.

The light was all but gone. The ambient glow of light from the snow was all they could see by. The ice particles, emptied out of the trees, blew over them and covered them in the refuge of their shelter. King could feel Lena hugging him tightly. She was scared, taking comfort in him, as much as trying to keep herself insulated from the savage wind.

There was a violent buffeting, a screech of

wind like that of an old vacuum cleaner, then almost as quickly as it had hit them, it dispersed, and the ice particles fell out of a still sky like a gentle fall of snow.

King let go of Lena and brushed the layer of snow and ice from his clothes. "What the hell?" he said, as he pushed himself up and dug out the rifle. He released the magazine, unloaded the live round from the breech. He looked at the round. .300 Winchester Magnum. A large calibre which could take down anything on land. He checked the barrel for snow by blowing down the breech. He saw his own breath at the muzzle and reloaded the rifle. He glanced and saw Lena staring at him. She had a hand inside her pocket and a look he recognised in her eyes. He would have bet his life her hand was wrapped around the butt of her service Glock 9mm. He held the rifle out to her and she took it cautiously with her left hand, took her right hand back out of her pocket. "Sorry," he said. "Force of habit."

"For Home Office investigators?"

King smiled. "So, what the hell was with that wind?"

"Arctic squall," she answered. "If the forecasters were right, then there's a lot more than that on the way."

"When?"

"A couple of days," she said, quickening her pace. "Back there, I'm amazed you sensed it coming."

"What?"

"The squall," she said. "I'm amazed you sensed it."

King said nothing. That wasn't what he had sensed, but in truth, with the suddenness of the squall, he had forgotten what had spooked him. It had been a moment of survival. The dramatic drop in temperature, the severity of the wind and the blinding ice storm. He had become lost in the moment. He looked to his right again, but nothing seemed at odds with nature now. It was quiet. Almost too quiet. As if something or someone had scared the animals away, long before they had arrived.

Chapter Thirteen

"We are here," Lena announced. She stopped walking and pointed across the clearing.

King nodded and looked around the clearing. "Show me," he said.

Lena studied the area. She looked uncertain. The trees all looked the same and the ground was white. She turned her back to him and King saw her remove a glove, hold it between her teeth and check her phone. She looked up decisively and led the way across the clearing. She stopped when they reached a series of ice ridges. "Over there, by that tree," she said, pointing to a large spindly spruce. The branches were thin and did not start until they were eight-feet from the ground.

King walked to the tree. He could see the scarring from a bullet. It had chipped off a chunk of bark and driven a groove through the wood. He looked at Lena, but she was staring at the ground. The squall had blown off the dusting of ice and there were blood stains in the snow. King looked back at Lena again, but she was studying the belt of trees at the edge of the clearing. She had the rifle gripped firmly in both hands.

"Are you okay?" he asked.

"I thought I saw a wolf," she replied. "But it's gone now."

"How was the body when you found it?"

"I…" she shrugged. "Horrible," she said. "Torn to shreds."

King stood up. "Did you notice the bullet strike?"

"He wasn't shot," she said.

"In the tree."

"What? No."

"It's as clear as day," he said. The irony that it was not yet three-PM and the darkness was fading rapidly. He pointed at the mark, a four-inch diameter piece of bark missing, new yellow-white wood underneath with a channel cut into it and lead colouring where the copper coating of the hunting bullet had split, and the soft lead underneath had deformed and left a tell-tale mark. To those who knew about such things.

"I must have missed that," she said.

King scanned the clearing, looked back at her, but focused on the rifle. It was pointed at his stomach, her hands unwavering.

"You never saw Fitzpatrick's body before this morning, did you? No, don't answer that. You hadn't." King watched her eyes, saw indecision in them. He thought of her reaction in the morgue. It had been a terrible sight, but if she had been at the crime scene, then she would have known what to expect. "You're not even a police officer. Who are you? And where is Senior Constable Mäkinen?"

She looked at him and smiled. "How did you know?"

"Where is she?"

"Dead, of course."

"And the doctor that Engelmann replaced? You killed him too?"

"Not me, personally. But yes, he was killed."

King looked at her, she had been playing a role. And she had immersed herself totally. Only her reaction inside the morgue over Fitzpatrick's body and her indecision out here had given her away. He wondered how much of what she had told him was the real Lena Mäkinen's life, or whether she had adlibbed the whole thing. Perhaps she used her own experiences. Either way, she had been utterly convincing. "Who are you?" he asked.

"Not your concern."

"Russian?"

She smiled. "Not your concern."

King looked at the rifle. It was still pointing at him.

"Who are you waiting for?"

"Someone to take care of you."

"The same person who killed Lena and the other doctor?"

"I imagine."

"And you don't do that sort of thing in the FSB?" She sneered, and he said, "GRU, then?"

She shrugged like it was no matter. "I could do that sort of thing. But that wasn't my orders."

"Don't be so sure. You almost threw up over Fitzpatrick's body," he said, taking off his gloves methodically and tucking them under his left armpit. He gripped them into fists and blew on them, warming them up and bringing some life back to them. "That's why I knew you hadn't seen it before. But I only knew for sure when you needed your phone to find the site. What was it, a text or GPS?"

"Clever man," she said quietly. "GPS. But not so clever with a gun aimed at him."

"So, tell me about the good doctor. One of Russia's finest sent to cover incidents like Fitzpatrick? Or to smooth over the crime scene of any potential defector who meets a vicious end out in those woods?"

"Both counts, I suspect."

"So, Russia knows it has people who want out, who want to sell what they have to the West. So much so, they put a team in to block their way, clear up the fallout."

She shrugged. "We think of everything," she said. "If we can manipulate a man into the White House from behind our computer terminals, we can get ahead of a few traitors."

"Well, looks like they thought of everything," King said sardonically. "Except for sending an amateur like you to do a professional's job."

"You don't look like such a professional from where I'm standing."

King dropped the massive brass cartridge onto the ice between them. She stared at it, but when she looked back up at him, he had the Walther in his un-gloved hand. She looked confused, hurt even. Like he had betrayed a trust and couldn't see the irony in that. Her expression changed to anger and the click of the bolt releasing and the rim that housed the firing pin striking the neck of the empty chamber sounded loudly in the stillness of the clearing. Even so, King flinched at the sound, relief that his gamble had played out. She glared at him and her right hand shot forwards and took hold of the bolt.

"Don't!" King warned her harshly.

She still tried to work the action, something in her eyes that told King it was a Hail Mary. Desperation. She was going for it. He saw the bolt pull backwards, the glint of brass as the cartridge in the magazine was exposed. She drove the bolt forwards then dropped to the ground as King fired.

He kicked the rifle out of her loose grip, kept the pistol aimed at her. The bullet had struck her dead-centre. There was a little blood at the edges of the clean hole in her jacket. He saw her look up at him. He had seen the same look before. Too many times to count, but enough to remember. Her right hand rested near her pocket. He remembered her doing this earlier, when he had checked over the rifle. He had thought it strange enough to hedge his bets then. A sleight of hand, and the weapon was locked down on an empty breech.

Amateurs and professionals.

The dying and the living.

King stepped onto her pocket. He could feel the form and hardness of the pistol even under his insulated boots. Her hand moved away from her pocket and dropped limply into her lap. She died looking up at him. She didn't try to say anything, didn't waste her last moments swearing vengeance or cursing his being. Most people didn't. The life left her eyes and he turned and picked up the rifle, shouldered it by the strap and made his way over to where the MI6 officer had died.

The squall had cleared the ground of ice crystals, taking the ground down to the last snowfall. The terrain was made up of layers. Snow fell, froze and each time the snow fell a new layer was made. The ice crystals were the result of moistness in the air at the warmest point of the day, then freezing rapidly as the colder night air froze. The crystals cast a layer on everything, like dew on spring grass. It gave the appearance of freshly fallen snow. The squall had blown it all away, no doubt depositing it many miles away when the wind's strength had blown out.

King could see the blood frozen into the snow. There was a lot of blood, but then a wolf or wolves had feasted on Fitzpatrick's body. For as long as it took to make forensic detection too difficult. A death camouflaged by nature. King suspected the real Lena Mäkinen had not been fooled by their attempts. That was probably why she had made Senior Constable. And certainly, why she had been killed. Engelmann's efforts had been thwarted, and whoever this dead female agent was had been called in at short notice. She would have been a dead-ringer for the Finnish police officer, but she would have been a last-minute recruit. Lena's substitute had clearly needed directions on her phone by way of text message or GPS. She hadn't been aware of the bullet strike either. That would have been noted by a half-competent police officer as they inspected the crime scene. Somebody had known that MI6 were sending someone to investigate their dead agent. In this case, quid-pro-quo by MI5 in the form of Alex King.

King surveyed the scene. The bullet strike on the tree, the blood in Fitzpatrick's final resting place. He closed his eyes, envisioned a man cornered, scared, hunted. He looked again at the bullet strike again. Tracked back along the ridge. He estimated the height of the embankment, an average-sized man taking aim with a rifle. The height of the bullet strike. He looked at the distance, estimated it at one-hundred metres. There would be little drop from a hunting round in one of the most likely calibres. He supposed .308 was the most popular hunting calibre. It was certainly the most widely available and covered the most bases in terms of hunting anything outside of the big five African game. The cold would denote a fifteen percent drop in trajectory. He made his way across the clearing and stopped at the top of the embankment. The squall had blown the loose ice away and it did not take King long to find two sets of footprints. He could see from where he stood that two people had paused here. Taken their time. One had stood still, while the other had moved around behind them. King placed his foot over the prints. He stood a shade under six-foot and wore size elevens. There were no hard and fast rules, but he could guess the sex of the owners of the prints. He would estimate average-sized males. One print was lined with modern treads, the other was smooth. The smoother print was shallower. This could denote weight difference, but more likely the smooth prints were from someone wearing traditional indigenous hide boots.

King shouldered the rifle and aimed across the clearing at the tree with the bullet strike. He lined the crosshairs on the mark, lowered it an inch and gently squeezed the trigger. The rifle kicked wildly against his shoulder, the barrel rose, and the clearing was filled with the noise of the gunshot. The echo resonated and cracked off the hard and frozen surroundings. He re-sighted on the strike and saw that he had hit the tree a fraction lower. Just about dead-on where he had been aiming. So, no drop from a .300 Winchester Magnum bullet. He trudged back across the clearing and studied the bullet strike. He touched the new wood underneath the bark which had been removed. The tail of the bullet was visible, almost flush with the wood. He knew the power difference between the .308 and the .300 Winchester Magnum. He could see that it was more likely to have been a .308 or a 30-06. The tree was frozen and the difference in power would have been enough to ricochet. King worked the bolt and applied the safety. He shouldered the weapon by its strap and looked at the base of the tree. He could imagine Fitzpatrick crouching behind, taking cover from the gunfire. Or perhaps he was done. Perhaps he was sitting down and resting. His back against the tree. King thought about the body in the medical centre. The wolves had taken one hand, but what about the other? That had been bloodied and frost-bitten. Two of the nails had broken away. King studied the ground at the base of the tree. He dug at the ice with the toe of his boot. There were two different textures, a split in layers. He bent down and dug his gloved fingers into the snow. He straightened up and used the buttstock of the rifle to loosen the ice further. He could see an orange glint in the snow. He reached for it, but a huge chunk of ice was blown out of the ground just inches from his fingertips.

King was already moving. He had taken in the eruption of ice, the noise of the gunshot, still echoing around the clearing. He made it to a nearby tree and was diving behind it for cover, already realising that it was no bigger than himself. A second gunshot hit the tree, but King had already subconsciously worked out the position of the gun before he hit the ground.

Standard hunting rifles used flush-fitting five-round magazines. King had dropped the round at the woman's feet. He had taken a shot with the rifle to ascertain the distance and approximate calibre of the rifle that had made the bullet strike. Which gave him three bullets. He had six more in the Walther, but the shooter was already too far away. With the extreme cold and thick Arctic clothing to penetrate, King wouldn't have much faith in the tiny weapon at more than twenty-five metres. And that was best-case scenario.

Another shot rang-out. The tree blocked the round, but it was close. King could feel the bark hit his shoulder. He got the rifle up to his shoulder and eased himself out for a peek. He did not use the sight yet, just needed to see some movement.

There was no movement, but there was smoke. The super-heating of the previously ice-cold barrel and the residue of hot propellant created both steam and smoke. He could feel a gentle breeze on his face, mirrored it in his mind, estimated the amount of dispersal the smoke and steam would make in the air as it left the barrel, and sighted two-metres to his right. He fired a round and was met with the sight of a figure clad in traditional furs jump to his feet and run back into the treeline. Something about the way he moved, the way the rifle dangled on its sling-strap. King worked the bolt. He had best-guessed and he had hit his target. But he knew it would have been a graze, a skim across the shoulder. Enough for the wound to have stung like a hundred bees and shock his attacker. King got to his feet, but he darted to his left before he made his way into the treeline. He needed to space himself, not follow directly. Should the gunman turn, take cover and wait for King, he wasn't going to have it easy. He'd have to be watching his flank.

King entered the treeline. He moved carefully, slowly. His clothes rustled, and the snow crunched underfoot. But he knew that if he had hit the gunman, then he would have his own problems. He no longer had the advantage. The man would be scared, and he would be in pain. Both these factors would raise his heartbeat, increase his breathing rate. Affect his decision-making.

King took another couple of paces, put a tree between himself and the direction the man had taken. He hesitated when he heard an engine behind him, followed by a rev of power that wound up to a crescendo. He turned and ran back through the trees to the clearing. He hesitated, stopped at the tree and bent down to retrieve the orange capsule.

It had gone.

King scoured the ice, dusting his hand over the surface. In a background of white, he knew he was wasting his time searching further. He could see faint footprints around him. Two dents in the snow where someone had rested on their knees.

He stood up, scanned the area around him, then went to the woman's body. He could see the flap of her pocket had been opened. He checked, and the Glock pistol was no longer there. He checked the other pockets. Her phone was gone too.

Another engine started, and King raced in the direction of the sound. He could hear the revs gaining, reaching as frantic a crescendo as the other machine. King ran as fast as his clothing and footwear would allow against the terrain. He caught sight of a snowmobile at almost one-thousand metres distant. The figure riding was clad in grey and white. The same person who had been shooting at him. The second snowmobile was following, five-hundred metres behind. And that put it at five-hundred metres from him. King shouldered the rifle and sighted on the figure. He moved the crosshairs ten-feet or so in front of the snowmobile and fired. He worked the bolt and gave the vehicle more of a lead. He estimated it was traveling close to seventy-miles-per-hour. He gave it a full fifteen-feet and fired again. The snowmobile and the rider parted company and the snowmobile slewed and rolled and came crashing to a halt fifty-metres further on. The rider was still sliding and rolling. King aimed at him and fired, but it was a miss and the man scurried over to the snowmobile and took cover. King ran back to the clearing. He picked up the loose round he had called the woman's bluff with and ran across the clearing to where they had both parked the snowmobiles. He started the engine and adjusted his goggles, then powered away, turning hard and traversing the edge of the clearing to come out on the other side. The terrain was bumpy and ridged with ice shelves, but after a few minutes, he found flat ground and headed down onto the frozen lake. He thumbed the throttle and found the tracks the other snowmobiles had made. He could already see the snowmobile on its side and he slowed and took out the Walther, moved it to his left hand, riding steadily with just his right hand on the handle grip and his thumb feathering the throttle.

There was no sign of the man. He could see that there were more tracks. The other snowmobile had come back for him in the time it had taken King to get to his snowmobile. He eased forwards, then got off the machine and walked over to the ruined snowmobile. King noted there was no blood on the ground. He could see smoke coming out of the snowmobile's fairing. There was the noxious smell of fuel, too. He could no longer hear the snowmobile's engine in the distance. He could track it easily, but he had only just realised how dark it was getting. As he surveyed the scene, he realised that most of the light came from the ambience of the snow on the ground.

King felt in a quandary. He could well follow, but if they stopped and took cover, then they would both hear and see him coming. They still had a rifle and local knowledge of the terrain.

King called it. He was still alive, and he intended to keep it that way. He walked back to his snowmobile and checked the compass and fuel gauge. He turned the machine around on the opposite heading they had ridden from and made his way back across the lake to town.

Chapter Fourteen

The town was in darkness. The streetlamps lining the main strip were sporadic in both number and layout and only illuminated the base of the lamps. The snow, as always, creating enough ambient light to make out the road, the sidings and the houses that had been cleared of snow and ice. King wondered how dark the place would be in the spring and summertime, but then he remembered that it would be daylight for most of the time. At least for the eight weeks of summer. It really was a strange place in which to contemplate living.

King parked the snowmobile outside the police station, next to his truck. There were no lights on within the building. He took off his gloves, opened the zipper to his jacket and tucked the gloves inside. He took out the Walther, switched over magazines, and with the already chambered round, this gave him eight in total and a further six in the other magazine, which he tucked into his left jacket pocket. He would have preferred to carry a different weapon, one with more power and capacity, but the Walther was a solid piece, both reliable and easily concealed. Its fixed barrel, though old in design, provided a solid base in these temperatures and the action would not be prone to contracting and this limited the potential for feed stoppages and jams. He reflected that it had been chosen well.

King took the steps cautiously and opened the door. He looked for a light switch, found a bank of them on his right and flicked them on. The corridor lit up, and the light above his head flickered and illuminated the foyer and desk in front of him. The door was locked, so King went behind the desk and looked for a release. Standard in law enforcement buildings around the world. He found it on the underside of the desk, pressed it and the door buzzed. He stepped back out around the desk and pushed the door inwards.

The office at the other end of the corridor was empty, but he suspected it would be. He made for the door at the other end of the office and tried the handle. Locked. He could see the keypad on the doorframe. He wouldn't be able to bypass it without tools and time. He didn't have either. He still had the .300 rifle strapped to his back. He took it off, released the safety and stood back. He aimed at the door hinge, or at least where he estimated it should be, eight-inches down from the top of the door. He chose the area on the jamb, rather than the door. If the bullet met resistance from the metal hinge, then it would deform and take out a large amount of wood and metal. King didn't aim, simply held the muzzle where he wanted the bullet to go and squeezed the trigger. The shot, in the confines of the office, was deafening. Time was now a factor. He didn't have much of it before someone would become curious. Or maybe the building would deaden it altogether? It was heavily insulated after all. He wouldn't take the chance though.

King had no more rounds left for the rifle. He propped it against a desk, picked up the Walther and aimed a kick at the door. It pivoted and spun in the frame, and after two more kicks, the bottom hinge broke out of its fixings and the entire door crashed onto the floor inside an area of cells and equipment lockers.

The room was warm. Well-insulated and heated. It was a holding cell, after all. And King could already smell a familiar odour. He didn't have to look to know there was a body in here. Maybe more. But he would have to look, have to confirm. Or maybe there was a morbidity to seeing, to linking the smell from olfactory to visual senses.

The female police officer was bound to a chair, her mouth gagged. A single, ragged hole permeated her otherwise faultless features. The bullet would have entered the back of her head and exited through her forehead. There was a lot of blood. That was the nature of headshots. The blood would pump around the body for as long as the heart received messages from the brain.

The hole was sizeable. It would have been like turning on a tap. King could see it had pooled on the floor and congealed.

King turned to the male police officer. He had fared better. He had been shot through the back of the neck and by the look of the absence of all but a few blood splatters, it would seem the spinal cord had been severed by the bullet. In both cases, a medium calibre pistol round. King would have guessed one of the missing 9mm Glock's from their holsters. Likely to be the Glock Lena's Russian imposter had been carrying, and that had been taken by one of the men at the clearing. The woman had admitted she hadn't killed anybody, so had she been present? From the way she had behaved when she had seen Fitzpatrick's body at the morgue in the medical centre, he suspected not. But he guessed the two people on the snowmobiles had.

King looked around the room. He could see a CCTV camera, but it would be useless; the wires pulled out and hanging limp. He glanced at his watch. He had spent enough time here. He needed to report this to somebody. But he would call Thames House first. He walked back out into the office. He had missed it earlier, but he could see wires stripped out of the wall above a CCTV receiver and recorder unit. There were no lights displayed on the unit. They had covered their tracks.

King zipped up his jacket and put the Walther back in his pocket. He put his gloves back on, hesitated as he decided whether to take the SUV or the snowmobile. He settled on the SUV, but circled the vehicle a few times, slowly looking for footprints around it. The vehicle had been parked there all day; it would have made a nice target for a boobytrap or IED. He couldn't see any footprints or tell-tale markings in the crust of ice. Nobody had swept the area clean. He took his chances and opened the door. The inside felt like a freezer. King started the engine. The heaters were still set to full from earlier. The air that rushed out was super-chilled. King decided to get the vehicle moving. He pulled out of the parking lot, the headlights cutting swathes of light across the snow, eerie shadows created by the many pine trees lining the road. He couldn't get his head around the fact it was not yet four-PM. He neared the medical centre, saw a light within. The vehicle hadn't even warmed to -10°C on the inside, so King wasn't reluctant to switch off the engine. He stepped outside, turned as he heard the high revs of a snowmobile roar off from behind the medical centre. He could see the headlights light up the forest, and within a few seconds, it was already out of view, the lights fading as it tore away and became a faint hum in the distance.

King frowned. It seemed erratic behaviour in the darkness. The forest may well be sparse this far north, but there would have been all manner of obstacles, not least the trees themselves.

The door to the medical centre was open, but there was nobody inside. Where a receptionist and assistant had sat earlier in the day, an empty swivel chair was all there was behind the desk. King took off the gloves, pulled down the zipper and tucked the gloves inside his jacket. He took out the Walther and felt that dream-like experience of déjà vu. The building was utterly silent and the feeling of anticipation in King's chest was becoming overwhelmed by a sense of dread in the pit of his stomach. He turned down the corridor and headed to the door he had been through with two Russian insurgents only seven hours before.

Doctor Engelmann was seated behind his desk, his head lolled to one side. His thick hair and copious facial hair gave the impression his head was twice the size of most men. The thick, over-sized spectacles seemed to close off the only part of his face without hair. King studied the way the man slumped. There was a great deal of blood and an empty vodka bottle on the desk in front of him. The man's wrists had been slashed and King could see a surgical knife on the floor beside him. King stepped closer, looked at the man's wrists and studied the depth of the gashes. Tendons had been severed and King could see at once that the man had not inflicted the wounds himself. One perhaps. But not both. He would not have been able to hold the instrument for the second cut. The man's murder had been made to look like suicide. Another resident, new to the area and unable to cope with the loneliness, the darkness and the cold. It happened in many places near the Arctic circle. The long hours of darkness in the winter, the midnight sun throughout the summer. It messed with sleep and eating patterns, occasionally turned people insane. It was the flip side to the happiest population medians on the planet.

King searched, but he did not find the receptionist. He made his way back outside and replaced his gloves, zipped up his jacket. And then he noticed the footprints around the SUV.

Chapter Fifteen

King found a torch in the desk behind reception. He was tiring of undoing clothing and removing gloves. The effort in simply moving around in a set of thermal snow clothes over the top of his clothing was becoming tedious. The shockingly abrupt temperature change from stepping outside a heated building was playing havoc with his lungs, as well as his eyes. The heat made his eyes water, then the cold outside air froze the tears. His hands were already gloved, so picking the frozen gems from the corner of his eyes was not an option. Every movement, every process was an effort.

He had taken a coat hanging from a peg in the foyer and spread it on the ground beside the vehicle and on top of the footprints. He needed to be able to move freely, so he removed his jacket and gloves. He knew he had only minutes to perform his tasks. The cold was biting him. His heartrate increased greatly, and he could feel perspiration at his armpits solidifying. He lay on the coat and pushed himself around the underside of the vehicle, shining the torch's meagre light into the wheel arches and behind the wheels themselves. He used his feet to scull himself, the coat sliding on the ice. He found the device wedged between the fuel tank and the chassis. He ignored it and continued his search. You never stopped the search on the first thing you saw. Many good bomb disposal specialists had slipped up in such a way. Usually through complacency because of their workload. The wars in Iraq and Afghanistan demonstrated this with copious quantities of IEDs. It made for over-worked personnel and bombers who had been quick to exploit this. Temperature was a factor and the Taliban and ISIS knew this. They would plant IEDs inside hot vehicles. Deep under the seats. A specialist in a bomb suit pulling up car seats could be working in 50°C or more. Sweat in their eyes, clammy hands, too hot to function, unable to breath. They found what they thought was an IED, called it and missed the main device as they exited the oven and made for fresher air.

King made his way around to the engine bay and shone the torch. He knew enough about engines to know what shouldn't be there. It all looked ok. He got out from underneath and got to his feet. He was freezing now, shivering. He looked at his hands. Shaking. Not what you wanted for removing a device from a fuel tank. He thought back to the upturned snowmobile. He could have given chase. And he could have walked into an ambush. He looked at the SUV and called it right there. Any device not connected to a door, boot lid or bonnet would only be detonated in one of two ways. Remote control; but then it would have gone off already.

Or movement. Doors and lids detonated a device by pulling a pin to open an electrical or fuse connection. Movement devices were almost certainly reliant on a ball of mercury which rolled to complete an electrical circuit. Removing one, if that was an option, was a complicated affair and not best attempted with shaking hands and a bad case of shivering.

He put his jacket back on, tucked the hood up over his beanie and put on his gloves. He was done here. It was time for a drink.

Chapter Sixteen

King dropped his bag at reception and put the key on the desk. He hadn't stayed in a hotel with a physical key for a long time. The brass tag with his room number on it looked old fashioned, but he missed those sorts of things more these days. Everything was seeming so clinical and characterless the older he became.

"How can I help?" the receptionist asked.

"How busy are you?" he asked but could see the confusion on the young woman's face. He added, "The hotel, I mean."

"Oh, about half-full."

"I'd like to check out," he said. "And check into another room."

"You are not happy with your room?" she asked.

King looked around, then leaned forward conspiratorially. The young woman did the same. King said quietly, "I'd like you to check me out," he paused, slipped a one-hundred-euro note across the desk. "I'm a writer, and I work under a pseudonym, a pen name. I'm being hounded by my agent to finish a project, and it's ruining my creativity. I don't want anybody knowing I'm still up in these parts." He slid the note over to her and she placed her hand over it. He kept hold of the note, bonding them in clandestine transaction. "This is for you," he said. "Just book me in for two more nights under a Finnish name, and I'll pay for the room in cash. I really appreciate your help."

The receptionist smiled. "No problem, Sir..." She looked at the computer screen and clicked the mouse a few times. She unhooked a brass key from the cabinet beside her and slid it across the desk. "Room two-ten," she said and smiled.

The room was one-hundred and fifty-euros a night and King slid another three, one-hundred euro-notes across the desk and returned her smile. He knew how hotels worked. Everybody had a scam – it helped get the staff through the unsociable hours, lack of respect from guests and low wages. A click of the mouse and a twenty-euro note to a trusted housemaid and King's stay could be made invisible. And that was what he was counting on.

"Thank you," he said.

Back inside his room, King left the snow clothes hanging on a chair in front of the radiator and took a hot shower. He soaped and shampooed twice and leaned against the tiles, letting the hot spray soothe his aching shoulders and the steam clear his sinuses. He felt cold inside. His efforts searching the SUV had left him frozen to his core. He had trudged back to the police station and taken the snow mobile back to the hotel. Changing rooms and checking off the register was a precaution. At least now he had a clean stay. He would source a vehicle in the morning. He did not intend to stay longer than tonight, but he would have a false trail planted if anybody investigated his stay, or indeed, put pressure on the young receptionist.

The hot water soothed his mind as much as his body. He had learned not to dwell on taking a life, but sometimes it was easier than others. He had killed terrorists and had never thought about them again. He had killed enemy soldiers in secret wars, seen their faces up close, and he had to justify that it had either been them, or himself. Sometimes, that didn't go far to making it any easier. But it was the job he did, and he had done it for so long that many of his memories had melded together. The haze of operations combining into one another. There had even been killings he was pleased to have done at the time. Such was the heinousness of their crimes. But he still did not dwell on them, and afterwards, he had felt no joy. The woman today would have killed him. But the fact that he had given her the chance to stop irked him. A waste of a life. He would always do what he had to do to survive, and that was why he was still here. But he found himself thinking about her nonetheless. Her weapon hadn't been loaded, and King had the advantage. Why had she ignored him? Why had she thought she could make it? King shook his head and turned off the tap. He ran a hand through his close-cropped hair and droplets of water flicked off like rain. The woman was dead, and he'd never know why she had taken the chance. He had been there before, given another woman an out. On a desolate hill in Northern Iraq. He had watched her die, comforted her even, all the while angry that she had not heeded his warning. He closed his eyes, then when he opened them he was resolute. He would spend no more time thinking about the woman who had died out there on the ice. She was history.

King wrapped himself in two towels and sat down on the bed. He picked up his mobile phone and dialled. It was terminated at a voicemail with no greeting, just an initial beep. King left his name, ended the call. Protocol. Nothing more.

He waited.

The phone vibrated silently on the bed beside him.

"King."

"Mereweather."

"Hello, Simon," said King.

"Problems?"

"Is the boss not available?"

"I am the boss. I've been briefed in."

"Then, yes. A few problems."

"Go on."

King filled in the Deputy Director, leaving nothing out. As he listed the events, he realised it had been quite a day.

"Amherst wants you up at that hotel," he paused. "The Eagle's Nest. You have twenty-four hours before that Artic storm hits the area. It looks imminent. You have a room booked already. He's taken precautions…"

"Precautions?"

"MI6 says the defector is uncontactable and we have to assume they will be on route as planned. There are hostiles in the area, so it will be safe to assume an intervention will take place."

"I'd say."

"You'll have to watch your back. I'm sending you details of an exfil. It's arranged, and you will need to follow several protocols. It's a last resort, so see what else you can arrange via Norway just in case it doesn't come off. As far away from Russia as you can."

King shrugged. He couldn't look at the text until he finished his call. Simon Mereweather was being a little too cloak and dagger for King's liking, but he had a sense that there had been developments he was not privy to. Most likely a powerplay. One of the reasons both MI6 and MI5 didn't work well together. He said, "I need to speak with their liaison officer. The person who sorted me out with a vehicle and the map. I'll need some more resources."

"I'll see what I can do," Mereweather replied tersely. "Oh, and King?"

"Yes?"

"Watch your back."

Chapter Seventeen

King did not want to be reactive to any threat. Inside his room, he was on the backfoot. He had taken the precaution of changing his room, going under another name. He would leave in the morning, but in the meantime, he was going to remain vigilant and hide in plain sight.

The bar was empty. So much for blending in. King waited at the bar. He positioned himself side-on. The Walther in the right pocket of his cargoes, the spare magazine in the other. He carried a folding lock-knife in his pocket. Easy enough to stash in his hand luggage because of its unique Teflon-coated ceramic blade. The wickedly sharp blade and polymer handle did not show up under metal detectors – even the fixings were fabricated from fibreglass composite.

As King waited for the barman to return, he cast his eyes on the various maps on the walls. He noted the border with Russia. The location of The Eagle's Nest Hotel was further North-West, just a few miles from Russia. The ideal location for a person on the run with a headful of secrets. But if King did not get the timings right, the impending storm could leave them vulnerable.

"Hello, Alex…"

King froze. He knew the voice, knew he was about the only man alive who would get the drop on him. Every time. He turned around slowly. "Peter," he said quietly.

The man held the pistol steadily. No waver. There wouldn't be. The man had his hand in his jacket pocket, the pistol's barrel poking out of the lining from a carefully trimmed hole. King could see the barrel was not one at all, but a suppressor. Or what people often incorrectly called a silencer.

"The tables have turned somewhat," he paused. "Since last I saw you."

King smiled. "But I still haven't pissed my own pants."

The Scotsman stared at him, lowered the pistol a touch. "You're not wired up right," he said. "Or you never actually believe your time is up."

"If I were wired right, I wouldn't be in this stupid job," said King. He glanced at the pistol. It was low and un-aimed, but the dangerous end was still close and lined up somewhat unnervingly at his groin. "You look well," he added. "I see retirement didn't agree with you."

The man moved the pistol, pulled his hand out of his pocket and smiled. "I think perhaps you actually saved me," he said. "But why go to all the trouble of seeking me out, drawing a gun on me and then let me go?"

King shrugged. "My world was in turmoil. I was outcast, I'd taken revenge and had disappeared. When it came down to it, I just couldn't see what difference it would make. None of the other deaths had. Not really. Vengeance doesn't change a thing. What's done doesn't get undone."

"Nothing to do with me being your mentor? Of saving you from a lifetime rotting away in prison?"

"Well, perhaps the sight of you pissing your pants..."

"Pity?" the Scotsman's eyes flashed. "Go fuck yourself, Mark!"

King smiled. He hadn't heard himself called by that name in twenty-years. "Mark Jeffries died while escaping Dartmoor Prison. He drowned in a bog on Dartmoor. It's Alex. You should know, you gave me the name..." King shrugged. "You screwed me over, Peter. I was angry."

"Survival," he replied callously. "You of all people should have understood that. Nobody has a survival instinct like yours. There's nothing you won't do."

"And you certainly exploited that."

The man shrugged. "It is what it is," he paused. "We all have jobs to do. And you always did yours. So, why let me live?"

"I guess I saw the rest of your days filled with shit daytime TV game shows, your wife knitting sweaters you'd feel you had wear to avoid offending her while she comments on her soap operas, of you sitting in your magnolia lounge in tartan carpet slippers and an M and S cardigan and thought it would be better revenge than a bullet," King paused. "Let you linger, rather than give you a quick release." He smiled. "Like an old, retired stud horse that has to stand limp-dicked in the corner of the meadow while the new stallion sorts the mares…"

"You're enjoying this, aren't you?" Stewart paused. "Bastard."

"Exactly right."

"Cruel bastard," he added. "I closed my eyes, waited for the gunshot…"

"They never hear it."

"I wanted it," he growled. "I closed my eyes and thought, you know, maybe this is better? Maybe this is the way I should go out…"

"What? Pissing your pants on a canal bank. Sorry to disappoint you."

"That's the thing," he said, ignoring the quip. "I was. Disappointed, that is. I opened my eyes and you were gone. A fucking ghost. The Reaper. Only you had done worse by letting me live. I knew I would die festering away in domesticated purgatory. Shit, I'd spent my life in the Paras, the Regiment, the Firm. I went back to MI6 and threw myself on my knees and told them I'd take anything. I'd go freelance, work for free even. I'd even drive rich little Oxbridge dickheads to the embassies. Anything. Just give me something to keep me alive. Keep the blood coursing through my veins!" He glanced behind him as the barman returned with a full ice bucket. The barman had made no noise, yet the Scotsman had known he was there. You couldn't teach that. Trained killers were only ever guided. Their skills honed by training. Instinct and reaction were either in you, or they weren't.

Fight or flight.

King looked at the man. He was in his mid to late sixties, but still fit-looking and as hard as nails. He had beaten King down, built him back up again. He had taken King to the edge – a place where death hovers like a foreboding spectre. A place where you learn what and who you really are. The foundation from which to build everything you choose to become. He had taught King how to fight – really fight, not brawl. Taught him how to use every type of firearm on the planet, how to survive every environment, every situation. And when he had taught him everything he knew, he had given him his assignments, debriefed him and taught him to be better through reflection. He had been King's mentor. But more than that, he had felt like a father figure. And King had never known one of those. King held out his hand and Stewart took it in his own calloused bear paw and King said, "The past is buried. Let's get a drink."

"Aye," the Scotsman said. "We'll make it a large one."

Chapter Eighteen

King chose the table. He never sat with his back to the room, and he knew Stewart wouldn't either, so they sat opposite each other, side-on to the room and the bar. King worked his left periphery, Stewart worked his right. There were two couples and a young family dining. The three young children were a little boisterous, but that suited the two men. No dangerous sudden silences where people heard a snippet of what they shouldn't.

Stewart drank down his neat whisky. Twelve-year-old scotch. Glenfiddich. Stewart's minimum standard. The amber residue ran down the sides and gathered in the bottom of the glass and he supped again. King downed his and placed the glass back down on the table. They had drunk to absent friends. It was a general toast; there wasn't enough alcohol in the hotel to drink to individuals no longer with them. Such was their trade.

The waiter brought their pâté and King asked for a Finnish lager to go with Stewart's second whisky.

"Poncing out on me?" Stewart asked.

"I want a clear head," he replied.

"Despite what has gone on, you're quite safe here. Nobody will risk anything in this hotel," he said. "Besides, the police are on the way."

"You know that for sure?"

"Yes."

"Who made the call?"

"Five called the office," he said. "They have spoken to the Finnish police, and units are being dispatched. They've been briefed with what you told your line manager. A few coppers at first to secure the medical centre and the police station, then the investigators will arrive in the morning."

"I'll be gone by then," King said.

"We both will."

"What are your orders?"

Stewart laughed. "I've got to nursemaid some young punk," he paused. "Probably have to clean up his mess. Like old times."

King stared at him dubiously. "You're assisting me?"

Stewart shrugged. He dipped his toast into the pâté and took a bite. "Fuck, that's strong," he said. He pulled a face like he'd been stung by a wasp as he chewed. "Well, now I know what reindeer liver tastes like after it's been in a blender with juniper berries." He took a forkful of diced pickles and ate quickly, washing down the flavour. "Yes," he said. "The vehicle and everything else were on me."

"I thought the map and acetate sheet seemed familiar."

"Never put a mark on a map, my lad."

"Quite."

King tried some of the pâté but didn't think it too bad. In fact, he smeared the velvety paste onto his sourdough toast eagerly. There wasn't much of either and he finished the dish quickly. The drinks came, and Stewart indicated that he was done, the waiter frowning as he took away the relatively untouched plate.

Stewart looked at him quizzically. "I've got to ask…" he said. "How in god's name did you end up working for Box?"

MI5's address used to be PO Box 500. Within the intelligence community, the Security Service had not yet shaken off the shortening to Box. It wouldn't either, because it was their wartime address because of the German bombing. If it wasn't going to lose the name for close to eighty years, it probably never would.

"Somebody found me, needed me."

"Charles Forrester," Stewart said. "The former deputy director. A good man. God rest his soul."

"Did you know him?"

"I know everybody worth knowing in this community," he quipped. "And you stuck around? I'm surprised. Not as much freedom on the other side of the river."

"I don't do badly."

"I gather that," he said. "Went a bit rogue though, got yourself and MI5 in a bit of a tight spot last summer. Or so I hear…"

King looked up as the waiter brought the drinks. His glass was tall and frosted. He'd seen enough ice for one day. Stewart savoured his Scotch, kept it in his hand long after he'd taken a sip.

"…Went on a merry little dance all over Europe," Stewart added.

"You do what needs doing," King said.

A waitress arrived with two plates. King had the reindeer steak while Stewart had the Norwegian crab claws. The Arctic Ocean was close, and the Alaskan red king crabs had been bought from America and released by Stalin to feed Russia, which was close to famine. Only now, they had over-bred and Norway paid fishermen a tax-free bounty to fish as many of the invasive creatures as could fill their boats. The waitress set down the plates and said she'd be back.

"That's the problem with getting involved with someone in the same line of work."

King's neck hairs bristled. His relationship wasn't on the table. "There's no problem," he said in a tone that would have shut most men down.

"Just an opinion," Stewart said coldly.

"Well, that's just it, isn't it?"

"What?"

"Opinions. They're just like arseholes. Everybody has one, but you don't always want one in your face…"

Stewart moved his elbow as the waitress set down a plate of assorted breads and a finger bowl. As she left, he said, "Did you think you could just walk away, take up with MI5 and have MI6 forget all about you?"

"It snowballed."

"I get it. You helped Charles Forrester out, served your country again. But then you went and fell for the golden girl of MI5. And then you couldn't just walk away. You were in too deep. Your arsehole must have been twitching every time MI6 was mentioned. Must have puckered up a bit when you found out you'd be working with somebody from the Firm…"

King bristled. He leaned back with his beer and took a large mouthful. He could see that his old mentor was enjoying himself. "I should have shot you," King said. "While you were pissing your pants."

"No doubt."

King sliced off a piece of steak. He dipped it in the pepper sauce and snapped it off the fork, his teeth scraping the metal. He knew it had been a risky move back then, but he had taken it nonetheless. Now he felt forces closing in.

Stewart broke open the long crab claw with the silver crackers and smothered the meat in spicy mayonnaise. He chewed and dipped his fingers in the finger bowl. He swallowed his mouthful, glanced around the dining room.

"Nervous?"

Stewart smiled. "It's a strange one, this," he said. "Hostile forces unknown. A defector coming in like it's Checkpoint Charlie in nineteen-seventy-eight or something. I'm in a John Le Carré or Frederick Forsyth novel." He laughed. "But, I gather the defector is an alternate. A spare. Somebody with something we want, but no way of getting out of the country. Not legitimately, at least. And they want a new life, with protection."

"They're on a tight leash, then."

"The tightest," Stewart said. He ate more crab, chewed as he spoke. "Your fiancée mucked things up for you in South Africa."

"I know," King conceded.

"Have you told her?"

"No. She's got enough on."

"Damned decent of you. She used your real name and photograph to verify the authenticity of the MI6 contact sent to help her when her back was against a wall. It was good thinking, but it's bitten you in the arse. That contact got himself into some bother of his own. He told tales to get himself out of trouble. MI6 not only found you, but MI5 know for sure who you are. Forrester had you down as a long-serving black-ops unofficial agent who he bought in and put in the system. It was a good way of seeing you legitimised. But your girlfriend cocked all that up."

King shrugged. "It wasn't her fault," he said. "She was in a tight spot."

"You love her?"

"Of course!"

"But she's on sabbatical."

"So?"

"Distance, methinks. She's letting you down gently, I expect."

"Fuck off..." King put down his cutlery. He'd lost his appetite.

Stewart shook his head. "If you get out of this..." he said, draining the remnants of whisky. "I think you should disappear properly. Lose the name, start a new life somewhere."

"Your arsehole in my face again?"

"Opinion."

King said nothing. He drained his glass and stood up. "I'll get the bill," he said. "You'll have to pay for your own dessert if you want one."

Stewart smirked. "I just thought you should know..."

"Know what?"

"To watch your back."

King said nothing as he walked away. He generally took such comments in his stride. But this was the second time he'd heard those words in as many hours.

Chapter Nineteen

King always travelled with two wooden wedges which he jammed tightly under his door. There was no tool created that could push the door inwards, short of blasting the hinges out of the doorframe with a shotgun and a Hatton round. It was a simple trick, but one he employed as a matter of course.

He had showered before bed and slept in his clothes. He placed the Walther and spare magazine on the bedside table. His snow clothes were folded on the chair and his bag was packed. Everything in place for a quick departure, although he only had the snowmobile parked behind the hotel, he would not be caught on their terms. He was ready for a fight.

The fight never came, and King showered and shaved and took everything he had with him to the dining room where he ate a good breakfast of scrambled eggs, bacon, toast and tea, which he took black and sweet to get past the suspect reindeer milk. He didn't check out, keeping his stay for another night as part of his false trail. He dressed into his overclothes in the foyer and stepped outside into a dark, clear morning. He estimated it to be around -25°C.

The Volvo estate pulled across the road in front of him and King was reaching for the comfort of the pistol in his pocket when he saw it was Peter Stewart behind the wheel. He made like he was itching a scratch on his hip and stopped walking.

"Getting in?"

"I have a ride, remember?" King said. He hadn't told Stewart about the IED he had found, but he suspected the MI6 man wouldn't have let him leave without an intervention. The ride would be handy, he hadn't thought much further than taking the police Subaru.

"Mine might be more practical," the Scotsman quipped.

"What makes you say that?"

Stewart hesitated, then said, "It's petrol and that old heap I got you is diesel. It will be getting colder where you're heading."

"I might be going out of your way."

"I doubt that. By happy coincidence, I find myself heading to The Eagle's Nest Hotel this morning, too."

King opened the rear door and dropped his bag on the seat. He opened the passenger door and slunk down onto the seat. The heater was on full and the car must have been running for a while because it was uncomfortably hot inside. King loosened his jacket and took off his gloves. He dropped the beanie in the footwell.

"How long is the drive?" King asked.

"How long is a piece of string?" Stewart

grinned. "There's only one road, but we have the delights of moose and reindeer on the road, snowdrifts, maniacal lorry drivers and the storm, which is heading straight towards us. The news reports are telling everybody to stay off the roads. But we didn't hear that, did we?"

"I don't recall hearing anything about a storm," King agreed.

Stewart moved off and drove far more quickly than King would have expected. The car held the road well, the snow chains on the front wheels gripping in the dry snow.

"I don't find this stuff too bad," he said, as if reading King's thoughts. "The snow we get in the UK is a bloody nightmare. Firstly, we don't get enough for people to be confident driving on it, or even have winter tyres fitted. Then the councils can't grit the roads fast enough, or have spent their gritting allowance on fact-finding trips to the Maldives, and after twelve-hours of utter chaos, it melts and that's it for another three years..." He accelerated up to fifty-miles-per-hour when the road both widened and straightened out. "This snow is dry. It's weird stuff, because you can't make snowballs out of it."

"You've tried?"

"Don't be daft! But I've scraped it off my car and it's like that sugar they make cake icing out of."

"What, icing sugar?"

"Yeah, that stuff."

King smiled to himself. Stewart knew his way around a ration pack, but he doubted the man even knew where the biscuits were kept at home. "I looked on the map and I couldn't see a road near The Eagle's Nest."

Stewart shook his head. "You're right. Well, technically. There is a track they dug out and gravelled for the summer and they keep it smooth and textured as an ice road in the winter. You won't find any clear roads in the winter... see?" He pointed at the road ahead. "This is about a foot thick. It's scraped and prepared, but they don't salt and grit it like in countries further South. There's no point. Not enough grit in the world. So, they drive everywhere on ice roads."

"So, there is only one way in and out of The Eagle's Nest," King mused. "I don't like that."

Stewart nodded. "No, but you need to think outside the box. On a snowmobile, there are no restrictions. Not even lakes."

"What is the plan for bringing in the asset?"

"You don't know?"

"No."

"The ball's in your court, then."

"Great."

"Didn't work out well for Fitzpatrick either. Hope your plan is better than his."

"What about the other asset?"

"Other?"

"The asset coming in is number two. What happened with number one?"

Stewart shrugged. "Who knows? Maybe the wolves got him, too?"

"Fitzpatrick was meant to meet you. Tell me more."

"Fitzpatrick was the handler. He liaised with the asset, built trust and arranged for them to come over to us. Using assets from other sources, he also gained the trust, or at least the cooperation of another. Somebody he kept in the dark, used as a spare. This person would have been cut off had the first rendezvous taken place."

"Not good for them," King mused.

"Big boys' games..."

"Big boys' rules..."

"So, the first asset doesn't show," Stewart paused. He squinted through the dull light, the snow and ice monotonously going on forever. The trees had thinned the further north they travelled. "He tried a secondary rendezvous, but no go. Fitzpatrick was to meet the asset, bring him to me and I was going to do the exfil. But Fitzpatrick didn't show."

"How long did you give him?"

"More than enough time. I had enough fuel to return. I set the cut-off by the fuel gauge. I went when it put me at risk."

"Fair enough," King said. He'd been there, too. He'd waited for people who would never show. He'd learned the hard way once. That had been the only lesson he'd needed.

"I didn't buy the wolf thing," Stewart said. "Sure, the man was torn apart, but I think only to cover the fact he was murdered."

"I saw cut marks on what was left of his intestines, lacerations consistent with a sharp knife. Nothing in nature could have cut so cleanly. He was gutted, I'm sure. Someone had wiped the blade on his clothing, too. It smeared the blood and made a faint cut. It was a razor-sharp blade."

"We can only assume the asset met his end before they got to Fitzpatrick."

"What sort of man was he?"

"Why?"

King hesitated as they drove perilously near a cliff edge. He hadn't been aware of any gradient on the drive, but as the road wound around to the left, there was only a stretch of steel barrier separating the road from a drop of several hundred feet. He caught sight of the snow-filled gully beyond. It looked like an abandoned mining project. But then he figured it would have to be a summer-only operation. He looked back at Stewart. "He tried to hide something," King said. "He'd dug into the icy crust. Hid something. His fingers were ruined, he'd ripped the nails out trying."

"What was it?"

King shook his head. "I don't know. Possibly a USB flash drive. It was orange and looked like it was a waterproof tube. I dropped it when I was shot at. Damn-near took my hand off. About an inch in it. Might well have hit whatever it was."

Stewart frowned. "Shame."

"About my hand?"

"No, you tit. Shame you didn't hang around to pick it up."

"Yeah, well, bullets can have that effect."

"But not on Fitzpatrick, evidently."

"Exactly," King paused. "I think the man was pinned down by sniper fire. I think he was done-in. He didn't waste time begging for his life or running for it. He hunkered down and tried to hide something important. That takes guts and a strong thought process. He was a family man, but he was an intelligence agent right up to the end."

"He was a desk jockey. He had basic training, but he worked in analytics and embassies, he wasn't a field agent."

"Well, maybe he should have been."

"I think he was a solid chap. I think he did his job well. I haven't heard anything negative. He had a wife and two children. He wasn't in debt, no more than a mortgage, anyway." Stewart shrugged. "You never know how somebody will perform until it's time. Our fathers and grandfathers proved that when they fought Hitler's Germany."

"Speak for yourself."

"Aye, lad," Stewart paused. "Well, even though you're a wretched bastard, the unloved son of a crack whore, maybe your grand-daddy did you proud!" He laughed raucously. "Perhaps he had a VC? A real hero?" He seemed pleased with himself. "Trust me," he said. "Sometimes not knowing who your father is can be better."

"How so?" King stared at him. He knew Stewart had a mean sense of humour. He wanted to punch him right now. He never had, but he'd come close several times over the years.

"Well, the older I got, the more I thought mine was an arsehole. Sort of ruined my childhood."

"I feel for you," King said without empathy. "Are you looking for sympathy?"

"There's a thought."

"Try the dictionary, somewhere between shit and syphilis."

"Class."

King rubbed his eyes. The gloom was lifting, but the darkness until now had made it difficult to wake up fully. He could understand the suicide rate. It could become wearisome. "It's getting light," he said.

"Marginally," Stewart said. "Another hour and it will be full daylight, but only until about three o'clock."

"Full daylight?"

"Well, okay, gloomy half-light," Stewart grinned. "Not a fan?"

"It's different," King admitted. He was tired, and he found the extra clothing cumbersome. He was positively over-heating now that the car was well into its stride and the heater was working well. He unzipped his hoodie top and loosened the collar of his shirt.

"What's your plan, then?"

"You don't have one?"

"Hey, I'm just the help. The Firm want me to give Box assistance. Or rather, not risk any more of their own personnel now they have something over MI5. I'm taxiing you up to the hotel. What more do you want?"

"Are you kidding?" King scoffed. "There is a defector, an asset, on the way. Nobody knows who they are, or where Fitzpatrick arranged to meet them. I can only assume that The Eagle's Nest Hotel is the obvious place. It's all that's there."

Stewart glanced at him, a smirk on his lips. "Well then, you have your location."

"But no clue as to the identity..." King looked ahead, strained his eyes against the whiteness of the horizon "Watch out!" he yelled.

Stewart snapped his attention back to the road, but it was too late.

The storm was upon them.

Chapter Twenty

The car stopped like it hit a wall. King was thrown forwards, his seat belt forcing him back in his seat. The inertia reel did not release, and he fought for breath against the restraint. He felt for the belt clip, struggled with the bulk of his jacket. Stewart shouted something, but King did not hear. There was a tremendous pressure inside the car, as if all the air was being squeezed from within.

The front of the Volvo lifted and the rear wheels, without the addition of snow chains, skidded as the car slid backwards. The front of the car dropped back down, and the car pivoted sideways, pushed broadside down the road. The pressure in King's ears was so intense, he felt as if he were diving too deeply underwater. The sky was black, and the blizzard covered the windscreen with snow and ice, the windows turning the interior into near-darkness. A solid gust spun the car right around, and the pressure gained in intensity until, with a shrill wail, the side windows shattered. King ducked down, the ice crystals peppering his face like birdshot. He clawed in the footwell for his gloves and beanie but could find neither.

The pressure had left his ears, but the intensity of the cold upon his face was unbearable. He fumbled with the hoodie and hood of his jacket managed to zip it up around his neck. His hands were frozen, already finding the dexterity to complete such a mundane task difficult.

King looked across at Stewart. The man looked panicked. King found himself realising he had never seen the man look like that before. Not even when they had once found themselves hunted by over one-hundred guerrillas in Mali, West Africa. The rebels had wanted the men's heads on spikes, and they had very nearly got what they wanted. King had been in his late twenties and the man seated beside him, now frozen in fear, had kept him alive. They had fought and fled, hidden and hunted their way to freedom. Those days seemed a thousand years behind Peter Stewart now.

The car pivoted again, lifted, and King grabbed the wheel and heaved it left with both hands. "Get your foot off the brake!" he shouted. Stewart snapped to, did as he was ordered. "Clutch in, now!"

The car went with the wind, tacked over like a sailing boat. The rear came around and the wind bore its brunt upon the square rear windscreen. The manoeuvre cleared the windscreen as the ice was blown clear. The car went with the wind.

Too easily.

"Reverse gear!" shouted King. "Play the clutch, just get a gentle bite!"

Stewart was on it now. He could see what was happening, and what King was trying to achieve. He selected reverse, allowed a little take on the clutch and feathered both the clutch and the accelerator to set some resistance to the wind. King steered, but felt the steering wheel played by Stewart. He released his grip and the Scotsman kept the car straight as they sailed down the road.

King could barely feel his hands. He searched the footwell again, found the gloves under his seat. It was an effort to retrieve them, get them on, but even when he had managed it, he still had no sensation of feeling below his wrists. He started to ball his fingers, fighting through the pain, knowing that it was imperative to get the blood flowing once more.

Stewart heaved the wheel and let out the clutch fully, his foot welded to the accelerator. King looked up, saw the precipice looming. The car had slowed, but the wind and lack of traction was coming out on top.

"Get out!" King shouted. "Now!"

King grabbed at the door handle but could still not feel his fingers. He tried to grip the handle, felt nothing through the thick gloves. Stewart already had his door open. It had been blown wide and bent the hinges, the wind smashing the door into the front quarter panel. He was already rolling away, swallowed by the vortex of ice. King elbowed the remaining glass from the window and pushed himself through. The wind-chill shocked him as he kicked his way out and used the seat as a springboard to get clear of the vehicle. The swirling ice and snow blinded him, and he felt the hard ground beneath him, unable to anticipate his fall. He hunkered down, his arms around his ears and his hands covering his eyes. He felt stable – the wind not blowing him away, but the buffeting was brutal – and he breathed through clenched teeth, doing his best not to inhale the powdery ice.

There was a grinding, crunch as the car hit the barrier, and then a moment of near-silence strangely audible against the hum of the wind, and the final crunching of metal on ice or rock. King could hear Stewart calling for him and responded as best he could, but he did not feel the sound leave his throat. He clawed his way across the ice, the sound of Stewart's shouts getting louder. He could see the shape of the man in the gloom, the colour of his jacket contrasting the white. He reached him, caught hold of him and together they clung on to await nature's mercy or wrath.

Chapter Twenty-One

The squall had died. Departing as abruptly as it had arrived. The snowmobile had been hastily, yet thoughtfully parked, wedged up against a substantial tree with the constant dominance of the wind driving the machine in place. Only if the tree had been uprooted would the machine be blown further down the road.

The loose ice had been dispersed, leaving the snow from a fall ten days ago in its place. The sky had cleared somewhat, the sun opaque behind low-lying cloud. But it was as light as it would be today, and the forest had taken on a pristine look. The trees were dark green in colour and cleared of heavy ice and snow, and the snow, three-feet deep above the forest floor, looked as if it had been swept clean. An Arctic fox trotted across the clearing, its ears pricked and searching the forest for food. An eerie calm had descended, noise somehow more perceptible since the storm had swept through and taken all the ice from the trees, detached the weak branches and driven the animals away or to ground.

Fifty-metres from the snowmobile a patch of snow started to move. The fox stopped in its tracks, its ears picking at the sound at first, then its keen eyes homing in on the slightest movement. It dropped low to the ground, its eyes and ears unwavering, its claws sprung out for purchase against the ice. Its back arched, and it looked set to take the twenty-feet or so in just two or three leaps. The crust of ice moved again, and the fox readied itself. A hare, rabbit or even mouse would be a good feed. Prey was not plentiful at this time of year. The snow moved again, and a man's hand smashed through the ice and snow and the figure got out of the snowhole, dusting his fur jacket and trousers off, a rifle clutched tightly in his left hand.

The fox was nowhere to be seen.

Chapter Twenty-Two

The squall blew itself out, dispersing as rapidly as it had arrived. King rolled away from Stewart, brushed the ice crystals from his clothing and got onto his knees. He had some feeling in his hands and fingers, but his cheeks felt like slabs of defrosting steak. He adjusted the hood around him, pulling down on the toggles until he was left looking out of a four-inch hole of fabric.

Stewart rolled onto his back. His limbs were stretched out like he was about to start making a snow-angel. He was breathing rapidly.

"Are you okay down there, old timer?"

"Aye, lad. And I could still out-fight and out-fuck you, so stick the old timer where the sun don't shine."

King smiled. He'd missed their banter. He reached down and offered a hand, was genuinely surprised when the tough Scotsman took it and hauled himself to his feet.

"That was interesting," said King. "I was caught in one when we went out to see where Fitzpatrick had died. Not as violent as that one, mind."

"We don't have much time," said Stewart. "The weather report confirmed there would be leading winds, like pockets of violent storms ahead of the main event. If the main storm hits us, we're done for."

"I agree."

"So, what now?"

"We're over halfway," said King. "Mission or not, we have no choice but to press on." He took his mobile phone out of his pocket and unlocked it, but it showed the charging icon and switched off. "Gone," he said. "It was fully charged, must be the cold."

"Tuck it down by your cock."

King looked bemused, but it was standard practice for cold hands, a phone should be no different. King tucked it down his trousers and the two men shared an awkward silence.

"Well, I'm not using it now," Stewart quipped.

The sky was starting to clear. It was as light as King had seen it since he arrived. He walked to the edge of the precipice and peered over the edge. The steel barrier had given way, leaving a Volvo-sized hole in its place.

"I'm surprised that gave out," King commented.

"Irresistible force."

"I've never known a wind like it."

"And you spend time down in Cornwall," Stewart grinned.

"Not anymore."

"Sold your cottage?"

"No. It was blown up. Long story."

"Sorry."

King shrugged. "We have to get moving."

"We need to scavenge the car," Stewart said. "Fuel and fabric. In case we need to hunker down and get a fire going."

"You can have a sing-song around a campfire…" King paused. "I'm going to be in a five-star hotel tonight."

"I thought I taught you to be thorough?"

"You taught me a lot of things, but we're wasting time here. That drop is three-hundred feet, and it's sheer. The exposed rocks are covered in ice, the ice and frozen snow is unclimbable without rope or at the very least, an ice pick." King looked at his watch, frowned as he looked up in search of the sun. The pale, white-yellow orb was just about visible through the clearing white cloud. As he stared directly at it, it seemed almost moonlike. He lined up the hour hand of his watch on the sun, looked at the minute hand and from there he ascertained north. He turned back to Stewart. "Are you up to a six or seven-mile tab?"

"Bollocks to you," Stewart said sharply. "I can out-run…"

"Well, let's see if you can add that one to your exclusively biased list, shall we?"

"What's your plan?"

King pointed across the gulley, out towards a thicket of trees a mile away. "We're traveling a long way just to come back on ourselves via a man-made track to The Eagle's

Nest. I estimate we're ten-miles maximum if we cut across the top of the lake. The weather has cleared, the surface ice crust will have been blown away by that storm, and the lake will be entirely flat terrain."

"Bollocks to that!" Stewart exclaimed. "We should abort the operation and head back to town. Or at least push forwards on the road. We could happen upon another vehicle. Or if we get down to the car, we can scavenge and utilise what we have in there."

King checked his watch again. He looked back at the man who was his mentor, his father-figure. His one-time friend. "We haven't seen a car for the entire journey. If we stick to the road, we have at least thirty-miles to travel. We'll never make it. Not before nightfall. The temperature will drop dramatically and the light fades around three o'clock. If another squall comes in, we'll have no protection, and no kit to dig a snow hole or get a fire going. If the storm they keep talking about, that everybody is worried about hits, we won't stand a chance."

"There's always a chance…"

King turned and started walking to the side of the road, parallel to the precipice. He looked over his shoulder as he walked. "Are you coming?"

Stewart hesitated a moment then begrudgingly followed.

The gradient was gradual and when the road branched off to the left and the barrier ended, King led the way down the slope to the edge of the basin. The ice was surprisingly grippy. A dry layer which stuck to the bottom of their boots. King tapped each boot on the side of the other, and perfect casts of his treads fell onto the ground.

"Have you ever seen stuff like this?" he asked Stewart, more to break the tension.

The Scotsman shrugged. "No. Only here."

A status quo had been broken. The two men had known each other for almost twenty-years, and in all that time, Peter Stewart had been the boss. King had operated alone over most of his time with MI6, but he was always sent out on his missions by the man, always debriefed upon his return. Stewart had often been the cavalry, the man at the end of the radio or phone, who could arrange the airstrike, the helicopter extraction or the boys in blue to make an arrest. He often reminded King that he wouldn't still be here had he not been in the loop. King had learned to rely on him. That said a lot, when he had never relied upon a single human being since he had his last nappy changed. And that was the way Stewart had worked him, played him. He had become the only person King felt he needed. Which was why the man's betrayal had been the most bitter pill of all. And even then, even after he had removed everybody in the chain who had wanted him dead, he still couldn't pull the trigger. The sight of his mentor trembling, his bladder and nerve gone on that canal bank, had made him realise that revenge did nothing. That was when he had left his old life behind, and with it, any reliance upon the man begrudgingly following him in the snow. King led, Stewart followed. The young lion had established itself and the old lion knew its place. Both men knew it too.

At the bottom of the basin King looked back towards the base of the cliff. He veered right and trudged over uneven mounds of frozen snow, which looked like a mogul ski run. As he reached the end of the series of snow drifts he stopped and looked at the wreckage.

"Glad we got out of that," he said.

"Going to scavenge the car now?"

King shrugged. "I didn't realise we could traverse across. Makes sense to get out bags, at least."

The vehicle was upside down and the windows were out. King reached inside for his bag. He grabbed Stewart's too and handed it to him. The Scotsman ignored it and got on his hands and knees. He reached in and got the glovebox open, pocketed his pistol and stood up.

"Want anything else?"

King shook his head. "Not unless you've got some skis in the boot…"

"Shit out of luck."

"Let's get out of here, then."

They crossed the basin and reached the belt of trees. King checked his vintage Rolex again. The sun and the minute hand gave him the direction of north and he physically used his outstretched arm to establish North-East. He used a distant peak and a strange wooded mound as a marker and led the way down towards the perfectly flat ground ahead of them.

The crust of ice crystals, like a sheen of fine hail, on the surface ice of the lake had been blown away to reveal a bluish white layer of ice which reminded King of a glacier. It was also the colour of King's eyes, hard, cold and unyielding. He studied the surface and stepped out onto it. He could see the water underneath. He estimated a metre of ice, perhaps more. Enough to drive a bus over. He took a few steps, started to slide and looked back at Stewart.

"We'll cut some poles to keep our balance," King said decisively. "A few hours and we'll be in the bar with a stiff drink and a log fire."

Stewart lifted the tail of his jacket and retrieved a knife. It had a stubby six-inch blade and a handle made from reindeer antler. He turned and pointed to the fringe of trees. "I'll get some branches cut," he replied.

King followed and when they reached the

trees he waited while Stewart hacked at the branches. The man was skilled in bush craft and cut wedges both sides, then set about pulling the branch one way and then the other to snap them. He tossed the branch at King, who took out his folding ceramic knife and expertly whittled off the tendrils and cleaned the ends, giving it a sharp point at one end to dig into the ice and a wide vee at the other to grip and wedge a thumb for extra purchase. He tested it, then dodged the next branch which Stewart threw at him. He said nothing as he trimmed the branch. Stewart was still licking his wounds. He hadn't been used to taking orders and it would take some adjusting to. King was damned if he was going to back down and appease the man. They had been close, but that had been a long time ago. There would always be the betrayal between them, the vengeance King had so very nearly handed him. There had been a lot of water pass under the bridge since then, and King had been pleased to reacquaint and pass an uneasy truce, but the two men worked for different services. King had a job to do, and he would do it with or without the man from MI6.

Chapter Twenty-Three

The man dropped the revs and the snowmobile slowed quickly as he reached the bend in the road. He could see the barrier had been broken. It was strange, because even at speed, which was difficult on the ice, most vehicles would have glanced off and slewed back across the road.

He cut the throttle altogether and the snowmobile stopped beside the precipice. He took the rifle out of its cradle and stepped off the machine. He looked around, checking the fringe of the forest on the other side of the road. A prime spot from which to spring an ambush. The trees were thinly spaced, and the recent squall had blown a thousand-tonnes of ice from their branches. There was nowhere to hide, nowhere to attack from. Feeling quite safe, he trudged across the ice road and looked over the edge.

The Volvo was on its roof. The snow chains were full of ice and as he looked back at the road and the skid marks, he could see why the barrier had broken. The car had been blown through by the devastating winds. He had lived in the region his entire life and he had never known a storm like this. And there was worse to come, by all accounts. He had seen his fair share of Arctic storms; his tribe were nomadic and followed the reindeer. When they reached the shores, they skirted the coast across Northern

Russia to hunt seals and Beluga whales. The winds there could be savage, but this was new to him. The series of squalls were both sudden and violent.

He looked back down at the Volvo and saw the footprints. He shouldered his rifle and used the scope to follow the tracks. Two people. One walking behind the other. So, they were heading to the hotel. The Eagle's Nest. A bold, but clever move. If they could hold the line and not veer left like everybody did, especially up here, deep inside the Arctic Circle, then they would have cut miles off their journey. But there were many hazards up here. And at this time of year, deep into the winter, the wolves were hungry. He knew the terrain. He would ambush the man who was asking the questions. And then, he would call in the wolfpack again. And like the Englishman before, he would enjoy gutting him alive.

Chapter Twenty-Four

With four sturdy poles cut and prepared, King picked up two of them and took to the ice first. He found that if he allowed the poles to take half his weight, he could slide his feet as though he were on cross-country skis and make satisfactory progress. Occasionally his foot would meet a stubborn piece of ice that the squall had not swept away, and he would have to save himself by putting more weight onto the poles. He turned and watched as Stewart fell and sprawled on the ice. He looked most displeased as he got back tentatively back to his feet.

"Bloody fool's errand," he grumbled. "Should have stuck to the bloody road!"

"And you'd be doing this the same time tomorrow morning," King said. He looked behind Stewart and mapped their progress. The tracks looked straight enough. In the Northern Hemisphere people tended to veer to the left. Hence the adage about walking around in circles. The further north, the more prominent the veer. Something to do with the tilt of the axis and the direction of the earth's spin. King had tried to counter this by leaning to his right and placing more weight on his right foot. He looked back at Stewart, who was breathing heavily and showing some pain on his face. The ice was as hard as concrete, and the man had taken quite a tumble. "Want me to carry your bag?"

Stewart did not reply, but his glare said it all. He adjusted his pack, dug both poles into the ice. "Are we moving, or what?"

King turned and led the way. He dug the poles in, then hesitated. Looking back at Stewart he asked, "Can you hear that?"

"What?"

"An engine," King held his breath, straining to hear more.

It was a distant hum. Monotonous and strained. King had heard the sound before.

"Shit," he said quietly.

"What? So, its an engine. Maybe we can signal for help?" Stewart shook his head. "Damn you! Now we could do with some fuel, some fabric from the seats or pieces of tyre to light a signal fire…"

King stared at him as he took off his right glove and got the Walther into his hand. He cursed loudly; his hand already cold. He got the glove back on and tucked the tiny pistol into a zip pocket on his chest.

"I think a signal fire is the last thing we need…"

Stewart looked towards the sound, already it was louder and had slowed in revs. "Why?"

King thought back to the clearing where Fitzpatrick's body had been found. He could picture the snowmobile taking off from behind the medical centre – the same tone. "Because I've heard that sound before."

"Big deal! A snowmobile in Lapland!"

"No!" King snapped. "The same tone, the same machine. Older, more emissions, a less efficient exhaust. Like a classic car or motorbike. It's an old model. Not super-tuned like the ones the police department have... I've heard that exact same engine. And the person on it tried to kill me, and certainly killed Doctor Engelmann."

"You're certain?"

"Absolutely."

Stewart struggled with his jacket and got his pistol clear. It was the same model as he had given King, and like King's, was good for twenty-five to thirty-metres in these temperatures. Maybe less so, given that anyone they would be shooting at would be wearing many layers of clothing. "Let's not mess about then, son." He dug his poles in and headed to the left. Easier progress.

King could see his reasoning but questioned him nonetheless. "You're heading towards the noise?"

"No cover out here and it's too far to keep on our course. We'll never make it and will be exposed. They'll pick us off for sure. Especially as everybody out here has a hunting rifle."

King felt a surge of adrenalin. He knew what was coming. He'd been there before. He followed his old mentor as the man raced towards the belt of trees that would by now be hiding someone who was hunting them. Like so many times before, the two men launched face on to their enemy. At a time when most people would have run the other way to escape, both men headed for a fight.

Chapter Twenty-Five

He had seen the two men on the ice. Sitting ducks. They were over eight-hundred metres from him and he would have to admit that was a sight too far for his .308 rifle with its short varmint barrel. He had the luxury of distance and could spot his misses and adjust his aim accordingly, but this would waste ammunition, and the men would undoubtedly run away and create more distance. He could pursue on the snowmobile, but he didn't want them dying on the ice. He would have to move the bodies back to the forest to call the wolves in – the animals seldom ventured onto the frozen lake. Too exposed. Besides, he needed to make the bodies look like they had been attacked by wolves. Bullet wounds would be too obvious. No. He needed to ambush them, hold them at gunpoint. Perhaps bludgeon them on the back of their necks. A few knife wounds to the area and the wolves would do the rest once they got the taste of blood on their lips.

He knew where he would do it. The men were heading for the furthest tip of the lake. The forest would provide him with the cover he needed, a place to hide the snowmobile and move closer on foot.

He had started up the machine and moved East. Losing sight of the two men on the ice, he threaded through the trees and finally came to a halt at the bottom of an enormous snowdrift. He cut the engine and listened to the forest for a moment. Utter silence. His machine would have scared off any birds or ground game. There was little left in the way of cover after the violence of the squall. The grouse, or ptarmigan, roosted in the trees and enjoyed the cover of the ice and frozen snow in the pines. They had fled at the first signs of the storm, and this area was devoid of either birdsong or the ruffling of wings and feathers.

The man took the rifle out of the cradle and carried it loosely as he trudged up the face of the snowdrift, which would afford him an uninterrupted view across the lake. From here, he would track them in his scope until they were near. A shot or two at their feet, perhaps even cracking the ice, and they would surrender upon his command.

He edged his way further up the drift, shouldered the rifle and eased himself into position. He checked the scope...

Nothing.

Nobody.

He craned his neck, forgot about the narrow field of view of the scope and shielded his eyes with his gloved hand as he looked out across the vast white plain. Almost at once, he heard a gunshot, felt the spray of ice in his face as the bullet struck the ground two-feet away.

He dropped back behind the ridge of the snowdrift and reached for the rifle he had managed to drop as he had thrown himself down. Another gunshot, this time head on, taking the ridge of ice apart. Another, then another. The gunman had his eye-in and was chiselling the ice away. A pop-gun in comparison with his mighty and trusted hunting rifle, but it didn't matter because he was the one cowering and taking fire. He steeled himself, took a deep breath and came up over the ridge a few feet from where the bullets had struck. He caught a glimpse of blue. The same blue jacket he had aimed at and missed at the gulley where he had previously butchered the English spy. The same man who had put a hole through the bulky shoulder of his reindeer skin coat, skimmed the flesh that had stung like a thousand beestings. A graze, but an agonisingly close call, which he had dressed in reindeer moss and a leather patch and would leave a thick and jagged scar.

The Sami was close for a shot like this, the blue jacket filling his scope, too close for the magnification of the lens. He sighted quickly, fired, then ducked back down as gunshots sparked from his right and ice chipped away at his feet. The bastards had pincered him. Come in on him from two sides and attacked simultaneously. He had nailed one for sure but could not see the other man who was raining lead around him. He fired in the general direction, then slid back down the drift and worked the bolt as he scurried across the snow back to the snowmobile. There was a pause to the gunfire and the man assumed that whoever was doing the shooting was now reloading. He slammed the rifle into its rack and jumped onto the snowmobile. He felt and heard the impact of a bullet hitting the machine and ducked down as he started the engine and revved hard, throwing a blizzard of snow up as the tracks dug in and he slewed away. He knew that with every ten-metres he travelled he was getting well beyond the range of a small pistol, and he swerved through trees to present himself as a more difficult target and to put obstructions in the path of a lucky bullet. He laughed, as much a product of adrenalin as the thought of having accomplished at least a part of his mission. He doubted the centre shot would leave the man wounded. And the cold and remoteness of the location would see that in his favour, too. The man he had shot would be dead. There was no question about it. It hadn't gone to plan, but he would have to be more fluid. He had not expected a gunfight. It was too late to make it look like an animal attack. He would have to put them through the ice. The river from the power station on the Russian side spewed out hot water at enormous pressure which created a current. If he took the bodies to the melt, tossed them in, they would move under the ice and be lost. Once the putrefied corpses lost their gases, floating against the underside of the ice, they would sink and the temperature at the bottom of the depths would make them sink forever.

He slowed the machine, spun around and took a course that he hoped would put him behind the second gunman. He knew he was getting into a fight now. He had speed and the ability to manoeuvre, and he had the firepower advantage. He would not be caught off guard again.

He had covered a lot of ground. Shutting down the engine gave him a thrill he neither understood, nor would have been able to describe. He had hunted his entire life. For food and for animal fat to use as fuel and for fur. He had killed his first tethered reindeer with a knife to its spinal cord when he had been five. He had shot his first seal at ten. Since then, he had taken many lives, but never human. Not until the man in the clearing. He had been paid well for his tracking skills, paid even more handsomely for killing the English spy. He had enjoyed it. He had never enjoyed killing animals, but it was a vital part of his tribal, nomadic lifestyle. His heritage. But the killing of a man had been a different and completely emotive experience. He had already killed the man in the blue jacket, the Englishman sent to investigate the death of his colleague, and now he would enjoy hunting and killing his older companion.

He opened the bolt and breech fed the internal magazine until he had replenished the maximum of five bullets. He closed the bolt and held the rifle ready as he walked, carefully placing his soft-soled boots on the dry ice. Even with the soft leather, the ice crunched underfoot. He listened intently as he walked, expecting to see the man in the green jacket at any moment. He was sure he would come in behind him. He raised the rifle to his shoulder and sighted the terrain through the scope. He took another few steps, paused and sighted again. The older man was kneeling in the snow. He was bending over the body of the man in the blue jacket. The Sami hunter smiled as he steadied his aim and released the bolt safety with his thumb.

And then he froze.

The blade of the knife was ice-cold. It had slipped in through his open hood, the tip of the blade digging into his neck, piercing the skin. A warm trickle of blood ran down his throat. An irritating dribble, tickling his cold skin. He realised he had stopped breathing, took a sudden breath and felt the blade dig deeper.

"Put down the gun."

The man did as he was told. He had cut enough reindeer throats to know how it worked. The rifle clattered on the solid surface of the compacted snow and he slowly raised his hands.

King pushed him hard in the back. The man spun around defiantly but stopped when he saw the pistol in King's left hand, the knife in his right. He was shivering, wearing only a thin sweater and a hooded sweatshirt.

"Peter!" King shouted, his eyes not leaving the other man's. "Bring my bloody coat!"

The Sami stared incredulously at him. He had been fooled by the blue jacket. He had taken a shot at it, obscured by the trees and the close range through the powerful scope thinking he had killed one of the men. And again, as the other man had lent over the 'body'. He did not seem angry, if anything, his expression showed respect and acceptance. He had been outsmarted. He was a hunter and he understood that sometimes there was no hunting some quarry. They always managed to get away. And that was partly the thrill of the hunt. But he wasn't a trapped beast that had accepted his fate, though. He studied King, who was so cold he was shaking. The pistol was no longer steady in his hand and the knife was held loosely by his side.

The man saw his chance and took it. He dashed forwards and kicked the knife out of King's hand but grabbed King's right wrist with two strong hands and pushed King backwards.

King smarted from the kick to his hand, but by grabbing his other wrist with both hands, the man had left King's other hand free. King swung a left punch, impacting against the man's right ear. His hood heavily cushioned the blow and King swung again, catching the man on the chin. It was a glancing blow and the man shook it off. But he drove King's hand backwards against a tree and the pistol fell onto the ice. King slipped and fell and when he looked up, the man had a knife in his hand and the dull steel was driving downwards towards his stomach. King kicked the man's kneecap and he yelped, stumbled and redirected his attack. King rolled to gain distance and reached for his own knife. He wasn't going to make it in time, so he left it and concentrated on defending himself from the wicked-looking curved blade scything towards him.

Stewart was running on the ice, making poor progress and fumbling with his pistol. He dropped the coat like it was an afterthought and steadied himself before stepping over a fallen tree. He still had fifty-feet to go.

King chopped the man's wrist and he smarted at the pain but kept hold of the blade. He thrust out straight, and that's when King knew he had him. He side-stepped, grabbed the man's wrist with his left hand, and gripped his elbow with his right. He pushed and pulled simultaneously, and the man's arm twisted, the knife fell, and he dropped onto his knees.

The gunshot made King flinch, as did the sight of the man's face disappearing in front of his eyes - brain, bone and blood spraying up into King's face. He released his grip and stepped backwards, the body dropping onto the ground. King looked at Stewart, who was crouching with the pistol still aimed, held steadily in both hands.

"What the hell?" King said breathlessly. "I had him…"

"Didn't look much like that to me."

"I locked his arm, he had dropped the knife…"

"Yeah, well, it looked like he was kicking your arse from where I was standing." Stewart tucked the pistol back into his pocket. "You know what I always say to my agents…"

"I'm not your agent, anymore."

"Well, you were for nearly fifteen-years, son. And what did I always say?"

"There's no rewind…"

"Exactly! No fucking rewind button in life. Especially on a mission. The guy had a knife, you were looking like you needed to get your arse back in the do-jo, or at least the boxing ring…" he paused. "Christ, don't they keep you field-ready in MI5?"

King bent down and scraped up some ice, he rubbed it into his face and cleaned the mess off. It took a couple of attempts and his face was freezing when he'd finished. He stared down at the body. There was something about blood in the snow. It looked redder somehow, the effect more final. King could see the entry point at the back of the man's skull. Dead centre in the synapse – the point where the spine met the skull. The old MI6 warrior hadn't lost his touch.

"Get my jacket," said King. He was still shivering, despite the recent activity.

"Get it your fucking self," snapped Stewart. He walked over, bent down and started to check the man over.

King wasn't going to argue. He needed the jacket and paced over to get it. He swung it over him, zipped and buttoned it tightly, then adjusted his beanie and hood. He looked back at Stewart, who had spun the body over and was checking his pockets. He stood back up and turned around.

"Nothing," he said. He held out his hand so that King could see the fold of notes. "Two-hundred-euros. No ID, nothing."

"A ghost," said King. He picked up the man's knife. "I'll keep this," he said. "Maybe it will have Fitzpatrick's DNA on it. I'm certain it will."

Stewart picked up the rifle. It was old and battered, but well oiled. He checked it over, then shouldered it on the sling. "Well, at least we have a ride to the hotel. He must have left the keys in the snowmobile."

King bent down and started to check the man's pockets for the keys.

"I've already done that," Stewart commented tersely.

"Missed these, though." King stood up, the three .308 bullets in his palm. "I'll check him again. If you missed those, then you may have missed something else..."

Stewart huffed and puffed and turned towards the direction the snowmobile was parked. He trudged away, uninterested in anything else King might find.

King continued to search but found nothing. He stood up and watched Stewart walk away, unable to shake off the nagging feeling that he had missed something. What could the man have possibly achieved in killing them both? And what reception would be waiting for them at The Eagle's Nest Hotel?

Chapter Twenty-Six

King checked the numbers as he walked cautiously down the corridor.

Your guest has gone on up…

He hadn't wanted to cause a scene. His reaction could create suspicion. Would have undoubtedly done just that. The manager had shown no surprise. Like it happened every day. But King knew these things almost never did. The room was booked to him, secured via London. Nobody should have known he was staying here, but somebody evidently did. And the Sami who had unsuccessfully hunted them out on the ice; he would have known where he and Stewart were headed. There was nothing else up this far north. The hotel was their most obvious destination.

King took his knife out of his pocket, opened the blade, and tucked it into his back pocket, the blade sandwiched between the fold of his leather wallet, holding it firmly in place like a makeshift sheath. It was ready, concealed and would save valuable tenths of a second in reaching for it. He placed the bag on the floor, checked the Walther and held it ready, down by the side of his leg. He picked up the bag, continued down the corridor. Trepidation in his chest, a leaden feeling in his legs. He tensed the muscles there, got the blood flowing and the acid build up relaxed once more. He thought back to the manager. Was it a look of disdain, incredulousness? Or was it a knowing smile? Hotel managers were the same the world over. They had seen everything, every trait of human nature. Or they thought they had. They saw infidelities; affairs happen under their roof. They heard what state the rooms were left in. What had been left behind, knowingly or otherwise. They saw more than they should. And with that came an air of arrogance.

Your guest has gone on up…

King hesitated one door down from his room. He placed the bag down quietly. What the hell was he walking into? He didn't cock the Walther's hammer. It would only give him away. The trigger would be a harder pull, but the following shots with the hammer locked back would be light. He breathed deeply, swiped the card and kicked the door inwards, covering the room with the Walther.

Nobody.

Bed, chair, table, luggage stand, wall-mounted television.

Suitcase on the luggage stand…

He stepped inside the room and allowed the door to close softly behind him. His heart was pounding, but he heard the gentle splash of water coming from the bathroom and caught hold of the doorknob. He opened it an inch, the pistol held at waist level with the muzzle touching the door. The punchy little 7.65mm bullet could cut through the two-and-a-half-inch pine cleanly at this range. He opened the door a touch and the aroma of bath salts hit him. Hints of pine and berries. Christmassy overtones. The steam had wet everything in the bathroom and he couldn't see anything in the glass of the shower screen or the mirrors above the sink.

"Just in time to wash my back…"

King applied the safety and tucked the pistol into his pocket without Caroline seeing. He smiled as he looked down at her, tantalisingly covered by bubbles, her wet skin glistening and turned pinkish from the heat.

"What happened to the sabbatical?"

Caroline held a finger to her lips and shushed him. "Afterwards," she said.

"Afterwards?" he asked, feigning confusion, yet starting to untuck his shirt and sweater.

"Afterwards," she smiled. "Now shut the door, you're letting all the heat out…"

King ripped the shirt and sweater over his head and kicked the door shut. He started on his boots and socks, pulling them off and tossing them on the wet, tiled floor, and was about to tackle his belt and trousers, but Caroline reached up and grabbed the front of his trousers and pulled him down on top of her, sending a huge wave of soapy water over the bathroom floor. She laughed as the waves continued to break over the back of the bath and swamped everything on the floor.

"Now," she said. "Show me how much you've missed me…"

Chapter Twenty-Seven

"So, are we a couple now?"

"What?"

"A couple. I mean, we're shacked up in the same room. We've been sleeping together since the summer…"

"On and off…"

"Splitting hairs."

"I just…"

Marnie sipped some wine and grinned. "God, you're a shithead. I'm winding you up."

"Oh," said Rashid.

"I must admit," she said, placing her wine glass down and picking up some ryebread and her butter knife. "It was a bit presumptuous of the office to get just one room for us. We're not a couple, never made anything public either. I'm not a field agent, and I haven't had any training for this."

"What, dinner and sex?" Rashid smiled. "You're an attractive, and dare I say, experienced young woman. What additional training do you need?"

She shook her head. "Now, you're getting presumptuous."

"Have you missed me?"

"No." She buttered the bread, cut it into quarters and popped a piece in her mouth. "You?"

"Of course," he sipped his orange juice and smiled. "You'll see how much later."

"Oh, promises," she sighed. "Still, I think either Director Amherst or Simon Mereweather assume a great deal of their employees."

Rashid laughed. "Well, actually, I'd better confess," he paused. "Neil Ramsay booked us two rooms. When I checked us in, I just thought, well, you know…"

"You thought you'd get lucky? Without putting in the ground work, for old time's sake? Not even so much as a bunch of flowers."

Rashid smiled. "Well, yeah, I guess that was it. And you'd get lucky too, of course."

Marnie laughed. She moved aside a touch as the waitress brought her smoked salmon salad and placed it down in front of her. The waitress walked around the table and placed Rashid's reindeer steak in front of him. She smiled, asked if they wanted anything else and was moving away as they said no in unison. Marnie looked back at Rashid. "Oh, you would be getting lucky tonight, had you not pulled that stunt on me. I'd have given you everything, and more…"

"Oh," he said solemnly. "I have a feeling I've crapped out."

"And then some," she said. She smeared the garlic and caper mayonnaise all over the salmon. "Shan't be worrying about my breath tonight, then."

"Bollocks." Rashid tore off a chunk of bloody meat and chewed hastily. "Well, can't blame a man for trying."

She frowned as he wiped some steak through a smear of dark, almost black sauce. "What's that?" she asked.

Rashid chewed and swallowed, took a sip of his orange juice before he answered. "It's a sauce made with local beer, berries and thickened with the blood from the reindeer after it was slaughtered, sort of a speciality around here."

"Oh, dear god..." she grimaced. "What does it taste like?"

Rashid shrugged. "I guess if I were to chew black pudding a hundred times and wash it down with a Guinness, we'd be getting close."

"Oh, that's gross!"

Rashid nodded. "Pretty much," he said. He ate the next mouthful without the sauce and picked at something that looked like spinach and thyme. "That's not much better, either."

"What was that?"

"Moss," he said.

"Moss?"

"Fermented moss," he clarified.

"How is it fermented?"

Rashid waited for her to take a forkful of smoked salmon. It was flaky and not gelatinous like Scotch smoked salmon. Satisfied she was still chewing, he grinned and said, "It's fermented in the animal's gut. When the beast is being slaughtered and butchered they empty the stomach contents out and fry it in butter."

Marnie looked like she was going to be sick. She picked up her glass and drank down her mouthful, swallowed hard and wiped her lips with her napkin. The knife and fork went down. She was done.

"Well, that settles it," she said. "There's no way in hell your mouth is going anywhere near mine tonight." She looked up as King and Caroline entered the restaurant. Caroline glanced at them both, but quickly ignored them. King didn't even look. Marnie looked back at Rashid. "They've just come in," she said.

"I know," he said tersely. She hadn't seen him look up. "Look, but don't stare."

"King didn't even notice us," she said.

"Yes, he did," Rashid said. "But he wouldn't have let you know he had."

"So, how do we play it?"

"Play it?"

"Yes."

"We have dinner. Then we have a drink in the bar. Then we go to bed. Separate beds, and on separate floors by the looks of it."

"You only have yourself to blame," she said. "That trick with the receptionist for one, that abomination on your plate, for another. So, like I said; how do we play it with them?"

"And like I said; dinner, then drinks and then bed. Separate ones, of course."

"And that's it?"

"What more do you want?"

"Meaning?"

"You're not a field agent. You ignore them until it's evident you don't have to. You are here to unlock data, if or when that time arises. I'm here for support. Muscle. But until either of them lets on, we just enjoy the hotel and the glorious unlimited expense account, curtsey of the British public."

"That's it?"

"You can study the other guests, the staff. If you see anything suspicious, at any time of night, just come to my room…"

She laughed again. "You're a sod, do you know that?"

Rashid smiled. "I have a fair idea."

Chapter Twenty-Eight

Caroline closed her eyes for a moment as she sat down. When she opened them again and stared back at King across the table from her, she couldn't have looked more content. He shared her expression. Their lovemaking had been frantic the first time; tender and caring the second, and more adventurous after that. They were in that wonderful state of contentment from both the physical exertion and release, coupled with bonding and rekindling a sense of closeness that had been lost in separation.

Their waiter handed them menus without a smile and asked what they'd like to drink. Caroline chose a gin and tonic and asked for a jug of water with some cucumber. King asked for a local beer.

"This is a shock," he said. "Or a surprise, at least."

Caroline reached out and placed her hand over his. "A pleasant surprise?"

"Of course."

"Simon Mereweather called me back in, said the sabbatical would have to wait."

"So, it's a temporary thing, then?"

She looked thoughtful for a moment. "I'm not sure," she said. "Don't get me wrong; I've missed you like crazy. But it just feels unfinished."

"It will do," he replied. He hesitated while the barman brought the drinks over on a salver. He struggled to unload the two glasses, the tonic bottle and the jug of water, fighting with the balance of the silver tray. He poured all the tonic into the glass, then turned and walked back to the bar. King continued, "You're too involved."

"I'm what?" she asked, somewhat hoity.

"You're too involved," King repeated. "You were abducted, subjected to cruelty, but you witnessed some terrible things those other women were put through. Added to that, the knowledge that it could well have happened to you. Had you not escaped, had my game with Helena Milankovitch not played out favourably, then your fate could have been very different indeed. That is what's driving you. It's personal. And you're too involved to be subjective."

"Well, don't hold back…"

King shrugged. "I say it how I see it."

"Diplomatic as ever." She picked up her glass and sipped. "God, I was missing you up until just now."

"You know it's true, that's why." He reached over and held her hand this time. "I've missed you like crazy, I want you to come back to MI5 permanently. But, if you're not finished…"

She sighed. "But I think I am," she said. "And you're right. You're a smart-arsed bastard sometimes." Her expression softened. "The people trafficking, and sex trafficking industry won't change. Somebody will always take the place of the people we put behind bars. In many cases, in Russia and Eastern Europe, the governments, and particularly on a regional level, are so corrupt that the people we trace and hand to them for prosecution are back on the streets in a matter of weeks." She sipped some of her gin and tonic and shrugged. "I could give my life over to investigating sex trafficking and I'd get one step forwards and two steps backwards. I only have another month with Interpol, I'm not sure what to do next."

"Don't beat yourself up," King said. "You could fight terrorism for MI5 and argue the same conclusion. That was one of the reasons Forrester took me on, so that he could be sure of shutting down a terrorist front for good. There's only so many times you can live with injustices and technicalities and know innocent people will die."

"I feel a fraud," she confided. "I set out to start a crusade and welcomed the chance to come back when Simon ordered me."

"You're no fraud."

She smiled, then looked up as the waiter returned. She passed on a starter and ordered crab fritters and a tossed salad. King, who realised he hadn't eaten since breakfast and was famished, ordered crab soup with extra bread and whole roasted partridge with a root vegetable dauphinoise.

"Oh, I am," she said, as the waiter walked away. "It sucks."

King sat up straight, his eyes boring into hers. "Right, let's get this sorted now. You went through a lot. You tried to make a difference, and you have. Now, get back in the room. Look around you. Ignore Rashid and the girl from analytics…"

"Marnie…"

"Right. Ignore them. We have a defector coming in. Sex and identity unknown. Thanks to MI6 and close handling, and the death of their handler in the case, we have no idea who or when. Only that their arrival is imminent, there's the worst storm in living memory boring right down upon us, and this hotel seems the obvious place for someone on the run to head for. All our eggs in one basket. Now, get with the operation and forget everything up to this point. Look around, what do you see?"

Caroline glanced left, then right. She picked up her glass, just surveying the room as she took a drink. She shrugged, placed her glass down. "Rashid and Marnie. The family with the noisy children and another couple."

"What about the staff?"

She hesitated then said, "What about them?"

King sipped some of his beer, placed the glass back down. "The waiter is built like a boxer and has a scar on his cheek."

"So?"

"So, he took our order and didn't ask whether we wanted potatoes, rice or the extras they have on the menu. Unless carb-free fads have made it this far into the Arctic, which I'm pretty sure they have not, then he wasn't doing a very good job. He has prison tattoos, too."

"You're a tattoo snob," she smiled.

"The barman never made a gin and tonic in his life. He poured all the tonic into the glass, and besides, he could barely carry the tray. And he didn't put the cucumber in the water. A good thing if you ask me, but still. He looks like the waiter, too. Tough, scarred and cropped hair. They're two peas in a pod. They look like Spetsnaz, and I've been up against enough of them to know."

"Anything else?"

"Rashid and Marnie have a waitress serving them, as do the family behind and the couple. Dining rooms are divided into serving stations. How is it that we have the Brothers Grimm?"

"I think you're paranoid," she said, but she smelled her drink nonetheless.

"They have no rapport with the waitress, either."

"And they should?"

"She doesn't have a ring on her significant finger, they should be chatting her up at least."

"You bloody dinosaur!" she said mockingly. "They may be gay, may have their own partners, as may she," she paused. "And bloody old fashioned, too! Not everybody gets engaged or married!"

King sipped his beer and said nothing. He sometimes felt like a dinosaur, too. Out dated, extinct. Or close to it. The last of his kind. He looked up as a man entered the room and looked for assistance. The waiter was bringing King's soup. He pointed at a table in the corner and walked over to their table. He placed the bowl of soup down, nodded and walked away.

"He forgot your bread, must be a Russian spy…" Caroline goaded him.

The waitress was clearing Rashid and Marnie's table. King asked her for his bread as she swept past. She nodded and smiled and returned less than a minute later with a basket of warm bread which looked like sliced ciabatta.

"Thanks," he said, then added, "The young man serving us; is he new?"

"Yes," she replied anxiously. "Is everything all right?"

"Oh, fine, yes. I just figured he hadn't been waiting tables for long." He gave her a knowing smile.

"No, he's from an agency. I understand he is experienced though."

"The barman, too?"

"Yes," she replied. "Both from an agency, short notice, I gather."

"Staff sickness?"

"No," she said. "Our regular barman and waiter left suddenly." She leaned towards King and whispered, "They disappeared. And then some money was found to have gone missing." She shrugged. "I don't really believe they stole the money. They were honest men. I'd worked with them for long enough for it to have been a huge surprise."

"And you don't know where they've gone?"

"No."

King nodded. "I suppose it happens all the time," he said. "Transient staff…"

"Oh, no. Christoph worked here for two years, Reiner had been here since it opened four years ago."

"And these two new men, the agency staff, they are both Finnish?"

"No," she said sullenly. "They are both from Norway."

"Norway?"

She nodded, then leaned even closer and whispered, "But they are lying," she said. "I have heard them talking to each other in Russian. I suppose it's better wages, and the

the euro is the currency of choice for Russians."
She asked if they required anything else, then
left and took the order from the man who had
been seated by one of the Russians.

Caroline shrugged. "Can't say much to
that," she said. "You're so bloody annoying
when you're right."

King supped his soup. He twisted in
some pepper and tore off a piece of bread to dip.
"The question is; what do they want from us?
Are they here solely to head off this defector? Or
have they identified us as a threat and are
planning to kill us?"

Chapter Twenty-Nine

Neil Ramsay watched Rashid and Marnie head out of the dining room and into the lounge. They ordered drinks and took a pair of facing sofas in front of the log fire. The hotel had many alcoves and corners, all with open fires or woodburning stoves. It was that sort of place. After enjoying the skiing, snowmobile safaris, ice fishing for Arctic char and trout, or husky tours through the forest, or even simply sitting on the many carved-out logs which served as ornate seating in the grounds to watch the Northern Lights, people wanted to shed their bulky snow-wear in the lobby, sit with warming mugs of hot chocolate or stiff drinks and take comfort and warmth from a fire.

He had not wanted to eat alone, always preferring to order room service when he was traveling alone, but it was a good opportunity to get the layout of the hotel and size up the guests. He barely glanced at King and Caroline, who looked to be in the early stages of their meal. The waitress had taken his order and he had chosen a half-bottle of merlot to accompany his meatballs and mashed potatoes with celeriac. Hearty food to warm him through after his drive and time spent waiting for the funicular to take him through the man-made mountain to the hotel. He hadn't travelled well enough prepared and only had a trench coat over his suit and a pair of thin woollen gloves. The receptionist and manager had looked at him quizzically as he had stood shivering at the desk, and the manager had disappeared for a few minutes while Ramsay had completed the check-in procedure and returned, handing him an all-in-one ski suit and pull-on thermal boots and gloves to use during his stay. He was a fish out of water in this environment and had taken his beer outside with him to sit on one of the ornately carved logs that dotted the front of the hotel to catch a glimpse of the Northern Lights, and after only a few minutes had discovered just how quickly an already cold beer could freeze solid at -30°C. He had returned to the lounge, watched his drink melt slowly back to something resembling a child's slushy in front of the log fire and reflected how he needed to get smart real soon. He had skied once as a teen with his university friends in the French Alps, but it wasn't even half as cold as this, plus he had spent most of his time drunk and chasing the affections of the chalet maid with little success.

The waitress arrived with his food and before he had finished, Ramsay watched both King and Caroline leave. King held his hand over the small of her back. He was a fair amount taller than her, at around six-foot, and he was twice as broad. The gesture was caring and protective. Caroline momentarily touched the side of her head against his shoulder. Ramsay smiled. It was good to see them together. He was as surprised as everyone else that she should take off to work with Interpol, especially at having been separated from King so suddenly, so dramatically. The service psychologist had reported that it was because she was suffering from PTSD. Interpol was her coping mechanism. It made sense, but it was good to see her back. He asked the waitress for another drink and studied a tall, sharp-featured man as he entered the restaurant and was ushered to a corner table by a waiter. A strong-looking man in his late twenties with close-cropped dark hair and Slavic features. Possibly Russian going by his tattoos, although he doubted that. But as he started to discount the prospect, he reminded himself how close the hotel was to the Russian border.

Ramsay tucked into his meal. The meatballs were succulent, but he had no idea what meat they were made from. The sauce was rich and buttery and extremely dark. The mashed potatoes and celeriac were almost half cream. It was a delicious meal and he was pleased with his choice. He watched the waiter and the tall man exchange a few words, and then the waiter left, presumably with the man's order. Ramsay was halfway through his meal when the waitress came to the man's table and took his order. He thought it strange. Perhaps the waiter had forgotten to pass the order onto the chef? For the rest of his meal, he did not see the waiter again. And nor the barman, who should have arrived with his drink by now.

Ramsay took out his phone and typed out a text. He selected multiple contacts and pressed the send button. He caught the waitress's eye and she ambled over. He relayed his drink order, asked if the barman had forgotten and got an apology and some mutterings about agency staff. He didn't particularly care, just wanted his orange and lemonade to wash down the rich meal. He made it a point to only drink one alcoholic drink when he was working. He needed to keep his mind keen, and besides, he always felt tired when he drank. He could not afford to lose concentration. The waitress returned with his drink and an apology. The drink was on the hotel.

"Is there any news of the storm?" he asked.

She nodded, her expression pale. "It is due to hit tomorrow night. In the early hours."

"Will it be as bad as they say?"

"I expect it will be the worse this area has seen," she said. "The weather forecasters are calling it a Polar Vortex. It will bring in colder air, and the chill factor will be unbelievable."

"Are you staying here?" he asked.

"Oh, yes. This job is a live-in position," she replied. "There are no houses up here; nobody lives for miles."

"Nobody?"

She shrugged. "There are the Sami. They are the indigenous people of Lapland, tribal and nomadic. Like the Inuit of North America."

"Where will they go?" Ramsay asked incredulously.

"Mister Huss, the owner of The Eagle's Nest, is making the hotel available to anyone in need of shelter and sanctuary from the storm. He has put out the claim in regular broadcasts on shortwave radio and over social media." She smiled. "Even people who live in huts and igloos have a cell phone! Probably get likes for posting a picture of them skinning a reindeer!" she paused, going quiet when she saw that Ramsay wasn't sharing her humour. "Anyway, anyone in danger can come and use rooms he has put aside. The hotel is quiet, mainly because of the storm forecast, so there are many vacant rooms."

"Interesting..." Ramsay mused. Security was going to be a nightmare. But the defector could walk right in without anybody realising. He nodded a thank you to the waitress and watched her leave, stopping to talk to the waiter who was hovering in the doorway to the lounge. He sipped his drink and decided he'd eaten enough. He would take a wander around the hotel, get a feel for the place. He had an hour or so free and decided to put it to use.

Chapter Thirty

Russia

The wooden table was pitted and scuffed. The edges were uneven, and several hundred people had either carved or written their initials or names into it over the years. The dates ran back to the mid-eighties, when the first phase of the hydroelectric station was opened. And although the facility had been expanded and upgraded, the last of which was the geothermal hot rock project, the room in which the table centred had not been decorated since. A perfunctory room where people, exhausted from their shifts in the power plant, sat in silence and ate a meagre meal, then returned to their shift. A half-hour break in a shift lasting fourteen hours. Seven days a week in the winter, six days a week in the summer. There was no union, no workers' representative, but wages were substantially higher than the national average, so people stayed. There were no transport links in the winter, so no way out other than the ice road. Fifty-miles to the nearest town. No vehicles were allowed at the plant, so the walk would be suicide. In the summer, a few people left and made the walk to town. They never returned. Some thought it strange that they hadn't shown up on social media, but others had their suspicions why. There were secrets here. And secrets were a dangerous knowledge to hold.

Natalia Grekov ate her meagre meal of vegetable soup and bread, whilst reading a four-day old newspaper. The papers came in every week and with them, the occasional magazine. She liked the Western fashion magazines the most. So glamorous, so out of reach. Russia had changed much in her lifetime, and at thirty-two, she could remember stricter times and a life with less opportunities than today. But this far north, this close to the edge of Russia's shores and the Arctic Ocean, she had travelled to a time warp. She had been glad of the employment, and the money was better than she would have got elsewhere, but the lack of amenities, communication and feeling of isolation was taking its toll. She was worn-out and the hours they were expected to work made her work feel like a prison sentence. A true Russian gulag, but with heating and occasional use of a television and the internet. She was no fool, though. She knew her time online was monitored by the facility's security. Like the old days of the KGB, they waited for people to slip up. People often did and were dealt with swiftly. Their employment terminated. But she was no fool. She knew these people, knew they wouldn't slip from society. She had searched for them online, but not too thoroughly. She had always planned to leave after a year. That would give her enough funds to travel to Europe, to seek visas and employment and a new life. She was a specialist in her field, and there were hydroelectric and thermoelectric concerns that would pay a fortune for her expertise. But the years had passed, and she was now five-years in and knew that she was a lost cause. She had seen too much. She didn't even bother requesting leave anymore. Not since she had stumbled into the lower sector. A favour for a man she knew she would never see again. And she would never forget the sinking feeling that day. The knowledge she had sealed her own fate. They would never let her go now.

And now the lifeline.

The message had come to her by a roundabout way. A mutual friend had been quoted, things written that only he could have known. The Northern supply route was now solid ice and the icebreakers were having trouble carving a route through. Her last message had come just after Christmas. There had been little in the way of supplies since then. Such was the location and poor infrastructure surrounding the plant, that resupply was taken from the port of Koll and transported on the ice road. Far easier than bringing it in by road from the South. Norway's infrastructure to the West put this region of Russia to shame. Although, there was precious little that far north to truly test the conditions.

So, a series of notes, transported by one of the crew of a freighter who had passed the note onto someone unknown. The notes had outlined what was expected of her, and what she would receive in return. Safe passage and a bounty of fifty-thousand pounds, with a well-paid job, a new identity, along with a house and car. The specifics were unclear on the latter, but she reasoned that any house and car would be better than what she already owned, and the chance of a fresh start in Britain appealed more than the material things. She assumed Britain, because of the currency, but anywhere would be better than the freezer she was living in now. And the hours and workload were breaking her down more than she could bear. She felt like an old woman, yearned to live again.

It was the passing on of the messages that she feared the most. That was what had taken her so long to decide whether she should take the bait. Because once she did, then there was no going back. Could it have been a trap? Almost certainly. Was it? She would not know until the game played out. She had spent more than a year in her quandary. She left her reply, unsigned and carefully written in her left hand to avoid a comparison with writing samples that would undoubtedly be held on file. The last message had taken three months to reach her after her reply. It had given the date and co-ordinates. Along with a four-hour window. No further messages would be collected from her dead-drop, and no more received.

She looked at her watch. She had less than twenty-four hours to go, and she had heard that a storm was coming. She had seen many storms living out here. There were only a few miles of frozen land and then nothing but sea ice until the North Pole. Storms were common during the winter months, she doubted this one would be any different. She turned the newspaper over and glanced again at the front page, the headline grabbed her attention:

MORE BRITISH LIES!
RUSSIA IS NO THREAT TO WORLD PEACE!

She thought back to the day that changed her life, the day that she had learned the unthinkable. She looked back at the newspaper headline and tossed the paper across the table. Tears welled in her eyes, and she wiped them with the back of her sleeve. She had lost her appetite for tinned vegetable soup. Tomorrow, she would dine in style.

Chapter Thirty-One

"Come on, I'll show you the ice hotel," Caroline said breezily. "I had a nose around after I checked in." She nestled her head into King's shoulder and said, "It's breath-taking, you'll see."

King looked at the double glass doors. They looked thick, the sort of perspective you got from walking through an aquarium tunnel, where the sharks suddenly halve in size as they swim by. Man-eaters to dogfish in the blink of an eye. He looked at the rows of snow suits hanging on pegs. All black with panels of red or blue. They appeared to be generic, utilitarian. He unhooked an extra-large for himself. Caroline chose a medium in blue. It wasn't personal preference, the blues looked to have a female cut and were generally smaller than the reds.

"It's like stepping into a freezer," she said. "But there's no wind chill, so it isn't anything like as cold as outside." She kicked off her shoes and stepped into the suit. It went on easily, and she was glad she had worn trousers instead of the cocktail dress she had been planning. Somehow, even in the warmth of the hotel with all its fires and cosy alcoves, a dress did not seem substantial enough given the extreme temperature outside. She pulled on a pair of loose-fitting and well-worn soft snow boots and looked up at King, who was dressed and waiting. "I'll never know how you get dressed so quickly."

King didn't enlighten her with tales of the older bullies in children's homes or of those early days in prison showers, the pecking order not yet established. He smiled and pressed the door release button. The doors opened with a satisfying whoosh like on the bridge of the Enterprise in Star Trek. The boy in him wanted to press it some more, but Caroline had already hooked her arm inside his and was leading him inside. A moment of intimacy for some, but all King could do was feel the unease at having his right arm clamped so tightly. He really did know little peace. He pulled her near, kissed her for a moment, then swung her round and took her right hand in his left. She squeezed tightly, blissfully unaware of his motives. He relaxed a little, the pistol in his right pocket, his right hand comfortingly close and unobstructed. He remembered a story as a child, how a man's sword hand dictated which side his female companion should walk. That the tradition carried on, all the way to which side the woman stood at the altar.

The difference in temperature was remarkable, but as Caroline had said, the lack of windchill made it more bearable on the exposed areas of skin. The excavation and carving of the ice was truly impressive. King had no idea how it was made, but he didn't imagine it had been tunnelled out. There was no reason why there should have been enough ice to do so. As a manmade concept, the hotel had been built on top of a purpose-built hill. There was no subsequent glacier to bore through with machinery. He imagined a frame being constructed, water pumped through, or even large slabs of ice cut elsewhere and bonded in place with water which would freeze within minutes. Then they would chisel at it to create texture and the illusion that it had been bored out. Regardless of how they had done it, they had constructed it with great skill and attention to detail. The walls and ceiling had a softened effect which looked like a jagged finish that had melted slightly. The ice had a blueish hue, glacier-like. King wondered whether they had added some dye to it. He smoothed his hand over, for the first time remembering he had not picked up gloves. The ice was dry to the touch.

"Amazing, isn't it?" Caroline marvelled. "Look at the lights in the floor, they're changing colour."

King looked at the electric tealights under the ice. They were blending from a cold blue to a warm red, with a thousand shades in between. Arguably tasteless under kitchen counters in most homes, but the lighting created a beautiful effect as it was accentuated by the ice. As they rounded the first gentle bend in the carved ice tunnels, King laughed out loud when he noticed a fire extinguisher set into the ice wall. Its own alcove with instructions on how to use it in various languages.

"Proof, if ever it were needed, that health and safety has gone mad."

She smiled. "You're such a cynic."

"And how, exactly, does ice catch fire?"

Caroline squeezed his hand and pulled him onwards. The tunnel curved to the right and a series of openings were spaced along both sides. Outside each opening there was a different animal's head carved in the wall. Caroline stopped outside one with an ornate eagle, wings in a vee and its talons splayed as if bearing down on an unsuspecting prey. The carving was truly exquisite.

"Here," she whispered. "They don't have doors, so I'm not sure how you tell if a room is occupied."

"I guess if you're meant to be here, you'll already know which room yours is."

"Smartarse," she said. She craned her neck to look around the curve of the ice, then simply walked right in. "It's okay... there's nobody home," she called behind her.

King shrugged and followed her inside. It was impressive, though hardly lavish. A raised plinth of ice acted as the bed, with what appeared to be a rubber mattress and a pile of animal skins, with rolled-up sleeping bags and pillows, with scatter cushions around the base of the plinth. The electric tealights made the cavern seem warmer, but it was still -20°C according to the thermometer which hung from a climbing piton that had been hammered into the wall.

"Nothing much in here," King commented flatly. "But I guess the people come for that…" He pointed to the viewing bay, which was glazed in the same quadruple glass as the entrance to the tunnel. Two sliding doors and a portion of roof that had been melted and bonded into the ice. An ice sofa had been carved and draped in the same skins and cushions. Beyond the glass, the sky was green and boiling. The Aurora Borealis, or Northern Lights danced and weaved across the sky in mesmerising beauty.

"Oh, my goodness…" Caroline trailed off. "It's beautiful!"

King stepped closer to her, wrapped his left arm around her shoulders. "It is," he agreed.

They watched for a good ten minutes, neither breaking the moment with talk that would only go to cheapen the experience. Nothing other than admiration for the spectacle. Eventually, King moved away. "We'd better get going," he said. "We'll see it again while we're here, I'm sure."

Caroline nodded, then gasped. "There's somebody out there!" she exclaimed. "Watching us!" She took a pace towards the window. "Over there, crouched down!" she pointed.

King turned and looked, only aware of a sudden movement. The thick glass had obscured their view, light reflecting from the ice room back to them. The lightshow in the sky had taken their attention and only the movement had made the person visible. He tried to focus through the thick glass and caught sight of a figure dashing out of view behind the next ice pod viewing bay. He looked at the doors, but they were operated by a card, the same as his own room's door.

"Come on!" he snapped as he turned and charged out through the chamber and into the ice tunnel, the lights turning to an eerie blue-green as he ran towards the outside exit.

Caroline fell in behind him, but in truth she was a faster sprinter than he was and was soon level to his shoulder and by the time they reached the end of the ice tunnel, she had streaked out a considerable lead. King slid to a stop behind her, but she already had the button pressed and the doors were sliding open with their *Star Trek* whoosh.

The frigid air engulfed them and the windchill was severe. King's first thoughts were that he should merely leave the person to the elements. But whoever had been watching them would have had to be committed in the first place. Why would they endure such conditions to watch them inside the room? Even a perverted voyeur would have to concede the likelihood of a couple getting naked at that temperature was non-existent. The ice rooms were designed for an entirely different experience. Fully dressed, wrapped and swaddled in blankets and sleeping bags, and encapsulated in the moment – of being in an ice chamber, watching the Polar Lights. It was an experience. Nothing else would matter – the ice rooms did not even have bathrooms, the guests having to use their own rooms within the hotel, or the public lavatories off the lobby. So, what else would a watcher hope to achieve?

King had the Walther in his hand, only now noticing how cold his hands were. He kept the weapon down by the side of his leg, unnoticeable, yet ready to bring to arm. He glanced at Caroline, who was blowing on her cupped hands. He looked at the ground. There were hundreds of footprints. The tunnel was an entrance and exit for the hotel, a main thoroughfare and part of the attraction. Even if they were not staying there, people all went and had a look. He couldn't hope to track somebody here. He walked around the first viewing pod. There were less prints, but still too many to single out the watcher. The next pod had a couple seated inside, wrapped and watching the light show much as he and Caroline had. He noted how cosy they looked. Obvious that was as good as it was going to get for a voyeur.

There were less footprints by far, and as King reached the pod they had been in, the pod denoted by the exquisite carving of the eagle, he could see just a few scuffed footprints on the ground.

He turned to Caroline and asked, "How close do you think they were?"

Caroline stepped forwards. She crouched low to the ice wall. "Back a bit," she said, standing up and walking backwards a few paces. She looked at the marks and scuffs on the compacted snow. "Here, I guess." She crouched down again, squatted close to the ground. She looked to her right. "This would be about right," she said confidently. "He jumped up and legged it that way."

"He?"

"I'm just supposing."

"What makes you think it was a man?"

She shrugged. "The build, movement…" Then she exclaimed decisively, "The suit! It was red and black. Not blue and black, which are the ladies suits."

King glanced down at his own, then looked at Caroline's. He led the way back to the tunnel entrance and pocketed the tiny pistol. His hands were raw and stiff. They would burn when they thawed inside. They said nothing as they walked back through the ice tunnel. The blast of warm air was both welcome and uncomfortable as they walked through the doors and they whooshed seamlessly shut behind them. Caroline stepped aside to allow a couple through. They beamed a smile, a knowing nod. They were looking forward to their night in the ice hotel and had paid a substantial figure for the upgrade. King barged between them.

"Come on," he said sharply. "We'll check the main entrance."

"Hey!" the man shouted after him, but it fell upon deaf ears.

Caroline pulled a face of apology then followed. They marched through the foyer, past the main dining room and the brasserie restaurant, and past the reception desk. The duty manager looked up then turned back to his computer screen. Just another domestic, the woman chasing after the man after a few cross words. He'd seen it all.

King stopped at the front entrance, bumping into Neil Ramsay, who was brandishing an expensive looking camera in one hand and dusting snow off his suit with the other. Red and black, issued by the sympathetic manager.

Ramsay ignored them both, turned to the man next to him and said, "The wind's getting up, I couldn't work out if it was snowing or just the ice dusting off the trees in the wind."

The man next to him was finishing a cigarette. He had a hooked nose and was particularly thin. "Yes," he said, his accent thick and distinctive. King had heard the accent many times. Russian, or at least Slavic. "Plenty of snow is on the way, by all accounts." He casually flicked his cigarette butt out into the wind and unzipped his identical red and black suit. "Well, goodnight."

King ignored them both and pushed past. He rounded the front left façade and past rows of people cradling steaming mugs of cocoa or mulled wine as they watched the Northern Lights, which were now starting to fade having put on another spectacular show for the evening.

Caroline stopped and called out. King turned around, but he shared her expression. There were too many people. Too many tracks to hide the ones they were after and too many people for the watcher to hide amongst. Resigned to failure, King walked back with her to the entrance.

Peter Stewart was climbing the last of the steps as they reached the entrance. He was holding a mug of mulled wine and the heady scented aroma of cinnamon, nutmeg and red wine hit them. He eyed King warily but chose to remain silent as he studied Caroline. He looked at King approvingly, then ambled into the foyer, loosening the top proportion of his hotel-issue red and black snow suit as he headed to the bar.

He drained his glass, obviously getting a top-up.

"Bugger," said King. "Safety in numbers." He stripped off, overheating from the thick suit, and yet his hands and cheeks were painfully tingling. He looked at Caroline and assumed his face was as red as hers. He wore his suit at his waist, the arms tied together. "Come on, let's put these back, and get our shoes. And then we can get a drink. I don't know whether I need to cool down or warm up."

"You can apologise to that couple first," she said indifferently.

"Right."

"I mean it," she said. "Crikey, Alex, what were you going to do if we'd caught up with whoever was spying on us? It could have just been innocent."

"Innocent people don't run."

"Well, they do if someone built like you looks at them like you did, then shouted and charged out of the room," she retorted, only half serious, downplaying the incident considering there was no positive conclusion. "Let's forget it and move forward."

King shrugged. "Nothing else we can do." He kicked off his boots and tore the snow suit off and hung it back on the peg. His trousers were damp from the exertion, but his cheeks and hands were numb. "Somebody tried to kill me," he said calmly.

"What?"

"Twice," he said. "And they killed somebody else, before they got the chance to talk. Or before I got the chance to interrogate them."

"What?" she looked at him incredulously. "Who? How? When?" She shook her head, realising just how stupid she had sounded. "What are you talking about?"

"A GRU agent held a gun on me," he said. "It escalated, and I killed her."

"Her?"

King nodded, an image of the woman going for her reload. He was still angry she had pushed him to it. "Yes. But somebody else tried to kill me, too."

"Did you kill them?" she asked, tearing at her own suit. "That's how it usually ends when somebody comes after you."

"Not this time."

"But they're dead?"

"Yes."

"Then who killed them?"

King shook his head. "That man with the mulled wine," he said. "I know him. And I need to tell you about him. So, let's get that drink, because it won't be quick."

Chapter Thirty-Two

From their own private alcove, affording the generous and comforting heat of the log-burning stove, King settled into the comfortable wing-backed chair and clearly observed the reception desk through the open concertinaed doorway. He had been about to ask the manager to look at any CCTV the hotel may have had of the grounds but had been put off by the in-depth conversation he had been having with both the Russian waiter and barman. There had been the air of conspiracy about it, although Caroline had been quick to remind him that he had effectively passed on their lack of hospitality skills with the waitress. What looked like conspiracy could well have been a stern word about standards and expectations.

King hadn't noticed any cameras on his ride up in the snowmobile. He had surveyed the hotel for a while, much to Stewart's consternation, but he wasn't going to change the way he operated for him. The man should have known the importance of a recce, even if it was just a casual observation. The two men checked in separately, thanks to King parking the snowmobile down the side of the hotel, out of the way of the main entrance. The winding road up the mountain, or what King decided was merely a huge mound – an almighty engineering feat, but no less a mound all the same – had been easy enough and King saw by the tracks that a caterpillar style machine had taken regular trips, compacting the snow as hard as concrete. It would have made sense to bring up the hotel's supplies from the carpark this way. The snowmobile coped with the corners and gradient effortlessly, but he could see why the funicular had been constructed. Cars would not cope at all, and the prepared carpark below had been full of all sorts of vehicles. He had counted a dozen. He assumed some would belong to staff, but otherwise it had meant the hotel would be barely half-full. He thought of the impending storm and considered it was just as well.

"So, you and he go back to MI6?"

King took his eyes off the reception desk and looked back at Caroline. "All the way. Another life," he paused. "It's not pretty, but I want you to know."

"You're scaring me, Alex," she said quietly. "Who is he?"

"He recruited me," he said. He stared into the fire now, the flames hypnotic. The drinks came, but he barely noticed. He was in another world.

Caroline edged his beer across the glass table closer to him. "Go on," she prompted.

"I haven't told you this, but I went to prison."

"I know," she said. "I guessed."

"You guessed?" King asked. "What does that say about me?"

She shrugged. "I can read you, Alex. Just snippets you say, or how you react to conversations, or dramas and films on the television. Little tells."

He shrugged. "I was in and out for all sorts. Fights and thefts mainly. I had nothing, and it's not an excuse, but I had to feed my brothers and sister from before I was ten. If I didn't, well she certainly wouldn't have." He had told Caroline about his mother before, but only skirted the issues. She had been a crack whore and the family had disintegrated into care after she had arranged a punter to be with her own twelve-year-old daughter. King had been unruly and far enough into his teens to be considered an adult and he had never seen his siblings again. He had found them though, many years later and had seen them right financially. Although, it had been an anonymous endeavour. "I started with the biblical loaf of bread to feed my family." He smiled. "And then the odd television or stereo…"

Caroline had been privately educated, went to a good university and entered the army as an officer. She attended Sandhurst and had childhood memories of her pony and skiing trips in the Christmas holidays. She bristled and felt entirely guilty when she heard snippets from

King's childhood. "It must have been tough," she said, aware of the emptiness in her words.

King looked away from the fire and took a sip of his beer. He nursed the glass, but the flames were a welcome distraction from making eye contact with her. He loved to look into her eyes, but not for this. "I killed two soldiers in a bar fight," he said. "I was an arrogant shit, and I boxed semi-professionally. They were back from a tour in the sandbox, pretty drunk and hitting it big with the women. They had their pay and were throwing it around. I was a tosser. There were words, insults and punches thrown. I was faster. But it didn't stop there. When they were down, I went back for more..."

Caroline saw that his eyes were glistening. Usually so cold and hard, they looked vulnerable for the first time. She sipped her gin and tonic, unsure what she should do. The distraction was welcome.

"I went to prison," he said. "For manslaughter. I had served a year, then one day I got a visitor."

"That man?"

He nodded. "Peter Stewart. Former Parachute Regiment, then SAS before he turned MI6 special operations officer. He trained his men, even worked with them on assignments. He told me what he could do for me, what my life could be like and I went with it. I'd made some enemies when I lived in London, and again in Portsmouth. I did some unofficial boxing matches, won when I should have lost, threw a fight when I should have won. I made a lot of money on the side bets, but the wrong people lost a fortune. I was a marked man. And there's no place worse than prison for a marked man. They always get someone to you and you can't get away. My time was running out, so I leapt at the chance. I was busted out of Dartmoor Prison, the body of a homeless man who died on the streets of hyperthermia was dressed in my clothes and dropped in a bog on Dartmoor and the autopsy of that poor fellow was passed off as one Mark Thomas Jeffries…"

Caroline reached out and touched his hand. "But you're a different man now, Alex. And you'll always be Alex to me."

"Am I different though?" King didn't take his eyes away from the fire. "I've killed people, done terrible things."

"For your country, though. A soldier in secret wars. Wars which could cost our country everything," she paused. "Look at your first mission for MI5, with Charles Forrester. There wouldn't be a country now, had Zukovsky got his way."

King sighed. "I can't leave Mark Jeffries behind. He's always there."

"No," she said. "Alex King is always here." She squeezed his hand. He was on his way to maudlin, and she wasn't having him do that. "Tell me about that man, Stewart."

King nodded. "He was my recruiter, my mentor. I spent so long thinking I owed him my life, that he betrayed me, and I just couldn't see it."

"Betrayed you, how?"

"It was before I worked for Five. Some people furthering their private business interests using government funds and assets thought I knew too much. They persuaded Stewart to come down on one side of the fence or the other. He was nearing retirement, needed the security, and sold me down the river." He shrugged. "We're all collateral in the end, I should have been ready for it."

"But you trusted him. In your mindset, he rescued you and changed you. He undoubtedly had a part in creating the man in front of me today, the man I fell in love with. A man with a sense of justice and duty, of doing the right thing, no matter what path must be taken to get there. So, his betrayal was everything to you. You wouldn't have seen it coming, and it wouldn't have been easy to get over," she paused thoughtfully. "So why the hell is he here now?"

King took a drink, draining a third of the glass. He placed it back on the glass table and shifted in his chair. The alcohol and the fire were making him tired. He decided he'd had enough to drink for tonight. He looked back at Caroline and said, "Last year was madness, it created a large footprint."

"Footprint?"

"In South Africa. You confided in that man Ryan Beard, the MI6 contact who helped you out after you had your run in..."

"I was abducted and driven to somewhere they could kill me and get rid of my body. I killed two men!" she said harshly. "And then I was ambushed and only just made it out alive..."

"There's no medals in this game," he said sharply. He caught her expression, softened his tone somewhat. "Whatever happened, MI6 caught wind of my existence. When Forrester took me on, I wasn't too bothered about using my name. Everybody involved in my last days in MI6 were either dead or retired. There were only a few people who even knew of my existence. I underestimated two things. The first was that a young man who literally drove me to an embassy on two occasions would be handed a picture of me and actually remember my face."

"And the other?" Caroline was irked. She had known from King's initial reaction when he found out what she had done, that she had made a mistake. She had just hoped it would be ok.

"And the other thing was I went too far off the reservation last summer. Searching for you, faced with the game Milankovitch forced me to play, I created a trail. That trail would have been fine, but for a loose end I failed to sever almost three years ago…"

"Peter Stewart," she said quietly.

"I was intent on killing him for what he did to me," King paused, casting his eyes to the fire. "But when the crunch came, I couldn't see what difference it would make. The man had become a father-figure to me over the years. I walked away. But I had no idea that he would come back out of retirement. He was desperate for recognition within the new MI6. He had no contacts worth a damn, but when MI6 found the link in South Africa, he must have stepped up and volunteered what he knew. Now MI6 have the Milankovitch affair hanging over Director Amherst, who in turn, has sent me up here on this fool's errand to clear up things for MI6. Amherst has his balls in a vice, and the new director of MI6, Villiers, is slowly turning the key."

"And Stewart killed the person who tried to kill you?"

King's mind filled with the image of the man's face blowing out, the sight of Stewart standing behind him, casually lowering his gun. No chance to overpower the man, get some answers out of him. King had the man, just needed another second to put pressure on the arm lock. Another second and the man would have dropped to his knees and started talking.

"He did." King looked back at her. "The man shot at me when I visited the scene of Fitzpatrick's death. I winged him, but he got away. There was another man, I shot out his engine, but he got away on his accomplice's snowmobile."

Caroline nodded. She had been brought up to speed in her briefing prior to leaving London. "Where is this man who Stewart killed?"

"About five miles away," King paused. "I've made a note of the GPS coordinates on my phone, but we couldn't bring him on the snowmobile."

"So, where does this Peter Stewart character fit in? Does he know I'm with MI5?"

"Oh, I'm positive," King mused. "He may not know the rest of the team are here, or who they are. But he'll know you from your South African escapade. And he'll know Neil Ramsay for sure. Simon Mereweather is deputy director. Ramsay is Mereweather's righthand man. He'll know him, will have looked at his file. Or whatever they have on him."

"But he won't know Rashid and Marnie," Caroline nodded. "We should keep it that way. It won't hurt to have two pairs of hands that only we know about. Not if you don't trust MI6."

King nodded. "I'm not happy about those two Russians either."

"The barman and the waiter?"

"Yes."

"You don't think it's just a coincidence?"

"I don't believe in coincidence."

Caroline took a sip of her drink, put it down and looked at him. "I'll lay off those for a while, it's easy to get caught up with thinking I'm actually on holiday, when really I need to keep a clear head..." she paused. "I'll get a coffee. Do you want a tea?"

King shook his head. "They don't do tea well here... It tastes like wood and they keep putting lemon in it. The milk tastes sour, but the courtesy tray in the room has UHT, which is passable, and Lipton tea, which is drinkable." He looked up as Caroline swung around in her seat as a commotion started at the front desk. King stood up and said, "Let's take a look."

It was a chaotic scene. The manager was calling somebody on the phone and holding up one hand to subdue the man thumping the desk with a fist. King couldn't understand a word of the language, but he got the gist. The man wasn't happy. He was clad in thick clothing made from animal skins, and had a rifle slung over his shoulder on a braided leather sling. King could see the rifle was a Mauser from World War Two. The scope on top looked from the same era. He suspected the man would be a superb shot. There was something about people who used a gun to feed their family. They learned not to waste a single bullet.

King turned his attention to the two women who stood quietly behind the man. They were rotund, red faced. He doubted he could guess their ages within twenty-years. To King and his limited knowledge, the three looked like Eskimos. Only he knew they were called Inuit now. And he doubted they still lived in igloos. He was aware that these people of Northern Scandinavia were the Sami, and he knew there were several types of Sami, like tribes. They were a semi-nomadic group and they travelled through Norway, Lapland, Finland and Russia. The Russians seemed to leave them alone. There wasn't much in the way of a hard border this far north.

A tall, lithe man of about fifty, with cropped white silvery-white hair sidled up to the desk. He carried an aura of calm and confidence. King watched as the manager seemed to breathe a sigh of relief and the newcomer started to talk with the Sami at the counter. The manager seemed bolstered by the arrival of the other man, and an arrogant expression took over where indecision and uncertainty had been merely moments before.

King caught sight of the waitress walking through, and he walked over and said quietly, "Excuse me, what's going on?"

She looked at him quizzically and frowned. "I'm sorry, but why are you interested?"

King smiled. "Well, the man was being aggressive, I'm hanging around in case the manager needs a hand," he said with a concerned expression. "I work in security, I guess it's a natural reaction. A habit, I suppose."

"Oh, I see," she hesitated, then said, "From what I gather, they have come here to take advantage of the owner's offer to shelter people from the storm," she paused. "It's coming tomorrow afternoon, or evening. No change to its path." She frowned, listening to the Sami and the man who had certainly calmed the situation. She looked back at King. "Nobody has seen his brother."

"His brother?"

"Yes," she said. "Apparently, he was going to meet them here, hours ago."

King swallowed. His heart raced, but years of operating on the edge had given him the ability to quell his nerves quickly. "And nobody has seen this man? His brother?"

"No. Not a soul."

"And is there CCTV?" he asked, then said, "Sorry, as I said, I work in security." He offered, to cover his inquisitiveness. He just hoped that there wouldn't be footage of Stewart and himself riding in on the dead man's snowmobile, of King hiding it down the side of the hotel amongst the spindly fir trees and concealing the man's rifle in his jacket.

"No," she replied. "It was all knocked out by the storm we had earlier. It was like a tornado crashing through. It was terrifying, but over in a few minutes."

"I know," he said. "It knocked our car off the road. We came in by foot."

"Oh, you were lucky to get here," she said, her voice full of concern. "It would have been treacherous."

"It was," King said sharply, hoping to deflect her somewhat. "I saw a man on a snowmobile, though. A Sami like them."

"Oh, then you should say," she said. She coughed and addressed the owner in Finnish. She spoke for a few seconds, then looked back at King and said, "Please, tell Mister Huss and these people what you saw…"

King stepped towards the desk and said amiably, "I saw a man dressed similarly to these people…" he motioned towards the Sami. "He was heading South fast on an old-style snowmobile. It was a noisy machine, more squared than the modern snowmobiles. He had a rifle on his back."

"When was this?" Huss asked. His English was excellent, and King noted how self-assured he was.

King backed-up an hour to allow for any disparity. "About one-thirty. I tried to flag him for a lift. My vehicle was blown off the road." He shrugged like it was no big deal and said, "He didn't stop."

"And he was on the road up here?" Huss asked, somewhat incredulously.

"No. Quite a way South-West of here. On the road. Like I said, he was heading South." King watched the man. He could tell Huss knew he was lying. That suited King, because the man would have to have a reason for this. He knew more than he had admitted, and certainly more than he had told the irate and impatient Sami.

Huss conversed with the Sami and the man nodded.

"Are you going to call the police?" King asked. "A man is clearly missing. But I suppose if he was heading South, he would be in town by now."

Huss shook his head. "I fear it will endanger further life. We must wait until the storm has passed." He looked at King. "There is much danger on the way."

King nodded, looking the man in the eyes. His stare was cold and unwavering. "Then we must be ready for it."

Huss smiled. "Always."

Caroline caught King by his elbow and peeled him away. "Well, that was awkward," she whispered. "He certainly didn't believe you'd seen him on the road," she said.

"I know," said King. "So, let's find out why."

Chapter Thirty-Three

The Inari Falls Paatsjoki River Hydroelectric Plant
Russia

The plant made up a string of hydroelectric plants on the Paatsjoki River, owned by Norway and Russia in a shared usage agreement dating back to 1957. The first in the line, and situated at the falls of the Inari River, the plant produced electricity from the torrents of water and sent it back to St. Petersburg via the northern grid. Natalia Grekov though, knew this to be nothing more than a front. The plant did produce electricity, and it did supply much of St. Petersburg as a privately-owned enterprise with its registered offices based in the city. But she also knew that the secondary plant built twenty years ago, and operated by a separate tier of personnel, was a secret Russian government department producing something completely different.

Natalia pulled the hood of her jacket over her head and opened the door to the gantry. The windchill clawed at the exposed parts of her face, and her eyes watered. Barely twenty-feet across the gantry and she could feel the crustiness of the tears freezing to her eyelids. She blinked hard, softening her eyelids. She breathed hard through her nose, felt her nostrils stick together. As she walked swiftly onwards, keeping her right gloved hand on the rail to steady herself, she negotiated the three steps down to the next gantry. Thankfully, the designers had not put in gradients due to the build-up of ice and snow, and every fifty feet or so, two or three steps dropped to a lower level gantry, until by the time she reached the next building, she had dropped some fifty-feet in elevation. The route was more difficult on the way back, especially as she would be walking into the wind as well as climbing all the way. There was no underestimating how difficult even moderate exertion made breathing at these temperatures.

She reached the entrance to the turbine regenerator house and pulled down on the metal full-section handle. Because of the harshness of the environment and the fact that everybody wore gloves for seven months of the year, the ergonomics of the plant had been thought through with fire escape style pull down bars on the doors, wider doorways to accommodate bulky clothing and two people entering at once. Nobody wanted to form an orderly queue at -30°C.

The regenerator turbine was not in use when the hydroelectric dynamos were actively spinning to generate electricity. Each time they stopped for routine safety checks or maintenance, the gas operated regenerator would fire-up and run, bringing the prop-shafts up to twenty-seven-thousand revolutions per minute, before the hydroelectric dynamos essentially geared in and took over the flow of the water. Once up to speed and running for ten minutes, the regenerator turbine shut down slowly over a twenty-minute period and finally disengaged gearing so that the only element driving the dynamos was the crashing waters of Lake Inari river falls forming the Paatsjoki River. From its elevation of almost seven-hundred feet above sea level, the river was a torrent of powerful white water all the way to the mouth of the Varangerfjord, which emptied its water into the icy saline of the Barents Sea, where the mix of waters formed mini icebergs that collected along the shoreline.

Natalia worked her way down the spiralled staircase of metal grating and descended the one-hundred feet or so to the rock-lined cavern. Now seventy-feet under the river bed, the rock walls were covered with a sheen of ice which did not defrost through the summer months. The rock had been blasted and bored, with water used to cool the blades of the boring machine that had frozen solid on the rock. A layer of permafrost which would remain frozen for millennia.

She checked her watch. She had a clear hour in which to work. She did not know who the inside person was. She had left and collected the messages from three separate dead-drops throughout the plant. She knew the person would have to be senior, but not top-tier. That would point clearly to one of four individuals. It would be suicidal for one of those to be involved. In any event, she knew once she had defected, the top-tier would be left in a difficult position. But she had weighed the situation and knew that she had little hope of leaving this place alive. Not now she had seen what she shouldn't have. The price would be worth it. Collateral damage, the agent had called it in one of her earlier messages. And in bringing her into the fold, they had already sealed her fate. From the moment she had returned the message and not gone straight to plant security, she had sacrificed the top-tier and undermined her own safety.

There was a row of steel lockers along the wall. Some were single full-length personal lockers and others were six-feet wide and labelled with the contents. Mainly tools and parts needed for the maintaining of the regenerator. Others were fuse cupboards and circuit boards. Few people had business down here, and but for a chance encounter, she would have been none the wiser. But an errand for a friend had brought her down here and she had seen that not all the lockers were as they seemed.

Natalia made her way to the furthest wide locker and she checked behind her as she opened both doors to reveal the hidden door behind and security keypad. She had been given the code but had memorised it and burned the note. She couldn't afford to be caught with such information. She punched in the eight-digit number, and the steel door opened inwards on a set of six thick hinges. She could see the rubber seals around both the door and the frame, shuddered at the thought of what secrets they would hold in here. Sealed in the airtight facility, the air capable of being sucked out under immense pressure and a total vacuum created within minutes of the alarm being sounded. Not just to kill what this facility made, but the living beings within. Personnel included. Certain death in little more than a minute.

Natalia checked her watch once more, knowing as she did so, that barely a minute had passed since she had last checked. She had been told it would be clear. Again, she wondered how this could be so without involving one of the top tier personnel. To recall security, to organise a shift pattern without an inter-lapping of personnel. But she cleared her head of such thoughts. It wasn't her problem. An out. That was what she had been given. And through her predecessor's contact, she had been given the chance of a fresh start. Clearly the man had failed to take all the information required of him.

Or perhaps he had merely whetted their appetite? Whoever they were.

The walls were different down here. Thermal tiles lined the walls, floors and ceilings. They conducted either heat or cold and held the temperatures required for days. She was not aware, but they were the same tiles used by the Russian space program for the re-entry of their forthcoming reusable rocket. She was not aware that through what was basically a heat generating turbine that the entire facility could be heated to over one-thousand degrees Celsius, or using liquid nitrogen, could get as low as minus one-hundred and ninety-eight Celsius. Again, protocols were in place to lockdown and sanitise the facility without the evacuation of its personnel.

The next door was constructed of Perspex and was the entrance to the air-lock. She entered the eight-digit pin on the keypad and stepped inside. She took her phone out of her pocket and placed it on the bench seat, then unhooked one of the orange suits and stepped into it. She pulled it over her shoulders, zipped it up and fastened the plastic overlays over the zip. After she had put on the rubber gloves, she used the insulation tape as she had been instructed. She sealed the wrists, slipped on the over-boots and taped the trouser legs in place. Next, she pulled on the plastic helmet and mask, and allowed the attached, heavily weighted flaps to roll down around her back, shoulders and chest. She checked that the door was tightly closed behind her and pressed the button marked: **Шлюз**.

Air lock.

The rubber seals expanded and there was a faint whoosh, and she felt her ears pop as if she were taking off in a passenger airliner. The light above her turned from red to green, and she used the same eight-digit pin on the keypad. The second door opened, and she picked up her phone and stepped out into the laboratory.

She filmed the laboratory. The work stations, flow charts, television screens, computer terminals and monitors, and the row upon row of scientific equipment that she had no idea of its purpose. She recognised test-tubes and pipette's, petri dishes and all manner of tools she would have associated with a medical theatre. She looked up at the bank of television screens. A vision of evolutionary terror. From tiny rhesus monkeys in cages, to chimpanzees in single Perspex units, to a lone and solitary gorilla, and to her horror – two Perspex units, each containing a man and a woman.

Her heart raced, and she felt herself go lightheaded. She couldn't take her eyes off the screens. She recognised both people – former workers of the hydroelectric station. She had thought it odd that they had left without word, had no further presence on social media. But people moved on with their lives, and jobs like this, they were a means to an end.

Natalia caught herself, realised she had started to urinate. Just a trickle, but she stopped herself, the sensation taking her back thirty-years to a time where she felt safe and loved and secure. Her legs were heavy and leaden, she willed herself to move, but could not. She did not know how long she stared at the screen, but she knew she had lost vital minutes, and her fear of being caught now was on an entirely different scale to her first fears. She knew that she could end up here, whatever this hell was.

She had been instructed to use video only. Stills could be taken from the film later, and she could not change the phone's settings while wearing the gloves. She filmed the television monitors, using the zoom function to give greater perspective. She filmed the last two screens longer for dramatic effect. Then she felt voyeuristic. The feeling sickened her, and she lowered the phone. She knew what she had to do, but it was at odds with what she knew she should do. She could no longer see her watch and could not take the phone off its camera setting while wearing the gloves. She looked for a clock on the wall, then relaxed when she saw eight. They were labelled: Site, Moscow, Vladivostok, Washington, London, Paris, Los

Angeles, Canberra. She frowned at the significance but looked at the clock labelled "site" and realised she was well over halfway through her window of opportunity.

But what should she do? She had instructions to film the facility and map the location using the GPS of her smartphone. She imagined that her predecessor had some information that had whetted the appetite of an outside agency but hadn't documented the smoking gun. She looked again at the bank of television monitors, a thought coming to her. If they wanted evidence, then what better than the subject of their trials? What better way to get somebody's attention than take a witness? She watched the man and the woman on the screen. What better way indeed?

Chapter Thirty-Four

"So, my mini bar takes the hit?" Neil Ramsay paused. "The accounts lot are going to love that, and it makes it look like I've got a bloody drink problem."

Rashid laughed. "It's a juice," he said. "And besides, from what I've seen, MI5 is fuelled on alcohol. You'd have a bigger problem if you didn't drink!"

"But there's wine gone as well," he replied tersely.

Ramsay had a large suite and it had been the obvious choice to act as a meeting room. Rashid was perched on the desk, an apparently expensive bottle of orange juice in his hand. King leaned against the wall and had reverted to a cup of tea. He sipped his half-decent cuppa and smiled at Ramsay's protests. Marnie sipped from her glass of white wine, the object of Ramsay's protestations. She had flushed at her cheeks and was looking embarrassed.

"Make the most of it, Marnie," Caroline laughed. "He'll ask housekeeping not to restock it tomorrow. If I hadn't had too much already, I'd join you." She was seated in a chair, pouring creamer into a cup of coffee. She'd found some cappuccino sprinkles and was juggling the cup, creamer and sprinkle sachet, the cup balanced between her knees.

"Oh, sod it!" Ramsay opened the mini bar and took out a miniature of brandy and a bottle of soda. "But nobody has any of that organic chocolate… it's ten-euros a bar!" He twisted the caps and unceremoniously poured both bottles into a glass. He took a sip and relished the taste. He looked up at King as he sat down in the chair next to Caroline. King remained stoically against the wall. "So, what have you found out?"

King shrugged. "It's not quite as simple as that," he said. He told them about Peter Stewart, his association with him in MI6 and their eventful journey up to the hotel. He glossed over much of his MI6 career. It was out of the bag now, and he knew it wouldn't be the last he heard about it. He had already started to think of an exit strategy. An archipelago in Indonesia or Malaysia, maybe. Somewhere he could disappear and live inexpensively. But would Caroline be willing to cut herself off? He glanced at her across the room. She had managed to construct a passable cappuccino. He loved her. Hoped she loved him enough to leave it all behind. He shrugged off the thought. He needed to finish this first.

"Simon Mereweather filled me in about Director Amherst's penance," he said stiffly.

King smiled thinly. "I know," he said. "It's my fault…"

"No more than mine," Rashid interrupted. "I was the new boy, but I did my share to upset the Russians. And I guess that is what has upset MI6."

"And it's not like Alex had a choice," Caroline chimed in. "What was he meant to do? Sit around and wait? It's not like the service got any rescue operation in place before you recruited Rashid to help. Frankly, I think about what was done early doors and it makes me want to find a new career…"

Ramsay held up his hand. "MI5 had things in place," he said a little contritely.

"Sorry to play Devil's advocate, but from the transcripts, wasn't it Deputy Director Mereweather's plan all along to get Alex to work off grid?" Marnie paused, looking at everyone. She looked like she'd started something she wished she hadn't. "Otherwise, why else would he have presented him with the letter? The news and instructions? Like a clockwork mouse. Wind it up and watch it go…"

King smiled. He didn't know Marnie, but he liked what he saw. She was a smart cookie. "Well, I'm glad that's out there," he said. "I knew why he did what he did. And I think he knows it too, which is why he's mopping this up for MI6, rather than tossing me to the hounds." He looked at Ramsay. "In other words, we're all in this together."

"Look, let's all get on the same page here." Ramsay could see the team were tight. He hadn't thought of them as a team until now, but this was what he saw before him. "This wouldn't normally be our bag, but MI6 have us over a barrel. We need to get this job done and move on." He looked at everybody in turn, then focused his attention on King. "I'm not happy with this MI6 spook, though."

"We need him," said King.

"We needed Fitzpatrick," Ramsay corrected him. "What we have now is an ex-spook who's back in the game, and lord knows what he's agreed in order to be taken back, and a defector whose original handler is dead."

"And a bloody great storm on the way," added Rashid. "So, kicking about in the woods isn't an option. Not for everybody, at least."

Ramsay frowned. "Meaning?"

Rashid stood up and opened the laptop beside him. He switched it on and said, "Marnie has run a topography program and we're left with a map that shows the three most suitable places for a person to come in by foot across the border," he paused. "Given the location of the power station and the hotel, and natural obstacles like ravines and cliffs that Fitzpatrick would have been aware of, it really narrows it down to one place. I can get out there, get a snow hole dug out and hunker down. I have the best clothing available and some modern aids, I can see out this storm."

Ramsay nodded. He couldn't help noticing the look of concern on Marnie's face. He looked back at King and said, "What do you think?"

King shrugged. "Couldn't hurt. If he gets out there soon it will not only act as a welcoming, but a good contingency if she is followed." He looked at Rashid and said, "I've got some kit you might be interested in. Come to my room after this."

"Am I going to want to know what?" Ramsay asked.

"No."

"But the storm?" Marnie interjected. "The polar vortex they have predicted will take temperatures as low as minus sixty!"

Ramsay held up his hand. "If Rashid thinks he'll be okay, I'll go with it," he said tersely. "Rashid are you okay with it?"

"Sure, no bother."

"Are we bringing in this guy, Peter Stewart?" Marnie asked. "I mean, if he's MI6, then surely we need to cooperate with him?"

"The jury's out for the moment," Ramsay said. "We'll have to bring him in at some stage, but for now, let's keep both you and Rashid out of it. He's working with King, so he'll know about Caroline and her..." he hesitated and said, "...troubles last summer. That's why MI6 are pulling one over on MI5, after all. I've moved up a notch with Simon Mereweather's promotion to deputy director, and with that, I imagine he will have an inkling who I am. We'll not assume, just take it as given that he knows me. But he will have no reason or even the means to know our newest field recruit, nor just a secretary and analyst."

"None taken…" Marnie said quietly.

Caroline smiled and gave her a wink.

King shrugged. "It won't hurt."

"You don't trust him?" Ramsay asked.

"No."

"Because?"

"Because he tried to pull the rug out from underneath me once."

"Any other reason?"

King took something out of his pocket. A small, orange lozenge. He turned it over in his hand and held it out for Ramsay. "Because he found this and didn't tell me."

"You took it off him?" Ramsay asked, taking it and undoing the cap to reveal a stubby USB flash drive.

King nodded. "Fitzpatrick buried it in the ice, moments before he died. It was important enough for him to spend his last moments trying to hide it. His fingers were ruined in doing so. The ice split his skin and he tore out a couple of fingernails. I found it but didn't get time to retrieve it before the Sami hunter shot at me. Stewart found it when he searched the body of the Sami after he tried to ambush us. I thought I saw him palm it then. He was so worried about finding it, he didn't check the body further. When I found a couple of bullets in the man's pockets, I knew I'd seen Stewart pocket something. It makes sense now, but at the time I was shocked that he had shot him. I was wrestling the guy down, tricky on the ice, but I was getting there. Stewart just shot the man in the back of the head. I was freezing and needed to get my jacket back on, so I wasn't watching him when he searched the Sami. When I turned around, I thought I saw him put something in his pocket. I picked his pocket as we got to the hotel. When we pushed the snowmobile into some brush to hide it."

"And Stewart hasn't twigged it was you?"

"He will have by now."

"So, he won't trust you."

"He doesn't anyway."

"No?"

King shook his head. "Not a chance."

"An uneasy accord, then," Ramsay mused.

"In which to bide my time," said King.

"For what?"

King looked thoughtful for a moment before answering. "Before he tries to kill me," he paused. "Or I kill him."

Chapter Thirty-Five

The Inari Falls Paatsjoki River Hydroelectric Plant
Russia

She checked the site clock. She was half-way through her window of opportunity and she still had to deal with the air-lock and remove the protective clothing. She wasn't sure she would make it, but she needed to speak to the two people – her two former colleagues. She needed to see if she could get them free or, with time so critical, just assure them that she would not give up on them, that she could give them hope. What evil was happening here? How could two people be caged alongside primates and monkeys? Who was behind this absurdity?

Natalia had entered the keypad pin she had memorised. It operated a second air-lock. The light went from red through to green and the second door opened with a whoosh. Her helmet was fitted with a fibre particle filter, but she had a sudden panic, as if it were too late, whether whatever was being tested here was an airborne disease, and whether the particle filter was enough to clean the air. She took a deep breath. It was too late now. And she was too close to those two poor souls to backout now. She walked past the first row of cages, close enough for the rhesus monkey to swipe an arm close enough to her for her to jump backwards. She glanced up at the CCTV cameras, realising that in her haste to see the prisoners, her former colleagues, she had put herself in clear view. On record. She panicked, picked up the pace as she walked past the chimpanzee enclosure. She could see that the enclosure was separated into four sections, with a solemn-looking beast in each cage. They did not share the rhesus monkey's enthusiasm for visitors. She caught the eye of one of the larger chimpanzees. Sad and resigned to fate.

The gorilla was a large male weighing in at more than four-hundred pounds. To her horror, Natalia could see that one of its hands was chained to the wall. Dried blood and torn flaps of skin had formed around the cuff on the chain, and the hair had been worn away. The beast shared eye contact with her, but the look was far more emotive than that of the chimpanzees. It wasn't fear, nor anger. It was pure rage. Before Natalia could cover the distance of the width of the cage, the gorilla lunged at her and smashed its left fist into the mesh, stretching it and straining the bars. Its right wrist was shackled, but she could see the chain straining against the steel loop in the wall. The wound around its wrist tore open and bled as it tried to get to her, the look in its eyes one of sheer hate. Baring its teeth, it let out a deep, resonating grunt. Its fingers had now gripped the mesh and it was using the chain to pull backwards, heaving at the barrier between them. Natalia ran, covering the distance between the two enclosures in seconds, despite the bulky over-boots and thick rubber suit. As she reached the enclosure with the two separate cages, her former work colleagues within, she noticed that the gorilla had forgotten about her and had returned to its bench, sitting contemplatively back down. Pure rage to sedentary in just a few seconds, with no apparent memory of what had incited it so.

Natalia hesitated outside the enclosure. Both the man and the woman were naked. Now that she was closer, she could see welts on their back and buttocks. Both rested on their sides, their backs to her. She approached the cage. The noise of the angry gorilla had not disturbed them, but she could not believe that had been the case. The noise would have woken an entire neighbourhood. She coughed, but neither stirred. She looked at the lock on the gate. A series of bolts recessed into the metal, so that only someone from outside, and standing at an angle to the enclosure could work them. She eased the three bolts backwards.

She turned around, checked for a clock, but there was nothing but a blank wall with the row of CCTV cameras spaced opposite each enclosure. Her finger and thumb still clenched on the last remaining bolt, she looked back to the cage, recoiled when she stared straight into the woman's face. She went to step backwards, but the woman had squeezed a bloodied hand through the mesh and had taken hold of the rubber suit.

Natalia screamed and tried to batter the woman's hand away with her gloved hands. She looked into the woman's eyes, but they were lifeless and yellow. Her face was blistered with tiny burns that looked like weeping pimples. She was perspiring and as Natalia looked down at the woman's vice-like fist, gripping at her clothing, she could see that the woman had lost bladder and bowel control long before Natalia had entered.

The woman's head lolled and swayed, and Natalia realised that she was in fact blind, merely turning her head as she sensed her presence, felt her clothing and listened for her erratic breathing.

"Let go of me!" Natalia wailed. The woman's head cocked to one side and she pulled hard at the handful of rubber suit. "Please! I'll help you!"

The man had got up off the bench. His eyes were not as yellow as the woman's. They were raw and red and wet. He too had lost control of his bodily functions, and he was covered in the same tiny boils. His teeth were broken, and his gums were bleeding. He stepped closer then lunged at the mesh, biting and chewing on the wire, teeth breaking and splintering to the floor. He had squeezed his fingers through the mesh, but the little finger did not fit, and he was breaking it slowly as he clawed at her. The web of the join of skin was cutting on the wire, and as he lunged, the little finger almost severed through. He did not seem to feel the pain, nor register what he had done. His only intent was to get to her.

Natalia punched and struck the woman's hand and fell backwards when she released her grip. She looked up at the two people, now no more than beasts, clawing and biting on the mesh. The cage door was opening outwards and she kicked it shut, the mesh hitting the woman in the face. The door did not clip shut. Natalia got to her feet but did not look back as she ran down the row of cages. Out of her periphery, she saw the gorilla charge at the mesh as she passed, heard the great smash of metal, the hinges bearing the brunt of three-hundred or more pounds of angry beast. She reached the airlock, typed in the code, but pressed the wrong digit and the unit sounded a short bleep. Two chances remaining. She could hear more cages rattling, the solid crash of metal as the gorilla smashed against the cage again. She glanced backwards, saw the bulge of the mesh. She turned back to the keypad but faltered and cursed as the bleep sounded again. Natalia could hear the cages rattling, the noise consuming her. She realised she had not breathed for the entire time. She could hear own pulse thudding in her ears. It was almost enough to drown out the noise of the cages.

Almost...

Natalia got the code entered and to her relief, the door hissed open. She turned to see the gorilla smashing out through the cage, its hand severed and bleeding. It looked up to see her and started to charge down past the cages. Behind it, Natalia caught sight of the woman stepping out from her cage. She had turned towards the noise and was walking tentatively down the corridor. Each step seemed laboured, and she swayed unsteadily, her equilibrium clearly off kilter.

Time stood still as she waited for the light to change. The gorilla reached the door and started to smash its fist and bloodied stump against the Perspex. The blood smeared and streaked, and the look of anger on the animal's face was insurmountable. The woman had reached the end of the corridor too. She stood alongside the frantic gorilla at the door, placed her fingers on the glass. The gorilla did not look at her, or even acknowledge her existence. She had cocked her head again, trying to sense her rather than see her. Natalia heard the whoosh of the airlock, looked up and saw the green light and breathed a sigh of relief as she bounded through and the door closed behind her, putting another door between herself and the hell on the other side. She could hear screaming, realised it was her own voice. She looked at the clocks, saw by the site clock that she was down to five minutes left in her window. She looked back at the bank of monitors, then down at the CCTV receiver. She could see it was a digitised unit. She snatched the USB out of the front and gripped it tightly. She still had her mobile clenched in her gloved hand, and it was still filming. As she ran for the second air-lock, she could see the timer running. It would make for chaotic viewing, but she doubted she would make it out alive to give to her contact. She would have to bank on the time window being a conservative estimate. Perhaps whoever had arranged this, had factored in some leeway. She certainly hoped so.

Inside the air-lock, Natalia picked up the spray cannister like she had been instructed and sprayed liberally all over the gloves, boots and suit. She paid extra attention to the helmet and hood. Satisfied she had been completely doused in the chemical, she ripped at the tape on her wrists and ankles and kicked off the boots. She tore off the gloves and removed the helmet. The air tasted better without the filter, and she breathed deeply, her heart still pounding. She unzipped the suit but winced when she reached her stomach. She looked down, horrified to see a section of the yellow rubber had been torn. She got the suit off, reached her fingers inside her cardigan and touched the wound. Natalia looked at her fingertips, suddenly feeling nauseous when she saw them glinting in the light, bloodied and wet.

Chapter Thirty-Six

They had separated. Ramsay had gone down to the bar with the aim of chatting casually to the waitress, who had been a free source of information. He would make a point of tipping her when she brought his drink, ask about the hotel and try not to look at her breasts. That had been Caroline's advice. Eye contact, sincerity and make it clear he wasn't hitting on her. He was twenty-five years her senior and his wedding ring had practically grown into his ring finger.

Caroline had gone down to the bar, where she was going to drink coffee and simply watch the world go by. She would scroll on her phone, apparently uninterested in her fellow guests, but take film and photos of anybody of interest. She would send them to Marnie, who would be in her own room connected to the Wi-Fi and comparing the photos to MI5's Russian personnel database. A hard-won asset that the Russian's had no idea had been compromised. In the meantime, Marnie would also be working on unlocking and viewing the flash drive.

King had taken the bundle out from under his bed and placed it on the bed for Rashid to examine.

Rashid unwrapped the coat to reveal the Sami's rifle, the barrel and magazine removed.

"This will be handy," he said.

"Right up your street."

"Ammo?"

"Just the five rounds."

"Not even enough to check the zero." Rashid looked deflated. "How am I going to know if it shoots straight?"

King shrugged. "Well, happy bloody Christmas…"

Rashid pulled a face. "You know what I mean."

"The Sami was around a hundred yards from me when he took his shot. I was reaching for that USB drive and he damned-near took my hand off. I reckon a hunter will zero to minute of accuracy at one-hundred metres, no more than one-fifty. It's a three-oh-eight, it can take deer, black bears and wolves, but it's pushing it for large bull moose and brown bears at a distance greater than three-hundred metres. So, he'd have to be close to cover the big game up here. I reckon it's zeroed for close kills. He'd stalk and get near. It's not a theatre of war, and nor is it a rifle range. It's the wild, and it's all about one shot, one kill. Protecting yourself and putting food on the table. The scope is only a four by forty. That would indicate one-fifty metres, say two-hundred tops."

"So, you're saying bank on it being accurate at those ranges?" Rashid shrugged. "I suppose it's all I can go on. Unless I can get some more ammo?"

King shook his head. "That's not going to be easy."

Rashid nodded. "Well, it's better than nothing, I suppose."

"Well, that's it," King said. "Socks for you next time." He watched as Rashid put the rifle together. It was a simple screw in the bottom of the fore-stock. Once the barrel had recessed into three lugs, the screw tightened it all together. Rashid used a coin to turn the head of the screw. "Keep the bullets as warm as you can, close to your body. Load them when you want to fire, and remember, with this freezing air, the second round will be the accurate one."

"Thanks, dad. But I learned a fair bit about warmed barrels and cold shots when I was with the SAS."

"Keep up the attitude and you'll get a ticket back there." King chided. "How is the Colonel's daughter anyway?"

"Bastard."

"I'd leave that particular piece of personnel integration off your CV if I were you."

Rashid smiled. "I've moved on, mate."

"I can see that."

"Meaning?"

"Nice and cosy with the analyst bird."

"She's got a name," Rashid said tersely. "Christ, you're as bad as Ramsay."

"Now do I go around taking Allah's name in vain?"

Rashid shrugged. "You can if you want. Two billion people can't be wrong."

"Well, by that logic the other five billion are barking up the wrong tree then." King smiled. "Or pillar…"

"I miss our intellectual chats," Rashid said. "Remind me when we start to have one, won't you?"

"Marnie, then," said King. "Nice girl. Unusual for her to be here. Ramsay must like her."

"Piss off," he paused, looking at King's teasing expression. "I like her. We're casual. I don't want anything to get in the way of work. Imagine if we got close, then some nutjob kidnapped her and I went off on a rampage that compromised the service, put people's lives at risk and stirred up troubles with foreign governments…"

"Okay, twist the knife," King conceded. "You're no fun anymore…"

Rashid shouldered the rifle and aimed at a spot on the wall. He worked the bolt, took up the tension on the trigger and dry-fired on an empty chamber. "That will have to do," he said. He took the rifle apart and smiled. "Thanks, it's the thought that counts…"

"When are you heading out?"

"First thing."

"It'll be dark."

"It's dark all the bloody time up here."

"Twelve to three if the sky is clear. That's all the light I've seen so far."

"They hire snowmobiles at the desk if you have a driving licence. I'll nip down in a moment and get one ordered. Then I'll go back to my room and get my kit together."

"Your room? Not sharing, then?"

"No. The consummate professional, me." Rashid smiled. "Marnie has her own room. We thought it would be better to resist mixing business and pleasure."

"Yeah, you lucked out there," King grinned. "I heard all about it. Women talk."

Chapter Thirty-Seven

The Inari Falls Paatsjoki River Hydroelectric Plant
Russia

Natalia had set the shower as hot as it would go. She had used neat sanitiser on the wound and scrubbed it with a rough flannel. She had used the sanitiser all over her body, wincing as it stung at her private parts, the wound and her eyes. She had then scrubbed herself almost raw and soaped all over until the whole bar of soap had worn down to a piece so small that it washed away down the plughole. She had been in the shower for almost half an hour. She had wanted to cry, but there was nothing there. She was beyond hysteria, merely as low as she thought it possible to be. She had lost track of time, passing like it was merely a few minutes.

When she finally stepped out from the shower, she wiped the heavy condensation from the mirror and studied herself closely. Some would describe her as pretty, but she had never laid stock in that. She wore her reddish-brown hair to her shoulders and never bothered with makeup. There was precious little reason to up here. She was slim and well-toned. She used the gym and ran through the woods and along the lake's shore in the summer months. Occasionally she would swim at the shore of Lake Inari where the super-heated water pumped out from the turbines. It was warm through the summer months and kept an area around the size of an acre from freezing throughout the winter.

She gently touched the wounds on her abdomen. Nothing more than a couple of scratches, really. And she had scrubbed them raw with the sanitiser and then the soap. Surely, she would be ok? It was with a heavy heart that she realised that she was being absurdly optimistic. But what could she do? To speak to anybody here would mean certain discovery of her antics. And she had seen how former employees had been treated. No, she needed to get out. Whomever she took her secrets to would have, or soon have the means to treat her. An antidote. It was her only option. She needed to bring forward her defection and get to the prearranged rendezvous early. She simply needed to flee this place before it was too late. The harsh elements would make it difficult, but surely not impossible?

The laboratory would be under lock-down, if not now, then imminently. They would play the footage back to see what had happened, how their subjects - or experiments - had gotten free, and when they did, they would see that the USB was missing. She imagined the unit would record digitally as well, recording over its own memory at certain stages, maybe weeks or months later, the USBs changed regularly to create a permanent log. She even wondered whether the footage saved itself to a cloud storage facility, in which case, the recordings would be infinite and accessible.

She had planned to leave in the morning. That would tie in with her rendezvous. But she knew she had little choice but to move now. The shift would be back by now. They would see the chaos and they would start working on their protocols.

She packed her rucksack with spare clothes, what few possessions she could not contemplate leaving, and a few supplies she had been taking over the past few weeks. Chocolate, UHT milk, tinned ham, long-life bread rolls and canned beans. Enough food for a few days if the rendezvous did not go according to plan. She had no money. The company paid into her St. Petersburg bank account and she had a debit card for transactions. She had some money saved but had been told by her contact to destroy her card and make no more transactions. It was a sure-fire way of being traced. She would be taken care of financially in her new life.

Natalia grimaced as she zipped up her suit. The wound itched and there was a distinct feeling like that of pins and needles. A strange feeling to experience from a scratch. She tried to ignore it. She had been stupid. But it wasn't over yet. She wasn't just bringing what she had been asked for, but a whole lot more. Up-close footage of the results of what was being created here. A secret facility producing quantities of substances the nation had signed and agreed not to manufacture. Biological weapons - and that was what her contact had been adamant was being produced – were illegal to create and stockpile. The fact that Russia was doing so was an act of war. The deadly agent Novichok that had been used in Salisbury on an ex-KGB defector and his daughter was just the tip of the iceberg.

She would be missed soon, so now was the time. She swung the rucksack over her shoulder and checked that she had the compass and map in her pocket. She removed the sim card from her mobile phone and dropped it down the plughole in the sink. She would have no communication now, not if she got into trouble – and out here that was a risk in itself - but in doing so she could not be traced either. The phone held all the evidence, and along with the USB, would be her bargaining chip – her fee for safe passage and a new life in The West.

Chapter Thirty-Eight

"The coach is optional, Sir," the manager paused. "But I would advise you take it. The storm is imminent. Reports are showing a first wave later this morning."

"So, being on the road will be riskier," said King.

"The coach will leave at eight-AM. The driver assures us he will make it to Kittila in time, and the report is saying that the storm should break over the White Sea and head straight for Archangel, in Russia. Kittila has been declared a safe zone."

"Should head for Archangel?" King asked. "That's quite a gamble. And why now?"

"Excuse me?"

"Why is there a coach available now? This place was the last refuge to all and sundry earlier today. The Sami, for instance."

"It's been arranged, that is all I know," said the manager tersely. "Shall I book you and your… lady friend, on it?"

"No." King said sharply and turned around. He made way for a family, both parents looking concerned. It was evident they wanted to be on that coach at all costs. Fair enough, thought King. But he had other matters on his mind.

He found Caroline in a conservatory-style room on the East side of the building. The glass was triple-glazed, and the square, open fireplace burned fiercely in the centre of the room. It was a curious looking fire, with a rack resembling a train track running from floor to ceiling on both sides, at a forty-five-degree angle. Each track held a row of logs, which were gravity-fed and constantly feeding the fire. King imagined the tracks could be filled with logs in the morning and run for twenty-four hours, simply dropping a log into the fire after the last log burned enough to make room for the next.

Caroline stood at the window. She held a saucer in her left hand and was sipping from a cup of coffee in the other. She glanced at King as he walked in.

"Fancy a bathe in a hot tub later?" she smiled, and he could tell she wasn't serious.

King stood at her shoulder and looked down on the arrangement of wooden hot tubs, each heated by its own log stove with a stainless-steel flue. Great clouds of steam drifted into the air, and the Northern Lights on the horizon danced across the sky, making the steam in the icy air take on a green hue. There were a few couples in the hot tubs, but they could see that the vacated tubs were being covered and the fires extinguished by maintenance men in bulky snowsuits. It seemed impersonal, but the remaining couples did not seem to hurry. It was clear that the maintenance staff were readying for the storm.

"I doubt we'll get the chance," King said. "They're trying not to be rude, but they're shutting those things down as quickly as they empty. I imagine they'll start chaining them down soon."

"How cold is it out there?"

"Minus thirty," he replied. He pointed to a row of red lights towards the ice hotel. "Those are saunas, and can you make out the piles of snow?"

Caroline struggled to see against her own reflection in the glass. "Yes," she said eventually. "Just."

"The snow has been loosened and sieved so people can run out of the sauna and dive into the piles."

"Oh my god!" She laughed. "Forget that!"

King smiled. "It might have been a thought, had we not been on official business and there not be so many people around."

She rested her head against his broad shoulder. "What are you like?"

He put an arm around her and pulled her close. "Sometimes I just want to get off the treadmill."

"I know," she said quietly. "I thought my sabbatical with Interpol would be a bit like that," she paused. "I was hell-bent on seeing this trafficking thing through, but it's just another perpetual situation that will never change, never be any different. Like what we do for MI5."

"Same shit, different day," King mused.

"Something like that."

"So, this must be the woman Alex King has gone all soft for…"

They both spun around, but King had recognised the voice before he had started to move. The silence in which the man had entered the room was unnerving. Hard floors, yet no noise. It took a while to master. But then King remembered the man had once been the best there was. Maybe he still was.

"Caroline, this is Peter Stewart." King looked at him and added, "Peter, this is Caroline Darby."

Stewart walked over and extended his right hand. Caroline shook it and smiled. "Alex has told me a lot about you," she said neutrally.

"All good?"

"Not at all."

"Well, he's probably right."

"I'm sure he is."

Stewart released her hand and looked back at King. "Sharp one, this." The comment could well have been construed as humour, but nobody kidded themselves. "How about a drink, then?"

King nodded. "I'll get them in. What are you drinking?"

"Scotch, of course," Stewart said. "Neat and warm."

"Let's go to the bar, then. It's a bit quiet in here," replied King.

"I thought that's how you liked it," the Scotsman said sardonically.

"Not when I'm trying to spot the players."

"There's no players," Stewart said as he followed them out of the room. "Just a lot of scared people trying to book themselves on a coach, and a few curious thrill-seekers who want to see what two-hundred mile an hour Arctic winds look like."

"Two-hundred miles per hour?" Caroline asked, somewhat incredulous.

Stewart ignored her and said, "There's someone of interest coming in. From the power station on the Russian side. There's no hard border here. No more than a rusted fence put up in the fifties. From a look on the map, there are only three places where crossing makes any sense. My money is on just one of them. It's the most obvious. Fitzpatrick knew this, but he had worked out an exact rendezvous point with the first defector. We'll have to cover the other two."

"And Fitzpatrick wound up dead," King said sharply. "So, don't tell me there are no players up here. That Sami hunter tried to kill us. And he tried to kill me earlier, or at least tried to scare me off. And he was with another man. That's two hostiles."

"Well, one more possible, at least," Stewart corrected him.

King caught the waitress's eye and she came over. He ordered Stewart's Scotch and a coffee for Caroline. An Americano. He settled on a tall ginger ale with ice. Despite the cold outside, the hotel was overly-warm. Stewart frowned at their orders but didn't say anything. He'd always drunk alcohol no matter the operation. King had never seen the man drunk. He must have been immune or weaned to Scotch from the teat.

"Yes," King said as the waitress left with their order. "Shame we couldn't question the Sami."

"Well, you should have put him down swiftly," Stewart countered. "Getting soft, from what I see," he added, glancing at Caroline.

"Or perhaps it suited you better for him to die?" King said.

"What do you mean by that?"

"Just musing."

"Muse away," Stewart said tersely. "But if you've something to say, laddie, then best get it said."

King said nothing as the waitress arrived with their order, but he watched Stewart intently. Had he rattled him? He hoped so. The waitress set down Caroline's coffee first, then Stewart's Scotch. King held out his hand for his drink and took a deep mouthful. The room was hot, and the air was dry. The waitress asked for his room number and King shook his head like it didn't matter. He wasn't about to give his room number away in front of Stewart. He gave her a twenty-euro note and told her to keep the change. He doubted it would amount to much considering the hotel's prices.

"What's your plan, then?" King asked.

"I thought MI5 were handling this?"

King shrugged. "Sure, we'll take it from here. I'll get you booked onto the coach."

"Nice try."

"Can't have it both ways," Caroline interjected. "Your man was killed, MI5 are on the scene, for whatever reason or political agenda, so like Alex said; we'll take it from here, enjoy the ride back."

"She gets sharper," Stewart said to King, swallowing his Scotch in one gulp.

"I'm right here," Caroline glowered.

"Clearly," Stewart said as he stood up. "We must do this again sometime…"

"Not likely…" Caroline sipped her coffee, turning away to look at the fire.

"I suggest we use your resources to cover the bases," Stewart said. "There's enough of you milling around here to have someone on all the possible locations."

King smiled. He didn't reply. Stewart may have been bluffing. He knew that the man would know Neil Ramsay. Ramsay had said to bank on as much. He doubted Stewart had spotted Rashid.

"Neil Ramsay is here," said King. "He's not really a field man. So maybe you can work one location, I'll take another, and Caroline will cover the remaining possibility?"

Stewart shrugged. "Works for me," he said. "We'll get out there after an early breakfast. I'll hire some snowmobiles." He looked down at Caroline. "Just make sure you've got a map and a compass as well as your clutch bag." He turned his gaze to her shapely legs and smiled. "You might want to wear something a little warmer, too."

Stewart turned and walked out of the bar and headed towards the reception desk.

Caroline downed her coffee and looked at King. An expression somewhere between sympathy and bemusement. "And that was the best you ever came to actually having a father figure?"

King shrugged. "Yeah, it sucked to be me," he said. "But I'm over it."

Caroline linked her arm in his and pulled him closer. "You don't need him, that's for sure. Come on, let's find a place to people watch," she said and led him out of the conservatory and into the foyer.

At the far end of the conservatory, the tall, thin man with the hooked nose sipped his vodka, the wing-backed chair still hiding him from view. He had watched the entire scene in the reflection of the window. He had heard more than he should have and certainly more than he expected. But not as much as he wanted. He smiled, catching himself in the reflection of the glass. The players in a deadly game had presented themselves to him. He was ready to make his move.

Chapter Thirty-Nine

The Inari Falls Paatsjoki River Hydroelectric Plant
Russia

He hadn't had much time. A moment's notice. He had gathered a team together, but it had been a hastily conceived task and he had still been communicating with Moscow via the satellite phone on the helicopter flight over to finalise his orders. He would have preferred to work with tried and tested men, men he had fought with, killed with and bled with before. But time was a valuable commodity and he was in deficit. Still, they were good men. They were security contractors who the Kremlin had recruited, vetted and deemed worthy to protect something he had no wish to know about. He had a mission, and that was all he cared about. Track, recover or kill Natalia Grekov. A thirty-two-year-old engineer who had fled the plant with Russian federation state secrets. An act of treason, terrorism and war.

He looked at the file, learning more about his team. Some had fought as insurgents in the Ukraine, others had played their part in Syria in the Cold War against Britain and the United States. All had faced battle, and all knew that to be called for, to work under this agency's banner was not to be taken lightly. They were all black-ops initiated, and they knew what had to be done.

In front of him, the table was loaded heavily with the tools of his trade. He had stood back and watched. He had briefed them, now wanted to see how much they knew. What they selected would tell him how good they were. He would leave behind those who failed. But this was the darkest of operations, and those who did not make the grade would get the short walk down the long corridor. Enough steps for him to draw his pistol and shoot out the back of their neck.

Two men approached the table. They had already put on their white snowsuits, gloves and hats tucked into their belts, zippers left open while they waited.

"Colonel," one of the men nodded, though did not salute.

The Colonel nodded back. "Call me Vasily, soldier. We are all private citizens here…"

Both men nodded. They knew him, of course. They were all ex-soldiers and one was ex-Spetsnaz - Russian special forces - they would know the legend, if not the man. And his reputation was fearsome.

Both men picked up the Makarov pistols, checked them over and helped themselves to three loaded magazines each. They were smart and dependable, they had done the maths and worked out how many magazines had been allocated. Neither were selfish, simply cogs in the machine. One man picked up the compact AK-12 assault rifle with familiarity. He checked the action, helped himself to six magazines and tucked them into the pouches on his belt. The second man picked up the Dragunov sniper rifle and checked the sight fittings. Vasily Rechencovitch knew him to be the sniper. He had managed to recruit four men at short notice. Sniper, medic, explosive specialist and rocket grenade/mortar operator. Of course, all the men were trained in each other's skills, but each man was a master of his speciality.

The medic arrived, nodded at Rechencovitch, glanced over the other men and picked up a pistol. He looked at the remaining weapon, picked up three magazines. Seasoned and reliable, thought Rechencovitch. He watched as the man went through the medi-pack and rearranged it in his own preference of order. When he had finished, he looked over the table and settled on an AK-74 assault rifle with a shortened barrel and folding stock that looked like it had seen some service. It was a favourite of Spetsnaz soldiers similar in appearance to the classic AK-47 but chambered for a lighter and faster round. Given the brief and the fact he carried a heavy medical pack, the former Russian Spetsnaz Colonel was pleased. The men, however long out of official service, still knew their business.

The last man in saluted Rechencovitch, and clearly knew one of the other men from the smile he gave him. He surveyed the table and helped himself to what was left. He loaded up his pouches and strapped the RPG (rocket propelled grenade) launcher to his pack and arranged the rocket grenades around the pack's pouches. There were three rifles on the table. A Heckler & Koch UMP machine carbine with five magazines stacked alongside it. The .45 cartridge was both heavy and slow-moving but provided a solid strike out to one-hundred and fifty metres. The next weapon was a shortened M4 in .223/5.56mm. It was arguably the best weapon in the room. Given that he carried a heavy rocket launcher, it would seem to be the obvious choice. The man glanced at the other men's weapons and then at Rechencovitch's own modern AK-12. He then settled on a standard wooden-stock AK-74. It was both long and heavy compared to the other two weapons, and had clearly seen years of service, but Rechencovitch approved. All the men had chosen the same calibre. If a weapon or man went down, then the ammunition and magazines were interchangeable. They were already operating as a unit.

Chapter Forty

King and Caroline sat down opposite Neil Ramsay at a set of sofas and a low, glass coffee table he had commandeered in reception. It was a good spot, affording views of the brasserie restaurant, the bar and the reception desk. Nobody could enter or leave the hotel without Ramsay seeing them, and the internal entrance to the ice hotel was also in full view.

Ramsay looked up, slightly perplexed, perhaps irritated.

"Peter Stewart knows you, knows you're with us," said King. "There's no point in pussy-footing about. I haven't declared Rashid and Marnie."

Ramsay nodded. "I thought he would. I must say, and I've communicated so to Simon Mereweather, Stewart being here means MI6 are keeping a full tab on our operation. I don't get it."

"I know," said Caroline. "I mean, we're either running an operation up here, or we're not. If MI6 still have an asset in play, then why are we here?"

"Where are Rashid and Marnie?" he asked, then paused. "Dare I ask?"

"Absolutely no distraction there," Caroline smiled. "Rashid isn't in her good books."

Ramsay shrugged. "I can't keep up with those two," he mused. "So, what are they doing?"

"Rashid is preparing for a jaunt out on the snow," said King. "He's convinced that he can get to the most obvious location and set himself up in an OP."

"OP?" Ramsay asked.

"Observation Post," Caroline interjected.

"Oh." He nodded. "Well, that should be jolly cold."

"He's tough, he'll be okay," said King.

"Alright. And what about Marnie?"

"She's working in her room," Caroline answered. "She's processing pictures I have taken and sent to her, checking to see if any of the guests are on Russian databases. She's working through GCHQ and they will bounce back anything that becomes red flagged. And she's also working on unlocking that USB drive."

Ramsay nodded, looked at King. "I'm not happy with MI6 playing an asset in the middle of this. And I'm not happy that asset has a history with you. There's a coach leaving tomorrow, perhaps he could be on it?"

"There's no way he's leaving," Caroline said tersely. "He's a stubborn son-of-a-bitch…"

"I didn't mean voluntarily…"

King nodded. "He's a wily bastard, but it won't be a problem."

"What are you going to do?" Caroline asked incredulously.

"He could slip on some ice?" Ramsay suggested. "Lord knows, there's enough of it around."

"Leave it to me," King said. "One way or another, he'll be on that bloody coach."

Chapter Forty-One

Russia-Finland Border

The chocolate had frozen solid but melted enough to chew after she had worked it around the inside of her mouth for long enough. The sensation was odd yet satisfying as the sugary chocolate gave her energy and comfort all at once. She had given up on the milk. It was as solid as a brick. She hadn't thought it through, but she was out of her depth. She did not have the survival skills needed for a trek like this one, although she knew her engineering skills should have foreseen the milk freezing. She had tried to wear the container inside her jacket, close to her skin, but the container was frozen solid and as cold as the ambient air temperature, which to her reckoning, was thirty-five below. She simply hadn't been able to bear the coldness of it and had returned it to her pack until she could find a way to defrost it.

She had left the facility without incident. The hydroelectric plant was a non-hazardous operation requiring little security in the way of fences and gates, but it operated a roving security patrol of heavily armed men, which she now realised was because of what she had discovered in the underground chamber. A secret that needed guarding but could not draw attention to itself. Now that she thought about it, the military style security contractors always seemed excessive for a hydroelectric power station, but they were a subtle bunch and kept themselves to themselves using separate living quarters and preparing their own food rather than opting for the cafeteria. Most probably a safer bet, given the quality of the tinned soup and the stale bread. In the summer months it wasn't too bad with fresh vegetables, fish, meat and berries, but throughout the winter the boundaries of what was acceptable was pushed daily. It reminded her of stories her parents would tell of growing up in the Soviet Union. The shortages and the gluts. Near-starvation, then months of nothing but potatoes and beets. Stories of how the butcher would have no meat, and the delivery, when it finally came, would be rotten. Or tales of workers who were not allowed to move the crop and watched it ruin; the word to transport it coming days too late. Fundamentally, much was still the same, only glossed over by state-controlled press and a new Russia where money was overtly on display, where the mega-rich created a façade under which the poor still lived, barely surviving.

Natalia chewed on some of the bread. It was solid to bite but melted as her lips warmed it. After a few attempts, she could get a mouthful off and chew. By the time she was ready to swallow, the bread was defrosted. She helped it down with a handful of snow, which tingled on her tongue. She had read somewhere that you should never eat snow, as it cooled you down too quickly, but she had little choice. Despite the cold, or even because of it, she was as dehydrated as if she were crossing a desert. She craved water, and the snow melted enough to slake her thirst, though never satisfy it fully. She would give anything for a cup of strong, sweet coffee.

Natalia pushed the rest of the bread down her snowsuit. It was cold, but not in the same league as the milk carton. It would be tolerable, and when she stopped next time to rest and eat more of the snow, she was sure it would be easier to chew. She looked around her, the darkness held off only by the snow on the ground reflecting what little moon there was. Enough light to move by, but not enough to see any great distance. It made the forest seem closer, inescapable. She closed her eyes, breathed steadily to assuage her fears. There was nothing to fear here, she told herself. And then, as if fate was privy to her thoughts, the lone cry of a wolf pierced the night air. She tensed, unsure of the distance. There were two more howls and a degree of resonance, of an echo. She stood back up and checked the compass heading. Natalia was scared now, needed to get moving. As if moving would make the threat go away. She started to pray for the first time since her childhood. The praying matched the pace of her footsteps, and she took some comfort in the fact that no more howls sounded, and the night became silent once more.

Chapter Forty-Two

They had made love tenderly. Not like earlier where want and passion had created the pace. Desire driving them towards a heady conclusion. This time King had taken control but was ever conscious that there could only ever be one driver. Caroline had started to take the lead and he was more than willing to let her set the pace and direction.

King was now in that state of consciousness where he slipped into a delicious and well-earned sleep, but was aware of Caroline's warm, damp body on him, the movement of her hand on his torso, her soft breathing against the back of his neck.

There was little King hadn't experienced. In terms of drama and tragedy at least. He often dreamed of people and places, lives lost, and the wake left behind by battle and conflict, death and despair. He would often wake with a start. A helicopter crash, an ambush, an explosion...

King was on his feet and had the tiny Walther in his hand as he covered the door. Caroline was awake but sat up slowly. She looked at him in the dim light of the room.

"What the hell was that?"

"An explosion," King said. He pulled on his trousers and hastily buckled his belt. "A grenade, I think..."

Caroline was out of bed now, rummaging through the pile of clothes to find her trousers. "How can you tell?" she asked but didn't wait for the answer.

King said nothing as he pulled on his shirt and sweatshirt hoodie. Caroline had flicked on the bedside light and he found his socks and boots. He debated whether to get into his snowsuit but decided on his thick ski jacket instead. He made for the door but did not pause at Caroline's protestations. He worked the lock, and as he opened the door, he could hear shouts and screams coming from the floor below and the other end of the corridor. Caroline caught him up as he reached the staircase. The shouts were growing louder, more frantic.

"It's an attack!" Caroline exclaimed, her face ashen. She had lost her former fiancé in a terror attack and the noise and shouts of fear and desperation had struck a chord with her.

King didn't pander to her. He was almost automaton, absorbed in the situation. He had his pistol in his hand and was edging his way down the stairs. He met the manager head-on, who froze when he saw the gun.

"There has been a bomb, an explosion!" He tried to ignore the pistol, but his eyes still couldn't quite leave it. "Everybody is to meet outside in the grounds, beside the hot tubs." He edged past King and ran up the staircase. At the same time, the fire alarm sounded and filled the air with its shrill uncertainty. King had noted the fire alarm meeting point on the list of health and safety initiatives fixed to the back of his room's door.

King bounded down the rest of the stairs but pocketed the pistol as he reached the lobby. The owner, Huss, was standing behind the desk watching the guests and staff alike make their way outside; some wearing snow clothes, others wrapped in blankets. The man seemed indifferent – neither authoritative and in control, nor caught up in the shock – and his sharp features and narrow eyes made him look hawk-like and predatory against the vulnerability of the terrified guests. To the side of the desk, a tall, thin man with a hooked nose looked on. King had noticed him earlier, noted he had sounded Russian.

Walking past the entrance and to the other side of the foyer, King bypassed the reception desk and made his way towards the entrance to the ice hotel, where staff members were gathering and putting on snow clothes.

"Sir!" Huss shouted after King, then stepped out from behind the desk to block his path. King pushed him aside, and the man was knocked backwards into the desk, his shoulder bearing the brunt of the fall. "What the hell...?"

King made no apology. The door to the ice hotel had shattered and the cold escaping the tunnel was raw. Two guests almost fell through the broken doors into the lobby. Staff members wrapped them in jackets and King noted that both Russian men - the waiter and the barman – were quick to expertly check them over for injuries. He observed they acted like experienced soldiers – calm, methodical, measured. It was clear both men had extensive battle-field medical training.

Caroline caught up and stood beside King. "What on earth has happened?" she asked, directing her question to an affronted Huss.

The man stopped rubbing his shoulder. Considering the cuts and bruises the couple had received, his actions seemed trite by comparison. He seemed to realise this, too and quickly forgot about his bump on the desk. "We think the ice hotel was struck by lightning," he said sourly. "There was a terrific thunderclap and some of the guests report seeing a great white light."

"The manager said it was a bomb," Caroline protested.

"It was," replied King. He glanced back at the desk, noticed the thin man with the hooked nose was no longer there. He looked back at the owner. "I'd say it was a grenade."

"It was a lightning strike!" Huss persisted.

"Nonsense," King said. "It was a grenade." One of the Russians looked up. King had forgotten who was who. He thought it was the waiter. King caught the man's eye. "Something you want to say?"

The man shrugged. "It sounded like a grenade to me," he said, standing up and dropping a wad of bloodied paper towel onto the floor. "I was in the military."

"In Norway?"

The man hesitated, then said, "In Russia."

"What?" Huss shook his head despondently. It was evident he had been lied to, but there was precious little the owner could do at this time. He shrugged and asked, "Why do you think it was a grenade?"

King stepped over to the entrance of the tunnel. "A dull, hollow thud drowned out almost instantly by what sounds like a secondary explosion." He shrugged. "You get to know what they sound like."

The young Russian nodded. He turned back to the woman he was treating and started to strap what was clearly a badly fractured arm. King could hear moans and screams down the labyrinth of carved ice. He looked at Caroline and said, "Stay close."

Caroline was tugging on a jacket and zipped it up as she followed. The cold bit at their skin under their thinner clothing. Caroline tucked her hands under her armpits and King kept his hands in his pockets, his right-hand gripping the butt of the tiny Walther. Ahead of them, a couple in their fifties stumbled towards them, their hair and clothing covered in a fine powder of ice and snow, as if a patisserie chef had dusted them with copious amounts of icing sugar.

"Are you okay?" asked King as they drew near. They didn't respond. "Is there anybody else down there?"

The couple still didn't reply, then King realised they couldn't hear him. Their hearing had been damaged, most likely perforating their eardrums. He waved them past him, pointed for them to continue down the ice tunnel.

Caroline put her arm around the woman's shoulders. "Keep going that way," she said loudly, mouthing every syllable so that she stood a chance of lip-reading her as well. "The tunnel is clear, and the staff are helping people at the end." She smiled. "They'll have hot chocolate and mulled wine on the go in no time…"

"My ears are ringing," the woman said feebly and started to cry. "Malcom can't hear a thing…" The tears came from relief. That the worse was behind them, and safety and comfort awaited them. She nodded a thank you and wiped the tears from her face and was guided past them by her husband.

King could see the epicentre of the explosion. The room they had looked at. The room with the ice sculpture of an eagle outside the open doorway. The room where somebody had been watching them from outside. Only now, the eagle was in shattered pieces on the floor of the tunnel. He bent down and peered through the doorway, could see the night sky from where he crouched. The entire roof of the sleeping chamber had collapsed in seven or eight huge slabs of ice, and the metal bars that looked like corkscrews and acted as a bonding and support agent for the ice had twisted and bent into a gnarled mess. King had seen it before, on a larger scale, the twisted mess of bombed-out bunkers in Iraq and Syria.

"What's up?"

King turned around to see Peter Stewart standing behind Caroline. Caroline moved away, not hiding her disdain.

"A grenade, I think," King said. "It's taken down the entire roof." King turned back to the doorway and heaved at a slab of ice. His hands stuck to it and he tore them away, breathing warm air onto them.

Stewart reached into his pocket and retrieved a pair of gloves. He tossed them at King, and he wasted no time in putting them on. Stewart stood beside him and together they got the first slab clear of the doorway.

Caroline followed them inside, gasped when she saw the grisly sight. "Oh, no…" she trailed off.

Two pairs of legs poked out from underneath the largest slab of ice, a six-foot by six-foot section of roof with metal all twisted and broken. The bodies were fully dressed, as was the protocol for staying in the ice hotel, and blood had already frozen solidly and somewhat macabrely to the floor.

There was a moan further down the tunnel and King said, "These people aren't going anywhere," he paused, looking at both Caroline and Stewart. "Let's see if we can help." He pushed past them both and said, "Come on!"

Three rooms down on the left part of the tunnel had given way. The entrance was pinning a woman down in the doorway. Her husband was trying to move the block of ice. He looked up and his face said it all.

"Oh, thank god!" he said. "Here, help me with this…"

King looked at the woman on the floor, then back at Caroline. He didn't know quite what to say. Caroline took the lead and stepped into the room, put her arm around the man's shoulder.

"She's gone," she said quietly. "I'm sorry…"

The man had clearly been unable to accept the obvious, given the woman's head injuries, but he seemed able to comprehend Caroline's words and her sympathetic tone.

"Come on," she said, easing him around his wife's body and both King and Stewart, who both appeared awkward and uncertain what to do next. "They'll take good care of her. Let's get you back into the warm and see to your injuries…"

The man did not seem to be aware of his bleeding forehead, or that his right shoulder looked considerably lower than his left. Whether it had been damaged in the ice fall, or whether he had dislocated it trying to lift the slab of ice would be unclear, but Caroline could see that he had just realised, and the pain was kicking in. He was about to follow, then fell to his knees and kissed his wife on the cheek. He whispered something to her, then allowed Caroline to guide him to his feet and walk with her down the ice tunnel.

King stared at the woman's body. He did not see her. His mind full of images of a note on the kitchen table, his sullen footsteps up a rickety staircase, the longest walk he'd ever taken. Ten paces that seemed an eternity. His wife's body slumped on the bed, lifeless and the smell of death in the air.

"Come on," Stewart said. He bent down and gave the woman's legs an almighty heave. "Ease the ice off her and I'll yank her out…"

King wanted to stop him, show more respect, but found himself heaving on the ice until the body pulled clear and Stewart stumbled back against the ice wall. He let go of her legs and stood up, breathless.

King tidied the woman's limbs and gently closed her eyelids. Despite the massive head trauma, she looked at peace. He stood up, covered her with one of the animal skins, and said, "Let's get back to that room and see what delights await us there."

They stood in the doorway and stared at both pairs of legs under the slab of ice.

King took a deep breath, sighed and said to Stewart, "Here, help me with the other end." He walked around the plinth which acted as a bed and caught hold of a corner.

Stewart stood opposite and heaved in time. The slab slid off enough to reveal the faces of the couple. They looked as if they had died sleeping. Whatever the case, death had been instantaneous. Their bodies were crushed flat.

"Oh, no," Caroline said quietly. They looked up as she spoke, then turned back to the macabre sight. "It's the couple we met as we left the tunnel." She looked at them, deathly still and silent. She noticed the resemblance the woman had to her own features. The dirty-blonde hair, a similar age. The man was tall and powerfully built. Much like King. His hair was brown and short. Not flecked with a hint of salt and pepper like King's, but close enough. "Oh, no," she said again.

"What?" King asked tersely. He remembered how rude he had been, barging past them in his haste to discover who had been spying on them.

"I think they were mistaken for us," she replied quietly. "Look at the woman," she said. "And we were in this very room only hours before, when someone had been watching..." she stopped herself from saying more and looked at Stewart. "You were coming up the steps," she said.

"When?" he asked, his tone hostile.

"Earlier this evening," she said.

"I went out for a mulled wine and a chance to see the Northern Lights," he replied.

"Convenient."

Stewart took a step forward. "Watch your mouth, young lady. Maybe somebody needs to shut it for you!"

"And it will be the last thing you ever do," said King from behind him, his tone low and menacing.

Stewart looked at them both, shook his head incredulously and said, "Forget it." He barged past Caroline and stormed off into the tunnel.

The two Russian men entered carrying a shovel and an iron bar. The manager followed, he was wrapped up from head to toe and carried a camera and a clipboard.

"We are recording what we see," he said. "For the coroner, when he can get up here. In the meantime, we will seal off one of the undamaged rooms and use it as a morgue," he said quietly. "It is cold enough, obviously."

"Too cold," said Caroline. "The bodies have to be cold, but not frozen. It will corrupt the results."

King touched her on the shoulder. "It will be okay, love," he said. "I think the results will be cut and dry." He walked back over to the slab and crouched down, then turned back to the manager. "Here, take some photographs of this." He pointed to a blackened area, peppered with hexagonal pieces of metal. "These pieces are shrapnel. They are the outer casing parts of a pineapple fragmentation grenade. Russian specification, I suspect." He stared at both Russians, but they clearly couldn't care less. They were as indifferent to him as his aspersions.

The manager nodded. He was photographing the damage to the ice and looked back at the doorway as Huss strode in.

"These people shouldn't be here!" he snapped at the manager.

"Well, Mister Huss," King paused. "In lieu of any police presence, we are the best you could hope for."

Caroline took out her MI5 identification card and showed it to the owner. "We're here to follow up a lead, with the full knowledge and cooperation of the Finnish government," she lied. "We can take over, utilising the skills we have and hand over to the police when they get here," she paused. "But I imagine that will be after the storm now."

Huss looked at the manager, and his look was returned by someone clearly out of their depth. He had other matters to attend to, like terrified guests and half his hotel's accommodation being destroyed, or at least, rendered uninhabitable. An ice hotel was one thing, but one without a roof and open to the elements of the biggest storm in modern history merely hours away. Huss looked back at Caroline and nodded.

"Okay," he said as he scrutinised her ID. "Miss Darby. Whatever you want, just ask. My staff will be only too pleased to help."

"Thank you," she said amiably.

Huss did not look at King as he left and walked back down the ice tunnel.

"I don't think he likes me," King said.

"Well, you could try not shoving him into the furniture for a while. That ought to do it."

King shrugged. "I'll see what I can do."

"Let's get back to the main hotel," she said. "Get warmed up and see if they've got the hot chocolate on the go."

King couldn't think what else to do, but now he was out in the open and had the cooperation of the owner, the CCTV system would be a good place to start. He didn't buy that the entire system had been taken out in the squall. He nodded. He could do with something warm to drink as well.

Chapter Forty-Three

The near-perpetual darkness had thrown him. He had never glanced at his watch more. In the end he had taken off his gloves, undone the strap and fixed the watch on the outside of his jacket, threading the black rubber strap through one of the toggles on the chest pocket. Like a ward nurse. He had managed to turn the luminous dials towards himself, so that no glow was given off, but even the few minutes without wearing the gloves had rendered his hands numb and useless. Now they tingled as they warmed through.

It was truly an inhospitable place. He knew the Sami lived here year-round. Tending to their herds of reindeer, hunting for meat and fur, and occasionally heading out to the coast where, in winter, the icepack made the hunting of seals possible by digging out holes through which the seals would breath, and waiting with a harpoon. He wondered how they could survive such a place but realised they would probably say the same about his native Birmingham. He smiled as he thought they'd have that in common. He tried only to return for family gatherings. Since joining the army, he preferred to be in one place no longer than six months. The SAS had certainly given him that, and MI5 was working out well on that front, too.

The hide he had made had utilised the terrain. The elements were such that he had to think smart. He had found the GPS coordinates of the rendezvous, or at least the location he had deemed most likely. Given that it was unlikely the defector had military or specialist survival training or experience, he had plotted the easiest route rather than the most direct. The location gave him a terrific overview of a small plateau fringed with wispy pines on all sides. It was the ideal place for a killing ground. And that was what had drawn him to it. While Ramsay had seen the operation as a defection, Rashid had seen it as an operation culminating in an assassination. Somebody had gone to great lengths to see that Fitzpatrick did not get what MI6 was after. The defector in that operation had either not shown or had been killed also. He would bet his life that this defection was lining up the same way. Rashid was playing a hunch, but he had played them before and he was still alive to tell the tale.

He had chosen the high ground. Rule one of any conflict. He had used a fallen tree for both cover and camouflage. It was a natural feature and he could dig below it using the snow shovel he had stolen from beside the main steps to the hotel. Once he had broken through the crust, he had dug out a tunnel just ten percent larger than his own mass. He used the excavated snow to create a ledge in front of the entrance. Rashid got himself into position, wriggling in feet-first and positioning himself back from the entrance with the rifle shouldered to utilise the scope, but without the muzzle protruding. He loaded the rifle, worked the bolt-action and pushed the safety forwards so that the weapon was ready to fire. Rashid no longer left safety catches in the 'safe' position. Experience had seen to that. When he needed to fire, he did not need extra obstructions to slow him down or cloud his mind.

Rashid had hired a snowmobile at the hotel desk. He had been issued with maps and a GPS tracker, which he had immobilised. He had also been warned to return the machine before eleven-AM – the time the storm was estimated to arrive – and under no circumstances was he to deviate from the prepared course that had been scraped and banked throughout the forest. A myriad of roads and tracks designed to take users to various lookouts and points of interest along the lake shore and through the hills surrounding The Eagle's Nest Hotel. Colour-coded markers indicated points, in conjunction with the map, and provided a safe environment in which to ride. Rashid had found the GPS unit affixed to the underside of the handlebars and left it beside the garage. If anybody checked, they would assume he had not left the hotel. The unit was rechargeable, and he estimated he would have approximately six hours before anything was noticed - that is, if they bothered to check in the first place. The machine was now parked up beside two fir trees about two-hundred metres West of his position. Rashid now used the reflected light of the snow and moon to watch the area below him in the gloom. He laid upon a silver thermal ground sheet, keeping himself away from the snow. He was dressed in his own clothing and then an all-in-one snowsuit with another ski jacket on top. Over these bulky items, he wore a white over-suit, like those worn by forensic officers. The hood covered his own beanie and only his boots and gloves remained uncovered. Beside him, a pack contained a thermos of strong, black coffee and a packet of biscuits. He had previously discovered that biscuits did not freeze because of the lack of water content. The same went for the packets of crisps. All of which he had swiped from Ramsay's mini bar. He grinned as he thought about the man's room bill and his near-constant battle with the Security Service's accountants.

Rashid studied the area ahead and below him through the rifle's scope. He suspected King was correct in his assumption that the weapon would be zeroed for hunting use. And a specific type of hunting at that. Close and practical, not for ego. A kill up here meant food and fur. And with quarry like bears, wolves and wolverines, you wanted them dead. Not merely pissed off. King was right about most things, and Rashid would trust him on this, too. He did not have the luxury of range practice and would know if his assumption had been wrong, the moment he squeezed the trigger. Like every other time, he hoped he wouldn't have to.

Chapter Forty-Four

The gunfire in the remote landscape seemed to echo for an eternity. Natalia had ducked down behind the fallen tree she had been using to take shelter from the windchill. The wind had increased, and the chill factor was off the scale. Simply being out of the wind had felt twenty degrees warmer.

It wasn't a hunter. She had heard enough gunshots since she had been here. Occasionally a Sami would wander into the facility dragging a deer in the snow, ready to barter or sell the fresh meat to the chef. Hunting was simply a part of life here, and she had heard the occasional single shot throughout the year. But this was different. A rapid burst with a metallic ring to it. Short, sharp and quieter than that of the hunting rifles the Sami used.

It hadn't occurred to her that she had been the intended target. Not until the second burst of gunfire and chips of bark shattered from the frozen trunk beside her. She had leapt up at first, then thought better of it and dived onto her stomach. She listened, waited. But then her instincts took over. If someone was shooting at her, then they could be edging closer as she took shelter. She needed to get moving. She had the advantage of the perma-dawn. It was at least another three hours before daylight. Enough to get clear. But how had they spotted her? She then realised it had been her profile. Enough to break the contrast of the sparse forest. The grey hue in which the half-light presented itself was pronounced by the snow. A sort of backlight. She had been readying herself to move. Adjusting her suit, her gloves and hat. She wore black and blue clothing. It would all look dark at any distance, most likely black. But the movement and profile had given her away. She knew she would be followed eventually; but so soon?

Natalia crawled away from the fallen tree. The scraping on the hard, impacted snow tore at the scratches on her stomach. She felt them burn, the tingling sensation of pins and needles was becoming more acute. She needed medical attention, expert treatment. As for the hundredth time since she had left, she touched her pocket containing the USB and her phone, checking they were still there. Her lifeline to another life.

There were no more gunshots, but she kept low and slid down the embankment. She gathered speed, all the time grimacing at the pain in her stomach. When she reached the bottom of the embankment, some twenty-feet or so, she scraped up a handful of snow and rammed it into her mouth. Perhaps it was the dry air, or the exertion, but she had noticed her thirst was insatiable. She had been shovelling mouthfuls of snow all through the night. But as she felt another surge of rawness on her stomach, she knew with a sinking feeling that there was more to it than that.

Chapter Forty-Five

Rashid had been drifting towards sleep. He snapped to at the sound of the distant gunfire and cursed his own stupidity. If he'd had a man serving beneath him who had fallen asleep on watch, he would have had him RTU'd, or returned to unit. Unceremoniously kicked out of the SAS and back in the guards or wherever they'd started out their miserable military career. How could he have been so stupid? So sloppy? He checked his watch. Perhaps the cold had gotten to him? He'd lost three hours. It was now six-AM. Damn this place! Damn the lack of dawn, the lack of birdsong! Didn't this place ever wake up? Rashid scanned along the plateau, then raised the rifle and started to study the treeline. Again, there was only just enough light to see by. The moon had moved halfway across the sky and was still lighting up the snow, but he was aware that it would get darker soon. The moon would disappear, and the darkest hours of the day would bring almost total darkness. Dawn, as it was, would start around ten-AM and daylight would be from around mid-day to three-PM. What a place! he thought.

He had been awake enough to hear the last of the gunshots. The burst woke him, but the final shot had been clear enough in his mind to draw assumptions, if not conclusions. Medium calibre, high-velocity rifle round, semi-auto. An assault rifle. But at what distance? How could the cold, dense air affect things? He knew that bullets travelled more slowly, that the drop was more acute at five-hundred metres when temperatures dipped below minus-five. Around twice that of a shot taken on the equator at low altitude. But what about noise? The pristine forest had nothing to absorb the sound. Everything was hard, the surfaces and surrounds offering nothing in the way of absorption, and even mundane things like getting off the snowmobile seemed to echo. Which meant his best guess at a mile or so away could put it considerably further than that.

Rashid could see nothing through the scope. But he hadn't expected to. Not with the shots taken at that distance. It was merely instilled drills. Nothing taken at face-value. He lowered the rifle and reached for the thermos. He drank the hot liquid straight from the flask, savoured the warmth, the anticipation of the impending caffeine hit. He squared his kit away and settled in behind the rifle. He had chosen this spot, of the three most likely places, because of its qualities as a killing ground. With the gunshots at such a distance, the other rendezvous possibilities were still in play. Nothing was for certain. He just hoped his gamble would pay off.

Chapter Forty-Six

"You've alerted her now!" Rechencovitch shoved the man in his chest, pushing him down onto his backside in the snow. "Idiot!"

The man glowered up at him, but hastily thought better of it. He knew the Colonel's reputation hadn't been built upon fantasy or speculation. "I am sorry, I thought I had the shot…"

"Too far away," Rechencovitch snapped. "Too cold."

He cursed as he studied the map with his red-filtered torch that would both make his position less visible and keep his night-vision unaffected. He knew that the icy air would slow the bullet, coupled with the elevation of their position and the deep ravine which would be trapping the cooler air, it simply made the four-hundred metre shot from the 5.45x39mm bullet impossible. What's more, the man now sitting on his backside in front of him should have known it, too. They were now faced with either a dangerous rappel and near-impossible climb, or a two-kilometre trek to get around the ravine.

The man's shot had been a Hail Mary. A fire and hope shot. But it hadn't paid off. It had alerted their quarry and given away their advantage. Now he was faced with the choice of time over safety. Could they rappel and climb safely in these temperatures, or should they press on and take the easier route, but put distance between his team and their prey?

The man with the sniper rifle had dropped into a prone position, scanning the area on the other side of the ravine. His more powerful 7.62x54mm weapon would make the distance easily. But as he got back to his feet and dusted the snow off himself, he shook his head at Rechencovitch.

She was long gone.

***

Natalia did not turn around and she did not stop moving. She knew that moving was key. She had to put time and distance between herself and her pursuers. The gunshots could only have come from the other side of the ravine, and she knew how long it had taken her to cross. She estimated she would treble her distance from whoever was hunting her, just so long as she kept moving.

After what she estimated to be a strenuous kilometre, she stopped and dared a look behind her. Her footprints were clear. A half-centimetre indentation in the crust of frozen, compacted snow. She felt deflated. Her tracks were so clear, so easy to follow, all that kept her separated from her pursuers was fitness. And she was feeling exhausted.

She looked around her, settled for a fallen branch from a fir tree. She trudged over and picked it up, used it as a sweeping brush to clear her tracks. It worked well. Pine needles fell from the branch, and she could make out a trail from the loose snow, but it was a hundred times harder to spot than her original footprints, and that would be enough to slow her pursuers down. She then looked at her map and the button compass. She strained her eyes to see in the dim light. As always, the snow and occasional glimpse of the moon giving off just enough ambience to stave off complete darkness. She had practised map reading in her room. Using the coordinates and memorising every detail on the map she had a feel for the surrounding area, if not the experience of walking it. But she had made her way to the ravine ahead of schedule and had been impressed by her efforts making it out of the facility and due West across the Russian border. Only the rusted and broken remains of a fence had remained. Further South a post was manned, and the border fence sprung up like Cold War Berlin. There was nothing here, though, and the elements were enough to put most people off.

Most people.

Natalia hadn't marked the map with a cross or circled a point, but she had folded it incorrectly, many times, but every time the same so that her destination was marked exactly by the point of the corner. At a glance, she had a mark that nobody would have considered. But she could see the spot clearly and she realised she was close. Three kilometres. Just three thousand metres and she would be safe.

Or so she hoped.

Chapter Forty-Seven

"What are you doing?"

"What does it look like?"

"Give me a few minutes and I'll come with you."

"You stay here. We're on this."

Stewart watched incredulously as Caroline swung her leg over the snowmobile. "And where is she going?"

King shook his head. "Peter, just leave it." He turned around and watched as Caroline fired up the machine and took off, tentatively at first, but gaining in speed as she headed down the track that spiralled around the hill on which the entire complex was built. "This is an MI5 operation. Things have changed. I want you on that coach in a couple of hours."

"Fuck off!" Stewart spat at him. "I'm getting changed, and I'm coming with you. Get me a snowmobile hired while I'm getting ready."

King looked at the man, shivering on the top step. Tantalisingly close to the warm foyer; uncomfortably cold in the early dawn. "You're staying. And then you're leaving. Like I said; things have changed."

Stewart spun around and squared up to him. "Don't forget who you're bloody talking to!"

"Nor you." King glared at him, his glacier-blue eyes colder than the outside air. "I mean it. MI6 have a right mess going on up here, and we're cleaning it up. MI6 aren't going to have a presence while we do so."

Stewart scoffed. "A lifetime working for the firm and now you're talking like you were never there!" He shook his head. "Where's your bloody loyalty?"

King grabbed him by the collar with both hands, turned his torso and moved his right leg side on. As he had anticipated, Stewart's knee to his groin in response glanced off his thigh. He pressed down with his hands and moved forwards a step, pushing the man backwards. Stewart was off balance, over extended and had nothing to reply with. "My loyalty ended the day I knew they were trying to kill me," he growled. "And my loyalty to you ended the day I realised you were working against me to feather your own nest!"

"But you pulled a gun on me!" Stewart rasped, King's knuckles tight in his throat, his grip like a vice.

"I let you live," King replied quietly.

"But…"

King glanced behind him, then turned his attention to the reception desk at the end of the lobby. It was unmanned. He pulled Stewart towards him, then dropped his right knee and shoulder, twisted and lifted all at once and Stewart sailed over King's shoulder and crashed down hard on the top step, his right leg taking all the impact against the tread of the step.

Stewart screamed, an agonising wail. He started to pant, the pain so intense and his expression one of both shock and disbelief.

King pushed the door open and strode up to the desk. The manager was seated in the back office, nursing a coffee, his forehead resting in his other hand. It had been a long shift. Three guests had been killed, many more superficially wounded, rooms in the ice hotel had been emptied and accommodation found in the main hotel, complimentary drinks distributed, and normality restored as best it could be. And now somebody was at his desk again.

"A guest has taken a fall down the steps," said King. "I think he's broken his leg. He'll need triage. I suggest those two Russians working for you will have the necessary training. And he'll need a place on that coach." He pulled down his glove and looked at his watch. Behind him, cases were stacked in readiness and a few early risers were at the breakfast buffet table in the main restaurant. "That's another ninety-minutes, so you'll need to make him as comfortable as you can. Do you have any strong painkillers?"

The manager put down his coffee and dialled a number on the switchboard. "We have some strong codeine. People break their limbs all the time… snowmobiles, skiing, the ice…" He spoke quickly into the receiver, turned back to King and said, "Our first-aider is on the way, and I've asked for Nikolai, he was extremely competent with the… incident, last night."

"Good," King paused. "I'll go and reassure him, you get him the attention he needs."

King walked back across the lobby and into the foyer. He could see that Stewart had struggled to prop himself up and sit on the top step, but he wasn't getting any further than that. He pushed the door open and gave Stewart a wide berth. He didn't fancy taking a trip himself.

"You bastard…" the man said quietly. He breathed short, shallow breaths to quell the pain. "You utter, fucking bastard."

"Yeah," King said. "But when you've heard it from your own mother, it means nothing coming from you."

He took the steps carefully then reached the snowmobile and swung his leg over, settling into the seat. He turned the ignition key and pressed the start button.

"Watch your back!" shouted Stewart venomously. "You bastard!"

King did not seem to hear as he gave the machine a load of throttle and sped off in a flurry of ice and snow.

Chapter Forty-Eight

Caroline pulled into the clearing and switched off the snowmobile's engine. The silence was eerie. The moan of the engine had filled her ears, numbing her senses. The stillness of the sparse forest was uncanny. She swung her leg over and stepped off the machine. She checked that the pistol King had given to her was still in her pocket. It was chambered and had been left with the hammer forward. It was ready to fire, but the first shot would require a firmer squeeze of the trigger.

She took her mobile phone out of her other pocket and checked the time and GPS coordinates. She was directly on target. The clearing was small and sheltered by a cluster of knolls to the East. She looked up to the peak of the first hill. It was some two-hundred metres to the summit, with pines and firs dotted across the face. She slipped the phone back into her pocket and took out the Walther. The tiny pistol was compact and heavy, and fitted in her gloved hand. She would be able to use it with her glove, unlike King, who had not been able to wrap his index finger inside the trigger guard with a gloved hand. With the weapon held by her side, she studied the terrain ahead of her. It did not feel good.

During her time in the army, Caroline had served in Afghanistan in army intelligence. She had been on many patrols and missions. She had walked into ambushes and she had lain in wait, ready to see who showed up to a weapon cache or to arm an IED. She had been on both sides of the first volley of fire, and she had grown to trust her instincts. This felt wrong, and she wasn't going to wait and see how it panned out. She needed to reposition herself, find somewhere with more cover from which to observe the clearing. She walked back to the snowmobile and swung her leg over the seat. She tucked the pistol back into her pocket and reached for the ignition key.

The gunshot rang out. Loud and dull, the echo of the high-velocity round breaking the sound barrier, ringing off into the forest around her. She felt the impact of the bullet striking the engine cover and plastic fairing and metal sparks flew up in front of her. The bullet passed through, throwing up a dusting of ice particles a few feet to her left. Caroline screamed and looked to her right. She pressed the starter button, but it just whirred away electronically. She rolled to her left to use the machine as cover as the second round hit the saddle and soft leatherette and stuffing showered down onto her. She had seen the muzzle flash further up the hill, high and to her right. She rolled and ran, sliding and skidding on the hard snow as she made her way into the treeline. She darted left, right, right again, then left... Another gunshot and snow puckered up to her right. She darted left again, right, right, then left. Never a uniformed zig-zag. A competent marksman would be able to anticipate the turn, give them enough lead. She made the treeline, kept going. She heard another gunshot but did not see or hear the strike. She reached another tree, dodged behind it and dropped to the ground. She rolled and looked up. There were many trees between herself and the treeline. That was good. Those same trees would be blocking the sniper's point of aim and arc of fire. She got the Walther ready in her right hand, then changed her mind and fumbled for her mobile phone. She needed bare fingers to work the touchscreen. She tore her gloves off with her teeth, pocketed the gloves and started to dial.

Chapter Forty-Nine

King felt the vibration of his phone in his pocket but could not stop the ascent he was making up the side of a steep hill. The snowmobile was working hard, and he was standing up out of the saddle, jockey-style, his calves gripping the sides of the seat as he worked the machine through a gulley hemmed in on either side by jagged rocks. He was at a point where it was make or break, so he thumbed the throttle all the way and the snowmobile headed skywards like a rocket at an acute angle of approximately seventy-degrees. He was about to slip off the back of the machine when it reached the summit and became airborne. King threw his weight over the handlebars and the snowmobile dropped back down, settling on the snow as he released the throttle. The machine glided to a halt.

The phone stopped vibrating but started again almost at once. King tore off his gloves and dug his phone out of his pocket. He could see it was Rashid's number, although he never assigned a contact to a number. He only had ten numbers stored, and all of them related to MI5.

"Yes, mate?" he answered.

"Forget the other two RVs, there's movement here."

King hesitated. "What's happening?"

"Someone has shown up in the clearing. I think it's a woman. Build and movements, like."

"How is she acting?"

"Unsure. Nervous. Constantly checking their 'six,'" Rashid paused. "And there were gunshots earlier. A short burst. Semi-auto, not a hunting rifle. By the way she's checking behind her, I think she's being pursued."

King hesitated for a moment. If the woman in the clearing was the defector, then being in the open would compromise her safety. But if Rashid was in an OP, then he would be perfectly placed to surprise any hostiles. But then he thought of the five meagre rounds he had given him, and the uncertain range the rifle had been zeroed for. "What's your status?"

"In a hide. Cocked, locked and ready to rock…"

"With bugger-all firepower if it all gets a bit shooty…"

"Suggestions?"

"Get down there, get them out. If you heard an automatic weapon and that genuinely is the defector, you could be in the shit if you fire on any hostiles."

"On it."

"I'll get there," said King. "I'll approach from the North-West." King could hear Rashid breathing heavily. He could hear feet crunching on the ice. "Good luck."

King ended the call and the phone vibrated instantly in his hand. He pressed the answer icon.

"Caroline. Are you alright?"

"Get over here!"

"What's happening?"

"I'm pinned down! Getting fired upon from someone on the high ground!"

King was already on the snowmobile. "Where are they firing from?"

"The high ground!"

"I know that! As you look at the clearing, where are the shots coming from?"

"The first hillock, the more easterly one…"

"Caroline?" All that King could hear was the dial tone. "Caroline!"

The snowmobile started on the press of the button and King thumbed the throttle to full revs and turned sharply to the right. The machine skidded round, the track throwing up snow and ice fifty-feet into the air. He aimed for the edge of the cliff, directly in line with the tracks he had made on the way up. As he was ten-feet short of the edge, he halved the revs and held on for all he was worth. The snowmobile shot out ten-feet from the edge, an ominous engine whine as the tracks lost contact with the snow, followed by silence as he plummeted fifty-feet before hitting the seventy-degree slope. The two front skids caught, and the tracks tore at the snow as it gained traction and powered down the precipice. The slope levelled out and the machine was traveling at close to ninety-miles-per-hour when King slowed and turned for the second rendezvous point.

Chapter-Fifty

Rashid had ended the call with King and pushed himself out of his hide, dragging the rucksack behind him. He put the pack back on, reamed the tags tightly. He had a feeling he was going to have to move quickly. Better if he spent a few seconds getting sorted than regret it later. He kept the rifle in his hands and started to make his way down the steep and unforgiving slope towards the lone figure on the plateau.

The figure looked his way, then started to run. Rashid increased his pace, sliding and leaping until the slope levelled out and he was on the same terrain. He was sure now, positive that the figure was a woman. The movements, the slight curve of the hips under the bulky snowsuit. He chanced it, called out, "Stop running, madam! I am with the British Government, your contact!" he shouted. "I'm here to help!"

The figure hesitated momentarily, then continued towards the trees.

"You have something for me. The defection is going ahead, but I've had to stand in. Your initial contact was killed!"

The figure stopped. Turned around. Rashid could see her face. Vulnerable, scared.

Rashid added, "Look, I have a gun, I would have used it if I wanted to harm you."

Snow and ice showered them, the burst of automatic gunfire tearing up the snow between them. Rashid watched as the bullets tracked towards the woman. He shouted, "Move!"

Natalia watched the bullets smash through the crust of ice and she darted to her right, towards the treeline. Rashid followed, the gunfire stopping while the gunman changed magazines. He caught up with her, gripped her by the shoulder and guided her to his left. "This way!" he shouted, the gunfire opening up again. The gunman had his eye in now, the bullets tracking closer to their feet. Rashid stopped dead, pulled her backwards and the bullets tracked onwards, paused, then came back. This time they were wide of them and he pushed Natalia onwards towards the treeline.

He risked a glance as they reached the trees. He could see the muzzle flashes high and right of their position. He pushed Natalia into the trees and threw himself onto his stomach.

"Get behind a tree!" he shouted. He ignored her, keeping his eyes on the ridge. She had been told what to do and he wasn't going to babysit her.

He shuffled over to a tree and used the trunk as cover while he tore off his pack and shouldered the old hunting rifle. He got his right eye to the scope and worked his way to the last position he had seen the flashes. The light was dim, but the scope coped well. He could see the gunman moving on his stomach towards a set of trees. Rashid kept the rifle steady but took his eye away and glanced to his right. He was midway between two sticks poking out of the snow. He tracked across the plateau, counting the sticks on a line with the far slope. He had placed them at twenty-metre intervals. The sticks marked a line some three-hundred metres to the line of trees at the top of the slope. He counted down three sticks until he found the man in his sights. He was still working his way steadily towards the trees. The cluster would give the man a perfect aimpoint and a good amount of cover. Rashid checked the markers again and his calculations put the man at exactly two-hundred and forty-metres. He thought back to King's reckoning that a bread and butter hunting rifle in these extremes being zeroed for one-fifty metres. Two hundred tops. He put the crosshairs dead centre to the man's forehead, then eased the rifle up so that the crosshairs sat a full two-inches above the man's forehead. He kept it there, tracked with the man until he rested still for a moment. The man was looking at a stick in front of him. The bark had been peeled away in several places and resembled an old-fashioned barber's pole. He craned his neck, saw another one twenty-metres further forward. Rashid saw the man's realisation as he squeezed the trigger.

Contrary to widely held belief – and impossible at this close range - you rarely saw the pink mist. The recoil of the powerful round and resetting of the weapon's aim meant that it was the sniper's companion – the spotter – who usually saw that. When Rashid got the sights back on target for a second shot, he saw that his first had been enough. The man was slumped forwards and his hat had gone. Which was just as well, because the man had nowhere to wear it. Steam was lifting from the cavity, clearly visible through the scope. Rashid imagined it was already cooling considerably in the cold air.

Rashid chambered another bullet and scanned the treeline for further targets. For that's all they were to him. He couldn't see any, but he would be able to return to the snowmobile without setting foot out of the trees. He looked over to the woman.

"I'm Rashid," he said.

She got out tentatively from behind the tree she had been sheltering behind and dusted the snow off her. "Natalia Grekov," she replied. "There are others," she said quickly. "We must get out of here."

Rashid nodded and got to his feet. "You look cold and tired." He picked up his pack and took out the thermos. He handed it to her and she snatched it, unscrewing the cap and drinking straight from the flask. It was hot, but she coped with it. "We'll get you food and more to drink when we get back."

"Who's we?"

"An extraction team," he said. "From the department I represent. To get you out safely and retrieve what you've brought for our government." He nodded. "This way, quickly..."

Chapter Fifty-One

Caroline dared not move. She had found herself in a gulley with trees on each side. She supposed in the spring it would act as a culvert, taking the vast quantities of water as the snow melted. But right now, it was frozen solid and acted as her lifeline. The sniper could not see her, but nor could she see the sniper. She had no idea whether he was moving calmly down the hill towards her to take a close-up shot or was still hunkered down and playing god at the top of the hill.

She held the Walther tightly. She knew the tiny 7.65mm bullet packed a punch up close, but what range would she have? She had never used one before and was aware that it was not as powerful as a 9mm, which she had trained with in both the army and with the small arms course in MI5. Although strictly forbidden from using firearms on operations on British soil, in recent years, MI5 had increasingly taken part in operations abroad and the small arms course had been hastily put together by SAS instructors at Hereford to give Security Service personnel enhanced security abroad. But the course had not factored in firearms some seventy-years-old in design. It had concentrated on modern security and law enforcement weapons such as the Sig P225, the Glock 19 and Smith & Wesson M&P 9. A couple of old service Browning Hi-

Powers had been thrown in for good measure as a comparison into how far technology had moved on. Caroline had carried a Browning in Afghanistan and had been familiar with it. Other UK units had used Sigs, but army intelligence had kept the older weapon for some reason. Possibly budget or logistics. Or maybe because most intelligence officers worked in an aircraft hangar and barely ventured out of the base. But Caroline had been into the field more than most, and she had used her SA80 rifle many times. She later admitted to King that she had fired a lot of bullets and wasn't sure if she'd hit anybody, but she was sure as hell she'd made the enemy keep their heads down.

This was different though. Out in Afghanistan she had been part of a unit. She hadn't been under-gunned either. Whoever was shooting at her now had a rifle and she felt she had nothing more than a pop-gun to respond with.

She knew that she should keep moving. She could not afford to let her enemy pin her down. She crawled along the gulley, the pistol held in front of her as she used her right elbow and left hand to crawl, keeping low and trying to watch the hill above her as she made progress.

The gulley led into the trees and she knew that if she could get further away from the clearing, then it would be near impossible for the sniper to see her through the layers of trees. It would not only provide her with cover from a bullet but would take her out of view altogether. If she could get there, she could be home and dry. Or at least safer. She still had no transport and was over five miles from the hotel with the temperature down to minus thirty and the threat of the storm on the way. But right now, getting out of the line of fire was all that mattered.

Chapter Fifty-Two

There was only one way to sensibly do it. Park the snowmobile a substantial distance away, far enough that the noise did not give away his position, and approach from the east. Behind the sniper and work his way down stealthily. He carried his knife but was armed with nothing more. But that hadn't stopped him before. He had faced worse odds. If he could get close enough for a kill, then fine. If he couldn't do this, then maybe he could get close enough to shout for Caroline to run and he could face off with the sniper, hope to get close enough using the trees for cover, but at least he would have saved Caroline. Or at least given her a chance.

Sensible. Measured. The best course of action.

And then there was the other way.

King gave the snowmobile as much throttle as he dared, damned-near full revs as he hammered up the peak. He was traveling close to sixty-miles-per-hour. The rooster tail of snow following him sprayed more than fifty-feet in the air, showering his trail behind him like a fresh snowfall. He had memorised the map, but there was no accounting for rocks or trees, so he steered by the seat of his pants, throwing the machine left and right as he dodged or skipped over mounds and obstructions.

As he neared the summit of the hill, he

steered hard to the left and traversed the slope.

He heard a gunshot over the engine's wail. And then another. But this time he saw the muzzle flash. Four-hundred metres distant and at this speed he would be upon the sniper within seconds. But he would also become an easier target the closer he got. He throttled back, veered higher up the slope and turned hard left, throwing up a hundred-feet of snow into the trees. He needed the sniper to take another shot. He needed a marker to aim the snowmobile at when he gave it a full throttle charge. And he needed the sniper to be working the bolt action of the rifle, not taking aim.

The shot came soon enough. Louder now, the muzzle flash wider and brighter the closer he became. King could feel the zing of the bullet tearing through the air close to him. He reckoned inches rather than feet. The gunman was a hundred-metres from him now and scrabbling to his feet. A tall, thin figure despite the bulky clothing. He shouldered the rifle, took aim, then fell to the ground, the rifle spinning out of his grip and into the snow. King released the throttle and the tracks stopped altogether, brought the machine to an abrupt halt. The gunshot that had floored the sniper resonated behind King and echoed throughout the clearing. King could see the man reaching for the rifle. He heard another shot, but the bullet struck the snow a foot in front of the sniper. King glanced behind him and saw Caroline heading out of the trees into the clearing aiming the tiny pistol. She had either had the perfect shot, or a lucky break. King suspected the latter because she was still eighty-metres distant and walking steadily towards her target. The man worked the action of the rifle, but the bullet from the Walther had struck the frame and distorted it enough for the bolt to stiffen in the action. He tugged at it, drew it back. King saw the brass cartridge eject and spin through the air. The man struggled to push the bolt forward. Caroline's next shot kicked up snow an inch from the man's foot. King pressed on the throttle and the man suddenly had to weigh up what posed the greater threat. Caroline's shots were getting close to him, but the snowmobile would reach him with a damned-sight more force. He pressed the bolt home, spun around and fired at King. The bullet struck the front of the snowmobile and the steering went to pieces. King was thrown to his right as the snowmobile veered left and rolled down the slope. He was winded, but instinct told him to move. He tried, but his movements were slow and unsteady. He could not get air into his lungs, and his chest felt as if an elephant was standing on it. He rolled, anticipating another shot, but all he heard was a steady volley from the tiny Walther below him. He looked up to see Caroline lying prone in the snow, aiming the pistol with both hands. The man screamed and hobbled backwards. One of the punchy little bullets had struck him in the thigh. He had dropped the rifle and was now scrabbling up the slope. King got to his feet and started to lumber up the slope after him. He tried to run but slipped and fell. He settled on a rapid walk, crouching low and grabbing at the slope in front of him to steady himself.

Caroline got to her feet. She had one round remaining and knew better than to waste it. She had wounded the man, her last shot needed to count. She made better progress than King up the slope. She neared him, but he waved her on.

"Don't run blindly over the ridge!" he shouted, but it came out as a croak, the air still not finding his lungs quickly enough. "Move left and head him off. He may be waiting..." he saw the rifle on the ground, decided to head for it.

Caroline did as he said, veered to her left, and pumped her legs hard to sprint up the slope. The sound of a snowmobile starting filled the air. She hesitated, decided to head back towards King. The tone of the snowmobile changed as it accelerated hard and became quieter by the second.

"He's gone," she said. "I wouldn't have made it over the ridge." She reached him and hugged him tightly. "Are you hit?" she asked, pulling away and looking at his torso in concern.

"Winded," he grimaced. "The handlebars snatched out of my hands. I think his bullet severed the steering rack. That snow is bloody hard…"

She pressed her hand against his ribs and he flinched. "I think you might have cracked a rib," she said.

"Where's your snowmobile?" he asked, ignoring her diagnosis.

"He shot out the engine," she replied.

"Great." King turned and headed for the upturned snowmobile. "Here, give me a hand." Together they rolled the snowmobile back onto its tracks. The skids were locked hard to the left. He pressed a button under the lip of the seat and the seat popped up. There were a few tools and a coil of rope stored in a recess.

"What are you thinking?"

"Well, we've got a working engine but no steering and a machine that will steer, but with no engine." He shrugged. "Where are you parked?"

"At the bottom, towards the end of the clearing. There's not enough light to see from here."

King swung his leg over the seat and started the engine. It spluttered for a moment, the oil had drained from the sump and the petrol had drained from the cylinders. He gave it a quick rev and it settled into an idle. He then swung his left leg over and stood with both feet on the right side of the machine. He worked the throttle gently and pitched himself out to the right. The snowmobile tilted onto its side and he feathered the throttle as he drove it down the hill. Caroline walked beside him. She marvelled at the skill involved but did not say anything. She knew King would simply laugh and say it was luck.

The snowmobile pitched twice. Once back onto its skids and track, the other time it rolled, and King was thrown onto the ground again. He didn't complain, but Caroline knew he was hurting. The fall at the top of the hill had damaged him. She would only know how much when they got back to the hotel and she could examine him.

Side by side, the two snowmobiles were junk. But they were identical models and as King studied the steering rack and pinion, he realised it was a straightforward nut and bolt job. He wasn't a particularly skilled mechanic, but he was a practical man. The light was dim, and he had lost all concept of time. Constantly removing his gloves to look at his watch was impractical, but when he saw the time, he felt anticipation and regret. The coach would be leaving the hotel by now. Peter Stewart would be on it. A chapter in his life had closed. But it did not rest easy with him. Like so many pivotal moments in his life, he knew chapters could be rewritten.

Chapter Fifty-Three

As Vasily Rechencovitch looked down at the body on the ground, the blood frozen solid and the mass of brain and bone and blood that used to be the man's head, now crystallised in the cold, he couldn't help thinking he had paid his penance from earlier. From alerting their quarry with his enthusiastic volley of gunfire.

The sniper on his team was laying prone next to the body. He rested in some of the blood, but it did not seem to bother him. As he got to his feet, the blood peeled away from the ice crust like a crimson-coloured pancake. It reminded the Colonel of cloud berry crepes and he realised he was hungry. He watched as the man used his mobile phone to zero in on the angle. An architectural app that measured distances, angles and worked out geometric values.

The sniper stood up and looked at Rechencovitch. "I reckon two-hundred and fifty-metres max." He pointed to the corpse and shrugged. "Calibre is anyone's guess, but I'd say from the point of entry it was a thirty. Three-oh-eight or thirty-oh-six, maybe. It was a soft-nosed hunting round for sure."

That accounted for there being only the fractured forehead in place. Everything else was missing.

"So, a shot uphill from those trees?" Rechencovitch pointed down the hill. "That's quite a turn of events, considering our man had the high ground."

"Whoever shot him knew he was coming," the sniper paused. "Or at least, knew someone would be coming."

"Why?"

"They put out markers. Like the British did in established battlefields. The American War of Independence, the Zulu uprisings and Arabia." He pointed to the row of sticks at twenty-metre intervals. "This was a confirmed rendezvous. The sniper had time to set himself up."

"A pro, then?"

"As good as it gets."

Rechencovitch nodded. "Well, let's get down there and see what else we can find."

Chapter Fifty-Four

"So, she's in a room now?"

"Yes. I've charged it to your account."

"Naturally."

"Don't worry, it's too early for the minibar to take a hit."

"Don't bet on it," Ramsay paused. "And I noticed mine is empty."

"Not the time to talk about your problems."

Ramsay ignored the quip. "What is she like?"

"About thirty, attractive but had a hard life, I'd bet."

"I meant; her state of mind."

"I'm not a psychiatrist," replied Rashid. "But I'd say she's shit-scared. We ran into some problems. She was being hunted. Numbers and specifics unknown, but I got the person shooting at us."

"Dead?"

"Yes."

Ramsay cupped his head in his hands, then rubbed his temples. He looked back at Rashid and said, "Is there a trail?"

"The body is still there. I had the asset and decided to exfiltrate. But I imagine, like Fitzpatrick, the wolves will be on it soon."

"Lovely," Ramsay said sardonically. "What about King and Caroline?"

Rashid shrugged. "I phoned King, told him my rendezvous was in play. I cleared out before he could meet me. I imagine he's on the way back."

"And Caroline?"

"No idea. But I presume King would have contacted her to reiterate."

Ramsay picked up his coffee and nursed it in his hands. "Okay, good work. And the asset is secure?"

"They're old fashioned locks. I showed her to her room, locked the door behind me. She's secure. But I said I'd return with food and coffee for her. I said she should clean up and expect a meeting with you within the hour."

"Fair enough," said Ramsay. "Go and get changed, then wait with her. Send for room service if she wants anything. I'll contact London, then make my way over. What's the room number?"

"Three-thirty-three."

"An omen, perhaps?"

"What do you mean?"

Ramsay looked thoughtfully into his coffee cup. "Times three-three-three by two and it's the devil's number. Six-six-six."

Rashid nodded. "You're right..." He scoffed, smiling when he saw that Ramsay had taken his reply as enthusiastic agreement. "And if my auntie had a dick, she'd be my uncle..."

Chapter Fifty-Five

King pulled the snowmobile into the trees and switched off the engine. He kept his eyes on the horizon, a dull and monochrome hue in the distance, surrounded by trees on both sides. They had been traveling down a wide clearing, which he had earlier realised was in fact a river. The water had frozen months before and the ice had been covered in snow, only ridges on both sides where the snow had built up on the banks distinguished it as such.

"What's wrong?" Caroline asked. She released her grip on his waist and stepped off the machine. "What have you seen?"

King couldn't put his finger on it, but he had the same feeling he had earlier with the woman who had been impersonating Senior Constable Lena Mäkinen. And again, with Stewart in the car on the way up to The Eagle's Nest Hotel. It was the way the sky looked mottled, like a mackerel. As he watched, the clouds parted, and he was sure they started to turn counter clockwise. Slowly at first, then gaining in momentum.

A biblical sky.

King swung off the saddle, his ribs catching him and making him wince. "Follow me!" he barked. He swung the rifle off his shoulder and trudged up the slope towards the trees. He found what he wanted. A fallen tree, with a build-up of snow caused by a prevailing wind. The other side of the trunk rested on the slope with a drop of a few feet before the ground levelled out towards the riverbank.

"What is it?" she asked again, but she knew better to stop and protest. King's instincts were to be trusted.

"The storm!" he shouted as he drove the buttstock of the rifle into the ice crust. "Scrape the ice and snow that I break up into a mound, either side of the hole I make."

Caroline dropped onto her knees and did as he asked. He punished the rifle, its ability to function would be over after this. The dented receiver had made the action difficult for the gunman to use, but its accuracy would now be ruined beyond repair. King upended the weapon and used the muzzle to loosen the ice, then turned it around and used the butt to dig and scrape. Caroline had banked up the loose snow and pressed it down with all her weight. She could see what King was trying to achieve and simply worked with him. They saved their breath, the exertion made it dangerous for them to breathe through their mouths. Just breathing through their noses warmed the air enough to save their throats, and in turn their lungs. They were perspiring, which presented more problems. Freezing sweat would cool them down too quickly. But one problem at a time, was all they could worry about for now.

"That's big enough," said Caroline.

King nodded. "Get in," he said. "Head first."

She did as he said, bent down and crawled inside. She turned onto her side, pushed herself against the ice wall to give him some room. King bent down and stripped the rifle. He pocketed the magazine and the chambered round, tossed the bolt aside and slipped the barrel out of the fore-stock. He jabbed the barrel into the roof of the cave and worked it until it pushed right through. He pushed the barrel until it was approximately halfway, then contorted himself around it and crawled in next to Caroline.

"What the hell?" she asked, looking at the barrel of the ruined weapon.

"If we get snowed in, or the cave collapses, then we have an air hole. Enough to keep us alive," he said. "We wouldn't know the air was being used up, because we'd just fall asleep with the lack of oxygen and then die."

"Is there no end to your general knowledge?" she asked light-heartedly.

"Just survival," he replied.

They were braced for the storm, but the lack of drama seemed an anti-climax after all the effort they had put into their shelter. They looked at each other, the whites of their eyes visible in the darkness, and not much else. They were so close, their faces almost touched. King leaned in and kissed her softly on the lips. She responded, her lips warm, her mouth soft and moist. They had spent so much time apart that the act seemed different, yet familiar. A strange mixture of emotions, that needed rekindling. The constant familiarity had gone. It was like starting a new relationship, but with a close friend.

Caroline pulled away and smiled. "I've missed you so much…"

She couldn't finish her sentence, because the world seemed to end outside. The howling of the wind was like a locomotive passing through a tunnel at full speed. The air seemed to disrupt, sucked out by the vortex, then swept back to their grateful lungs as the pressure equalised.

King hugged her tightly and she slipped her arms around him and nuzzled her head into his neck. He risked a glance at the entrance to the tiny cave and saw the blizzard of ice and snow and debris of pine needles, pine cones and branches. Throughout the storm, they heard great crashes that could only have been falling trees dropping around them. They just hoped that one did not come crashing through the roof. But neither said a word, merely hugged one another to keep warm and took solace that they were together.

Chapter Fifty-Six

Ramsay knocked on the door and waited. He wasn't a patient man at the best of times, so in the brief time it took for the door to be answered he had already started to pace around in a circle. The door unlocked, and Marnie peered through the crack, the security chain pulled taut and a curious expression upon her face.

"Progress?"

Marnie closed the door, unlocked the chain and pulled the door wide open. "Yes," she said. "And no."

Ramsay tutted as he stepped over the threshold. "Meaning?"

Marnie led the way over to her laptop. "It was difficult to get in, but I bounced it to GCHQ and one of the techies got through the data encryption. GCHQ bounced it back. It is clearly scientific, and I'm guessing biological and chemical, so I sent the file back to GCHQ to be sent to Porton Down. They're the people for that sort of thing."

Ramsay glanced out of the window. There was a faint howl of the wind through the triple glazing, but the snow and ice crystals in the air looked like a snow globe. It was wild and all-consuming in the darkness, and he knew that King and Caroline had not returned. He glanced at his watch, uncertain what to do. It wasn't like there could be a search party put together. He looked back at Marnie. "And?"

"I haven't heard back," Marnie paused. "But it has a priority order on it and I'm on a direct link with Cheltenham, so we should know more soon enough."

"Okay, good work."

"Wow."

"What?"

"Nothing," Marnie blushed. Ramsay wasn't known for his praise. "Just one more thing…"

"What?" he asked, his manner terse. He looked like he was trying to order a thousand things at once in his mind and basic conversation skills had left the building.

She leaned over the laptop and opened a file. She stepped back, and Ramsay watched. A series of high-quality photographs filled the screen.

"Jesus Christ…" he trailed off.

"Be careful of the defector," she said. "We don't know what we are dealing with yet."

"I've sent Rashid in to wait with her…"

"Oh no…"

Ramsay shot for the door, Marnie followed. They ran down the corridor, Ramsay bustling into a tall, thin man who was limping. He was covered in snow and looked frozen under his snowsuit, his face ruddy and crusted with ice. He wore a permanent grimace, obviously in pain. He mumbled something as Ramsay apologised and ran onwards. Marnie moved past him and caught up with Ramsay as he reached the stairs. They climbed the staircase two treads at a time and darted into the corridor. Rashid was at the door, the key turning as he looked back towards them curiously.

"Wait Rashid!" Ramsay shouted.

"Don't!" Marnie added.

Rashid shrugged and stepped back from the door.

"Have you unlocked it?"

Rashid shook his head. Marnie went to step forward and hug him, but Ramsay caught hold of her and pulled her away. "No!" He looked at Rashid, who squared up, looking as if he was about to hit Ramsay. "Just wait," he pleaded. "Rashid go back to your room. Strip off those clothes and put them into a laundry bag, along with any possessions. Take a shower and meet back at my room."

Rashid frowned, but he soon worked it out. "Is she contaminated?"

"We're not sure," said Ramsay. "But I'm hoping we shall know soon enough."

Marnie had tears in her eyes. She smiled at Rashid, then turned and followed Ramsay back along the corridor. She had only just noticed the noise. As if a dozen vacuum cleaners were working on every floor. "Is that the wind?"

she asked incredulously.

"It is," Ramsay replied absentmindedly. "King and Caroline are still out in that."

"Oh my god…" she said quietly.

Chapter Fifty-Seven

The silence was eerie. It happened at once. No warning. One minute the outside world sounded as if it would come to an end; the next moment silence fell, and with it, the pressure that had squeezed their ears, sucked at the air from their chests. The wind dropped, and the world lived on.

"Are we in the eye of the storm?" Caroline asked. "Like in tropical hurricanes?"

King shook his head. "I don't think so. This happened before; both times. It was violent and intense, then simply gone. Blown out. I think we can get out of here now."

She kissed him again and said, "Shame."

They were in complete darkness. The mouth of the cave had snowed over. King wasn't sure if the rifle barrel had saved them, but it would have provided the snow hole with air nonetheless.

They struggled and scraped their way out, discovering just how difficult it was to crawl backwards. They kicked at the snow blocking the entrance. It had already started to freeze solid. King finally got his right foot through, and that gave him something to kick at. He made the edges of the hole larger with every kick. By the time they fell out through the hole and down the slope, they were exhausted and soaked in sweat. The droplets of sweat on exposed parts of skin had already frozen to tiny icicles.

"We've got to get going," King said. "That was another squall. If this storm is as bad as people are predicting, then we need to get back to the hotel."

Caroline nodded. She looked around for the snowmobile but couldn't see it. King searched too, but it was gone. There was a distant glimmer of light on the horizon to the east. It did nothing to illuminate the dimness, but it signalled there was a reprieve on the way.

"It can't have just blown away," she said incredulously.

"Well, it has."

"Wait. Is that it over there?" she asked, pointing to a speck in the middle of the river.

King squinted, could pick out the solid colour against the pristine white of the snow. With no trees or scrub to deflect its presence, it stood out, but was a hundred metres away at least. He nodded. "I think so. Let's go and look."

It didn't take long to see the machine wasn't going anywhere. The forks and skids were buckled, and the handlebars had snapped at the centre fixing. Fuel was leaking onto the ice and a thick ooze of oil was gathering to one side.

"Well, that's that then." Caroline punched King on the arm. "Looks like a tab."

"Well, don't go getting all competitive on me," he said. "I've got broken ribs."

"Ahh, diddums," she grinned. She looked at the crack of light in the sky, then turned the other way. "Due West, I make it."

"That's about right," said King. He fished out his mobile phone and pulled off his glove with his teeth to thumb the device open. He opened the GPS app and set the pre-entered coordinates of the hotel as their destination. "Five kilometres."

"Back in time for breakfast, then."

"If the chefs haven't bailed out on that coach."

"Well, as long as your friend Stewart has, then that's alright by me."

"He has."

She glanced at him as they paced through the snow. "So sure?"

"Absolutely."

Chapter Fifty-Eight

Stewart knew that human nature, the kindness part of it at least, was merely a façade. He had been to the worst parts of the planet, dealt with the worst people imaginable. And what separated these people from their kind-hearted counterparts was circumstance. Circumstance, fate and solution. Simply put, people had no lower limits. Society was nothing more than a veneer that could so easily be peeled away. There was nothing they wouldn't do when pushed over the edge.

The edge in question had been a squall, the like of which they had never seen, and the coach – their lifeline – being taken off the road by the monstrous winds. Trees had blown down across the road, making a return to The Eagle's Nest Hotel improbable, if not impossible. The windows of the coach had been sucked out by the drop in atmospheric pressure, and when the ferociousness of the winds slewed the coach sideways and hammered it into the trees on the opposite side of the road, tilting it onto one side and threatening to topple it over, his fellow passengers had not been the compassionate, caring kind. They had hastily gathered their carry-on luggage, their loved ones and piled out into the trees. They had barely glanced at the weathered and worn man nearing seventy, with the broken leg and the dazed and confused expression brought on by the strong opiate-based painkillers. They had simply left him to his fate. He had seen their indecision, then their decision. He would slow them down, put them at risk. It was amazing how soon people lived with the most inhumane of decisions when it suited them.

Stewart had grimaced through the pain of being thrown about, but he had cared little about their fate as well. He had heard many screams above the wind, and now that the storm had departed – as quickly as it had arrived – he saw few people as they staggered back to the coach. Some would have been hit by debris, others would have simply fallen to the searing cold and the elements. He cared as much for them as they had for him.

Stewart pulled himself up and placed his broken leg on the ground. It throbbed and pulsated from his ankle to his groin. He left it a while before moving. The strapping had been expertly applied, and tighter than the hospital would eventually cast it. In fact, by the way it throbbed, he suspected it was too tight. But that would serve purpose. He reached up and took a pair of skis and poles out of the ski locker. He doubted the owner would be back for them. He winced as he lifted them down. He had swiped the painkillers back at the hotel, and the young Russian had not bothered to protest. Stewart opened the bottle and took three. That would be enough to sedate him, but not for what he would be doing. He wasn't going to be sitting on his arse and taking deep breaths. He was going to push his body one last time. By the time he finished what he had started, his leg would be unsalvageable. But he did not care. He had a job to do. And damned Alex King. He would do what he was meant to, and nothing would stand in his way. He would push on back to the hotel. He would end things right there. He was a killer and he would kill again. And he didn't care if he went down doing it.

Chapter Fifty-Nine

King as watched as the two men walked down from the slope to their right and turned towards them. They slid down the bank and onto the frozen river. They were on course to meet them in another hundred metres. Both men carried rifles and wore utility vests. As he watched, one of the men slung the rifle over his shoulder and let it hang on the sling.

King turned to Caroline. "Give me the Walther," he said sharply.

She was a competent shot, but she didn't argue. She knew King had lost count of the close quarter battles he had been in. She could still count them on one hand and they kept her awake some nights, too. "There's only one round left," she said as she passed it subtly into his hand.

"You're trigger-happy," he said.

He slipped it into his pocket and loosened the fastening to his glove. He took the glove off, stuffed it into his other pocket and took hold of his knife, opening the blade with the thumb stud and putting it back into his pocket. He worked off the other glove and then stuffed his hands in his pockets.

"Who are these clowns?" Caroline asked.

"No idea. But they don't fit in here. These guys are after our asset. I'd bet a month's savings on that."

"You don't save that much a month…"

King nodded to them as they drew near. "Hi," he said. "That storm was something else. And there's more on the way."

The men nodded. King could see they were armed with Kalashnikovs. Not your average Finnish hunting rifles.

"Why are you walking out here?" one of the men asked.

"I don't see what business it is of yours," King smiled thinly. "Why are you hunting in between storms?" He stepped closer. "Surely the animals have all taken flight?"

"The prey we are hunting is still out there…" the other man answered. "And we get what we hunt for."

"I think hunting is cruel," Caroline said. King rolled his eyes. There was no stopping her sometimes. And then he remembered that was why he had fallen for her in the first place.

The other man patted his assault rifle. "Not really," he said. "I can make it quite painless."

"I'm sure," she said. "Any fool can pull a trigger."

The man went to say something, but the other man tapped him across the chest with his forearm. "Are you staying at the hotel?"

King stared at the man for a long time. He could see both men started to feel uneasy. He smiled thinly and said, "Where else would we be staying?"

The man shrugged. "We are going there," he said. "To shelter before the real storm hits. We will accompany you, yes?"

King nodded. He glanced down at the man's legs, saw the dried and frozen blood on his knees. He looked up and took in the sniper rifle hanging from the sling. A Dragunov, 7.62mm. These men were soldiers, not hunters. And the only creatures being hunted if he allowed them to travel with them would be Caroline and himself. These men were part of a team hunting the asset. He was certain of that much. And what of the man shooting at them from the second rendezvous? Was he part of this hunter team? King suspected he'd find out before long. Maybe these men would lead them right into another trap. In fact, he knew they would.

King turned to Caroline and winked. When he looked back at the two men, he already had his right arm scything through the air, the edge of his hand striking the man with the sniper rifle in the throat. He allowed his own momentum to throw him towards the second man, and swung a haymaker left fist into the man's jaw. The man went down, but his finger caught the trigger of his rifle and a fully-automatic burst filled the air and threw snow and ice fragments over them as the bullets riddled the ice at Caroline's feet.

There was a crack like gunfire as the ice shattered all around Caroline, her weight accelerating the effect. A spider's web of snow crust, widening until the blueish ice was visible underneath. Caroline looked up, stared directly into King's eyes for a fleeting moment, then with a final crack, that echoed all around the valley, the ice gave way and Caroline fell through and disappeared.

King stared at the hole, the water lapping at the edges. He took a step forward, then hesitated and turned back to the two men on the ground. One was moving, moaning and reaching for his weapon. King raised his foot and pounded down on the side of the man's head. He dropped lifelessly. King suspected he was merely unconscious, but wasted no time following up with another stamp. He did the same to the other man, who was clutching his throat and staring at the sky. King ripped the Dragunov sniper rifle off the man's shoulder and worked the action and dropped the safety. He dug through the man's utility vest and found a tactical torch and switched it on. The red light cut a swathe through the gloom and King shoved the handle in his mouth, bit down hard and took a deep breath, before sliding on his stomach over the lip of ice and into the water.

The water shocked his system, but he had been ready for it. He needed to move and not let the shock take over. Every ounce of his being wanted him to breathe in, but he willed himself not to. The cold water hurt his eyes and ears, but the water was thankfully crystal-clear, and the torch illuminated the underside of the ice and created a halo of red around him. He felt the current take him, and once he had established the direction of travel, he kicked and clawed with it with all his might.

Twenty-seconds in and he was fighting the need to take a breath, but he could see the dark shape in front of him, floating eerily in the current and scraping the underside of the ice. He gripped the rifle with all his strength, powered his legs and left arm until he collided with Caroline's lifeless form and wrapped his arm around her chest. He already had the muzzle of the rifle scraping against the ice and he jammed it in hard to stop them in the flow. He fired, and the muzzle flash reflected against the ice like sheet lightning, but the sound was faint and suppressed by the water. He fired again and continued to squeeze the trigger as he breathed out the last of his breath and felt himself go lightheaded. He had lost count of the gunshots, and he was losing his hold on Caroline. He shifted his grip on her and realised that he had to let the weapon go. He pounded the ice amongst the bullet strikes and felt it give. He powered his legs to keep him near the ice, but with his breath gone he had lost all his buoyancy and he was sinking fast. With the desperation to force an intake of breath almost too much to bear, he attacked the ice with punch after punch, not noticing the searing pain of his knuckles cracking, nor the fact he had started to taste the water as he sucked in minute breaths in his bid to break through the ice.

He could see the ice broken, the shards floating and bouncing on the surface, the torch lighting them from underneath. But they might just as well have remained solid, locking them in their watery grave, because without the buoyancy, the air in his lungs, he could not get them to it. He watched, the ice getting further and further away as they sunk and caught the current. He closed his eyes. Just for a moment, he promised himself. Just a little sleep...

Something snapped to within him. It couldn't end like this. He had been so close. He pulled Caroline with him, but it was no use. She weighed him down, anchored him to the purgatory beneath the ice. He glanced at her, her eyes closed, her face peaceful. He released his grip on her and fought with the last ounce of strength left in him. Hand over hand, legs pumping as he surged upwards towards the cracked and broken ice; everything that had been good in his life beneath him and sinking into the depths.

Chapter Sixty

King powered out through the ice, the air tearing his lungs and bringing the light back to his eyes. His head steadied, and as he grabbed hold of the edge of the ragged hole, he could feel the water already freezing on his face. He took another breath, deep and steady, then pushed himself back down. He caught hold of Caroline by the ankle, pulled her against the current and heaved her close to him, hugging her with both arms and frog-legging towards the hole. He had dropped the torch, not sure when or how, but imagined it would have been as he breathed and gulped like a landed fish on the ice. He could see the hole, a faint circle where the water lapped, and the ice shards bobbed in the wake. He heaved Caroline to the edge, the hours spent training each week paying off, the weights and pull-ups, the press-ups and squats giving him just enough strength to get her out of the water. He almost collapsed, slipped back under with the exertion, but kicked and clawed, thrust and heaved until he was clear.

Caroline's lifeless body lay face down in the snow. Her soaked clothing starting to freeze. King could barely move his arms and legs. He crawled to her, rolled her over and felt for a pulse. He couldn't even feel his own fingers. He put both hands on her, midway between her chest and stomach and pumped six times in quick succession. Water pumped out of her mouth, and he kept pumping another two revolutions. He then clamped her nose shut and breathed into her mouth, a full and steady breath. He moved to her heart, linked his fingers and pumped out to the Bee Gees song Staying Alive. An ironic title, but the lyrics worked in perfect time with CPR. He stopped and breathed for her, repeated the process. More water seeped from her mouth, but she still wasn't breathing, and when he tried to check her pulse, all he felt was his own fingers burning as if he'd touched the stove. He was getting desperate, could feel his stomach knotted and his chest pounding. He was getting lightheaded again. He knew that he had to get warm, or the elements would claim him. And if he did not continue, then death would claim Caroline. He pumped her around the chest and stomach again, then breathed for her and started chest compressions. He had done this before, and he had seen it done. He knew enough to know that it wasn't looking good.

He looked across at the two men laying inert on the snow. They were thirty-metres further away. That was how fast the water had been running, how long they had been under. He pushed himself up, staggered in the snow towards them. He fell onto the sniper. The man moaned, and King hit him in the face, but it was a feeble attempt. It did nothing more than shake his head a little as he slept. King crawled over him and tore at the pack on the other man's back. He recognised its squared form. Designed to carry a specific item, or various items in compartments. He could not release it, but instead he drew the knife on the man's belt and sliced through the strap. He pulled and fell backwards onto the snow. He pulled at the tabs, his fingers barely able to grip them, but he opened it enough to see the medical supplies within.

King crawled most of the way, his legs too unsteady to stand. He emptied the contents onto the snow, pulled through the items looking for something that would help him. A defibrillator would have been ideal, but he found the next best thing. He opened the packet and took out the syringe. He removed the cap to reveal a wicked-looking needle over four-inches long. He tore at Caroline's clothes, opened the zippers and Velcro enough to get to her chest. He knew where her heart would be. He did not need to feel. In his time, he had reached people's hearts with bullets and knives, it had been second nature. He held the syringe, placed his thumb on the plunger and struck down hard, driving the four-inch needle directly into Caroline's heart and releasing the shot of adrenalin. Almost at once, her back arched and her limbs went rigid. King clamped her nose tightly and breathed for her. He pounded out six chest compressions and breathed for her again.

Water spewed from Caroline's mouth and he turned her head as she started to cough and splutter. He could hear her breathing hard. Huge intakes and sharp and ragged exhales. King got unsteadily to his feet, caught hold of both her ankles and dragged her the thirty-metres to the two men. He dropped onto his knees and picked up the man's knife. He saw Caroline looking blankly at him, like a child woken in the middle of the night by the bedroom light. He couldn't spare the time to reassure her, but he told her he loved her and that she would be ok as he cut and slashed at her clothing and started to strip one of the unconscious men bare. He tore off her boots, pulled on the man's clothing, warm and dry from his own body heat. As King got more of Caroline dressed, she started to come around more. He kissed her cheek, before wrapping the man's hood over her head and pulling his military-style beanie down over her ears.

"C… cold," she said slowly.

She sounded drunk. King hoped and prayed she had not suffered brain damage from the rush of adrenaline. But it had been a Hail Mary and he had no other option. What he counted on was the freezing water shutting down her body in such a way as to put her to sleep, rather than suffer instant cardiac arrest.

"It's okay, my darling," he said. He found himself thinking of his wife, Jane. How he had discovered her body, still and peaceful. How he had hugged her close and talked to her, reassured her for hours. He had known she had died, but he couldn't find it in him to say goodbye. He remembered his tone, echoing in his ears, his senses nulled from grief. He sounded the same now. He stroked Caroline's forehead.

"C… cold," she said again. She looked at the ground, an expression of bewilderment upon her face. She wasn't coherent. She was seated upright, but there was no attempt to get to her feet.

King was fading fast. He could barely feel his hands and feet. He sliced himself out of his clothing and tore off the other man's snowsuit. He got it on, felt the warmth of the other man's body heat. King pulled on the boots. They were far too small, but he couldn't feel his feet anyway. He looked at both men. He could clearly see one of the men breathing, although he was starting to shiver now. The other man lay still. King picked up the two utility vests and put them over his shoulder. The AK-74 was empty, so he dropped the magazine to save weight and slung the strap over his neck, letting the weapon dangle. Then he pulled at Caroline, heaved her to her feet.

"Move!" he shouted. She flinched, looked at him like he was mad. "Get moving!" he shouted again. He pushed her forwards and she stumbled on the snow. "Move your arse, woman!" This time, he punched her in the kidney and she howled. He did it again. "Move! Left foot, right foot!"

"Stop…"

"Shut up!" he snapped. He jabbed her again. The sharp punch made her wince. But it also got her breathing rapidly, sent the flow of blood around her and spiked her adrenalin. It broke his heart to hurt her, but he didn't stop there. She floundered, and he punched her other kidney. "Move, woman!"

"Please… stop…"

"What's my name?" He shoved her hard, kept his hand on her shoulder and pushed her onwards as he broke into a jog. "My name, what is it?"

"Please…"

"My name!" He punched her again and she yelped. "My name, damn it!"

"Alex…"

"Your name?"

She hesitated. "Caroline."

"Surname?"

"Darby."

"Age?"

"Thirty-seven…" her answer sharper this time.

"Right, now pick up the pace and breathe only through your nose."

"Okay," she said sharply through ragged breath. "But punch me again, and I'll kick you in the bollocks."

Behind her, King smiled. "That's my girl," he said quietly. "That's my girl…"

Chapter Sixty-One

"Well, you should have shut the bloody door behind you!"

"I was more concerned about Rashid!"

Ramsay scoffed. "I knew that people in relationships and working together is no bloody good in this game," he paused. "What were you thinking?"

"I'll have you know; Rashid and I are not in a relationship, and I was as worried as you that my colleague, and friend, may have been in trouble," she glared back. "And King and Caroline are working together..."

"And if they weren't together, then last summer wouldn't have happened and we wouldn't bloody well be here!" He looked up as there was a sharp rap on the door. He walked over and opened it a touch, the chain stopping it from opening further than six-inches. He saw Rashid, then stared blankly at him. "What the...?"

"Just let me in."

Ramsay eased the door to, took off the chain and opened the door. Rashid walked in and Marnie stared at him with the same blank expression as Ramsay had.

"What..."

"Oh, shut up," he said. "Neil got me all wound up thinking I'd been contaminated with something, so I took precautions..."

"I can see you've done something," she said. "But what precautions were they?"

Rashid walked over to the mirror and sighed. "Well, I scrubbed all over, used a full bar of soap, then I saw the bleach down beside the toilet brush..."

"Oh," she smiled. She looked at Ramsay, who was trying not to laugh.

Rashid shrugged. "I'll shave my head."

"No, don't," she said. "Red really suits you."

"Red?" Ramsay laughed. "How about orange?"

"Ginger?" Marnie countered.

"I like the way it flows," Ramsay commented. "You've done a cracking job at streaking and highlighting. If this intelligence work doesn't work out for you..."

"Piss off," Rashid said with a smile. "Anyway, what's with all the shouting?"

"I didn't lock the door," Marnie said. "We rushed to you and while we were charging down the corridors, somebody took the laptop."

"And the USB that King took off Peter Stewart was still plugged into it."

"Thanks," she said succinctly. "But all of it was sent to GCHQ. They can quite easily send the files back."

"To what?" Ramsay asked laconically.

"I..."

"I'm pretty sure we can use a computer from the hotel," Rashid interrupted, winking at her. "We can save the data to a cloud facility and delete the files from the hard drive. Marnie, you're the techie, you should be all over that," he paused and smiled at her. "And thanks for your concern."

Marnie smiled and nodded. Her phone sounded in her pocket and she took it out and scrolled down to her emails. "That's GCHQ, the scientists at Porton Down have confirmed that, in their opinion, the data shows that the virus is not contagious. As such."

"As such?" Rashid asked. "Not feeling good about this…"

She looked at him earnestly and said, "It's early days, but they sent back the salient facts for us to deal with this as safely as possible. The virus is a biological agent designed to be air-dispersed. It renders the population incapacitated. Such symptoms as rapid heart rate, thirst and hunger are common," she read. "Sensory breakdown, sometimes leading to complete blindness. The Russian's research, as far as Porton Down can decipher it, has tested it in animal trials, including strict vegetarians like gorillas, and found that when the hunger persists enough, they will eat flesh. In short, cannibalism."

"Sounds like some horror flick," Ramsay mused.

"Sounds like a bloody zombie apocalypse," added Rashid.

"Apparently, the Z word was never mentioned, but Porton Down consider that after initial air-burst dispersal, it then goes on to be spread by saliva and blood."

Marnie shook her head. "Jesus…"

"Allah and Buddha," Rashid added.

"What sick minds invent such things?" Marnie said quietly.

"We do," Ramsay said. "And the US. Or at least attempt to. A virus dispersed by air, just once, that can be spread by the population by the simplest of means. Hunger. Incapacitate, degrade, turn that person into the most primitive form, and instinct will prevail." He looked at them both in turn. "Humans are pretty rubbish on the primal scale. We are intelligent. But we were born to be vegan, if you think about it. We do not have the natural tools - the claws or teeth - to kill, dismember tough hide and eat an animal. We had to evolve and turn to using weapons, traps, cutting implements and preserve or cook the meat. So, when someone has been returned to a primal state and has lost most function, all inhibition and has a terrible hunger, what will be their easiest prey?"

"Other humans…" Marnie said coldly. "But we don't make such awful biological weapons. This is pure evil."

Ramsay shook his head. "You are naïve, my dear. We have wanted a weapon like this, the Americans probably more so, ever since it was first imagined by science fiction writers in the fifties. The Russian's simply beat us to it, that's all."

Rashid shook his head. He was a soldier. He had been trained to kill and outsmart his enemy, but the idea of weapons such as this was something he would never get his head around. His idea of what was intolerable in battle ended at conventional smart bombs. If chemical and biological agents were needed, then perhaps the war wasn't ever going to be won, or even worth fighting in the first place. Time for the politicians to work harder. "Alright," he said. "But who stole the laptop?"

Marnie put her phone away and frowned. "I'm convinced it was the man who Neil bumped into in the corridor. He was near my room, he would have seen the door ajar as he walked past."

"Well, let's go and find him," he said. He turned to Ramsay and said, "And we can't forget the asset. She will be hungry and thirsty."

"But hopefully not too much…" Ramsay said thoughtfully. "Hopefully not too much."

Chapter Sixty-Two

They had pushed it. Driven each other on. Not a long march by any means, but the ice and snow, the freezing air and the exposure to the water and elements afterwards had sapped them, drained them to their core. Caroline had recovered enough to walk, but not much else. She was quiet, subdued and concentrated solely on breathing. King knew she inverted into herself when she was scared, concerned or uncertain, so he did not push in getting her to talk. There were many concerns on his mind, not least secondary drowning – whereby water still in her system, her lungs and throat, collects and drips back into the lungs where it pools, and drowning happens all over again – as well as the effects of the adrenaline injection – sending too much to the brain resulting in brain damage. The heart and lungs themselves suffer from the effects of oxygen starvation, as well as the brain. But the cold had been Caroline's saviour. She had held her breath for as long as she could, had passed out from the cold and starvation of oxygen, but had thankfully succumbed to just one intake of breath and sucked in the icy water, which in turn would have shrunk her lungs to half the size. The fresh water did not induce gag reflux in the same manner that seawater did, so there had been no multiple respiratory function to flood the lungs. King knew that his best bet would be to use the shot of adrenaline to kick start her heart, but the damage to the heart from the needle would also have been less because of the extreme cold, tightening and hardening the muscle of the heart wall. Like many things in his life, it had been a gamble. He would only rest easy once she had seen a doctor, but he had done the only thing he could have and right now, she was alive. Every fibre of King's being had wanted to hold her, to say how much he loved her. He wanted to sweep her up in his arms and carry her, but it had been essential for her to get warm and this could only happen through exertion. Her muscles needed to work and pump oxygen around her bloodstream, and her lungs needed to work to drive the residue of water from them and oxygenate the blood. He had stripped their snowsuits off and put the dry clothes on over their wet underclothes. Once they got moving, the damp clothes warmed and created an insulated layer which warmed them more quickly than if they had simply put the snowsuits on over their cold, bare skin. Similar in principle to how a wetsuit worked.

The two Russians had been collateral. He hadn't tried to kill them; simply incapacitate them. And he had been given no choice. He knew they were hunting the asset. And in any case, the blood on the sniper's clothing had not come from a deer or a wolf or an elk. No hunter knelt in their kill. And skinning and gutting a beast did not create the amounts of blood needed to make the marks it had. That sort of blood came from the kill. And they were soldiers; not hunters. King had stripped them to their clothing underneath. He knew they would not last long, but he hadn't given them a second glance as he left. He wasn't about to administer a coup de grâce, the elements would have done that soon enough.

The going had become easier with the belt of sunlight that was gleaming on the easterly horizon. Dawn would be breaking soon, and with it the anticipation of seeing daylight and escaping the gloom of near-perpetual night. It lifted their spirits, and with that, the going became easier.

They were on their last legs by the time they completed the spiralling climb to the Eagle's Nest. There were welcoming lights on within the hotel but, unlike before, there were no people milling around outside. The fires in the hot tubs were unlit and the thick thermal covers had been strapped in place and chains tethered them to one another. King thought the water inside them would weigh a ton, so the expectations of the impending storm must have been grim. Snowmobiles were parked up in lines and the maintenance men had chained them in place to metal railings. There were two spaces left, ominous loose chains waiting for their return.

King placed his hand on the small of Caroline's back and guided her up the last of the steps. He was cold and exhausted, but he had a few more paces left in him. The arrival at their destination, the completion of their trek was too much for Caroline to bear and she collapsed at the top step, falling into the foyer. King helped her to her feet and pressed the button to the glass door. It whooshed open and the warm air washed over them. Almost at once, the manager hustled over from the desk and crossed the lobby.

"What has happened?"

"We fell through the ice," King said. He sagged onto the floor, trying to fight the will to succumb now that he was inside. He realised his voice was shaky and his hands were trembling. Now that he had stopped moving, he was suddenly aware just how cold he was.

The manager clicked his fingers at the Russian who had so expertly administered the first aid. The man had been sitting in an alcove near the fire, taking a more casual and familiar break now that the hotel was all but deserted. He trotted over, bent down and swept Caroline up. King realised he had probably misjudged the man. He tried to resist as the manager helped him to his feet, then relinquished and used him as a crutch to bear his weight.

"The saunas, now!" the manager said, leading the way across the lobby. As they passed the desk, a bemused woman looked on. It was the waitress, but she was not dressed in uniform. The manager snapped at her, "Brandy, Michelle, now! And hot coffee! To the saunas!"

They veered away from the shattered glass doors of the ice hotel. The draught was immeasurable, even though maintenance had done their best to board up the opening with timbers. As they neared the saunas, King could feel the heady essence of pine and coals in his sinuses and the back of his throat. The manager opened the door to the nearest one and bundled King inside. The Russian placed Caroline down on the bench, eased her backwards so that she leaned against the hot pine wall. The manager ladled some water onto the coals from a bucket on the floor and stepped back, clearly offended by the heat. He disappeared for a moment, then returned with a bundle of towels.

"Take off your clothes and wrap yourselves in the towels," he said, pausing as the waitress appeared at his side with a tray of coffee cups and brandy. She had thoughtfully added two glasses and a jug of water to the manager's request. Regardless of the cold, they would be dehydrated from the dry air and their efforts. The waitress stepped into the heat and placed the tray beside King. The manager added, "We'll leave you alone for twenty-minutes and then we'll be back with bathrobes and accompany you to your room."

The heat intensified once the door was closed, and King ladled on more water. The coals hissed, and the steam filled his nostrils and warmed his throat. He tore off the snowsuit and then turned his attention to Caroline.

"I feel awful," she said weakly.

"Here, get some water down you first," he said and poured a glass, handing it to her. She caught hold of the glass and drank thirstily. "That's it," he said quietly, passing her the double measure of brandy. He took a glass of water for himself and downed it in one. He followed with the brandy and felt the warmth flood through him.

Caroline sipped at the brandy. "Thanks," she said. "I... I'm not really sure what happened..." she confided. "I remember going through the ice... the shock of the cold. Christ, it was so cold. I don't really remember anything else after that..." She finished the brandy and reached for the coffee. It was strong and black, but the waitress had spooned in dark-brown sugar making it syrupy and sweet. The caffeine and sugar were just what was needed to bring back some energy levels.

"It was my fault," King said.

"It wasn't."

"Yes, it was. I took the men down, because I thought we were at risk. Their manner, their weapons, the blood on the clothes of the man with the sniper rifle…" He tore off the rest of his clothes and kicked off the poor-fitting boots. He stood in front of her, naked and steaming from the heat. He started to help her off with the rest of her clothes. "He fired at the ice through poor weapon handling skills, rather than to shoot us. I didn't foresee that," he paused, wrapped himself in a towel and draped another over her shoulders. He ladled on some more water and could feel the perspiration trickling down his back. "I'm sorry," he said.

She shook her head. "You obviously saved me. I just want to know what happened."

He shrugged. "You went through. I wasn't sure if you would pop back up, but I couldn't help you until I knew that both those men were out of the equation."

"You killed them?"

"I don't know. I knocked them out for sure, but I had to be quick. I got a torch and the Dragunov rifle and went in after you."

"But, it was as cold for you as it was for me."

King ladled on some more water. He rarely drank coffee, but he started on the large cup and enjoyed its warmth. The sweetness helped the bitter liquid down.

"I trained years ago in Norway and had to go through the ice wearing skis. I remember what hell it was, but I guess I knew what to expect this time," he said. "There was no shock factor for me. Well, not so much, at least. I imagine you snatched a breath and that was that."

Caroline pulled her legs up to her chest. She adjusted the towel and King threw another over to her. The door was made from glass and King imagined that somebody would be returning to check on them. The position of her legs, the way she cradled them, made her look vulnerable.

"And how did we get out?"

"I shot out the magazine," he said. "Made a hole. I figured if the AK74 could break the ice, then the Dragunov with its more powerful ammunition would have no problems at all. Even if it was fired underwater, the bullets wouldn't lose velocity or energy straight out of the muzzle. It would take a few feet for that to happen, but it would happen abruptly. I had the barrel practically touching the ice, so muzzle velocity would still be high."

"And, was I unconscious?" Caroline shuddered. "Or was I..."

"You were gone," King said. "I couldn't get a pulse, but then, I could barely feel my own skin. You weren't breathing, and CPR wasn't doing anything. It's hard with drowning, because the water is in the lungs, so you can't just keep breathing in air for someone or they'll split. You have to pump out the water, but you have to work the heart, too, and that means pumping two different areas."

Caroline shuddered. "Jesus…" she trailed off. "That's twice you've had to do that to me."

King had a vision of her. Hands tied, face down in the bathtub. The room otherwise derelict. A bare bulb hanging from the ceiling. He closed his eyes. He'd saved her then, but he'd left her to go after the person responsible. A chain of events that had ultimately led him here. He thought if he hadn't have saved her at the river, then events could have turned full circle.

"It's getting to be a habit," he said, hoping to ease the tension.

"I don't recall a thing," she said. "No lights at the end of a tunnel, no deceased family members waiting for me… nothing."

King had been there. He'd seen the afterlife and it was as black as coal with no hope of anything metaphysical. He had been technically dead for almost five minutes. He always assumed his personal experience of death and the afterlife was down to the life he had once led and the path he had taken. But Caroline was a good person. She had killed, but only in self-defence. She was the most honest and sincere person King had ever met. Her experience simply confirmed his belief that mankind was so self-indulgent, so full of entitlement as to think they were due a second existence. But that hadn't stopped him from praying in the depths of despair. Soberly, he shrugged it off as merely hedging his bets. Human nature at its most egocentric.

King held her hand but said nothing. Sometimes people just needed their own thoughts. He looked up as the door opened and was surprised to see Ramsay and Marnie peering inside. Caroline adjusted her towels, smiled at Marnie as her expression said it all.

"I'm okay," she said.

"What happened?" Ramsay asked.

King gave the abridged version. He stopped talking when he noticed Rashid peer around the doorway.

"What the hell happened to you?" he asked.

Rashid ran his fingers through the bright orange-red hair. The sides were yellow and caught in the light. He shrugged. "New look. Get over it."

"Well, at least it isn't a man-bun and skinny jeans, I suppose…"

"Maybe that comes next?" Caroline chuckled.

King laughed and grinned at Rashid as he said, "I always wondered why more Pakistani men didn't dye their hair," he smiled. "Now I know why."

Caroline punched King on the arm. She did not look subdued anymore. Whether it was the water, the brandy, the coffee or the warmth, was unclear, but the laugh about Rashid's disastrous hair colour had certainly made a difference.

"I need to know what happened," she said. She turned to Marnie. "Was this your idea?"

Marnie smiled. "I don't think anybody could class that as an idea," she said, trying not to laugh.

Ramsay cracked a rare smile then said, "We'll debrief," he said. "My room in thirty-minutes." He left without further word.

Marnie caught Rashid by the elbow. "Come on," she said. "Let's leave them to finish up here."

King called after Rashid as the door swung closed. "Billy Idol called, he wants his look back…"

"Too young to know who he is, old timer…" came the reply as the door shut behind him.

Chapter Sixty-Three

The two men were wrapped in silver foil space blankets, the clever amalgamation of plastic and foil reflecting their heat back towards them. Rechencovitch had ordered the rocket specialist to get two gas stoves running to warm the pop-up survival tent, while he fed them both hot chicken soup from self-heating packets of rations. A simple foil packet, that when opened, mixed two chemicals in the outer lining, heating the contents in a few minutes. Both men were subdued. One man found it difficult to breathe from a ruptured larynx and the other nursed a broken jaw. They were bruised and broken, but they had lived through their ordeal. Both men wanted revenge, but that would have to wait until they warmed through and got their strength back. Rechencovitch warmed his hands on the gas stove in front of him. Within the confines of the tent the air temperature had risen quickly. It was now so warm, he had undone the zip of his jacket a good few inches.

He had already administered glucose drinks with some cocaine and codeine that he poured in from a homemade silver foil sachet. He had used this before and called it Marching Juice. What soldiers needed to maintain their pace, to lose their fear and inhibitions, and to ignore ankle twists or blisters until the mission was over. He could see an improvement in both men and as they warmed through, they would be faced with superficial injuries, nothing more than his soldiers usually sustained through a weekend of R&R and vodka. The next drink of marching juice would give them the courage to take on the man who did this to them. And win.

"He may have drowned, as well," the man said. He had contemptuously sneered at his bested companions. He hoped it would stand him in good stead with the Colonel.

The sniper shook his head and rasped, "No, I don't think so. Who else would have taken our clothes? No, the woman drowned, and he stole our kit."

The other man mirrored his expression. "I started to come around, I had the medical pack," he said. "I tried to get up, but the blood went to my head and I…"

"Fainted?" the other man mocked him, glancing at the Colonel.

"Passed out…" he glared. "When you got to us, when I came around, the medical pack had gone."

"Who do you think he was?" Rechencovitch asked.

The man shrugged, winced as he did so, his jaw causing him some discomfort. "One of us," he said. "The same line of work. An ex-soldier, I would guess. Someone used to fighting, someone with good situational awareness."

"Better than yours, at least." The other man goaded.

The Colonel held up a hand. "Do not interrupt again," he said.

The rocket specialist shrugged and picked up his own ration pack of chicken soup. He creased the corner and started to drink it down.

"I think he is British intelligence. Meeting the woman from the power plant would be my guess," the man said. He rubbed his jaw soothingly. "He was fast." He shrugged. "I guess five years doing security, I'm not as fast as I thought I was."

"You can say that…" The man was cut short as Rechencovitch chopped him in the throat. He clasped his neck, fell to the ground and started to gag.

"I warned you…" Rechencovitch said coldly. "And perhaps your situational awareness isn't what it used to be either?"

The man's two comrades smiled. He did not look in a hurry to get back up. His soup had spilled over him and his expression was sheepish, his cheeks blushing.

The sniper said, "The woman was возбудитель," he rasped. "Goading us about hunting. She was either situationally unaware, or just provocative." He rubbed his throat and said, "I suspect she doesn't know how to back down."

The Colonel shrugged. "Then we will have to force her hand," he said. "And the man, too. Drink your soup, change your clothes and we will go and see this man and woman. And we will make them pay for their audacity." He held out a hand for the man laying on the floor. The man took it and the Colonel pulled him to his feet. He handed him his own carton of soup and said, "We have a job to do. As a team. We have lost a member, and we shall avenge him. They have given us a bloody nose, but we will cut their hearts out and watch them die. We will kill this traitor of the Motherland. We will kill her for taking secrets. And we will kill anybody standing in our way."

Chapter Sixty-Four

"And you haven't gone in to see her since?"

"No. The information from Porton Down has hampered us, somewhat," Ramsay said matter-of-factly. "Be my guest if you want."

"For god's sake, Neil," King said sharply. "She's got no food, needs a change of clothes and we have to start a debrief. Porton Down have said how this virus works, but we don't know, have no reason even, to suspect she's infected."

"I understand, but..."

"Neil, Alex is right," Caroline said. "It's bloody well hell on earth out there. She's nothing short of a miracle to get that far across the terrain, and being hunted by mercenaries..."

"If we can assume they were mercenaries," Rashid interrupted. "If they are official Russian forces, then we have to get the hell out of Dodge."

"With you," said King. "Any news on this storm?"

"Within the next hour," Marnie said. She had a weather program running on a monitor. The computer tower sat on the floor amid a bundle of cables and an internet hub. Ramsay had requisitioned it from the reception. Marnie was running everything through a guardian program at GCHQ. "It's set to last for over twelve hours, before heading east towards

Archangel in Russia."

"Can we assume this hunter team will come here?" Ramsay asked.

"You can bet on it," said King. "I'm not sure if those two guys made it, but I suspect there's more in any case."

"We will need to hold them off until we can extract," said Rashid. "What have we got?"

King took out the Walther. "I only have one round for this," he said. He had the two men's utility vests. Both were stab-proof and contained a Makarov pistol and two spare magazines as well as a tactical knife and one vest still contained a torch. There were four magazines for the AK74 assault rifle. "These even the field a bit. I'm bagsying a pistol..."

"Bagsy the other!" Rashid said.

"And that's it? Bagsy? What are you both, ten?" Caroline shook her head.

Rashid smiled. "Then learn to bagsy quicker," he said to her, then looked at King. "I've got four cartridges for the rifle," Rashid said. "Two inches above for two-hundred-and fifty metres," he said to King.

King nodded and tossed over the bullet he'd taken from the man's rifle on the hill. "Point three-oh-eight," he said. "So now you have a full magazine."

Caroline snatched a vest off King and took out the Makarov. "I'm overruling your pathetic bagsy with my own," she said to Rashid. "You've got the bloody rifle."

Rashid frowned and looked at Ramsay. "Is there a precedent in MI5 for an overruled bagsy?"

"Oh, bloody grow up, the pair of you!" he snapped.

King smiled. "I'm convinced somebody on the hotel staff will have a rifle for bears or wolves," said King. "Ramsay, you can ask. You seem to have an in with whoever you got the computer from."

"The manager," he said. "Huss, the owner is a strange one. And he was talking to that man with the hooked nose who we think stole the laptop. Conspiratorially, so."

"Agreed, I saw that too," said Caroline. "What about staff? How many are left on the premises?"

"I'll find out," Ramsay answered. "I'll see how many paying guests decided to stay as well. Are we recruiting?"

King shook his head. "I'm not sure. It's a trust issue. We need more equipment to defend ourselves, though," he paused, sipped some of his tea. "I'll find out where the maintenance chaps are and whether they have anything in their units. There'll be a hut or workshop. It's too remote here to rely on going back to town to buy things or have them mended."

Marnie looked up from the monitor and said, "There's more from GCHQ regarding Porton Down's findings. This virus can't be caught like a cold. It's a first-strike weapon. A way to degrade a nation and cause chaos. The only way to become infected, after initial airburst, is for it to spread itself. The degradation of the subject and subsequent hunger issue is one thing, the infected infecting others through primeval instinct. Or, to encounter an infected subject's blood, saliva or semen. The virus bonds with human DNA to enter phase two. Without phase two, the initial airburst simply disperses. Weaponised, it fires and forgets. The people do the rest. Without their DNA, it can't incubate and will die."

Caroline shook her head. She nursed a black coffee. Her colour had returned, but she felt tired, and looked it. "Who thinks of things like this?"

Ramsay didn't tell her of his knowledge that both Britain and America had been trying for years. He sipped some of his coffee and asked, "So, what first?"

"Call room service and get the poor woman some food and drink," said King. "I'll wait outside and take it. I want to talk to her. While I'm doing that, Neil I think you had better talk to the manager about staff and guests. Get a list or manifest of who they are and the rooms they're occupying. And I want to know where this chap is you suspect of stealing the laptop. Have a word about a rifle or shotgun for bears. There must be something with people going out into the forest. Maybe it's time to lay our cards on the table and bring the bombing of the ice hotel into it to persuade him further. Explain who we are and that the person we are protecting is under threat," he paused, realising he was jumping way ahead of the hierarchy order, but he was the field expert here, not Ramsay. He looked at Rashid and said, "You look for vantage points. Somewhere to spot anybody coming. And exits as it would help if we could leave quickly if we must. Marnie, you're doing cracking work. Keep a line running with GCHQ and push the Porton Down angle. We need to know more about this virus." He stood up slowly and reached into his pocket. His ribs were sore, and his actions were both slow and deliberate. He gave her a piece of paper. Caroline had bandaged his knuckles, they were split and bruised from punching through the cracked ice. "And I'd like you to get that sorted for me, as well. You'll need Director Amherst for that."

She took the piece of paper and looked at it. She glanced at the others, but they knew enough about intelligence work to operate under their own brief. If King hadn't shared, then it was probably better not knowing. She slipped it into her pocket and opened an email. She looked back at King. "GCHQ have sent back the photos the asset took. I haven't told them they were lost, just that we had computer issues."

"Good thinking," King said. He hadn't worked with Marnie before, but he knew she worked with Ramsay and Rashid searching for Caroline last summer, and he liked what he saw in her. "Let's have a look," he said.

Caroline and Rashid bunched up towards the screen. King stood back to allow them a better view. Ramsay had seen them once and didn't look keen to see them again. Marnie clicked through, settled on the video. It was unsteady, but they saw enough. The room was quiet for a good while.

Rashid broke the silence first. "I'm glad I bleached myself now."

"Oh, I don't know," said King. "You haven't got to look at it…"

Caroline smiled. "He's got a point. I mean, you couldn't look much worse with blisters, boils and a hunger for flesh."

"Are humans and apes Halal?" Marnie chimed in.

Rashid shrugged and walked to the door. "Great. I'll take my chances with minus thirty and Russian mercenaries over you bloody idiots…"

They watched him leave and smiled. Gallows humour. Tougher times ahead.

"What shall I do?" said Caroline. "Before you say anything; I'm not sitting this out."

"Wouldn't dream of it," said King. "You wouldn't listen anyway. Go with Neil and find out who this character is that could have stolen the laptop. I don't buy that it was a casual theft. If he took it, then he's a player. And if he's a player, then he has what we have and that's not good. Find out who he is and if he poses a threat, put him down."

Chapter Sixty-Five

"You did well to make it," King said. "It's an extremely hostile environment."

Natalia nodded. "There were times when I didn't think that I would make it," she paused. "Times when I wished I hadn't seen what I had seen."

Natalia was perched on the end of the bed. King took up the chair next to the window. The gloom outside was lifting, daybreak only an hour away. Sunset three hours after that. Natalia nursed a steaming cup of coffee, discarded dishes from the hotel's room service menu lay strewn on the table. The ubiquitous club sandwich and fries with a six-euro surcharge to carry a tray one floor and thirty paces further than the restaurant.

"And what are your thoughts on that?"

"What? The secret bunker with unspeakable crimes against humanity?"

"Yes."

"What do you think?"

"I'm asking the questions."

"Dumb question."

"Dumb answer," King paused. "At the moment, we have a phone and a USB. We have thousands of square miles of snow and ice and the worst storm on record heading this way. Not to mention a team of security contractors with military weapons hunting you down. There are no written contracts here, no guarantee of your safety. Want to know the best way for my team to avoid bloodshed?" She said nothing but shrugged. "Leave your ass on the steps outside," King paused and sipped from his cup of tea. The room courtesy tray was better stocked than the restaurant for his choice of brew. "Now, I'm a man of my word, and I took on a job to meet you and hand you over to my government. I'll try my utmost to do that, but if I feel you're not worth it, I'll put my team before my orders. Every time."

"Okay, I get it."

"Good. So, let me rephrase that. Did you suspect something like this was going on there?"

"No."

"Does anything make sense of your work and the location now that you know there was more to the facility than hydroelectricity?"

She shrugged. "I guess so. I mean, some people disappeared without trace. Not a word on social media. Two of them were in the cells in the bunker..." she trailed off, a distant look in her eyes.

King nodded. "And the security?"

"I suppose, now that I think of it, they were heavily armed and patrolled constantly. I mean, we convert the flow of water to electricity. Short of copper piping and wiring, the machinery itself, there's nothing worth taking.

Nothing that requires four men and Kalashnikovs on rotating shifts. They were all ex-military as well."

"And no visitors?"

"Sami tribespeople trying to sell reindeer meat and skins. Our cook did deals for fresh meat."

"But only occasionally?"

"When they pass through. Twice a year. Maybe a couple of tribes."

"Who runs the plant?"

"A director. He's a Swede named Ben Jorgenson. He is a hydroelectric specialist and has worked all over the world. Then the rest of the top tier. A woman called Casey Daniels. She's Canadian. The other two are Russian men. Mikhail Soltanovich and Gregor Vavilov."

"And they would know?"

"I can't see how they could not."

"But conversely, someone tipped you off."

"Yes."

"Were you worried it was a set-up."

"Completely. I was paranoid for months."

"And how did you contact London?"

She smiled. "I wasn't aware it was London until now. I knew it was an intelligence agency. I hoped British," she shrugged. "Everybody wants to come to Britain, don't they?"

"So, how did you make contact?" King asked, undeterred.

"Letter drops. The first was in my bed. It creeped me out. Over the months I studied the rotas, the shift patterns to see if there was a pattern. Like holidays, night shifts, that sort of thing."

"And?"

"No connection that I could make. Other than the orders from outside always happened on a resupply. I figured it came via a sailor or sailors in merchant vessels. The supplies come South from the Arctic shipping route. But I always thought it would have to be one of the top tier who made initial contact. And to pass the communications on, for sure."

King had jotted down the names. He did not know why, but he had circled the Canadian woman's name. He circled the Swede's name too. Now he drew a line connecting them. The boy in him wanted to finish it as an aerial view of a Mexican pissing in a bucket. Despite his life, the seriousness of the situations he found himself in, or even perhaps because of that, part of him had never grown up.

"Tell me about the people in the cells," he said. "What did they seem like to you?"

"You haven't seen the footage?"

King had. They all had. But the image was shaky, and the woman would be the first to say that it felt ten times worse for real. People always did in a crisis. "I have," he said. "But how did it feel?"

She shuddered. "Like hell," she said quietly. "The smell, fetid and inhumane. Like they had become beasts. Caged beasts, uncared for and abused."

"You had a helmet on, didn't you?"

"Yes."

"And you could smell through that?"

She thought about it for a moment. There was a particle filter fitted. Could she really have smelled the cells, or was it her imagination? She shrugged. "I'm sure I could," she said.

King scribbled underneath the two Mexican's. He would research particle filters. He had worn an NBC suit once, couldn't remember if he could smell with it fitted over his head and face or not. He looked at her, hesitated for a moment then said, "I don't really want to use the word, but…"

"Zombies?" she asked. "Yes. Like the living hell of the walking dead. Like those horror movies and shows. The worst parts. It's all I've been able to think about since."

King thought about it. He wondered whether Ramsay had been right about Britain and America wanting such a weapon as this hideous virus. But it didn't take much thinking about. He already knew the answer.

"I can't really get my head around the fantastical nature of it," he said. He was a man who had dealt with the cold, hard truth of death. People died. They died in all manners. Some brave, some sobbing, all with the same outcome. Organic matter devoid of life. They died, rotted, the end. He did not believe in an afterlife, in ghosts or the paranormal. He certainly didn't see the walking dead. But he reminded himself that this virus created symptoms. These people would die all the same. There would be no beheading, no destruction of the brain. They were not already dead; merely people rendered in an enhanced comatose-state. Their primal instincts searching only for food. Everything else was secondary. People infected with this would be sick. Nothing more sinister. Still, he never thought he'd see the like. "What about the animals?"

She shuddered. "They were just angry," she said. "And the gorilla just wanted to attack me. It was obvious. But it severed its hand getting out of its tether, didn't seem to feel the pain or realise what had happened."

King said nothing, but he knew that the fact that the creature had not felt pain was significant. If the people infected with the virus felt no pain, then they would not be easily destroyed, and certainly not effectively restrained to be treated. Perhaps there was some stock in the fantastical version after all.

"So, who's hunting you?"

"My guess is the security guards."

"My colleague killed one when he met you. So, three more?"

"I imagine. There were four full-time guards on that shift. More off shift and more on leave."

"And you feel in good health?"

"I do," she lied. "Never better."

Chapter Sixty-Six

Rashid had dressed in his thermal snowsuit and walked the perimeter of the hotel. The ice hotel took up a substantial area, being a single-story construction. Against any attack, this was the weak spot. The grenade blast had destroyed the roof of two rooms and blown out the glass doors to the room occupied by the unfortunate couple. Now boarded with planks to stop the cold penetrating the main body of the hotel, the deserted structure would be easy for attackers to breach and get through. Any attack would be won or lost in the lobby.

He made mental notes as he walked the area. During his time with the SAS he had worked on close protection and security advance details for visiting dignitaries. He knew how to order and write a threat assessment, and he knew how to approach a target from an attacker's perspective as well. Which was why he was having the most uneasy feeling that the building was nigh-impossible to defend.

The rifle was slung over his shoulder in a ski bag he had found in the utility room where snowsuits for the guests and the hotel's equipment was stored for guests who did not have their own. Since the departure of the guests on the coach, the hotel had taken on a deserted feel and walking down the corridors was akin to a scene from The Shining. Rashid felt more comfortable with the rifle and knew that the team of mercenaries would not be far away. They were likely out there, watching the hotel and making plans of their own.

The hotel sat, in turreted and glass magnificence, resplendent in its modernity, yet harking to the past. As an architectural exercise, it worked, but possibly because there had been no neighbours to rebuke the bold plans. It was seated proudly atop the man-made mountain on a flat piece of ground fringed with pines and firs on the South and West sides. To the North was plain and dropped to the steepest edge. This was predominantly ski slope all the way to the bottom where it levelled out and then dropped further down a natural valley. Two runs of chair lifts serviced the slope with a short traverse mid-slope between lifts. To the east and running all the way through South and West the access road meandered up the mountain in a series of S-bends. Rashid had travelled in and out on the snowmobile and the route had been well maintained and kept clear of snow by maintenance, who used a Caterpillar truck that ran on tracks. This was the vehicle that towed in supplies, most likely in the early hours while the guests were asleep. And that left West. Under the pines and firs, a funicular travelled underground to the carpark below. A safe and weather-friendly method of transportation that a added a little more theatre to the guest's experience. The track terminated fifty-metres short of the hotel and offered another act of theatre – an ice tunnel to the bottom of the hotel's steps. Lit with coloured lights, gentle background music of Scandinavian folk tunes, and ice carvings like that denoting each room in the now ruined ice hotel, it made arrival to The Eagle's Nest Hotel an event.

Rashid made his way down the steps to the funicular. A pair of steel gates were opened and pinned back against the concreted walls. He saw that the train must have been at the bottom of the tunnel, as all he could see was a pair of tracks at a forty-five-degree angle disappearing into the darkness. He turned to the control panel and studied the switches. An electrical cut-out button, on and off switch and a dial for what he gathered would be speed control. The other two buttons denoted up and down. He looked above him and saw the monitor on the wall, the train was parked at the bottom and nobody was on the screen. He switched the on button upwards, pressed the up button, then gently turned the dial. The train moved steadily out of the frame and he could see that the waiting area was empty. He listened for the approaching train, heard nothing and twisted the dial further around.

It all happened at once.

The beams from the headlights hit him, blinded him and the train appeared. He was aware of a great wind rushing over him, forced up through the tunnel – an icy draft. He turned the switch back, but it was too late. The train crashed into the barrier and the noise was like canon-fire. Rashid was bowled over as the shock travelled through the barrier and into the control booth. He got up, looked a little sheepishly at the train and then at the monitor. He switched the down button on, eased on the dial and the train moved steadily away. He changed the direction and brought it back, parking it considerably more gently than before. Satisfied he hadn't broken a million-pound's worth of funicular, he switched the panel off. The wind ahead of the train had shown how tightly the train fit in the tunnel, and with the train at the top of the tunnel, he hit the master switch and hoped he had sealed off another weak point.

Chapter Sixty-Seven

"All of the guests have gone."

"Not all."

"But they have, I saw them to the coach personally," Huss persisted. "Only your party, my manager and four members of staff remain."

"There is a tall, thin man with Slavic features," Ramsay said. "A hooked nose, to be precise. He was limping this morning, came back covered in snow and ice. We bumped into him on our floor."

"And you suspect this man to have stolen your laptop?"

"Yes."

Huss shrugged. "The coach will have reached Kittila by now, I do not see what else I can do…"

"He won't have left. He is still here, I'm positive of that."

"But I can assure you, all of the guests have departed. I insisted they all leave. We could no longer guarantee their safety. Not with the bomb and all."

"I thought you were insisting it was a lightning strike?" Caroline interjected. "That was what you were insisting last night."

"Perhaps I was wrong…"

"But you remember this man?" she ventured.

"No."

"Strange," she paused, feigning confusion and bemusement. "You were talking to him at the reception desk."

Huss shrugged. "I talk to a lot of people," he said. "That is all part of owning a hotel. Now, I think I have answered enough of your questions. You have insisted that you can investigate this matter, what do you propose to do?"

"Very little, now that most of the potential suspects have boarded a coach out of here," Ramsay replied.

"Then, why are you still here?"

Ramsay looked at his eyes. He was trained to spot liars, their tells. Everybody had one. "There are men coming," he said. "They have hostile intentions."

"Towards my hotel?"

"Towards somebody staying here."

"But I told you; apart from your party, there are only a few staff. Enough to keep it running, but in truth, they are live-in workers with nowhere else to go," he paused. "So, if these hostile forces are after you or your group, and putting my hotel at risk, then I am going to have to insist you leave."

"Good luck with that," Caroline said, taking the Makarov pistol out of her pocket and holding it down by her side. Huss stared at the weapon incredulously. "Let me know how it works out for you," she added.

"What are you doing?" Huss asked. Ramsay looked at her, as if reiterating the owner's feelings. "This is my hotel!"

"I think we've gone way past diplomacy," she said. "Mister Huss, for the next twenty-four hours, possibly more, this building has been requisitioned by us, for our needs and protection. You can cooperate with us, or you can see out the storm locked up for your own protection." She looked at Ramsay, who was still not quite on board with her decision. She turned back to Huss. "Actually, you know what, lets make that the case." She turned back to Ramsay. "We don't know who to trust here and that's putting the team at risk." She looked at Huss, raised the pistol. "Gather all your staff together now."

"But…"

She cocked the Makarov's hammer. The weapon would fire on the double action with the hammer down anyway, but it was always good for effect.

"Okay!" he protested. He picked up the phone in front of him, pressed a button and after a few seconds spoke quickly and tersely into the receiver.

"And you still maintain that the man with the hooked nose boarded that coach?" she asked.

Huss hesitated. "Yes," he said. "I mean, I think so…"

"You think so?" Ramsay shook his head. "Now, Mister Huss, I'll ask again. And if I think you are lying, I'll ask my colleague here to shoot you in the kneecap."

Caroline walked around the desk and aimed the pistol, her elbow rested on the desk to keep her aim steady.

"I…"

"Quiet, Mister Huss," Ramsay said quietly. "Now, the tall, thin man with the hooked nose; did he get on the coach?"

"I… I can't be certain," he said hesitantly, his eyes on the pistol. "No!" he added. "No, he didn't…"

"He didn't?" Ramsay nodded. "In that case, where is he?"

"I don't know." Huss was perspiring now, a pallor to his face, despite the temperature of the reception and lobby.

The manager appeared with the waitress and a man wearing chef whites. He surveyed the scene and the three of them looked at each other in concern. He said something in Finnish to Huss, then looked at Ramsay. "Nikolai and Mikael have gone," he said. "They are agency staff and I have no contact details for either of them."

"Convenient," Caroline said tersely.

"What do you mean?" asked the manager.

"I suspected they were Russian," she said. She tucked the pistol back into her pocket and pointed at the waitress. "She said as much, too."

The waitress shrugged. "I thought they were, but they both claimed to be Norwegian."

The chef nodded. "They were Russian," he said. "But they are good men." He looked with uncertainty between his manager and the owner, the waitress too, like he was about to betray a confidence. "They are both AWOL from the Russian military. They were left demoralised and ashamed after a tour in Syria. Mikael was a helicopter pilot, Nikolai was the weapons operator. The gunner…" He shook his head, as if trying to imagine what horrors and injustices both men had seen. "They simply ran away. If they are caught or return to Russia, then…" He left the sentence unfinished, but everybody seemed to understand the ramifications of their actions.

"And you don't know where these men are?" Ramsay asked, somewhat incredulously.

"No," the manager replied.

"Please, tell us what is happening," the waitress pleaded. "Why do you have a gun, and why all the questions?"

Ramsay glanced at Caroline, then conceded. He looked at the group and said, "We are trying to protect a Russian defector. They are at risk, and so is anybody standing in her pursuers' way. The storm and circumstance has conspired events and The Eagle's Nest Hotel has become the place where these events will conclude," he paused and looked at Huss. "You lied about the man we seek. I believe the tall man with the hooked nose and Slavic or Russian accent is a crucial part of this. He was posing as a guest. You were disingenuous when questioned." He looked at Caroline. "Put Mister Huss under arrest, please."

"Wait!" Huss exclaimed. "I own this place!"

Caroline aimed the pistol at him. "What about the others?" she asked without taking her eyes off the owner, or her peripheral vision from the other three.

"I don't wish to take such measures," Ramsay said. He looked at the manager. "I would greatly appreciate your knowledge regarding the establishment. Your staff can cater for my team, informally of course. If trouble comes, then perhaps we can adhere to a plan of action. A place they can go to and take refuge while matters conclude?"

The manager nodded. "The wine cellar is secure and even houses a generator. The temperature is habitable, as wine keeps best at fifteen degrees Celsius. A thermostat sees to that. We could take food and drink, blankets and toiletries down there. There is running water for the beer cellar equipment."

"Sounds ideal," Ramsay agreed.

"But…" Huss protested.

Caroline cut him off. "Be quiet." She waved the pistol, saw the fear in the man's eyes.

"Caroline, take Mister Huss to his quarters and see that he is locked securely inside." Ramsay looked at the chef and said, "Be a good fellow and make some sandwiches for my team," he paused, caught the waitress's eye. "Some coffee as well. We'll take it in the conservatory. Then take some time to yourself."

Huss looked as if he were about to explode, his colour several shades brighter than normal. Caroline could see his fists clenched. She noted he was close to losing his temper, made a point of standing several paces behind him as he led the way to his quarters.

Ramsay watched them go, then said to the manager, "Do you have any weapons on the premises? For bears or wolves?"

The man shook his head. "Wolves are shy creatures and you never really see them. As for bears, well guests would consider themselves lucky to see one."

"Aren't they dangerous?"

"Yes, but they don't come around the hotel. In the forest, it's a different matter entirely. We have cans of bear spray, though. And air-horns, to scare them away. We also have bangers. You hang a string of them on a tree, light the bottom of the fuse and a loud banger explodes every ten minutes. They are good to use if bears are persistent, but they never have been, so..."

"So, nothing to kill them with?"

The manager smiled. "This isn't America. We don't encourage killing animals out here. There are hunters, of course. The Sami mainly. But our hotel is all about the beauty of Lapland, we do not cater for hunters. Only fishermen and nature lovers in the summer months, snow-sports enthusiasts and Northern Light watchers in the winter."

Ramsay nodded. "What's bear spray?" he asked.

"Like pepper spray, but stronger."

"Show me," he said. "Show me everything you have."

Chapter Sixty-Eight

"I've called you in here to get a situation report and throw about any ideas before…" Ramsay paused, his tone ominous. "Well, before the storm hits, or we are hit by hostile forces."

The plate of sandwiches had been devoured, the coffee too. King sipped from a glass of water with lime. He'd given up getting tea anywhere else but the rooms. Generic 'English breakfast tea' bags and miniature cartons of UHT milk. He was developing a taste for it now.

Rashid said, "The ice hotel is the weak link. It's not secure, easy to gain access to and only boarded up from the main hotel with planks of wood and plastic sheeting."

King put down his glass and walked over to the window. It provided a panoramic view of the grounds along the whole front entrance of the hotel. "Then we can boobytrap it," he said over his shoulder. He turned and pointed to the crates of bear spray and bangers. "Rashid, there's enough there for a man of your expertise to get a couple of nasty IEDs put together. Bleach, sugar and baking soda in the kitchen. There's petrol in the storage sheds as well. Nails, nuts and bolts, too," he paused and smiled. "Just don't go setting your hair on fire…"

"Might not be the worst thing," Marnie smiled.

Rashid sneered at them both, then said, "I've brought the funicular up to the top, as well. A handy method of escape, and the seal is tight enough to keep intruders from using it to get close to us."

"Good thinking," said Ramsay. "Glad to see you used your head."

"Did that even work?" Rashid asked, bemused.

"It was a good effort," said Caroline. "For Neil, at least."

Rashid shook his head. "Seriously though, I only have five rounds for the rifle, but I can see three sides of the grounds from upstairs. Not simultaneously, but perhaps the staff could act as spotters?"

"There's the trust issue," said King. He turned his attention back to the view. He held the AK74 loosely in his left hand, the three spare magazines were tucked into the pockets of his cargo trousers.

"I can't watch all the sides anyway, so there's nothing to lose."

King shrugged. "Okay, but Huss stays where he is."

"Agreed," Ramsay added.

"Entrances?" Caroline asked.

"Five," King answered. He perched on the window ledge and said, "The front entrance, the ice hotel tunnel, a rear entrance to a courtyard from the kitchen, and from a service area to the same courtyard, and a side exit to the West."

"More than we can cover. Practically, at least," Caroline mused. "I think IEDs on the rear exits, as well as the ice hotel. That will leave the two main exits. And IEDs going off will act as a warning to us as well."

Rashid smiled. He'd had history with Caroline during an assault, back when he had been in deep cover with an ISIS terrorist cell. Caught up in the fluidity of the attack, he had managed to do enough to maintain his cover, but had taken the opportunity to run, aiding an injured terrorist to avoid suspicion from the rest of the cell. He had been the only member of the cell uninjured. Caroline had put up quite a fight.

"Weapons-wise," Ramsay paused. "Caroline and King have Makarovs and twenty-four rounds a piece?"

"Correct," said King.

"Rashid has five rounds for the hunting rifle, and there's the Walther with just one bullet." He looked at the box containing the bear spray. He reached inside and took out two, gave one to Marnie and held onto one for himself. "I'll take that Walther," he said. "One bullet is better than none."

"Should have bagsied," Rashid chided.

King took out the Makarov and walked over to Ramsay. "Take this, Neil. I'll hang on to my Walther. I've got the Kalashnikov, and you'll do better with eight rounds and couple of spare mags."

"Thanks," Ramsay said. He hadn't done any formal training with weapons, but he figured he had the gist of it. He turned it over in his hand.

"It's made ready," King said. "Point this end at whoever you want to kill and pull the trigger. Don't try aiming, just point and shoot. Press here to eject the magazine, insert the magazine with the lead pointing forwards, slam it home and pull the slide to chamber a round," he smiled. "And now you're all up to speed."

Ramsay handled it as if it would burn him, kept his finger off the trigger and the muzzle pointed to the floor. "Thanks, Alex."

King turned back to the windows. "This meeting is over," he said over his shoulder. He turned and looked at them as he pointed towards the horizon. "I've seen the sky look something like that before. The storm is on the way. Only those clouds look darker and angrier than it did before." He looked at them earnestly. "There's a truck outside. I'll find the keys and get it parked against that side entrance. It may be enough to make them consider it a non-starter. Rashid get some IEDs in that ice hotel. Make one for each rear exit, too. After that, get some elevation and take the watch on the front and both sides. Be sure before you shoot anybody. We don't want to plug some unfortunate person taking shelter from the storm. Neil, use the waitress and the chef as watchers. Tell them to alert Rashid if they spot somebody. Caroline, check our asset is okay, then get her locked up and secured."

Caroline nodded. "I've already given her a change of clothes and some toiletries. She looks exhausted."

"What about myself and Marnie?" Ramsay asked.

"Marnie, check your communications from GCHQ. Download everything. Neil, you can then destroy the computer. After that, stay with Caroline, who will be fluid between the first floor and the third. Or you can spot for Rashid."

"What about the manager?" Ramsay asked.

"I'd forgotten about him," said King. "Go and recruit him into spotting from the top floor. Rashid only has five bullets, and believe me, it will suit us far better if he gets to use them at a distance, than if they bring the fight to us at the door."

Chapter Sixty-Nine

The treeline served their purpose well. Keeping at least three trees from the edge of the forest, they had been able to dig into their two observation posts unseen from the hotel.

Rechencovitch was seething. His orders had been to capture or kill Natalia Grekov, and he would. But he wanted the man who had bested his men. Humiliated them. He wasn't sure if the same man had killed one of his own at the ridge, but he would find out and kill that person, too.

He could see activity on the third-floor. Through his binoculars, he could see a man and a woman peering out of various windows. They were not professional in their approach. On the second floor, he could see movement. A slender-looking man with combed brown hair and a woman with a dark bob and rectangular spectacles were standing further back from the windows. He could see they were on a route. Covering many windows, returning every few minutes. Occasionally, he caught a glimpse of dirty-blonde hair. Long, in a ponytail, but he could never quite make out the woman's build or features.

It was evident that they knew they were coming for them. Which suited the Russian warrior. He liked his enemy under duress. When the time came, they would not be ready for the onslaught. Rechencovitch had his rocket and mortar specialist holed up at the edge of the clearing. He was out of sight from the hotel, had a clear line of sight and trajectory and would be able to rain down terror onto the hotel at his command. The specialist had ten 40mm mortars at his disposal, enough to bring most of the hotel down. He also carried a rocket propelled grenade launcher, or RPG. Another ten 40mm rockets loaded with a variety of ordnance from anti-personnel rounds like shrapnel and fleshettes through to phosphorus to provide smoke for an attack or to take cover and fall back behind. Frankly, they didn't stand a chance.

Spare kit and clothing had been used up and weapons redistributed. The dead man's assault rifle replaced the one taken by the Englishman, and the sniper had been given the dead man's pistol. Two pistols and an assault rifle had been taken from them, along with vital ammunition, but they had enough firepower between them to wage war on this place. And that was exactly what they were going to do.

The Colonel had finished looking at every window. He could still see the man and woman on the top floor. They were too obvious to have training. He doubted he could take them both out from here with his assault rifle, but once the shells started to drop, and he closed his distance under covering fire, he was sure both could be taken out efficiently. He frowned, feeling the vibration of his phone in his pocket. He looked at the screen and studied the text. A short message followed by a number. He let go of the binoculars around his neck, pressed the highlighted number feeling a rush of adrenalin as it was answered.

Chapter Seventy

Caroline checked every floor. Both the waitress and the chef were peering out of the windows on the third floor. She nodded to Rashid, who had pulled out a sideboard and was using it as a bench rest for the rifle. He had set up similar rests in two other rooms and could now fire from three sides of the building. The SAS trained sniper had spread pillows on each sideboard to steady his aim and positioned the pieces of furniture several metres back into the room, so he could use the rifle without the barrel being in view, or the subsequent muzzle flash becoming visible from outside should he have to take more than one shot. Caroline had tried not to snigger at Rashid's hair but had failed. Rashid had flipped a middle finger and turned back to survey outside through the sight of the rifle. As she had walked back along the corridor, she told the waitress and the chef to stand further back from the windows. They nodded, but she could see from their expressions that they were well outside their comfort zones.

She found King in the lobby. He looked at her and the two shared a moment, like a couple at a party neither wanted to be at any longer but had managed to shake off their friends long enough to sneak a quiet word or a kiss.

"Huss is no longer in his quarters," Caroline said. "I've just checked, and he's gone. I locked him in, but I suppose it wasn't a stretch to have spare keys hidden somewhere."

"I suspected as much," King said.

"Somebody may have released him."

"I think that's a given."

"But who?"

"Were the waitress and chef upstairs the whole time?"

"Yes. I think so. On the third floor, a roving patrol checking out of the windows."

"And the manager?"

"I passed him on the stairs. He is armed with a can of bear spray and has been guarding the stairwells. He's joining Marnie and Ramsay on the second floor. And then there's the two Russian workers. There's no knowing where they are," she paused. "It's one thing having an enemy out there, but if we can't guarantee the safety inside... What are we going to do?"

King smiled. "Nothing."

"Nothing?"

King held up his phone. "Marnie organised this," he said. "GCHQ are scanning the hotel. With a triangulation of satellites. Anybody making a call has had their mobile phone intercepted and now I'm able to track their GPS. I don't know who is denoted by which signal, but the person who received the text and made the call is outside and directly in front of us. That is undoubtedly a member, most likely the leader, of the hunter team. But two people have used their phones from the hotel. One internally, and the tracking doesn't allow for floors or rooms, because none of those architectural diametrics have been entered. But another was outside, to the rear of the building. I have a copy of a text that has been sent as well. And a recording of the conversation."

"And?"

"Somebody has sold us out," said King.

"Who?"

"It's complicated." He walked past her and glanced inside the bar. The rooms were public areas and now that they were empty, they took on an eerie feel. He looked back at her, then pointed towards the windows of the conservatory. "The storm is here," he said. He took out his phone and dialled Rashid's number. "Be aware. I think they'll move under the cover of the storm," he said. "Keep your head down."

"I'd best come down, then. Won't be able to hit anything in the strong winds anyway."

"No, stay," he replied. "If you can get one of them in open ground, they'll take a big psychological hit. And be aware, Huss is no longer contained and must be viewed as suspect."

"I already did. I only trust the team."

"Well, err on the side of hostile, then."

"Check."

"And there's at least one other. Somebody in collusion. Marnie's app has shown two people have made a text or call."

"That's it?"

"Sketchy, I know, but that's all I can tell you." King ended the call and looked at Caroline. "Both signals are in the grounds, not the main hotel. One is in the maintenance huts at the rear. There is no access to the hotel without triggering the IEDs. The only way in is through the front door, or the side door. The other signal is coming from the side of the hotel. Where I parked up the maintenance truck. Now, there will be another set of keys for this, so I think we should expect this hunter force to come through there."

"Someone here is in contact with the hostiles?" Caroline exclaimed.

"Looks that way. Text message and a short conversation."

"And what was said?"

"The text passed on a telephone number and said that the person was onsite and could be trusted."

"And the conversation?" Caroline asked incredulously.

King said, "It detailed how many of us there are. My Russian isn't great if it's spoken at speed, so I got the gist of it, but not in detail. It was between the leader of the hunter team and this mystery man. Either Huss, the manager or this hook-nosed man who seems to have disappeared. Marnie said she suspected him of stealing her laptop, and I would agree. Ramsay and her both said he had a limp and was dusted with snow when they bumped into him. The timing fits. And that ties in with him being the same man who was shooting at us. You winged him for sure. I don't think he's part of this hunter team, but there is most certainly a link. And I suspect he knows about how Fitzpatrick, the two police officers and the doctor died. I'm certain he was present at those murders. So, I imagine he will use the hunter team, guide them as best he can."

"We need to take them down."

"I'm not entirely sure who. On the surface it looks like it could be both of them. But what if it's the Russian waiter and the barman? Maybe Huss and the manager have simply bottled it and run away? They could be innocent."

"Can't GCHQ discover the phone records prior to this?"

"Yes, in time. But all of this will be over before they get that far."

They both tensed as a tremendous roar engulfed them, as if a jet airliner were taking off overhead. Caroline found herself pulling close to King, and he hugged her, both ducking their heads at the noise. Almost at once the glass blew out in the conservatory and the wind tore through the hotel, pushing them backwards across the lobby and into the reception desk. King let go of Caroline to try and regain balance. He caught hold of her and pulled her with him to the stairwell. The wind did not reach here, and as they took shelter, they watched glass, snow, ice and debris blow past them and pepper the desk and office behind. King took out his phone, but all signal was gone. He wanted to call Rashid, get him and Ramsay to come down and cover the lower floors. No way could he see anybody in this wind and debris, let alone take a precision shot. King's only solace was that he doubted anybody could expose themselves in the storm to attack.

He was wrong.

Chapter Seventy-One

The explosion ripped through the lobby and picked them both off their feet. King landed heavily on the stairs, his cracked ribs taking the brunt of the fall. Caroline landed on top of him and he fought for breath as she knocked the wind from his lungs. He breathed hard, rolled over and gathered the assault rifle, shouldering it and backing away to take in both the side and front entrances in his periphery. Movement came from the side, the East exit. King crouched, saw the figure in white and fired three shots. They went wide, marginally so, but a miss is as good as a mile, and the figure returned a volley of fire that sprayed over King's head and into the desk, splintering the wood, some of the bullets going high and smashing the glass in the door to the ice hotel. King aimed, but the figure ducked back outside, and he did not want to waste ammunition peppering the door, unsure of who could have been outside. He got back to his feet and signalled for Caroline to go upstairs. She shook her head and he glared at her.

"Too much wind and debris here! Go up a flight and keep it covered!"

She conceded and took the stairs two at a time. King was sure she thought he'd follow, but he ran across the lobby, battling with the ferocious wind and checked the scene outside.

King could see a figure in white running across the open ground. He raised his rifle and aimed, ready to fire a burst in front of the man as he ran, but the figure fell to the sound of a single gunshot. King smiled as he thought of Rashid upstairs. If anybody could make a running shot in one-hundred-mile-an-hour winds, then it was him. He doubted anybody else on the planet could make such a shot. King got closer to the front entrance, sheltering in the lee of the supporting wall. He ducked his head, but when he looked up he saw the attacker getting to their feet and hobbling towards cover. King shouldered the rifle, but the man had reached cover, diving over a low wall and into a line of fir trees.

King battled with the wind but could take the cold no longer. He found himself running back to the stairs, his own survival instinct moving him on, aided by the strength of the wind. He took the stairs two at a time, shouted as he rounded the first flight. "Caroline, it's me!" He took the next flight, saw Caroline aiming the pistol at his face. She moved the weapon away, beckoned him up. "We need to get snowsuits on," she said. "It's colder in here than it was outside this morning!"

King didn't answer, but he was cursing himself. The hotel had been so warm. He should have anticipated the ferociousness of the storm, the vulnerability of the glass. He ran with her, stopped as they reached their room. King crouched low and aimed his weapon at the stairwell.

"Get the suits," he said. "Put yours on, then get upstairs and get everybody to regroup down here. Get the chef and the waitress to lie low…" he was cut off by the blast of an explosion, followed closely by two more. The hotel shuddered and above the cacophony of the wind, falling debris was clearly audible.

"Oh my god!" Caroline exclaimed. She was pulling on her suit, the door to their room open. She tossed King's suit to him and he put down the rifle to get his legs inside. He pulled it over him, slipped the spare magazines and Walther into the outer pockets. The gloves and beanie followed out through the door and King was grateful for them. He asked Caroline for the extra jacket. She was changed now, handed King the jacket and said, "Are they grenades?"

"Mortars," King said. With that a dull thud sounded and the hotel shook. He looked at Caroline. "IED," he said.

"They're on all sides!"

"Get Rashid and Ramsay down here," he told her. "Then get the asset. Keep her close, but remember where she was working and the exposure she had to god only knows what…"

Caroline looked at him, then flung herself forward and kissed him. He responded but pulled away and shouldered the rifle.

"Be careful," he said.

"Where are you going?" she asked.

"Hunting," he said. He turned and made his way down the corridor taking out his phone and looking at the screen. There was no signal, the storm was simply too violent for that, but the positions of the two dots had frozen in an automatic screen-shot activated when the signal died. He studied the layout. It wasn't current, but it was a good place to start.

Chapter Seventy-Two

King checked the side entrance. It had been forced open and the truck had been pulled forward. The storm outside was battering the trees all around and many had fallen or been uprooted. The wild, relentless and unidirectional vortex rocked the truck from side to side. The loose ice which had been covering the ground and trees in a fine powder of crystals had blown away, and now the swirling debris was predominantly broken twigs, pine needles and fir cones. The noise from the wind was like nothing King had experienced before. Now that he was outside, the sound unmuffled from the inside of the building, the storm sounded as if a helicopter was manoeuvring overhead. With the minimal daylight swallowed up by the dark clouds, King cupped his face to protect himself from the debris, strained his eyes in the gloom and tried to look out towards the wall where the wounded man had taken cover. He couldn't see anyone, but he suspected the man would either be lying dead behind the wall, having succumbed to his injury, or long gone – the bullet absorbed by a flak jacket and trauma plate. King certainly wasn't going to risk stepping out into the open to check. The debris alone would make it risky and the storm created too many variables, too much distraction. The risk of walking into the line of fire from either the hunter force or Rashid from above was simply too high.

King stepped out into the maelstrom, the dense clouds now creating an early blackout with precious little ambient light to see by. He took the steps tentatively, aimed the rifle down the side of the hotel, then stepped back and aimed the rifle down the other side. He couldn't make out any unnatural shapes. No shine, shadow or silhouette either. He started out over the snow, but the night turned to day and the sky tore itself apart with a monstrously bright pulse of sheet lightning. The sky flickered, then turned blacker than before. The rumble of thunder carried on, indicating that the lightning was directly overhead. King blinked the white out of his eyes, his retinas temporarily burned, but he heard the whump of a mortar round and ducked down before it exploded into the hotel. The explosion rumbled through the open door and again, he could hear debris falling. He just hoped that Caroline had taken cover, then felt a pang of betrayal to Marnie, Ramsay and Rashid, as he thought of the mortar round tearing through the roof, ceiling and floors.

**

In the darkened room Rashid had been looking through the scope as the lightning broke across the sky, a sheet of electric white light that was still making itself heard with the loudest thunder he had ever heard. He had lost his night vision, the images he had been looking at now burned onto his retinas. The lightning had been directly overhead, the thunder sounding like a Howitzer shell landing on top of them. And then had come the mortar round. Quieter in comparison to nature's wrath, but almost certainly deadlier. The explosion shook the floor beneath his feet, rocked him and made his internal organs feel like they had been turned to liquid. He realised that he had not been breathing and took a grateful intake of breath.

But he had seen something significant. In that flash of fury from the storm, he had seen deep into the forest and could make out a clearing beyond the fringe of trees. He kept the rifle aimed, closed his eyes as he recaptured the moment. How tall did the figure appear in his scope? Two inches? Crouched. Almost certainly over the mortar tube which had just unleased hell down upon them. He opened his eyes, mentally calculating. The rifle scope was a 4x40 with no aperture adjustment. So, four times magnification and 40mm objective lens. About average in terms of light admittance through the lens. Through the sight at two-hundred and forty metres, the man he had shot whilst lying down at the summit of the hill had filled the lens. Rashid calculated the size difference from laying to crouching as a factor of two-point-five.

Which put the figure he had seen at the wrong end of five-hundred metres. He calculated the arc of fire, this time elevated to a firing position of approximately sixty-feet. And then there was the head wind. Which although wouldn't deviate the yaw of the bullet, would slow it considerably. Rashid estimated a two-feet of elevation. He settled into the stock of the rifle and waited.

"Have you got a target?" Caroline asked from the doorway. She peered around the jamb, the pistol held in her right hand.

Rashid didn't move a muscle. He was breathing steadily, half-filling his lungs, to keep the rifle true. He didn't answer.

"Well, has he?" Ramsay asked over Caroline's shoulder. He looked on, glanced at Caroline and flinched as the night was turned to day.

The room was as bright as if someone had turned on the light. The great sheet of lightning filled the sky and Rashid moved the rifle just once before he fired. The rumble of thunder was instant, almost suppressing the sound of the gunshot. The light dimmed, then flashed brighter for two more seconds before the room switched back to darkness and Rashid slowly stood up and picked up the rifle.

"No. Not anymore," he said quietly. "Not anymore."

***

King moved up on the maintenance huts. He could see a dull glow of light from within, shining under the door. The huts looked like two converted shipping containers that had been welded together. There was only one door, cut into the side of the structure, but it was a double affair which King assumed allowed for large items of equipment to be stored.

The huts lay in the lee of the hotel which afforded some shelter, but the spiralling wind was still blustering at fifty-miles-per-hour and it was an effort for King to remain steady on his feet. The blustering effect made walking difficult because of the start-stop effect, causing King to overcompensate when the wind dropped. By the time he corrected his stride, the wind blew him off balance again. King reached the hut and studied the door. The vertical bolts of the shipping container had been replaced with a regular pull-down door handle, and King tested it as gently as he could. The door gave, and the wind did the rest, blowing it wide open. King went with it, ducked inside and moved to his left for no other reason than the open door blocked his movement to his right.

The hut was an Aladdin's cave of equipment, past and present maintenance projects and tools. King couldn't see anybody, but he could see where they had been. A primer-stove and dirty coffee cups were scattered on a workbench and there was the aroma of coffee in the air. King closed the door behind him and started around the hut, picking his way through and around the equipment. Two snowmobiles were in pieces, tools and parts left on the floor. King picked his way around them, side-stepped a broken wardrobe and that's when everything went blank. He was aware of falling, his ears ringing and a flash of white behind his eyes. He landed heavily amongst the tools and parts, felt a searing pain to the back of his head, followed by a groggy numbness. He fought unconsciousness, his inner voice screaming at him to fight. He felt someone step on his foot, and he rolled onto his back in time to see Huss coming at him with a wrench raised above his head. King kicked out with his other foot and caught the man in his groin. Huss wasn't used to pain, and he did not take it well. He grimaced and halted his attack, which gave King enough time to kick out again, harder this time and to the side of the man's kneecap. Pain was a fickle emotion, and inflicting it was a science. The man's groin was already flared, and the brain was sending endorphins to numb the area. Another kick to the same place, and the effect would be partially anesthetised. The kick to the knee sparked a whole new experience, and the brain would already be struggling to prioritise. King dropped his heel onto the man's instep, and Huss went down not knowing where to hold or comfort, his survival instincts overtaken by three areas of excruciating pain. King sat up, picked up the wrench and struggled to his feet. He looked down at Huss, raised the weapon above his head and raked it down onto the man's knee. There was a crunch of bone shattering and the man wailed, his entire body clenching before he writhed on the floor.

King was angry. He didn't appreciate somebody trying to kill him, but he had been given enough time to make the decision to wound the man in front of him and not drive the wrench deep into his skull. Timing was everything, and he had been given enough time. He looked around the hut, found a length of rope and snatched it up.

"Who are you working for?" King asked, looping the rope into the start of a slipknot.

Huss grit his teeth and sucked through the pain. "I'm not," he grimaced. "Not willingly, at least."

King bent down and slipped the rope around one of the man's wrists. He pulled him over, yanked the other arm behind his back and fastened both wrists together. He pulled Huss to his knees and pressed him to the floor through his shoulders. The man screamed as his knee took up pressure, and he gave him a moment to counter the pain.

"What do you mean?"

"My family," Huss winced. "They've got them under watch in Helsinki. If I don't cooperate, they will kill them."

King hesitated for a moment but looped the rope around the man's neck and trailed it back to his feet. He cast another slipknot, looped it around the man's ankles and pulled tightly. Huss grimaced, then sobbed. He was bent unwillingly into the foetal position, before King tested the gap around his throat and neck. Satisfied that the man was going nowhere, and if he tried he would tighten the rope around his own neck, King stepped back and leaned against the desk, his head feeling light and verging on dizziness.

"Who?"

"I don't know," Huss said. He was clearly in pain, but it would be easing. Well, all but the shattered knee. That would smart for a while yet. The hog-tied situation he found himself in was a more immediate problem for him. "They send pictures of my daughter on her way to school, of my wife when she goes to the gym. I am up here all winter and they have told me to tell my family not to visit, but to stay down in the city."

"Where's your phone?"

"In my inside pocket."

King retrieved it and looked down at him. "Passcode?"

"One-zero-nine-four."

King got into the phone and studied the texts. There were plenty, but nothing suspicious. He looked at the call lists. One recent in-coming.

"What did you tell them?" King asked.

Huss hesitated. "That the side exit was safe, the front entrance, too. That your force numbered five and that my staff were to be spared at all costs."

An explosion sounded and although they did not feel the rumble of the detonation, the noise was enough to cut out the howling wind for a few seconds.

"And does that sound like they give a shit about your staff?" he asked, picking up the assault rifle.

Huss tried to shake his head. "No," he said solemnly. "It does not…"

Chapter Seventy-Three

Caroline led the way, scanning in front of her through the tiny sights of the Makarov pistol. Marnie was tucked in closely behind her. She carried a can of the bear spray. It was more like a weed-killer gun with a co2 canister screwed into the bottom. The manager had informed them that it had a ten-metre range and was good for four shots. Ramsay followed, the pistol held towards the floor, his finger off the trigger. Rashid stood behind Natalia and brought up the rear. He reached around her and tapped Ramsay on the shoulder and passed him the rifle.

"Sorry, mate, but I'm taking that." He took the pistol out of Ramsay's hand and the man took the rifle more out of reaction than choice. "You get behind me and carry that for me."

"What? I'm your bagman now?"

Rashid smiled. "Bagman, side-kick, that sort of thing…" He eased Ramsay back by his collar and aimed the pistol over Caroline's right shoulder.

"Consigned to carry your equipment?" Ramsay said indignantly.

"Well, when you've put twenty-thousand rounds onto targets in the Killing House at Hereford, or half a million rounds down the range," Rashid paused. "Or a couple of thousand on the battlefield, then you can argue who carries the most suitable weapon and who carries the spare kit…"

"Boys, boys, boys," Caroline chided. "Now isn't the time. Whoever is covering, peel off and check the stairwell as I make my way down."

Rashid did just that, using the gap between the staircases to take up aim.

Ramsay looked at the rifle in his hands. "Is this ready to fire?"

"Yes, but I'd rather you didn't. There's only three rounds left…"

"Oh, I'll just fling myself in front of the bullets if you like…" He shook the rifle. "Use this as a bloody club!"

"That's good of you, thanks." Rashid grinned. He looked past Ramsay and said, "We've got company…"

The chef and the waitress were running down the corridor towards them. They had been told to take cover under the beds in a room at the rear of the hotel but had clearly had a moment of panic.

"We'll come with you!" the chef shouted. "I'd rather take my chances outside than with the rockets!"

The waitress looked terrified, nodded enthusiastically.

Caroline looked hesitant, then relented. "Okay," she said. "But hang at the rear and follow us. We're not babysitting you, though.

There's a vehicle parked up on the West side. Get in it and take cover…" They both nodded, and Caroline looked at Rashid. "Ready?"

He nodded and aimed the pistol down over the bannister. Caroline eased her way down the flight of stairs and when she reached the bottom, Rashid guided Natalia forwards then made after her, overtook her and Caroline, and Caroline covered the next flight of stairs with the pistol as he took point. Ramsay nodded for the chef and the waitress to follow, and he closed the rear holding the rifle in a manner akin to one of the cast members of Dad's Army. He had already decided that if he lived through this then he was going to get some weapons training. He hadn't signed up for this, and always preferred his comfortable office over anything he'd done this past year. But if he continued to find himself in these situations, he was going to bring more to the party.

Rashid checked the area of the lobby he could see, signalled for Caroline to join him. The wind swirled through, raining debris on the reception desk and office wall. It was difficult to see, and the temperature had dropped twenty degrees from upstairs. Rashid pulled up his collar and zipped his suit up tightly. Caroline copied him but crouched when she saw a movement. Rashid hadn't seen it, but he dropped down all the same and aimed his pistol in the direction she had been looking. There was a flicker of flame as the muzzle flash flared in front of them and bullets slammed into the stair treads above them.

Caroline fired twice and ran out to the reception desk, taking cover behind the thick oak. She signalled to Rashid for him to cover her and when he fired three successive rounds, she leapt up, kept low and made her way along the length of the desk. There was a burst of gunfire and when it stopped she dodged out and fired two shots. She was buffeted back into the desk, but she had seen a splash of red against the white snowsuits and had heard a howl. The injured man in front of her turned and kicked his way through the wooden boarding and charged into the ice hotel. Caroline was about to follow, but heard Rashid screaming for her to stop. She remembered the IED setup that Rashid had constructed, and she ducked back to the cover of the desk.

The sound of detonation was deafening and shut out the howl of the wind for a moment as the series of explosions tore through the ice passage and large chunks of ice blew out through the opening and peppered the walls adjacent to the reception.

"Stay put!" Rashid shouted above the wind. He half ran, was half blown across the lobby to her. "There are two devices in there. Low yield, but maximum effect. He'll be crushed flat by the roof to the tunnel. Leave him."

Caroline tucked in beside Rashid as they made their way back to the staircase. "What the hell was that?"

"Those bear-scaring bangers, some fuel and few things out of the kitchen. A trip wire and a rough-pull fuse. A bit old-fashioned, but deadly." Rashid shepherded her into the lee of the stairwell, out of the wind. There was a lull and he found himself shouting too loudly. "We're doing the bloody conga here with these two tagging along," he said, nodding towards the chef and the waitress. "Let's get them someplace safe and find King. What about the wine cellar?"

"But that will not be safe!" the waitress said incredulously. "There are bombs dropping, people with guns and the storm is still raging. We are safer staying with you!"

"I think she has a point," Ramsay said from behind her.

"The mortar rounds have stopped," said Rashid. "I got the man operating the mortar from upstairs." He shrugged. "That's three with the guy in the ice hotel and that makes four with the man I took down when we rendezvoused with the asset…" He looked at her and said, "Sorry, I mean Natalia." Natalia shrugged like it was nothing.

"So, there are still more unaccounted for. And where is Niles, the hotel manager?" the waitress asked. "And the two Russian workers?"

Rashid spun around as a metallic scraping was clearly audible, and a cannister around twice the size of a soft drinks can rolled through the lobby and came to a stop against the reception desk. He turned back to the group and shouted, "Grenade!" Before crashing into Caroline and landing on top of her amid an explosion of smoke and shrapnel and a flash of hot white light.

Chapter Seventy-Four

The service stairs were just like others that King had seen in expensive establishments around the world. Smooth concrete, no carpet and narrow. A way of getting the staff to where they had to be without cluttering up the stairs for paying guests. The lighting warranted no shades, just simple low-energy light bulbs hanging from bargain-budget ceiling roses above each landing. It was a stark reminder of the façade of a hotel. That people worked hard behind the scenes but were never wanted in sight unless they were waiting on or serving drinks. Nobody wanted to see a fifty-year-old chambermaid who earned minimum wage struggling along with armfuls of soiled sheets and used towels.

King kept the AK-74 ready. He had ditched his jacket in the hall below and wore his all-in-one snow suit undone to the waist like a wetsuit. He was sweating in the heat of the sealed stairwell. The destruction of the glass and the roof meant that much of the hotel was well under minus-twenty. The wind had died down, and the cloud was now blocking out the sky to the East which gave some ambient light in which he had been able to view the destruction to the grounds. Many trees had fallen, and the once pristine snow was now covered with a thick layer of pine needles and twigs. King could not see any of the hunter force in the treeline, but the mortar rounds had ceased. King had rounded the ice hotel but would not chance the boobytraps that Rashid had put in place. He had entered the hotel from the main entrance and made his way down the ground floor corridor, where he had picked up the service stairs and started to climb. He had heard an exchange of gunfire and the unmistakable sound of one of Rashid's IEDs detonating somewhere in the distance, and if he was not mistaken, a grenade from somewhere in the body of the hotel. He had resisted the urge to meet the gunfire head-on and continued to climb. He wanted to find Caroline and the rest of the team and the best place to start would be at the top of the hotel and work his way downwards.

There was no electric upstairs. The mortar rounds had taken out wiring as they had impacted and torn through the floors, taking an entire electrical circuit with them. The air was savagely cold, a blustery sixty-mile-per-hour wind still blowing ice crystals and debris through the corridor, the glass having blown out in most of the rooms. Some doors had been left open, and the wind cut through the corridor with savage effect. King paused, took a knee and pulled the snowsuit over his arms and shoulders. His perspiration had almost frozen in the fifty or so paces he had taken from the sealed service stairway. He stood back up, semi-shouldered the rifle. He had passed three rooms, the doors all blown off their hinges. The ceiling was hanging down in front of him, and the floor beneath was creaking under every footstep. He listened for movement, but the wind made that too difficult. Shards of glass dropped from the frames, shattered as they hit the debris on the floor.

King stopped as he reached a service door on his left. He stared at the floor, the discoloration on the carpet visible in the half-light. He stepped aside, checked the handle but it was locked. He bent down, touched the stain. It had frozen, but he could tell it was congealed blood. His heart started to race as he thought about Caroline. Then the same pang of guilt as he thought about the rest of the team. He stood back up and aimed a well-placed kick with the sole of his boot at the door beside the lock. It didn't give, but after two more, the frame started to splinter. King stopped, caught his breath and checked both ways down the corridor. Satisfied it was clear, he lunged in for another kick and the door gave and crashed inwards. He brought the weapon up to aim but knew he wouldn't need it. He relaxed his guard but was far from comfortable at the sight. He had seen worse, but that wasn't something he'd ever brag about. That was for him alone to live with, and the longest hours before dawn was when he thought about those things and sleep was a lost companion. The Russian barman and waiter had been trussed tightly. Seated on the floor, back to back, their hands bound in front of them, their ankles tied together tightly as well. To stop them working their way free, they had a long length of rope wrapped around them, cutting tightly into their elbows and stomachs. They had been gagged, too.

The manager was sprawled on his back, unbound and frozen in the horror of his last moments. Most of his head was missing and had splattered on the Russians behind. King could see a ragged hole in the manager's right hand. He could see how it had gone down. The Russians had already been captured and contained. The manager had been thrown inside the room. He would have been scared and panicked, unable to comprehend what was happening. Possibly more so when he saw the two men already imprisoned. But whoever had killed them had aimed the gun at the manager first and out of reflex the man had shielded himself with his hands, most likely begging for mercy. The bullet had travelled through the man's hand and into his forehead. The Russians would have been terrified now, knowing their fate. A single gunshot to each man's temple had turned this prison into a tomb and as the bodies ticked and twitched their way to stillness, that same person had calmly closed the door behind them. King pulled the door to, leaving it open just a crack on stretched hinges and a broken lock. He drew a deep breath and shouldered the weapon again. Further along the corridor, the gallery walkway ended, and the north-facing rooms started. King couldn't kick in every door he came across, but he stopped at the first open doorway and could see where Rashid had made his firing point. The bench, cushions and ejected brass on the floor. Four rooms on, and it was much the same. Another ejected bullet case, cushions propped up on a sideboard in the middle of the room. King hoped Rashid had found his targets. The man's sniper skills were legendary in the SAS. Although not committed to paper, his antics were exaggerated in the mess and bar, not even Rashid knowing the proper distances anymore.

As King neared the stairwell, he heard a noise. Distant, but consistent. Footsteps on carpet, getting closer. He swung himself out onto the landing and lowered himself in a crouch with his weapon trained on the woman at the bottom of the flight of stairs. He recognised her as the waitress, and the fearful expression on her face said it all. She was terrified.

"Please, help!" she exclaimed.

"What is it?" She started up the stairs, but King stopped her by raising the weapon motioning her backwards with the muzzle. "Tell me…"

She wiped her eyes with her sleeve. She was wearing just a pair of trousers and a blouse and cardigan. She was shivering, but King suspected it was as much from fear as the icy temperature. "We were gathered at the foot of the stairs, in the lobby," she said, then added, "Your friends and I…"

"What's happened?" King asked, unable to hide his concern.

"A grenade…" she trailed off.

King had heard it. Muffled and distorted by the service stairwell. He strode down the steps and put a hand on her shoulder. He squeezed and gave her a little shake. "Tell me."

"You need to see for yourself," she said. She turned and led the way. King felt as if his legs were made from lead. His heart pounded, and he felt himself go light-headed. He grabbed the rail, took a deep breath and continued. They got to the last flight and King could already see the body of the chef. His whites were pitted with red spots of blood, but it was his head which had taken a large piece of shrapnel. He would have died quickly judging from the wound and the amount of blood around him, already congealing in the cold. King felt her touch his shoulder, ease him into the foyer and around the corner of the corridor.

He froze.

He'd been stupid and now it could cost him everything.

The man held the assault rifle, the barrel just inches from Caroline's head. King studied him, recognised him as the thin, hook-nosed man he had seen talking to Huss. The same man that Marnie suspected of stealing her laptop. And if that tied in with his snow-covered clothing and the limp, he could very well be the same man who had shot at both King and Caroline at the second rendezvous.

King felt the cold metal touch the nape of his neck and the deception was complete. The Russians didn't only have a man in the hotel organising, communicating and indeed, blackmailing Huss; they had a woman, too. King imagined this hook-nosed man dealing with the two Russian staff. Perhaps the woman, a colleague, had lured them away, and together they had trussed them up. But who had done the killing? Not that it made any difference now, but he might feel better with the pistol against his neck if he'd known what part she had played. Or maybe not…

"Drop the rifle," she said. He did as he was told, and it clattered on the wooden floor a few feet from him. "Hand's on top of your head," she added.

He did so, begrudgingly and surveyed the scene before him. Ramsay was lying down, his hands taped behind his back with duct tape. He looked groggy, as if he were coming around from unconsciousness. King could not work out whether it had been concussive shock from the grenade, or if the man with the hooked nose had struck him down with the butt of the rifle.

Rashid must have put up a fight, because he had a tremendous lump on his head, his unfortunate bleached hair matted with blood. He had been forced to sit on his backside with his feet cross-legged and his hands on the back of his head. It was an awkward position, and one that was difficult to spring to action from. He wasn't tied, most likely because the man feared getting too close to him. Better to put him in a stress position at gunpoint and keep a weapon on someone he wouldn't chance endangering. King knew the feeling. He'd been on both sides of that scenario. Rashid was seething, glowering at the floor, murder on his mind. Which was probably why the man hadn't got any closer to him.

King looked at Marnie, who was also on her knees, her hands placed firmly on top of her head. She was sobbing, and King noticed she was bleeding from her neck and shoulders. Nothing life-threatening, merely tiny pieces of embedded shrapnel.

"What a mess!" the man said above the whine of the wind. He eased himself around

Caroline a step, and it was clear he was favouring his left leg. King found himself wondering how badly he had been wounded. The man pointed to Natalia, who was next to Marnie, the same stress position taking its toll as she shivered against the cold. "First one traitor," he said, and then sweeping a hand towards Natalia he said, "And then another!" He shook his head. "And then the British fool sent to take the traitor in, and now all of you..."

"And two innocent police officers," said King.

The man laughed. "And let's not forget a young woman from the GRU who you killed!" He smiled. "And the poor Sami fool, whose services I bought for an iPhone and the promise of a new snowmobile..."

"And the doctor?" King said. "Where did he fit in?"

"Well, at least you followed the breadcrumbs!" The man laughed again, although it was mirthless. "He was paid, but he drank too much and developed a conscience. Or at least, a higher price for it."

"And the poor couple in the ice hotel?" King sneered. "You thought that was us," he said, looking at Caroline.

"Regrettable," he said, but without emotion.

"And the manager and two Russian workers?"

King felt the muzzle of the pistol dig into his flesh and he was pushed forwards harshly.

"No, that was me," the woman said.

King shrugged. "So, what now?"

"I have your laptop," he said. "And I have my traitor."

"Well, you win. That's not even détente. You've got everything. Just walk away…"

"Sorry," said the man lightly. "For all I know, you have forwarded on the information from the USB drive. If that's the case, there is little I can do about it. But, I can't leave any loose ends. You look like an experienced killer to me, I'm sure you understand how the game works?" The man glanced suddenly to his right, struggled to make sense of what he was seeing. He had the weapon pointed at Caroline, but he had been outflanked.

Peter Stewart half limped, half dragged himself inside, his pistol held out in front of him and an expression of rage, pain and confusion on his face. He dragged himself through the glass and debris, his leg bleeding through the material and clearly misshapen under his torn snowsuit. His aim was remarkably steady, though. And the other man knew it.

King could feel the barrel against his neck, but he could also sense the indecision, a shakiness to the woman's grip. He tested it, moved a little to his right. The woman followed, but King guessed it was so she could see more and get a better idea of what was happening.

"Got yourself a Mexican stand-off," King said. He was no more confident - a three-gun stand-off meant someone would generally die – but now the man had a fair idea of the pecking order. It wasn't looking good for him.

The man did not respond, but he pressed the barrel of the assault rifle against Caroline's skull for good measure. She flinched, the weapon so hard against her that she could no longer see King, her gaze instead pushed towards Stewart.

Stewart smiled. He chanced another step. The man seemed to tighten his finger on the trigger and Stewart stepped all the way in, his pistol no more than a foot from the man's ear. He looked over at King and said, "Well, this is a wee little mess you're in, Alex," he paused. "Just like old times." His eyes flicked down to Caroline momentarily. "Sorry, lassie, but I'm not here for you…" He fired the pistol and the shot went through the man's neck, punching out vertebrae and spinal cord. He fired again, not aimed, merely the follow-up to his double tap and put the bullet through the man's head as he fell to the floor. His finger still on the trigger, but no reflex followed as the weapon clattered to the floor. Caroline fell forwards, turned a shoulder to break her fall and started to scrabble for the rifle.

King moved to his right and was flailing his right arm to sweep the gun away, but she was quick and fired two shots before her gun arm was knocked away. She glared at King defiantly, but he lunged forwards, striking her in the throat with outstretched rigid fingers. He caught hold of her throat and tore backwards, struck his own hand with his other fist to jolt the force downwards. There was no blood, but he had ruptured her windpipe and she dropped the pistol and clutched her throat in reflex. She stared at him in horror, making sense of what had happened, and what was to come. She knew she was dying, her face already changing colour as she found it impossible to breathe. King picked up the silenced 9mm MP-443 pistol and aimed at her. She held a hand in front of her, eyes pleading. King thought of the manager, the two tethered Russians who had met their end in the closet and shot her through the palm of her hand. The bullet carried on through her forehead and she fell backwards. He turned around and looked over at Caroline, who was getting unsteadily to her feet. She was looking down at Stewart but turned slowly and stared at back King.

"Alex…" she said.

Stewart was on his back. Both bullets had hit him in the chest and he was bleeding badly from one, his breath rattling and wheezing from the other. King bent down. He could see a lung was gone, the aorta had been clipped by the other. He had seconds remaining rather than minutes.

"You came back..." King said, bending down and kneeling next to him. He took the man's hand in his own. Both wore gloves, but King could feel the man's grip weakening by the second. "Why?"

Stewart rasped, "Because I let you down once..." He struggled to put his other hand around the back of King's neck and pulled him near. He whispered something into King's ear as he exhaled but he did not inhale again. He was gone.

Chapter Seventy-Five

The worst of the storm had passed, but as King weaved the snowmobile through the debris left in its wake, he couldn't help but to marvel at the sheer power of nature.

They had gathered up the weapons, shared out the ammunition and helped themselves to supplies from the kitchen. Ramsay's wound was superficial – he had cracked his head on the floor in the shockwave of the grenade - and Caroline had made a cold compress for him, joking whether she could find any ice. Huss had been loaded onto the caterpillar truck, his leg bandaged, and a similar compress given to him for the journey. They would take the truck down the winding track and take one of the SUVs they had travelled up in. The truck was fitted with a snowplough and would lead the way, all the way, if needed back to Kittila. King would return to the hotel and take the other SUV, meeting them in Kittila the next morning. It was as good a plan as they could hatch, but news of his separate mission had been a surprise to all but Marnie, who under King's instruction, had arranged it through Director Amherst.

King wound the snowmobile around another fallen tree, following the GPS on the instrument panel. It was a simple route - North.

Natalia held on tightly. The acceleration from the machine was savage and as King increased the power after every obstruction lying in their path, inertia forced them both backwards. Natalia had adopted a complete wrap around, locking her hands together around his waist.

They traversed frozen lakes – by far the easiest terrain – but a series of steep hills made for tough riding and snow drifts, frozen solid into shapes resembling breaking waves became impassable. King was forced to ride parallel for up to a mile to get around these natural barriers. Each time, the GPS pointed them northwards, a simple correction of the steering was all it took. King likened the experience more to sailing than driving.

The trees had thinned considerably, but ahead of them, in their place, great mountains jutted out of the ground like shark's teeth. There were no foothills, like arriving in the Rockies or the Alps and gradually climbing to a point where the mountains started to noticeably rise to their summit. These simply appeared, adorning the landscape with breath-taking magnificence.

King slowed the snowmobile and checked the GPS. He could see his path, between two impressive peaks, the fjord cutting between them, the Arctic ocean several miles beyond.

"Can we stop?" Natalia asked. "I feel sick."

King brought the machine to a standstill and used the opportunity to make fists and squeeze some life back into his hands. He winced, his bandaged knuckles aching from where he had pounded the ice. "It's the motion," he said. "I can see where we're going and make the decisions. Your brain has to play constant catch-up."

"I guess..." she said.

King rubbed his face. His cheeks had been numb and were now burning. He took off his gloves and held his hands to his cheeks, warming them and adding to the burning sensation. His eyes were watering, the tears frozen to his eyelids. He picked at them, like mini stalagmites. Natalia had released her grip on him and was rubbing her face as well. King turned and looked at her. Her eyes were red and sore. Neither of them had goggles. With the hotel abandoned and now lying in ruins, there had been little equipment to find, and time had been critical.

"Don't rub them too hard," said King. "They look sore and you'll damage them if you're not careful..."

He didn't get to finish his sentence. The explosion knocked them both off the snowmobile, snow and ice hitting them like shrapnel. King's ears were ringing, and he was experiencing everything in slow motion. He could see Natalia was feeling the same. Only

King had been here before, he knew what had done this to them, and he knew the importance to keep moving. This time, he saw the flare of the rocket, the trail of smoke and the rocket getting ever-closer. He was about to shout for Natalia to take cover, but even under such duress he knew the absurdity of it. They were in the open and had little hope of evading it.

The second rocket landed further away, but not by much. King had time to press his face into the ice and hunker down, his shoulders muffling his ears. The impact was felt in his chest and through his stomach, and especially in his bowels. The same feeling as one had before a bout of diarrhoea; as if every part of him had been shaken loose. He scrambled over to Natalia, who had not seen the second rocket and had been blown several metres across the ice. She was in shock, but apart from a peppering of lacerations on her cheeks from the ice, she was unscathed. He pulled her over, pushed her to her feet as he got unsteadily to his own. The snowmobile was lying on its side and King caught hold of the handlebar and stepped onto the footplate. He leaned back with all his weight and the machine righted itself. King swung himself on, started the engine and felt Natalia catch hold of him. He swung left, then tracked right. He corrected the steering and straightened up, an explosion detonating twenty-metres away. He felt shrapnel tear through his snowsuit, a searing pain in his lower leg. Natalia screamed, but held on tightly. She started to sob.

King grit his teeth, a burning, yet wet sensation on his leg. He wriggled his toes and tensed his calf muscle. It was all working, but excruciatingly painful. He chanced a look and saw scorched tatters of material and the tails of fleshettes poking out, like miniature arrows the size of sowing needles. Natalia was saying something, but King had shut her out. He was working on getting between the mountains to the fjord beyond. He checked the tiny mirror on the right handlebar and could see a snowmobile behind them, its rider dressed in an all-in-one white snowsuit. The same as the hunter force. A survivor.

King knew the man could not use a rocket launcher while pursuing them, so he relaxed into the task at hand. But not for long. He knew he was heavy, topping the scales at fourteen stone, and he estimated Natalia to be around ten stone. Which gave the machine a power deficit over their pursuer. He checked his mirror again. Was he closer? He doubted it just yet, putting the distance at three-hundred metres, which would tie in with the effective range of an RPG. King was still calculating whether he would reach the fjord before the rider closed in close enough to stop and take an easy shot, when he hit a lump of snow and was thrown airborne onto a ribbon of wonderfully new and well-maintained tarmac road. The machine landed heavily and sparked underneath, but he managed to hold on and correct it before smashing through the snowdrift and back onto the flat compacted snow.

He checked the mirror again, saw that the man had crossed the road without incident, and he gradually let out a little of the throttle. The machine slowed and the image in his mirror grew rapidly. King tore at his gloves with his mouth, and then gripped the heated handlebars. He slowed some more, and then as the machine got down to around thirty-miles-per-hour, he elbowed Natalia and she fell to the side. King lurched the steering, powered on full throttle and drove head-on towards the snowmobile. The rider had a moment of indecision and pulled to his left. King took his right hand off the handlebar and the machine slowed as he reached for the Makarov pistol in his pocket and aimed at the rider. He let go of the other handlebar, steadied the weapon in a two-handed grip and fired three shots in quick succession. The rider fell backwards, the RPG spinning out from where he had wedged it under his armpit as he hit the ice. King waited for the man to come to a halt, then fired twice more into his back. He pocketed the pistol, manoeuvred the machine around and drove it back to Natalia, who was still getting to her feet. He noticed she had shrapnel wounds to her calf, looked down and saw the mess of his own. Strangely, it had stopped hurting. He thought perhaps the cold air had started to freeze the flesh around the wound.

Keep moving forward...

He could almost hear Stewart shouting at him. He closed his eyes for a moment, thought of his old friend and mentor dying in the hotel lobby. He had been wrong about him. But that was the world he lived in. Smoke and mirrors. Bluff and counter bluff. A world of deception and death. Of playing cowboys and Indians and hoping it made a difference.

The GPS was showing he was near. He slowed the machine a little and checked his watch. He needed to time it just right. Ahead of him, the frozen fjord loomed, hemmed in from both sides by the terrific triangular mountains, like jagged snow-capped pyramids.

"Where are we going?" Natalia asked. "There's nothing here."

Ahead of them, three-hundred metres from the frozen shoreline, the ice peaked and broke, driven thirty-feet skywards by the immerging coning tower of the Astute class submarine. King slowed the machine even more. He wanted to time it, so he could get to the base of the coning tower as the vessel settled. Hatch up, asset and himself onboard, hatch down, dive. Job done. Home.

There was movement from the top of the coning tower, and two of the crew fixed a rope to the railings and tossed the coil out and down onto the ice. King stopped the snowmobile fifty-feet away and switched off the engine. He got off but had to help Natalia off the machine and onto her feet.

"Are you okay?" King asked.

"No," she said. "You knocked me off the damned bike and I've hurt my stomach. Shrapnel has torn my leg up, and my eyes are raw..." She forced a smile. "But other than that, I'm fine!"

King chuckled. "Well, it's been quite a day." He guided her to the rope and tied it around her waist. He gave a little tug, and the two crew members hand-overhanded her to the top of the coning tower some thirty-feet above the ice.

The rope was dropped back down, and King caught hold of it, gave them the curtsey of climbing as well as he was pulled up the soaking hulk of metal, now starting to freeze in the icy air.

"God almighty, you stink!" one of the men grumbled.

"Thank you, Able Seaman Archer!" the older man snapped. He looked at King. "I'm

Chief Petty Officer Patterson, welcome aboard the boat."

"The boat?" King asked incredulously.

"Yes," another man replied from below the hatch. He climbed out and stood with them, squashed like sardines, but submariners were used to that. "Secret squirrel stuff and nonsense," he said wryly. "I'm Commander Faulks, by the way. Captain of this vessel. No mention of the name of the sub on this mission. Skull and crossbones stuff."

King nodded. The Commander seemed as if he'd been teleported in from 1944. He imagined him to be from a long line of socially awkward men from a family with a long-standing naval tradition. No doubt, some grandfather or great uncle had been an admiral. He turned to the young seaman and said, "And that's fresh air, in all its glory," he smiled, recalling an anecdote how submariners become so used to recirculated and sterile air, that they can smell the men who have been 'up top' from a huge distance. The men's crewmates would smell the air on them, no matter how pure and fresh from the Norwegian wilderness.

"It's overrated, Sir," the young Able Seaman quipped, expertly coiling the rope around his elbow and shoulder.

The Commander stood aside and helped Natalia through the hatch and down the ladder. He looked back at King and his expression changed from mild curiosity to terror. "In coming!" he shouted and ducked down into the confines of the coning tower.

King felt the whoosh as the rocket propelled grenade shot past and missed the coning tower by mere inches. It carried on its flat trajectory and after nine-hundred metres detonated automatically. Molten-hot shrapnel showered down on the ice and the cloud of smoke spiralled in the wind. The thunderclap of detonation reached them a moment later.

King turned and saw the figure on the ice. He was staggering, reloading the launcher as he walked. King looked up at the seaman as he swung around the ladder and slid down onto the hull. "Get the sub out of here!" he yelled. "Now! And don't wait for me!"

The Commander was back on the coning tower and shouted, "We can't risk the boat!"

"I said, don't wait for me!"

King sat down and slid down the hull of the vessel, hit the ice slab and carried on sliding until he was on the icepack. As he sat astride the snowmobile he could already hear the sub sinking under the ice, and the whoosh of another rocket propelled grenade heading his way. This time, it found its mark and detonated against the thick slab of ice before the shrapnel bounced harmlessly off the coning tower. A direct hit would rupture the steel and the sub would be put out of action. If he managed to hit the hull, then it would sink to the bottom of the fjord.

King saw the man reloading from a canvas satchel. He was closer now, and he could see the man had at least one more rocket after that. He pressed on the throttle and the snowmobile tore off, accelerating savagely and throwing a rooster tail of ice twenty-feet into the air.

Colonel Rechencovitch shouldered the launcher, wincing at the pain in his shoulder. His body had taken the bullet from King, but his ballistic vest had taken the rest. The shot that had found its way through the seam of the vest had gone through, but he knew he would likely bleed to death before long. His clothing was soaked in blood, he could feel it congealing on his snowsuit, yet feel the wetness creeping over his skin underneath. The fragments of bone had nicked an artery. No matter. He would finish the task assigned to him, and his record would go unblemished. It would never be made public, but both Spetsnaz and the GRU would know, and his legend would live on. He watched as the snowmobile drew near. He didn't want to waste a shot, but he couldn't take another shot at the submersing vessel with this man coming at him. He crouched low, took aim and fired.

King took his thumb off the throttle and leapt to the side. The grenade impacted in front of the snowmobile and the machine was flung in the air in a shower of shrapnel and chunks of ice and landed back down on the edge of the hole created by the detonation. It started to slide into the water, its engine and manifold hissing as the cold water enveloped the craft. King had hit the ice hard but kept rolling. When he tucked into a crouch, he had the pistol in his hand. The man wasn't where he thought he'd be, but was running on the ice, getting closer to the sub as he reloaded the launcher. He tossed the satchel aside, oblivious to King, who had got to his feet and was starting out in pursuit. King fired, clipped the man's shoulder and he went down. He scrabbled back to his feet, picked up the launcher, again ignoring King as he fired. The bullet caught the man mid-torso. He fell, but the ballistic vest had stopped the bullet and done no more than break a rib. He sucked air in, staggered to his feet again, but his aim was unsteady. He dropped to his knees at the edge of the hole in the ice. The snowmobile was half-submerged, hanging on by its front skids.

King glanced at the submarine. It was pushing forward through the ice, its coning tower carving a path through, still fifteen feet above the ice and dropping slowly. He looked back at the man, stubbornly ignoring him and working on the aim for his final shot. King aimed at the man's head. His last shot. He fired, but the bullet clipped the man's neck. The man swiped at the wound as if he had been bitten by by a horse-fly.

He looked at the blood on his fingers, glanced back at King, then steadied his aim on the submarine.

King was running now. He closed the gap, threw the pistol at him but it sailed past his face. Enough to trouble his aim. King was diving through the air in a rugby tackle. He landed hard, barrelling into the man and pushing his aim off. The rocket launched and sailed off into the sky. King had hold of the man and they slid over the ice and into the hole and the freezing water.

Rechencovitch was thrashing about in the water. He wasn't just shocked at going in, but incandescent that his final attempt had sailed harmlessly into the night. As if to drive the fact home, the grenade detonated on its nine-hundred metre limit and the darkness was briefly illuminated in its impotent glare. He caught hold of King, growling in rage. King punched and kicked, then rolled onto his back and every kick aimed at the man propelled him to the edge of the ice. One kick caught the Russian in his mouth, and his ferocious attack slowed and put some distance between them. King reached the edge and clambered out. As the Russian reached him, he pushed off him with his right foot and got clear of the water. He was shaking, but as the man reached the ice, he had enough strength left in him to hammer a fist onto the man's clawing hand. King rolled over, staggered to his feet and looked down at the man as he tried again to reach the side. This time, King managed a boot and the man yelped, withdrew his hand and sunk under. He came thrashing back and stared at King. He knew he'd lost, and his glare said as much. He thrashed through the water, away from King and reached for the other side of the hole. King got there in time to kick his hands back off the ice and watch him go under the water again. He bobbed back up, clawing frantically at the water, but almost at once, he seemed to flounder and stop thrashing altogether. He stared at King, his eyes boring into him, but King's eyes were the coldest the man had ever seen, and Rechencovitch took the sight of the man standing victoriously on the edge of the ice, his stare unwavering, to the bottom of the fjord, where death was waiting for him in the darkness.

Chapter Seventy-Six

The temperature was positively balmy compared to Lapland and London was clearly entering spring with fervour. Buds of green were springing from the branches of the trees lining the streets and mature daffodils filled the borders of the lush-looking grass in Parliament Square. The sun was low in the sky, but there was finally some warmth behind it in the clear blue sky. It had rained earlier and now everything had a sheen that reflected the light with a golden hint of promise for the milder weather to come.

King sat in silence in the rear seat of the Jaguar. He ached, and his left hand was still bandaged from the frostbite. He had avoided surgery, but both hands were burned and discoloured. In his right hand he squeezed a squash ball. The gripping action worked the capillaries and kept the blood flowing to the deadened skin. He had been lucky.

King had stripped naked and rolled in the snow to insulate himself from the water. He had wrung out his clothing as best he could, but the windchill had been like a thousand blades on his skin. Once he had gotten the damp clothing back on, shivering so violently, his body looked like it was going into spasm, he had used the residual heat from the engine in Rechencovitch's snowmobile to bring some warmth into his hands. He had burned himself on the manifold several times, barely noticing the change in temperature before it was too late. He had rummaged through Rechencovitch's pack and pulled on the man's spare over-suit, which cut out the wind and allowed his own body heat to warm and steam the wet clothing underneath.

With the rest of the team en-route to Kittila, and without enough fuel showing on the gauge of the snowmobile to return to the ruins of The Eagle's Nest Hotel, King resorted to heading north on the E6 highway. The road he had crossed, and the northernmost road in Europe, which skirted the shores of the Arctic Ocean. After thirty-miles, he found an all-night truck stop. He nursed strong, black coffee with a lot of sugar and ate scrambled eggs and bacon with extra rye toast. He finally warmed through and the waitress helped him bind his hands with cooling burn gel and bandages from the truck stop's first aid kit. King paid with his card and used the payphone to leave a message on Simon Mereweather's voicemail. The MI5 deputy director returned his call and listened intently to King as he relayed the salient facts. Mereweather put King on hold for a minute or two, then told him to get to Karlebotn, where he could contact the police and arrange passage to Bergen through the Norwegian Intelligence Service. Mereweather would arrange a liaison by the time King arrived, and the police would be expecting him. King had smiled as he put down the receiver. Because of his actions last summer, he had allowed MI5 to be manipulated by MI6. Now he suspected the service would be owing Norway a favour or two down the line. He started to suspect fallout would be imminent and the thought of disappearing had been playing on his mind more frequently. He had history of playing musical chairs and having nowhere to sit when the music stopped. He wouldn't be caught out that way again. He looked out at the murky waters of the Thames as they crossed Vauxhall Bridge. He'd given his best years to keeping this country safe from those who sought to harm.

"Good work up there," Director Amherst said. He was seated by the other window. Neil Ramsay was sandwiched in the middle.

King didn't respond. Ramsay was the case officer. His name would be on the sleeve of the file.

"We all played our part," Ramsay said quietly. "I think it's fair to say King brought us through."

"Nonsense," said King.

"I'm not stroking egos, and I don't require modesty from either of you," Amherst said. He stared straight ahead and added, "SIS threw us a curve ball. But it's done now."

"Really?" King asked.

"Almost," Amherst said. "The asset, did she show signs of illness to either of you?"

"No," Ramsay said emphatically.

King saw her looking at him, her eyes red-raw. The tears on her cheeks. His own eyes were raw, burned by the cold as he had driven the snowmobile to the rendezvous. He hadn't thought more about it until Amherst's question. Could she have been infected? Could her eyes have been part of the symptoms? He covered himself, hedged his bets. He wasn't a scientist. He didn't even have a GCSE. He shook his head. "No," he said. But there was a nagging doubt now.

"The submarine has gone missing," Amherst said gravely.

"Missing! Where?" Ramsay asked, but seemed to realise how absurd he sounded and added, "I suppose if we knew that, then it wouldn't be missing..."

"Quite," Amherst mused. "But therein lies the problem. Those vessels are made to be undetectable. They have an unlimited recirculated air supply and desalination systems for unlimited water. Naturally, nuclear power means they have unlimited propulsion and electricity, but typically only ninety days of food. The whole point of a sub is that it makes next to no sound, applies stealth tactics and launches a torpedo on a ship, or a missile on a target without being traced."

"And there was no distress signal?" King asked.

"Nothing at all. The submarine must surface or draw near to the surface to send or receive messages. Part of its protocols is to do this twice a day. But the admiralty has heard nothing."

"What about homing devices in the event of emergency?"

Amherst sighed. "There are systems in place, but without the sub coming close to the surface, then they cannot be triggered."

"And it was close enough to Russian waters to cause an international incident," King said.

"Exactly. The last thing we want is to have an emergency beacon activate and be left with egg on our faces."

"But what about the crew?" Ramsay asked sharply. "We can't ignore the lives of around one-hundred men!"

"We can't afford a war with Russia!" Amherst snapped.

"Then perhaps we should stop..." Ramsay caught himself and said, "Never mind..."

Amherst shook his head. "The transcripts of conversations have been intercepted and the data wrung dry from the flash drive. GCHQ, the scientists at Porton Down and our own analysts have come up with the same conclusion. There is a missing piece that is key in the creation of this biological weapon. The potential of it being of use to us is to have a subject infected with it. Without that, we have nothing."

"Just as bloody well," commented King.

"So, the Russians have an apocalyptic weapon, and we have no chance of replicating it?" Ramsay asked.

"Yes," replied Amherst. "But what we want most is the antidote to such a weapon. And for that, we need the complete biological formula."

"I'm sensing a return trip on the cards," King commented flatly.

Amherst shook his head. "No, nothing like that. In fact, there is going to be a terrible accident at that facility soon. Imminently, I'd say. It's in the planning stage, but do you know what happens if a super-heated water source flows directly into geothermal shafts?"

"I'm guessing it boils?" King said. "Or super-boils?" He wasn't a scientist, but it wasn't difficult to work out.

"That's right," said Amherst. "There are people planning how to make it look like that. A sizeable enough reaction to devastate the facility and everyone, or everything in it."

"How to spin it after the bomb drops?" King asked.

"Something like that," Amherst replied.

"If we can't have it, then neither can the Russians. The experts think that what the Russians have is ninety-five percent complete. As they were still clearly in the infancy of human testing, they most likely don't have the delivery system in place. This way, we nip it in the bud."

King watched the guard ahead of them signal the car to stop. Amherst's driver lowered his window, showed the pass and was waved through to the underground parking. "Well, if the disappearance of the submarine means what I think it means, then you have your infected subject already. Or at least, a hundred of them. You just need to find the sub and get some fool to get onboard..."

Amherst shuddered. He had seen the photographs, the footage caught by Natalia. It did not bear thinking about. "We're here now. And remember, play the tough guy, okay?"

King smiled. "Trust me. It won't be a problem."

Chapter Seventy-Seven

Director Villiers looked up as the door opened. He smiled warmly as Amherst and Ramsay walked in, then frowned when he saw King. Naturally, Ramsay and the MI5 director both wore suits and polished shoes. King wore his cargoes, a polo shirt and a scuffed leather jacket. His size eleven desert boots had seen action in Syria and Iraq. Villiers stood up, walked around the desk and shook Amherst's hand.

"I didn't expect so many of you from across the river," he smiled. He looked at King and said, "Dangerous times, I suppose a bodyguard is desirable. My chap tends to wear a suit, though."

King smiled. "But he's not here, is he?"

"Meaning?"

King walked past him and stood at the window. The Thames was murky wherever you viewed it from. He turned back and said, "Take a seat, Director Villiers."

"Now, look here..." Villiers started, but was cut short by Amherst.

"Sit down, for Christ's sake. It's over!"

"What is over?"

King walked back and shoved Villiers in the chest. The man dropped into his chair and it slid backwards a few feet on its casters. King dropped a photograph on the man's lap. He followed up with two more.

"What's this?" He looked up at Amherst. "Enough of the theatrics. Explain yourselves. And what the bloody hell are you doing with pictures of my family?"

Ramsay and Amherst had each taken a seat opposite Villiers' desk. There were no other chairs but that didn't bother King. He perched on the director's desk and looked down at him.

"Peter Stewart told me about you before he died," he said. "He didn't trust you, could see right through you. He convinced you that he would be the ideal person to send up there to aid Fitzpatrick. He suspected you were working for the Russians. He also suspected Fitzpatrick at first, but when he was murdered, he knew that it had to be you. It was the phone call he made to you, you see. And when he was ordered back, he slipped off the radar," he paused. "Because by then he found out that I was going up there to look into it, and he wanted to watch my back."

"Very touching," Villiers said. "The word of a dead man. And a desperate alcoholic wash-out, at that…"

King lunged forwards and kicked Villiers' in the chest. Ramsay stood up, but realised he wasn't going to do anything, and sat back down again. He looked at Amherst, who had remained impassive. Villiers was winded, and his head was lolling from side to side as he struggled to suck in breath. King grabbed the man's lapels and pulled him close. Villiers tried to resist, but he knew he was outmatched physically. He tried to pull away, but King's arms remained locked solid, his biceps forming under the leather jacket that seemed to threaten the integrity of the stitching.

"You were thwarting Russian defection, in collusion with the FSB or GRU. What was it, money?"

Villiers glared. "No!"

"Ideals, then?"

"You don't understand!" He looked at Amherst expectantly and said, "Call off your goon!"

King pulled him closer, spoke through gritted teeth. "You're a traitor!"

"No! I was working with the GRU, in a joint intelligence operation!"

"Bullshit!"

"I was preventing sell-outs from jeopardising vital research!"

"Their research."

"I had an inside line, a way in to something we've wanted for so long! When it was complete, my contact was going to get it to us. We had to put off the defectors until it was ready!" Villiers said desperately. He looked at Amherst again and pleaded, "For god's sake!"

"The GRU would never work with a foreign agency on a project like that," Amherst said coldly. He took a fold of paper out of his pocket and opened it up. "These accounts are in your wife and children's names. Offshore accounts, but I'm sure neither of them are aware they're knocking on the door to being millionaires."

Villiers' shoulders sagged. King gripped more tightly just in case it was part of the man's plan to lull him into a false sense of security. King looked down, saw the damp patch soaked into the area around his groin and doubted he had it in him.

"So, what are you going to do?"

Amherst stood up. "My man here wanted to break your neck," he said nonchalantly. "And trust me, he's more than capable. But we've had a chat about the bigger picture and he agrees, of sorts. You'll be far more useful to us on a leash. An extremely tight leash. Of course, your wife and children will only be safe for as long as you cooperate. And it goes without saying that you'll be under surveillance twenty-four-seven. In short, we'll know what colour toilet paper you use. Which, we do already. And the man who has just made you piss your own pants will be all too pleased to twist your neck if you fail to fall in line with us." Villiers went to say something but seemed to think better of it. "Your accounts have been frozen, and your assets seized. Your passport has been flagged and you will hand it over to us when you come in to Thames House tomorrow morning at nine for the first in a series of meetings. Naturally, you will still retain your position, for now, but I am appointing Simon Mereweather as my liaison. He will be working fulltime in the River House until further notice. We'll call it a joint MI6/MI5 operation. He's on his way over now, but I thought I'd spare you the embarrassment of him being in on this meeting. He'll hear all about it later, of course." Amherst stood up and casually adjusted the sleeve of his jacket. "We'll start this new venture by maintaining your relationship with the Ruskies. And then we'll gradually trickle-feed them disinformation. By the time we've finished with you, the Russians will be thinking how to get Novichok on your door handle. By then, of course, we'll be your only salvation. Your only protection. So, play the game, stay onside and you might just have a future."

King gripped tightly, pulled Villiers out of his chair and the man put up no resistance. A ragdoll in his hands. "Make no mistake," he said coldly and threw him back into the stained chair. "The Security Service own the SIS now. And if you think about doing a runner, you have been warned. I'll hunt you and I'll find you, and I *will* kill you…"

Chapter Seventy-Eight

"He's a slippery one," Ramsay said. "But I think he understands."

"He'll hang himself," said King. "Metaphorically speaking, that is."

"Do you think?" asked Amherst.

"He's arrogant. He'll dust himself off, regroup, build his ego back up and he'll cross the line again," King said. "Which is fine with me, because I meant every word."

The sky had clouded over, and it was raining. So much for the promise of spring. The spray from the vehicles had made a greasy smear in the windscreen wiper's tracks. Seated in the front passenger seat, Amherst's bodyguard cracked his window down an inch and checked his own rear-view mirror for the hundredth time since leaving the River House. King wondered how much the man had listened to, but noted he was probably too situationally aware to care. Parliament Square looked less colourful than before as they followed the road to the right and headed for Thames House.

Amherst said, "The documents mention a name several times. Someone who oversaw the project from its conception. This person is of interest to us. A former communist hardliner. A general who ran a subversive wing of the KGB. His involvement in this horror show project is compelling, because he will no doubt have further information. Undoubtedly more than we have gained thus far."

So much for nipping this in the bud, thought King.

"What's his name?" Ramsay asked.

"Vladimir Zukovsky."

King felt the wall of his chest tighten, his heart skip a beat. Adrenalin surged through him, and he found he was gripping the door handle so tightly that his knuckles had turned white. His mind raced and for a moment he was caught up with images of things he'd rather forget. Of bodies and blood, of timers and detonators and cannisters of plutonium. He looked at the palm of his hand, the ragged scar from where he had cupped the detonator - a reminder of how close to oblivion the country had come. He closed his eyes and thought about Caroline, of the cove in Majorca, the engagement ring he had bought her after the operation had gone according to plan. Of the start of a new life ahead of them and Vladimir Zukovsky found and placed under permanent arrest. Simon Mereweather had been acting director, taking the helm after the death of Charles Forrester, and King had put together the hastily conceived abduction plan while he was still on official sick leave. Caroline had been none the wiser.

"Are you alright, dear boy?" Amherst asked. The car swept past Downing Street and

King turned and looked out of the window.

"I'm fine," he said. But like so many things in his life, he thought he would never be able to truly outlive his past. The feeling that he would forever be haunted. And the feeling that whether he wanted it or not, a new and deadly chapter in his life would soon open. He looked back at Amherst and said dubiously, "Never better."

Chapter Seventy-Nine

There was very little to signify that the well-tended gardens in which he stood belonged to the family of a man long since deceased, but ever immortalised in the annals of history. A piece of land bought in 1921 by the Cumming family to commemorate Captain Sir Mansfield George Smith Cumming, KCMG, CB and the work he did in founding what had become the Secret Intelligence Service, or MI6. A simple plaque honoured this man, and a plaque had been added for every agent lost from 1914 to 1918 throughout Europe. From 1942, the garden of rest had become a Home Office registered graveyard of sacrosanct land. Not every agent had been buried here, but those who had all bore a matching gravestone, and those whose families had opted for their loved one's body to rest elsewhere had still been honoured by a commemorative stone, identical to (C's) own. Each stone was engraved with the name, date of birth, date of death and their time in service with MI6. No details were added according to one's grace, standing or fortune, except that a single gold star denoted death in the field.

In 1961 a fund from MI6 had taken over lease of the land and undertook maintenance of the garden and subsequent licensing and registrar fees in accordance with births, deaths and marriages. Other than that, the garden was known by few, even within the walls of the River House.

King studied the newly-dug grave. Tiny shoots had already protruded from the soil, and before the summer took hold, he imagined the mound would flatten and settle and the grass would cover it completely, leaving just the headstone in place, and no clue whether someone had been laid to rest, or merely commemorated along with so many others. King had read all the stones on another occasion, marvelling at how many dates fell within the first and second world wars. Another rise had been in the mid-sixties and early eighties, though few would know why or where. From the fall of the Berlin wall, the numbers had been less. Sometimes years without a soul immortalised by a stone with a star.

Peter Stewart's name and star were bright, the stone glistening in the May sunshine. King took out the bottle of twenty-five-year old Haig. King did not know whether it was good or not, but he cracked the cap and took a swig, let the amber fire settle on his tongue and reach the back of his throat. It tasted like whisky to him, but the man in the wine and liquor merchants had said it was good, and the price would have King agree. He took another swig and it tasted better this time. He poured the rest on the earth and a little on the headstone, then put the cap back on and pressed the bottle into the ground and worked it into the soft earth until just the neck remained in view.

"Rest easy, you old bastard," he said. He wiped the corner of his eye, before it threatened to turn into a tear and added as he walked away, "Thank you."

Printed in Great Britain
by Amazon